Kane

Wolfwere Series Book I

Dick Wybrow

Dee Dub Publishing

Chapter One

The woman behind the counter nearly dropped the jar of pickled pigs' feet.

Jemma Lamberth was getting on in years, she knew that, but this time, her body's betrayal hadn't been caused by the arthritis that had meal-wormed into her knobby hands. Not this time.

She didn't blink as she watched the giant who'd just walked into her quiet country gas station. Jemma thought if she did, he might snap back into the ether. Like one of those mirages she'd seen in that old Peter O'Toole movie. The one with all the mean camels.

The film had turned her off camels for life. Not that opportunities to employ such an aversion came up often in Wisconsin.

Jemma and her late husband, Gerald, had owned their shop for over thirty years. She'd seen all types pass through her door. It kept life interesting.

The people she knew.

The people she didn't, the strangers.

"'Stranger' just means they're a handshake away from being a friend," Gerald had liked to say. Still never explained why he'd preferred Jemma talk to the new faces.

Although ever since they'd laid down the new expressway out of Madison, she'd seen fewer and fewer new faces; mostly just the old ones getting older.

The man casting shadows onto her coolers was *definitely* new. A stranger. And after one look at his size, she wondered whether, in testing the stranger-converting powers of a handshake, she might lose sight of her hand. To the elbow.

Pickle jar now firmly balanced in her hands, she watched him step from one frosted-glass display door to the next. Surprisingly, the word "graceful" came to mind.

Although not *entirely* graceful.

Years earlier, her husband had gotten a bee in his bonnet and dragged out one of the ladders stacked against the back wall of the store. They never sold, but this was a small, blink-and-you'll-miss-it town and theirs the only store for miles. It felt right to have them on offer.

Gerald would use them from time to time, rotating through the stock, so each would wear evenly. Just in case someone did come in to buy one. No one ever did.

On that morning years earlier, he'd hefted his sagging belly up the ladder to hang a bell above the door to alert them when someone entered.

It also served another purpose.

Those dinging the bell would know they'd been announced. According to other shop owners in a Facebook group she belonged to, this would deter more skittish thieves with plans for a quick grab-and-go.

When the large man entered, he'd actually announced himself twice. Once with the door, the second time with his brow. He'd banged the damn bell with his head.

Jemma offered a smile—"the *only* thing free in the store," according to another of her husband's sayings—and got a blank expression in return.

"Anything I can do you for?" She grunted, resuming her struggle with the jar. "If'n you need to use the bathroom, we do like that you buy something. Pays for the water and air freshener." She chuckled, but the man didn't even look up. Only let out what sounded like a low belch. "But it ain't a rule or nothing."

When he ambled away from the coolers, he didn't walk so much as stride through the shop.

As cluttered as it was—although she'd never have called it cluttered; she preferred "well stocked"—he didn't knock anything off the shelves. Not even down the trinket aisle, which never really sold much and, over the years, had just gotten more and more weighed down until the thin metal shelves had begun to slump.

The old woman turned to see if she had any of those rubber circles somewhere behind the counter. The ones people used to open up stubborn jars, which was what she had, all right. Good for hot pans, too, those. Not for opening them, just for putting the hot pan down on the red circle so it didn't scald the countertop.

Not seeing one in the piles of stock that still needed, well, stocking, she turned back and nearly yelped.

The large man stood before her at the counter.

"Holy horsefeathers," she said and clutched the jar to her chest, making its contents slosh back and forth. "I didn't even hear you walk up."

The man frowned. "I could hear your labored breathing by the glass door with the very tiny frozen fish."

"The what, now?" She looked around the man to see what he'd been referring to. No small task, looking around him. She'd had to take two steps to her left to do it. "Oh, the bait? You a fisherman?"

"No, I am not a fisher-man," the giant said with a strange accent she couldn't place. To Jemma, it looked like he'd stepped right out of an MTV music video from the eighties. Long wavy brown hair, neatly trimmed beard. No earring, thankfully. She didn't care much for those in men.

He stared at the half-gallon jar in her hands. "What is floating in that liquid?"

"These? Son, these here are pigs' feet."

"Pigs. Feet?"

She grunted again, gripping the lid harder. "Mighty tasty, if you got a taste for them. If you ain't had 'em before, you should give them a try." She strained, her face turning pinkish. "If'n I can get the jar open."

Without another word, the large man reached over, grabbed the jar by its lid, and placed it on the counter. He stared at it for a moment, bending down to look through the glass.

Jemma blinked, wiping her hands on her apron. Only then did she realize she'd been sweating.

The man said, "I would like to see the pigs you have removed these from. I am curious about how they must walk without feet."

"It—what?" the store owner said then shrugged. "Can't help you there, but if you want to give the lid a try, I'll let you have one for free."

He blinked once, held the base of the jar, then put his massive palm on the lid and twisted it open as simple as flipping a light switch in a dark room. His eyes had never wavered from the floating, wrinkled feet inside.

"My, my," Jemma said, her voice uneven. "You're a strong one. You must be one of them body builders. Like Arnie Schwarzenegger or something."

"No."

"Well, then your father must have been half bear, son!"

"Not bear." The man with the strange accent turned to look out the store's bay window. His eyes seemed to focus on nothing. "Bears are stupid but can be troublesome when angered."

The woman smiled and peeled a sticker from a sheet she'd prepared earlier. It marked the price of the pickled pigs' feet at $1.99. A steal, really.

"Well, your daddy must've been a big 'un, that's for sure."

"My father was wolf." As he straightened, the man lifted his enormous head.

Jemma watched it go up and up and up, wondering if it might hit the ceiling.

"My mother, also wolf."

She laughed and clapped her hands together. "Yet somehow, they had a beautiful boy like you!"

"I was born wolf," the large man said. "But bitten by a man, so now I am a man." He stared out the window once again, just for a moment, then looked back. "Most of the time."

"Do what now?" the woman said, her smile fading.

A young woman burst through the door so fast the bell banged hard against the ceiling. The short purple hair framing her face swished left and right as she scanned the store. Fierce green eyes that looked like emeralds against her olive skin. When those eyes landed on the large man at the counter—and then noticed the expression on the woman's face—she waved her hands in the air.

"Don't mind him," Emelda Thorne said with a wide grin. "He's French Canadian."

Chapter Two

Over the past two weeks, I'd learned to hate stopping in small towns.

Years ago, I used to love it. When I was a kid, I spent summers on my uncle's farm. It had been carved out of eastern Minnesota's lush, flat, never-ending carpet of green, about an hour out of the Twin Cities. A fifteen-minute ride down the interstate would have taken you to Wisconsin, only to have you arrive and assume you'd made a wrong turn and ended up in the exact same place you'd just left.

At least once during those hot and humid months, my uncle would pack us all up into his rusted truck and take us for some winding trip across the Midwest, pulling an old, hulking camper. On the road, I'd seen nice caravans, slick and long, stripes down the side. Some had faded script across the back announcing the owners' retirement years earlier.

The camper Uncle David dragged across interstates, highways, and gravel roads was not slick. If he'd ever gotten it into his head to sell it, the local PennySaver ad would have included the phrase "spare parts."

I was never convinced he'd been a big camper guy. Maybe getting one was just what white people did when they got older. Maybe he just felt guilty about leaving me under the charge of my two older cousins and had grown weary of the cuts, bruises, and scrapes I'd earned from their "games." They hadn't felt like games to me.

For the prey, it never feels like a game. Just survival.

Not that I'd been at risk of death by paintball. However, running around the massive farm and its thicket of trees, bushes, and impossibly high scratchy grass, there were plenty of times I felt like my heart would burst right out of my chest and scurry down the same holes I kept tripping over.

They always found me.

On those camper trips, when it was time to sleep, the oldest cousin used to get the couch, which converted into a bed. Her brother, younger by one year, got the lower bunk in the back—roomy and almost like a very tiny apartment. The youngest, I got relegated to the top bunk that had to be folded down from the wall.

The space it left for sleep was cramped. The mattress had to be thin, or I would have never fit up there.

And my cousin below would threaten to close me in during the night, so I never got much sleep. Bad dreams about being eaten by a lumpy clam. Weird.

Back then, long drives to some boring destination got broken up by stops at tiny stores on the highways. Full of all sorts of treasures. And, as lame as it sounds, roadside bathrooms always fascinated me.

Most were horrible. Disgusting.

But every now and then, you'd come across one that wasn't exactly pristine, but you could tell the owner had taken some pride in it. As if they'd once considered entering it in some competition in *Gas Station Toilet Magazine*.

In those rare nice ones, the floors were clean. The sink and toilet gleamed. The room might smell like lavender or lemon. Probably just the cleaning solution but pleasant enough.

I still remembered one gussied up like an old woman's powder room. A plastic floral arrangement. Light fixtures that looked like seashells. A small framed picture of some cool building with columns, which looked foreign. Maybe a favorite photo memory of the owner or the image of a dream vacation never taken.

Now, stopping in small towns led to all sorts of problems.

Kane kind of problems.

After I'd gassed up, I looked to the passenger seat where *I'd told him to stay* and saw that, once again, he'd totally ignored me.

"Don't mind him," I said as I'd burst into the store, unsure what he'd said, but, given the look on the woman's face, I was sure it had been horrible. Or just weird. He'd said a lot of weird shit since I'd met him. Although it all sounded less weird each day I spent with him. "He's French Canadian."

Thankfully, she laughed.

Kane turned to me, frowned, and pointed at a massive open jar. "She has taken feet from pigs."

Walking up, I said, "Everyone needs a hobby. Can I pay for the gas? And anything he might have done?"

The woman behind the counter waved a hand in the air. "He's fine. Opened up my jug for me." Her eyes lit up as she turned to him. "Which reminds me! I owe you a taster." She dipped her hand into the bloodred brine and held out a pink porcine foot to Kane.

He stared at it for a moment. "Would you like me to return it to the pig?"

"Heavens no! You eat it, son."

I stepped in and grabbed his arm, which was as big as my leg. I couldn't pull him away, but I'd hoped the mosquito-like pressure on his bicep might give him the idea it was time to leave.

Putting a hand between them, I gave her a smile. "He's not a big fan of, um, pickled stuff."

Kane asked her, "Do you have a raw one?"

The woman gawked. "Raw?"

"Canadian humor. Doesn't translate well, sorry," I said and tugged until my large friend finally got the clue.

He waved politely at the woman, who was still holding the dripping hoof out, and followed me toward the exit.

When we were out of earshot, passing a display of jumper cables that had faded in the sun, I asked, "Did you tell her you're a wolf?"

"Yes."

"Can you *not* do that!" At the open door, I pointed outside at the old Audi. He crossed the threshold, and a bell banged against his head but didn't chime. Must have been broken.

Once my feet hit the dusty cement outside, I strode up beside him. "You don't have to tell that to everyone you meet."

"Wolves do not lie," he said and stood by our car. "People lie."

"Yes, but at the moment, right now, you *are* a people, right? Human. So, when in Rome and all that."

"This is Wisconsin."

Kane looked around, and before he could say anything else inane, I rounded the car, jumped inside, pulled on the passenger-side handle, and pushed the door open. When he got in, my car dropped at least six inches.

I fired up the engine, and he closed the door.

Kane asked me, "Can we go see the pigs with no feet?"

"No. We're heading to this Menomonie place." When he stared blankly at me, I added, "To the car show. Remember?"

"I would very much like to see the pigs with no feet," Kane said. "I have many questions."

I hit the gas, spitting gravel as we bumped and jostled back onto the highway. "You and me both, Kane."

I reminded myself that I'd had worse jobs than this. Far worse.

Some part of me also felt that since I'd saved his life, for now, he was my responsibility. That and I am an animal lover. I wasn't exactly sure how much animal was within a lumbering, six-foot-seven man, but I had seen his other side the first time we'd met.

And despite his claims to be "wolf," that was *not* what I remembered. Far from it. But what I *had* seen had changed my entire outlook on the world. Made it even more confusing than it had been. Confusing but with a touch of magic I hadn't known it had.

Whatever he was or had been, the one truth I knew was that the big dude couldn't drive for shit. Either he was just terrible with machines or something about being... whatever he was... had left him bereft of any ability to coordinate his limbs to drive a car.

Or read well.

He'd needed help, and I'd needed a job. Or just a better job than the one I'd had.

So for as long as he kept paying me, I was his driver.

Despite what I'd seen that day two weeks earlier, I didn't put too much stock in his story about being a dude who'd once been a wolf. He hadn't been able to explain much beyond that.

What I did know was that Kane just saw the world differently than anyone else on the planet.

Chapter Three

Kane

When I had entered the glass-and-steel lair on the perimeter of the petrol station forecourt, I instantly smelled death.

I have no fear of death. She awaits me at the end of my journey with her warm embrace to assuage my unrealized aspirations and slake my incessant thirst for blood. I do hope it doesn't hurt when that end does come, however.

Pain. Not a fan.

That is an expression I have learned from Sad Girl. "Not a fan." I like it.

I easily pass through the shop's weak defenses without injury except for, maybe, a tiny red mark on my forehead from the tinkling bell.

This lair has a confusing jumble of contradictory scents. Both organic and chemical. Rotting and sickly sterile. And much plastic and cardboard packaging.

My keen wolf senses notice a woman to my left. Behind a slate-rock counter that still smells of river. She battles with the top of a large glass container, and it shakes under the strain. There are strange wriggling pink things within. Are these her prey?

Such savagery in a woman so old!

What wrong have the pink wiggly creatures imparted upon her to illicit such brutality?

To have lived to such an age, she must be a skilled hunter. I will have to approach her cautiously.

The fleshy aroma of fish beckons me, and I approach a clear door. On the other side of the glass, tiny ice crystals had formed into snowflake patterns, which entrance me, remind me of the winters in what the humans call British Columbia.

When the lakes would freeze, still, there were fish beneath the thick water glass. But I could not get to them. The fish knew it; I was sure of that. The way they would stare up, unblinking. Of course, fish have no eyelids, so this seemed like a standard fish expression.

Still, they would taunt me.

Laugh if fish could laugh.

Similarly, now, these fish are also behind glass but not water made. When I pull on the metal bar, an icy blast of air boils over me and spreads down to my feet. The fish are there for the taking!

Alas, they are dead. And very cold to the touch. And incredibly tiny.

"Mighty hunter!" The woman behind the stone slab calls out to me with her words and expression. "How may I serve you, my better?"

I ignore her. If she were attempting to mate with me, she would find no match here. Far too old, sure. And I am already betrothed to another. My wolf wife. She awaits my return.

"If you need to pass your water, I will require payment." I hear her make a strange, coughing call with her throat. Laughter. Was she mocking me? I growl low. "But for you, this will not be required."

Aha!

I have cowed you, old hunter woman. You have shown your true self and have been found lacking.

It is still strange to have two voices of my own. One that I make with my human mouth and another that slithers around in my brain. I do not remember this when I was a wolf. It may have been there, but recalling my former self is confusing.

Closing the cooler door, I look up to see she has returned to struggling with the helpless, glass-encased creatures cradled under an arm. What had the tiny beasts done to deserve such torture?

Silent as the night, I shift my weight and pad between two rows of colorful items hanging on metal hooks. Hundreds of them. Many smell musty. Most carry the same scent as the old woman. These were her prizes, then? Previous foes now put on display?

Warnings to others who may think of crossing her?

I will not be cowed by such small victories. And they were small. Several of them were also "half off," which, I wager, may have been the manner in which she slew them. Split down the middle.

A formidable foe if she were an enemy.

I would have to be careful. Stealthy.

"Holy horsefeathers!" the woman exclaims as I approach her. "Intrepid hunter, how silent you move through my lair!"

Human communication will always confuse me. The words they say with their expressions and manners do not always match the ones that escape their lips. Too often, they contradict. But the wolf reads others by twitch and shift. Furrow and frown.

This is the currency of one's true thoughts. I interpret these while also taking in the human words. Trusting my instincts, which have always served me well.

As a sign of respect, I explain she revealed her inattentiveness in the manner that she breathed. And that I had taken a minor interest in the tiny frozen fish.

"Are you more than just a fine hunter—clearly, this is true—but also one who can snatch fish from the water? A fisher-man?"

Man? I am no man!

"No," I say, growling my words so she would know of my disapproval. "I am no fisher-man."

Afraid, naturally, she offers me food, hoping to buy my favor. She identifies the prize within the glass, the pink squiggly creatures, as the feet of pigs.

What vile terror only eats the feet of helpless porcine creatures?

Cautiously, yet boldly, I remove the glass trap from her clutches and lay it before me. This may be a trick of hers, so I must be careful. Quick!

With a flick of my wrist, I do what the old woman could not and toss down the lid to declare my victory.

Naturally, she showers me with praise. Odd praise I did not understand.

"Like Arnold Schwarzenegger or something," the woman says, eyes sparkling with lust. She then attempts to begin a fruitless mating ritual. She will fail! I am not so easily swayed.

And she'd called me a bear.

"Not bear. Bears are stupid," I say with my mouth words, considering whether I should eat her, "but can be troublesome when angered."

I forgive her for the stupidity. She is old. Feeble. And eating her would only upset my stomach and likely give me the hind waters. I have found the older humans tend to do that. All of that flaky skin, perhaps.

To quell her desires—or at least to let her know she could not hope to be a mate of mine—I regale her with my pedigree. How I came to be.

I had been a wolf, happy in the forests of British Columbia and responsible for a pack of five. I protected them with my alpha female. My mate for life. My wolf wife who awaits my return.

But first, I must find the man who turned me into this abomination. He will have my answers. Answers that will help me once again be wolf. Then, most likely, I will eat him.

No, I definitely will.

Before I can explain my story fully, Sad Girl enters to interrupt me. She interrupts me a lot.

"Don't mind him," the Sad Girl says, flashing her teeth at the woman. "He's French Canadian."

Chapter Four

I jerked the wheel of the old Audi hard to the right, pulling the car back into the lane. "Shit!" I barked out, then chastised myself. "Pay attention, Emelda."

Navigating via my phone's map app had nearly gotten me and the big guy flattened. Although I was pretty sure he had a fifty-fifty chance of surviving a head-on collision.

I'd been searching for a less direct way to get to the Menomonie Car Show. The fewer people we had to encounter along the way, the better. Especially the police.

We'd never been on good terms.

The electric-blue eighteen-wheeler truck blared as it rolled past, the Doppler effect of its air horn rising and falling as it rumbled and warbled away.

"Jesus!" I said, twisting my locket necklace between trembling fingers. My grandmother had given it to me years earlier, and fiddling with it calmed my nerves. Sometimes. "Didn't you notice that I'd drifted over?"

"Yes," Kane said.

"Why the hell didn't you say anything about the truck, then?"

He squinted, focused on the road ahead. "I think I could have taken it."

"No, Kane!" I gripped the wheel tighter. "There is no 'taking' semis barreling at us at a hundred miles an hour."

"How do you know until you try?"

"Because I don't *wanna* try," I said as my heart rate finished up its drum solo. I fanned my face because the A/C hadn't worked since I'd acquired the car from my old neighbor two weeks earlier. "Truck means death. Can we get that straight?"

"Okay."

"I want to hear you say it!"

"Truck means death."

"Good," I said. I considered looking back at the digital map then thought better of it. One close call like that was enough for the day.

"Death for *truck*," Kane said, grinning. "If I were to bring the fight to it."

My groan rolled into a low chuckle. "How the hell are you still alive?"

Kane shrugged, a human trait that he'd obviously grown to like. "I am powerful. I am mighty."

"And dumb as an oak stump."

"No, this is not true. I am regal. I am kingly."

I poked him in his shoulder with a red-flecked fingernail that desperately needed new polish. "You didn't look so kingly when I found you in the garbage."

"Not in garbage," Kane said, shifting his weight, which made the vehicle's suspension creak, even at seventy miles an hour. "Next to garbage."

I double-checked the map app, quickly this time, and saw the exit was about an hour ahead.

At the end of that stretch, we'd find the car show that had been advertised on several of the hot rod websites I'd scanned. Odds weren't high we'd find the "purple car" at this show as the two previous ones had been a bust. But how many purple hot rods could there be out there?

"Just keep in mind that if I hadn't shouted those boys down, you'd probably be dead."

Kane stewed about this for a moment. "That is possible."

"So if Kane wants to stay alive, what should Kane do?"

I turned to him, keeping one eye on the long, long ribbon of gray highway ahead. He sighed and spoke in a monotone, as if repeating a lesson from school.

"Kane needs to listen to Sad Girl."

"Right," I said. "And don't call me that! *Emelda*. We've known each other for nearly two weeks. At least you can get my name right."

"Sad Girl is two syllables." He held up a pair of fingers with one hand. With the other, he did the same, adding a finger. "Emelda is three. Easier to say with mouth words."

"You got a daily syllable budget?" I shook my head. "Mel is fine. One syllable, right? Even simpler."

Kane shook his head. "Mel is too close to 'mal.' This I do not think is right."

"Why?"

"In French, 'mal' means bad," Kane said, his eyes softening as he looked at me. "You are helping me, so you cannot be bad."

"You're *paying* me to help. Drive and read because you're shit at both, right?"

The big man fell into the quiet brooding I'd come to know very well. The radio was only finding pop or country music—although it was getting harder to tell one from the other—so unless I wanted total silence for the next hour, I'd have to say something to lighten him up.

"We've all got a bit of bad in us, my furry friend." I flashed him a smile. "And some of us have a bit of wolf in us. Or at least you do."

"Incorrect. I am wolf. I have a bit of man in me."

"Been there, done that," I said. "Ain't nothing to get too excited about."

Chapter Five

Following the snapping red flags of men and women dressed in orange high-vis vests, I turned off the main road into the vast, hilly field. On that sea of green floated the flotsam of hundreds of different vehicles.

Cars, trucks, buses, vans, motorcycles.

Rows upon rows of them, snaking across the crests and valleys, kept mostly uniform by flag-waving parking attendants.

Kane eyeballed each vehicle we passed.

"So many cars," he said. "Purple car must be here."

"Ha, not likely."

"Then why have we come to the Menomonie Car Show if not to find the car I seek?"

At the grinning insistence of one of the helpers, I pulled into the shadow of a souped-up truck with fat, knobby tires. Once in the spot, I dropped the Audi into park.

"This part isn't the car show, Kane," I told him. "This is where people who can't afford fancy muscle cars park their shitty cars so they can go *look* at the fancy muscle cars."

"To acquire them?"

"No." I killed the engine. "To buy ten-dollar corn dogs and dream."

Sitting in the roasting car, I watched children without a care in the world run through the grass, giggling and playing, while adults leaned against their rides and swapped stories. The scent of freshly cut grass wafted through my window, mingling with the aroma of gasoline and leather.

We exited our car, and the midday heat felt like we were walking on the surface of an angry star after a rainstorm. Kane scanned the vast make-shift lot, then stopped and seemed to lock onto something.

"If these people no longer require their vehicles, we could take something better than old Audi."

"We're not stealing a car," I said, then added, "again."

The big guy frowned. "What?"

I waved him off, indicating it had been a joke.

He said, "In Audi car, my knees bend at uncomfortable angles. A larger vehicle—"

"No, Kane."

He followed me as I wove through the field of trampled grass and rusting metal. In the distance, we could hear a hollow voice chattering over some fried speaker system and the burbling sounds of crowds, engines, and the occasional custom car horn.

"I would like to try driving when we return to Sad Girl's car."

"What? No."

"It may help me stretch my legs to be in the more accommodating driver's seat."

"No way. I do not have a death wish," I said. "Not at the moment."

I stumbled on the uneven ground and was surprised I hadn't fallen right on my face. Then I noticed Kane's hand holding my arm. He'd caught me before I face-planted in the dirt.

Pulling my arm back, I straightened out. "Thank you."

"If there are many vehicles here, we could acquire a second. Then we could both drive."

"What's with the need to take the wheel all of a sudden?" I looked up toward the ticketing booth, wary of what weird shit Kane might say when we got there. I'd have to be quick about it. "You hired me to drive and read"—I drop my voice low—"'troublesome mouth words.'"

I didn't have to look to know he was glaring at me.

"You trying to fire me?" I said it as a joke, but the acid in my stomach churned. I'd left a shitty job for this one. I didn't want to get stuck in the middle of Wisconsin broke and getting more broke.

Turning to him, I placed a hand on his chest. "Let me do my job. And it would be better for everyone—you, me, and the entire state—if you just sat with your hands folded in the passenger seat."

Kane looked down at his massive fingers and grimaced. "The hands of a hunter should never be folded. They should be gripping and tearing and fighting."

I turned away from him, glad the conversation had moved away from me losing my sole source of income.

"The way you drive," I said, nodding to the ticketing attendant ahead, "the hands of a hunter would have metal bracelets on them with a tiny chain linking both."

Behind me, Kane muttered, "I could easily break a tiny chain."

* * *

From our vantage point, standing in line, the car show looked like a salvage yard of well-loved vehicles the owners couldn't part with. Shined up with wax, chrome, and disposable income.

The ticketing booth listed slightly. It looked like little more than an old tool shed with a window cut out of it and a tiny shelf nailed below that. Because that was exactly what it was.

The woman inside beamed at me since, I guessed, I dropped the median age of attendees by a decade. The air around me cooled as something large blocked the sun. I saw the woman lift her gaze up and up. She scooted back a few inches.

"Boy that big, might have to charge him double," she said, eyes widening.

Kane frowned, leaning down to the gap between the glass and the wooden counter. "I am not a boy. I am w—"

"Willing to pay what everyone else does."

"Right," the woman said and pointed to the handwritten script on a sheet taped to the window. "Twenty bucks each, unless one of you is a student. Then it's ten."

Kane nodded. "I am a student."

I held up a hand in front of his face. "No, he's not."

"I am studying the ways of humans," Kane said, pushing my fingers down so he could see the woman. "So that I might find the man who cursed me with this form and return to my pack. Return to my wolf wife."

"You got a student ID for that?" she said, plastering her smile on again. It hung a little crookedly on her face.

"I do not."

"Then it'll be twenty dollars each. And today, every ticket gets a free soft pretzel."

"Great." I pointed at Kane and stepped aside. "The student of humans is paying."

The woman peeled off two tickets and put them on the wood slat. "Card or cash, hon?"

"I have tiny pieces of paper, which I got from my adoptive parents."

She lifted off her chair to see the wad of bills clutched in the massive hand. In charge of the bank card, I'd stopped at an ATM when we'd pulled into town.

"Grab a pair that got a two and a zero on them," the ticketing woman said, "and I'll give you your tickets."

Kane did so and handed them over. She grabbed their corners, her hand a third the size of his.

She exhaled when she pulled the money inside. "You best tuck that wad of cash deep into your pocket. We got thirty thousand people coming here today, and I can't vouch for all of them. Someone might want to take it."

I slid the tickets out with my fingertips and dropped both into my black leather jacket. A few sizes too big, it had been a parting gift from my ex-boyfriend. He couldn't have taken it with him anyhow. Prisons have what you might call a strict dress code.

"I have much more money than this," Kane replied but did as the woman had said, stuffing the large roll of bills deep into the front pocket of his jeans.

"Must be nice to have wealthy parents, hon."

"They were kind."

I tugged on his elbow, but he didn't move. "Come on, Kane."

"Found me in the forest. Took care of me," the large man said. "But they died in a fire."

The woman in the booth put a hand to her throat. "Oh dear. I'm so sorry to hear that."

"I was also sorry."

I pulled harder but felt like a kitten trying to drag a Greyhound bus. "Kane! Come on, let's get ins—"

He said to the woman, "I fed on their charred remains to honor them, but much was only soot. Very sooty."

The color ran from her face, her mouth hanging open.

"He's only just learning English," I said, kicking Kane in the shin, finally getting him to turn. "He's French Canadian."

The woman in the booth nodded to herself, clearing her throat. "Well, it's always nice to have folks from overseas."

I furrowed my brow then urged Kane on, getting him to finally walk side by side with me.

"She was very nice," he said.

"How about you don't talk to anyone for a while. You're not very good at, you know, discretion."

He shrugged. "I am wolf."

"That's exactly the sort of shit I don't want you to tell people," I said, heading toward a row of shiny vehicles. "Let me do the talking, and maybe we'll get a line on that purple car. But don't get your hopes up."

Kane sniffed the air. "I would also like to try a free soft pretzel."

Chapter Six

Kane had told me his story the morning after we'd met. Of course, had I not seen what I'd seen, I never would have believed something as batshit as a wolf who'd transformed into a man. I would have hightailed it out of my own apartment, leaving the nutjob far behind.

But I'd been inclined to give him some latitude.

I'd been working part time at a North Minneapolis bar filled with crooks, derelicts, and burnouts. The customers weren't much better.

Given my colorful past, I should have been happy to have any job at all. I wasn't. I'd hoped to save enough money so I could head west. My mother had moved out there years earlier, tired of the punishing Minnesota winters. I never could understand how she'd gone all the way out to California but hit the brakes about ninety minutes from the coast.

Not Los Angeles or San Diego or any place cool like that.

She lived in San Bernardino.

As if on clear nights, she might be able to see, in the distance, that she'd stopped just short of paradise. Maybe she was torturing herself. Some self-imposed penance for all the hell she'd put me through.

Or, hell, maybe she really did like San Bernardino. Can't imagine.

I'd heard stories, good and bad, about people trying to make a living in LA, but I'd been drawn to San Diego.

A year ago, I'd found a novel discarded in the bus station I'd been sleeping in, about a woman who'd owned some antique shop near San Diego. Some beautiful place where the sun always shone and seals frolicked on rocks in the bay. I wanted to live in a place just like that.

Work in a small shop. Eat my lunch at the beach, watch the seals play, and let the waves drag my troubles out to sea.

That sounded like paradise to me, and one day, I'd go and drive all the way to the water.

But that took money, which was why I had been working in the crappy bar. Each night when I got home, I felt worse than the morning before. Like the act of living merely shoveled me lower and lower into the earth.

The night I met Kane, I'd arrived at home feeling at an all-time low.

There'd been a fight at the bar. Well, a scuffle initially. Keith, the bartender, three times my size, sent me over to calm it down.

What a puss!

People love to tell me I've got some rage issues. So maybe it should have been no surprise that when one of the guys from table 17a put a sweaty hand on my shoulder to push me away, I'd grabbed a beer bottle and smashed it over his head. When the glass had sprayed, bar lights turning the shards into glittering stars around me, only then did it occur to me that maybe all those people had had a point.

Trying to hide that long-neck *indiscretion*, I'd jammed what was left of the beer bottle into my smock.

Sure, okay, it may have been an overreaction. I just didn't like random dudes putting their paws on me.

Sweaty Guy was bleeding from the head, so I was the bad guy. To calm things down, Keith the Puss had sent me home. Probably so he could take some credit for "handling it."

The upshot was me getting paid a half day of a shitty wage. Hell, my asshole boss probably charged me for the beer I'd smashed over the asshole customer's head.

So, back in my dank basement apartment, which I could not afford, I was home early from work, which I could not afford. I'd hit some gutter-ball lows in my twenty-four years, but at that point, I would have had to crane my neck skyward to see those former lows.

My nightly shower was always the best part of my day. But I'd been too tired. And my towel hadn't seen the inside of a washing machine in more than a week, so what was the point? Washing away the night's grime only to slather on the leftovers from all the days prior.

I sat down at the rickety table in my apartment and felt sorry for myself. Beaten down by the day, by a succession of shitty days, I toed off my shoes. When I'd attempted to remove the second one, the sole had split from the fabric.

And I broke.

One shoe on, one off. I stared at the one I hadn't been able to remove because it sucked at my foot like a gray leech. Didn't even know I'd been crying until I saw the damp stains on my bar smock. Well, I hadn't washed that either, no coins for the machine, so at least my tears were starting to get part of the job done.

Limply, I pulled at the ties around my neck and back, releasing it. When I let it fall to the floor, I'd heard a thunk. I leaned down and gripped the lump within. The sharp edge surprised me, and I snapped my hand back.

Reaching inside, I pulled out the long neck of the beer bottle, the brown glass split and shattered below. I held it in my hand for a long, long time, staring at those ragged teeth. A dark impulse, one I can usually quiet, had found its voice and was growing louder.

Mechanically, I laid my forearm on the table. In the dull overhead light, it looked like the slick underbelly of a frog. I knew kids in high school who'd dissected frogs, but I'd never had the chance. With my other hand, I gripped the bottle's neck and held it over that soft, exposed skin.

A thought repeated in my mind: *I'd never had the chance.*

I heard an odd yelp.

Startled, I spun around to see where it had come from. I didn't have a television. Not even a radio. And the building didn't allow pets of any kind, so...

When I turned toward the window just below my ceiling, alley-side, I saw a shuffle of feet. Yappy barking. A few more yelps then an animal howling in pain.

Something about that sound triggered me. Like a chemical reaction, an activator dropped into the emotional cocktail in my brain, the sound of someone beating the dog outside turned my black thoughts to instant and over-the-top rage.

Jumping up, I kicked my door open and ran up the steps into the dark alleyway, screaming at the two teenagers kicking one of the tiniest dogs I'd ever seen. Both of the guys were big, but that had never stopped me before. Two older cousins had cured me of that sort of hesitation.

My fists balled, I screamed at them, "What the hell are you doing?"

One of the young men stopped and turned on me, the ropes in his neck popping as he did. He opened his mouth to shout me down, but windows had started opening on my building. Residents not supporting me—that was never going to happen—but instead shouting down to tell us all to shut the hell up.

The two punk assholes bolted away.

I saw the little yippy dog beat to hell, wedged between two trash cans. Face bloodied, eyes half open. I'd always loved animals but didn't know the first thing about caring for one. I turned my face up toward the building, and in that moment, all the screamers above slammed their windows shut.

I laughed.

They didn't want any part of it, either.

But I couldn't leave the thing. My heart isn't that cold. At least, not for nonhumans.

I ran inside and grabbed the blanket I used to keep crumbs off my couch and returned outside. The dog hadn't moved, lying there motionless. I wrapped it up and brought it inside.

For an hour, I just watched it breathe. Occasionally, it would crack an eye open to see, maybe, if I was still there. Or just to confirm it wasn't dead yet. That thought brought out another laugh from me. Obviously, I was anthropomorphizing.

It was just a dog.

There were no existential thoughts trotting merrily through its canine brain. It was probably looking to see if anyone was offering treats.

At one point, the dog fell into a fit of tiny, plaintive whines. I braced. Would it die right there in front of me? On my couch?

"Shh," I said, unsure whether to approach it. "They don't allow dogs in here. You can't make any noise."

The craziest thing happened. Well, the craziest thing up to that point.

The dog stopped its whining. And it looked like—but of course it didn't—it looked like it nodded. Just two dips of its head. Then it fell asleep.

I walked over to my bed, plopped down, and pulled up the sheet. I watched the tiny creature's chest rise and fall. Rise and fall.

It hadn't had any collar or tags. Maybe it had one of those chips embedded in its shoulder. The ones a vet can scan to reveal its owner. In the morning, I'd take it to one of those. Or rather, drop it off, so they wouldn't think to charge me for the procedure.

As I drifted off to sleep, I wondered if such a small animal could be a stray. How would it survive a week on the street? Well, it nearly hadn't.

I couldn't keep it. I'd get kicked out. But I did feel a connection. Two strays just breathing in a dark, moldy basement, hidden far away from an uncaring world. Just for a moment, the two strays were safe.

Seeing the helpless thing lying there, sleeping but shuddering now and then from its injuries, I wasn't sure if it would make it through the night.

I began to cry. Silently, tears rolled down my face and onto my pillow. Only once did I see the creature stir, briefly opening its eyes.

It stared at me as I wept for it. Only for a few seconds, and then its eyes fell closed once again.

Soon after that, I drifted to sleep.

When I awoke the next morning, the dog was gone. Instead, a large, very *large* naked man was lying atop my couch, sleeping. He awoke seconds later.

Probably because of my scream.

Chapter Seven

The Menomonie Car Show had been staged in an area originally designed to house horses not vehicles.

Cement-and-steel stables had been converted into booths to sell engine parts, decals, helmets, and various straps and hoses. Several of them had display cases with tiny model cars similar to those just outside. Die-cast metal cars, many of them looking old and weathered. I wasn't sure if that had been by design—"distressed" I'd once heard that called—or if they were just old.

I couldn't determine if the little toy cars had been for sale, though everything else seemed to have a sticker price, or whether this allowed the owner to show off their collection. As if, having now earned their retirement, they could now make their case for a life well lived.

Or, maybe, just not wasted.

At least to them.

Humidity hung thick in the air, like invisible campfire smoke, clinging to the car lovers and the family members who loved them enough to tag along and not mention they'd rather be somewhere else.

Attendees—revelers might have been a better description, given the beatific expressions on their faces—ranged from the very young to the impossibly old. Clearly, some had dumped their coin jars to scrape up the entry fee. Others could have purchased half of the vehicles on display with the spare change that had fallen into their couch cushions.

Fry cooks and pilots, trash collectors and lawyers—they all left their vocations at the gate, mingling and talking to strangers as if they were old friends.

And despite the cost of their clothes, the fashion trend this season was sweaty chic. Everyone glistened in the Wisconsin sun. Or, since this was a celebration of automobiles, maybe they could be described as well oiled.

"I do not see any purple cars like the one I seek," Kane grumbled. Grumpy, too, since he hadn't spotted the soft pretzels that the ticketing woman had promised.

"When did you see it? A *year* ago?"

"Yes, I believe so."

"It's just not much to go on, Kane. Shiny purple car." I wiped the sweat from my forehead with a black leather sleeve.

"There was also bird. Bird on car."

"Right, 'bird on car.' Gotcha."

This search felt exactly like the one we'd embarked upon the previous weekend in Blaine, Minnesota. Except, this being Wisconsin, the cheese quotient was far higher.

That Blaine car show search had turned up zilch. Ah well, I still got paid. In fact, the longer we didn't find his purple car, the longer I would keep getting paid.

So, yeah, I wasn't looking *very* hard.

Not for the first time, my hand drifted to the inner pocket of my jacket, and I thumbed around until I felt the hard edge of a bank card.

After that bizarre morning finding a naked French Canadian on my couch, we'd gone a few streets over and found his clothes under some busted pallets behind a restaurant. He returned my ratty, old blanket to me, which I chucked in the trash. As he stood there, butt-ass naked, getting dressed, he offered me a job.

Kane needed to find the guy who'd bitten him. A story I would have not believed in a million lifetimes had I not seen, well, what I'd seen that morning.

The day before, he'd been checking out a car show at the Minneapolis fairgrounds when he'd run into some trouble. When I pressed him for details—I'd already seen a hundred years of trouble in my twenty-four—he instead told me that since becoming human, two things continued to be a problem for him.

Driving and reading.

And since he occasionally lost his clothes when he changed, I'd also hold his passport wallet.

"There is bank card, inside," he'd said, motioning to the leatherbound booklet. "My human parents' savings, which they said was mine to use when I needed it. They are gone, and now I need this money to find the Biting Man."

At least once an hour, my hand dipped into my pocket as I considered making a run with the card. I'd seen the balance several times when I'd pulled cash out of the machine for gas and motel stays. That kind of money? I could live off it for years.

I pulled my hand back as we wove through the milling crowd and moved deeper into the belly of the show-grounds beast. Then a low rumble rattled the compact dirt beneath our feet. Kane flexed and spun, arms raised.

I heard the screech of tires on the dust-covered concrete and turned to see a man riding a wooden motorcycle, no helmet, staring wide-eyed at the large French Canadian who looked ready to fight his bike.

"Whoa now, big man," the middle-aged man said in a thick Midwestern drawl. He sat on his bike like a redneck king on his throne. His crown of sweaty stray hairs stuck to his balding head. "I'm just looking to get through. Don't want you turning my girl into splinters."

"*Qu'est-ce que c'est?*" Kane asked, baring his teeth, hands still rolled into sledgehammer fists.

The heavy guy blinked as the bike rumbled beneath him. He looked my way.

"Did he just swear at me?" The man's voice trembled as he spoke. But that might just have been because of its rattling motor. "No cussin' at the car show, now."

"No, no, he's, you know, foreign," I said, slipping out of the sun into the blissful shade of a massive display shed, which, days earlier, had been a stall for at least a dozen horses. Admiring the man's ride, I asked him, "Is this made out of *wood*?"

He laughed and patted the chassis. "Sure is! Beautiful creature, ain't she?"

"It's unique." I shook my head. "Where did you get a wooden motorcycle?"

"Didn't *get* it, miss," the man said, leaning back in his seat and crossing his pink, fleshy arms. "Made it."

Kane looked at me, a fierce look in his eyes. I waved his hands down and sighed.

"It's *just* a motorcycle."

"I know motorcycle." Kane eyeballed the machine. "This is not a motorcycle. It is made from tree."

The man on the bike laughed. "Well, yeah. My missus forbade me from buying a motorcycle. Said if I went and did that, she'd be out the door," he said, grinning. I could tell this was a story he loved to tell. "Mind you, it was a very tempting offer."

"Nice," I said, giving him the prompt he needed to continue. I'd always liked older people. They reminded me of my grandmother, the kindest person the world had ever squeezed out.

"Couldn't buy one, so I built one myself. I can do a bit with engines and the like, but I ain't no welder," he said. "During all that lockdown business, I had some time on my hands, so I just started banging bits of wood together and, well, just kept at it."

I smiled. "And it became... this?"

"Took me ten months, but I kept my promise to the wife." He grinned with a brilliant, perfect smile. "I didn't buy a motorcycle. I made one."

"Is it safe?" I asked.

"People get the wrong idea about bikes." He leaned over the handlebars, the effort eliciting one of those retiree groans, and crossed his hands at the wrists. "Motorcycles aren't dangerous. What's dangerous is all the drivers around them. Without those folks, you're perfectly safe."

Before I could say another word, an ear-splitting engine roar screamed into the covered paddock. One moment, Kane was standing there. The next, it was all black and chrome and smoke.

And Kane was gone.

Chapter Eight

I stared at the empty space for just a moment, my ears still ringing from the motorcycle that had rocketed past, just inches from me. For that moment, my visual world had become only chrome, leather, and a shiny, deep-black streak.

Snapping my head to the left, I could see the man on the wooden motorcycle, and he looked as shocked as me. I turned to where he was staring, his eyes like those of a meth freak tweaking out of his mind.

Nearby display cases had been smashed into a jumble of splinters and busted plexiglass. Only one hadn't been destroyed.

Dreamily, I realized I hadn't even heard the crash.

There was also a large French Canadian on the ground, face half turned into the debris.

On top of Kane was a man dressed in combat fatigues. He seemed barely thirty but had a crewcut of silver hair. Oh, and he was straddling a black motorcycle that looked as big as a Volkswagen. Which, if it's not clear, was on top of my new boss.

Had this happened in a mall, people would have been running and screaming, heading for the exits. However, this was not a mall. Actually, do people even go to malls anymore?

Not the point.

No, this was a car show. People who lived for the smell of exhaust, the screech of tires, and the roar of engines. Rough and tumble and a bit of blood. None of this was new to them.

Two large men in bikers' leather, head to toe, no sleeves, were instantly on top of the guy on the bike, throwing him to the ground. The motorcycle tipped, falling and shattering the last standing display case. The leather dudes bent down to check on Kane.

This was not their first rodeo. And by rodeo, I mean the first time they'd seen someone run down by a bike.

A woman strode up, face like an orange left out in the sun, clipboard under her arm, and punched the man in the army fatigues just as he was standing. He tumbled back to the dusty concrete floor, shouting and cursing.

From the ground, he wiped some blood from his mouth and pointed at Kane, who was slowly being helped to his feet.

"Kane, how the fuck are *you* here?" he shouted as three others, two men and a woman, also dressed in what appeared to be secondhand army gear, ran up to him. They circled the guy like an honor guard. "You've been told to stay out of this!"

Kane shouldered himself away from the men who'd been helping him and pointed at the guy who'd run him down. He looked like he was about to throw some heat back at him then noticed his finger was bent at a right angle.

He reached forward and *straightened his broken finger*. When it popped into place, all the big tough men and women around us went, "Eeew."

One of the attacker's crew, a massive gorilla of a man, pulled the short, muscular dude away.

"Come on, man. Not the place."

The boss growled at him—yeah, the guy growled—and extended an arm so fast I didn't even see it move. His lackey, twice his size, flew back against the side of the enclosure, his feet never even touching the ground.

From the opposite end of the enclosed paddock, a group of five large men, each carrying a bat or pipe in their hands, were running in, itching for a fight.

The two standing goons helped the gorilla guy up, and then all four turned and bolted into the sunlight. As they exited, a black truck wheeled up, forcing gawkers to leap out of the way lest they get flattened. High off the ground, the vehicle had an enclosed cargo bed with darkened windows and was spiked with antennas. Below, the truck's throaty wraparound pipes looked like fat, shiny lower intestines.

They all hopped in and raced away, kicking up grit, which turned the surrounding air into a whiteout.

The dust settled after a few seconds, and I heard a thud.

Kane was back on the ground.

"Jesus, are you okay?"

"I will be fine," he said, coughing in the haze. "But I had motorcycle man on my chest, and it was quite heavy. I will need a minute."

One of the sleeveless leather guys came up, checking my friend's eyes and neck. Then he pulled out a pocket watch—dude had a pocket watch—and put two fingers to Kane's wrist.

"Wait," I said, looking at the gruff man. "You're an EMT?"

"Sorta," he said then called over to the guy who'd been on the wooden motorcycle. "Dock, you got a minute?"

The heavyset man rose from his seat and headed toward us.

EMT-Sorta Guy hooked a thumb in the waddling man's direction. "Bunch of us are in the medical field. Or were. Dock's retired but knows this stuff better than me."

The guy with the wooden motorcycle knelt, picking up the conversational thread. "Former doctor. Pediatric surgeon. But I've spent plenty of time in emergency rooms," he said and slowly shook his head. "You friend must be in some kind of shock. I mean, his heart should be rabbiting right now. But his ticker is thumpin' along like he's reading the paper."

"I do not read papers," Kane said, trying to sit up. "I am wolf."

The former doctor scratched his neatly trimmed gray goatee and looked at me, popping his eyebrows. "I think he got a bad knock to the head."

"No, it's okay. He's French Canadian."

The first guy who'd tended to Kane stepped over and exchanged a few hushed words with the guys carrying the bats and pipes. They looked disappointed there hadn't been a fight.

The man next to Kane looked at me with soft eyes. "Listen, miss—"

"It's Emelda."

"Right, Emelda," he said and flashed me a grin. "I'm Dale Brubaker, but people call me Dock."

"Makes sense. You are a pediatric surgeon, sure."

"No, not Doc. It's Dock," he said. "Because I'm the only one around who's got a boat. Built my own dock outta the trees on my property. Sometimes, we all go fishing—"

I interrupted him. "He's okay, then?"

"Maybe," Dock said. "I think he needs a—"

"Kane doesn't do hospitals."

Dock smiled at me. "I wasn't going to say hospital."

"Oh."

"I think your man needs a *beer*," he said and fished into the pocket of his overalls, pulling out two red ticket stubs. "I'm one of the organizers here, so I get a mittful of these. Why don't you and your big buddy here go put your feet up."

I laughed. "He's not really a put-your-feet-up kind of guy."

The former surgeon looked between us. Kane had lost interest in our people talky-talk and was digging into the rubble next to him. Must have seen something shiny. Or maybe he was thinking of eating a bug?

Dock motioned to the toppled bike Camo Guy had run down Kane with. "That there motorcycle belongs to one of our regulars and has to weigh over 500 pounds. Add another 200-odd pounds for the asshole who was sitting on it, and you're talking a third of a ton pressing down on your boy's chest," he said. "That should have cracked his rib cage if not crushed him down to a tortilla. It didn't, but that doesn't mean he's not injured. He needs to take a moment."

"I'll take care of him."

"He *seems* totally fine. Just had his bell rung." Dock looked over and laughed. "Playing with the toy cars from the busted-up cases, so I'm not too worried."

All I did was nod.

"Y'all grab a beer at the tent over there—the big one with the yellow and white stripes. I'll make sure nobody bothers you." Dock stood and walked toward his buddy and the disappointed men with the sticks of wood and metal.

When I turned back to Kane, he was still lying on his back, covered in dust and broken bits of plexiglass. I brushed a few shards away then pulled my arm back and punched his chest.

He grimaced at me. "Why are you tapping me with your tiny fist?"

"What the hell was all that about?" I said, keeping my voice low. We had people watching us, but they didn't feel nosy. It was actually comforting, like they were just making sure we were okay. "That guy knew your name!"

Kane grabbed my wrist and slowly turned my hand over. Then he dropped the toy car he'd been holding into my palm. "This is car," he said. He spat out some grit and sat up. "This is car I saw in the woods that terrible day."

My jaw hanging down, my mind whirring, I just stared at the toy vehicle. It had been in the prize collection of an older man who'd been taken to the medical tent. Trying to wrap my head around what Kane had just said, I squinted at it.

"This is yellow." Holding the car up to the light, I frowned. "Are wolves color blind too?"

"Is same sort of car," Kane said, standing.

Dust drizzled down onto me as I examined the die-cast replica. Then I felt his meaty hand on my arm, and he lifted me to my feet.

"Has bird on hood. Except car is purple."

"Right. Well, when you said bird, I thought...." Hell, I hadn't known what he'd meant. The guy was confusing. "It's a Firebird? Who the hell drives a Firebird anymore?"

Kane looked out at the rows upon rows of vehicles. "This is why we go to car shows."

I dropped the tiny model into my pocket, eliciting a frown from Kane. Before he could speak, I put a hand up.

"I'm not taking it, just borrowing it," I said, knowing too well how he felt about rules and laws. "I'll give it back."

"It is not ours to take. What is someone's is someone's. What you have acquired is yours."

"Right, whatever," I said. He started to walk past me. I put a hand up on his chest. Sure, it wouldn't have stopped him. I could have jumped at Kane's chest, and it wouldn't have even ruffled his curly hairs.

He saw my hand, stopped, and turned to me.

"Who was that asshole, Kane?"

He sighed, shaking his head.

I pressed. "Are those guys after you?"

He shook his head. "Not after me. We are seeking the same."

"What?" Again, I threw my hands up. "What does that mean?"

Kane reached into my pocket and pulled out the tiny metal car and held it in front of my face. "We both seek the man in the purple Firebird."

Chapter Nine

Kane frowned as the woman in the *I'm Spending My Kids' Inheritance* t-shirt slid the orange plastic tray toward us. I couldn't help but smile. To me, life didn't get much better than when free food and beer were involved.

The dining tent buzzed with chatter and laughter that floated on heady aromas of fried food, ballpark condiments, and dirty boots. Families with young children and the old people who'd dragged them there sat at picnic tables covered in bright red-and-white checkered cloths.

My boss stared down at the two tinfoil-wrapped hotdogs like a cat being shown a magic trick. He didn't much like processed food. Not pasteurized, not seasoned, and especially not cooked.

But he did have a sweet tooth.

"My friend got attacked over at one of the paddocks," I said to the lady behind the counter. She tugged and twisted a lock of her graying auburn hair, wrapping the end of it around her finger.

"Heard about that." She eyeballed Kane, taking a step back to take him all in. "Brave."

"Ha, he got knocked on his ass, so not so brave."

"Nah," she said with a grin as her fingertip turned pink. "I mean brave of them to attack a man like this. Good lord, boy, how tall are you?"

"200 centimeters," Kane said.

She turned to me. "Is that a lot? It looks like a lot."

I ignored the question. "I'm afraid he got a poke to the eye. Do you have, you know, a raw steak I could put on it? I'll pay for it." I blinked. "He'll pay for it."

She dropped the hand from her hair and went to a large stand-up refrigerator that looked older than she was. Returning with a steak wrapped in cellophane, she dropped it on the tray next to the dogs.

"Don't worry about the charge," she said, lowering her voice. "We don't like when our visitors have a bad time of it. Beers and dogs and the steak are yours. Hope the rest of the day goes a mite better." She pointed at the entrance of the tent. "A couple of our boys chased down the jerks in the fancy truck but couldn't keep up. Which is saying something, because these fellas, they're looking for any reason to floor it. Boys in the truck smoked 'em. Although you won't likely hear anyone around here admit that outright."

We grabbed one of the open picnic tables, and the instant we sat down, Kane started to unwrap his steak. I put a hand on his hand and shook my head.

"First, you tell me what the hell you dragged me into."

"Not dragged." Kane frowned. "You offered to help if I pay."

"Right, sure, but you only said you were looking for"—I imitated his voice—"'pur-ple car.' In the past two weeks, you never *once* said anything about the violent-assholes factor. All I know is we're looking for a car. That's it!"

Kane grinned at me. "You know I turned from wolf into man during the night on your smelly couch."

"Ah, no. Not wolf. Dog. *Lap*dog."

That darkened my big friend. "It is sometimes confusing. Even for me. Especially for me."

"Whatever."

Kane folded his hands in front of him. "So, wolf who turns into man, this is okay? But angry tech sergeant with mean crew, now this is too far?" He grinned at me with teeth that looked ready to chew on a grandmother.

I leaned back and crossed my arms. "Tech sergeant?"

He looked at me like the cat that ate the canary. Or the wolf who ate whatever he wants to, I suppose.

"This Biting Man I am looking for, he is also being sought by another," Kane said, avoiding my eyes. "The tech sergeant is troublesome man who I have tried to avoid. I do not understand how he is also here."

"Probably had the same idea you did. Car shows." I leaned my elbows on the table and snapped my fingers to get him to look at me. "What the hell have you gotten me into?"

"You offered to help, Sad Girl."

"I offered to get *paid* to drive you around," I said, tapping my finger on the table. "Read maps and road signs."

"My reading, this is not so good."

"Yes, yes. You are wolf. Noted." I folded my hands together. "So who the hell is this tech sergeant? Do I need to be worried?"

Kane went to grab the plastic-wrapped meat then pointed at it and raised his bushy eyebrows.

I shook my head. "Story first."

"Okay," he said and licked his lips. "The Biting Man with the purple car is someone who is known to Tech Sergeant Gregor."

"Gregor?"

"Yes, he is a very angry man. He is little, sure, but all humans are little." Kane lifted a shoulder then winced. He'd gotten more injured than he'd been letting on. "However, Gregor is far stronger than he looks."

I barked out a laugh. "That's rich coming from you."

"I need to find Biting Man, because he is the only one to tell me how I can return to wolf. He has the secret of what has happened to me."

"And how do you even know that?"

"Because he is who do this to me!" Kane roared, fists hitting the table. The dining tent went silent.

I gazed around at the faces staring at us. Strangely, they'd all started watching me, not the big man who'd made all the ruckus. I realized they were looking to see if I needed any help. I had to defuse it quickly.

"Sorry, we're just, um, practicing," I said with a wide grin. "Renaissance fair coming up. Me and Sir Galahad are just going through lines. We'll keep it down."

The gazes fell away, and when I finally looked back to Kane, he'd twisted his face into a half scowl, half smile.

"So you have knighted me now?"

"Oh, right." I pointed at him. "You know about knights, but you don't know a damn thing about anything else."

"My human parents, they used to watch the *Throne Games* show. I have learned much from this show."

"Probably not," I said. "Wait, how did that even happen? You've always been a bit cagey about that shit."

"Cagey?"

"Not forthcoming," I said, knowing this would not clear it up for him. "They just took a random naked guy in?"

"It is unimportant."

I leaned forward. "I've taken that line from you for weeks. Now we've got a cadre of asshats, violent ones, sniffing around. Spill it, wolfman. How did you come to live with your parents?" When he frowned, I crossed my arms again. "We don't leave this car show until I get an answer. Unless you like walking."

Kane darkened, his eyes distant. Slowly, he nodded. "They had pity on a boy in the woods. I knew nothing of the world of people."

"Well, yeah."

"But they were kind. The times that I find myself disappointed with humans—"

"Like the night I found you. Those guys in the alley trying to kick you to death."

"Times like those, yes, certainly," Kane said softly. "I remember the kindness of Mère and Père. They were very good to me."

Something he had said confused me. "Wait, as a boy? How old were you, um, before?"

"I do not know in human numbers, but Mère had said when they found me, I was young teen, as she'd told me."

That didn't jive with what I knew.

"But you said you'd been with them for only a year." I leaned back in the chair and looked around to make sure no one was listening in. "Is that more bullshit?"

"No. This all began last warm season. And it was a very pleasant and loving year. Despite looking like a stupid human," he said, dampness making his eyes shine. "They were kind. And they knew I was different. Knew I would have to leave. This is why they often spoke English in the home, not only French, which they preferred, of course. They also knew of the Biting Man. It was Père who had seen this. He had told me because those images at the time, they confuse. Père told me of the purple car with the bird."

"Wait, wait," I said, throwing my hands up. "What you're saying is last year you were a 'young teen,' but you look thirty-five. So where did those twenty years go?"

Kane looked around the room then settled his eyes back on me. "Mère noticed this first," he said, the memory softening his words. "'You grow so fast, Kane. You will be a fine, strong man.' But Père was a harder person. Love there, but harder. He says I grow too fast."

"Too fast?"

"He tell me I grow much faster than normal humans, but, of course, they knew I was not normal."

"Can't argue with that."

"Last year, near this time, I am teen. Now I am older."

"So like twenty years for every one or something?"

Kane shook his head. "Slow at first, I think. Speeding up over the months. In first few months, not so much. Then following month, a year. Next, another two. These are just guesses, of course, and not my own."

"I'll deal with guesses. So it's speeding up?"

The large man nodded. "Wolf is not supposed to be man. And this is what is happening."

"How... how do you even know this?"

"My parents couldn't take me to *l'hopital*. Too many questions. They did know of an old man in town who had been a doctor many years ago. They took me to see him."

"And so these guesses, some of these are his?"

"Much is his, yes."

Trying to piece the story together in my head, I asked him, "So you left to go find Biting Man because of the aging thing? Running out of time?"

Kane shook his head slowly. "No, it was only a short time after we go to the old doctor," he said. "One night, I awoke to our home in flames."

"Burning?"

"Yes, burning." He said, his voice hitching. "I go to my parents' room, but it is all flame. I run through to grab them, but they are not moving. I heard shouting outside. Men, I don't know."

"Did you run?"

"I think. Maybe, yes."

"What the hell does that mean?"

He sighed. "My parents, they learned this," he said. "They say do not step into the moonlight. For you, moonlight is dangerous."

"Dangerous how?"

"It changes me."

I sighed. "Jesus. Okay, I've heard that. Stories. Thought it was all bullshit."

"Many bullshit stories come from truth place." Kane stared into his large hands, which clenched into fists. "But when I went to the window to see the shouting, I was angry. My parents burning next to me. The moon was out. I rarely had seen it, because they had never allowed this."

"Okay. Then?"

"I am confused by what happened then. I woke up when morning comes, and, as the first time, I was once again naked in the woods. But this time covered in blood." He sighed. "It was not my blood."

Chapter Ten

After I had finally given the go-ahead, Kane had unwrapped the bloody, raw steak and smelled it. He grinned.

"If you're going to chomp that down," I whispered, "do it kinda fast. I don't want people to see you—"

Kane chucked the entire steak into his mouth, chewed twice, and swallowed.

"—eating that." I fought back some of the rising bile and stuck out my tongue. "Bleh. Gross."

"Is good," the big man said, licking his lips.

I began gathering up the trash on our table. "Well, we've got that toy car. That's a start."

He nodded, a silly, satisfied look on his face.

"I suppose we could..." My voice trailed off as the rumble of a motorcycle filled the tent. I braced for Round Two with Gregor.

Instead, when I looked up, I saw Dock on his wooden bike, scanning the group of casual diners. He was looking for us.

"Time to go. Get a move on." I stood up, ducked my head, and headed toward the row of large red trash cans tucked at the edge of the tent.

When I turned around, Kane was gone.

At first, I panicked at the idea of getting ditched.

Alone.

Then I realized part of me *wanted* to run. I hadn't signed up for this kind of madness. Despite being the keeper of the bank card, I had no money other than what Kane had paid me so far. Well, that and the cash he'd given me for my neighbor's old Audi. The old guy hadn't driven it for more than a year, and I told Kane he'd sell it to us for two grand.

I just, you know, hadn't told my *neighbor* that. He wouldn't miss it for a while. I liked the old guy and had gotten him groceries now and again. I'd just borrowed the car.

All added up, it was the most cash I'd had all at once in my entire life. $3,214 stuffed into my backpack. I couldn't remember the last time I'd had more than a hundred bucks to my name.

And he'd promised more.

Was it worth it?

This bizarre chase after some Biting Man phantom? The threat of Tech Sergeant Gregor, who'd already knocked the big man down once. And not to mention my boss was part wolf. Or at least part lapdog.

However, when I thought about running—an appealing idea that was getting more appealing by the minute—I realized something.

I had nowhere to run to.

But the truth was Kane *needed* me. I was ashamed to admit it to myself, but that was worth even more than $3,214.

"Sad Girl!"

I snapped my head toward the entrance of the tent. Kane was standing next to the man with the wooden motorcycle, who'd donned a straw cowboy hat to block the sun from cooking his bald head.

"I wish he'd stop calling me that." I chucked our trash into the big plastic bins and headed over.

When I came up, Dock was sitting on his bike and staring at something in his hands. The tiny yellow car. He turned it over a few times.

How the hell had Kane snatched that from my pocket?

"You got this from Johnnie's collection, didn't you?" Dock flicked his eyes up at Kane. "He's going to want it back. He don't have any real cars anymore. All he's got left are these antique replicas."

"He can have. I do not want," Kane said, his head low. I realized he'd been ashamed for taking it. "But have you seen another like it? Purple color."

"Hell, we see thousands of cars, so yeah, maybe," Dock said, dropping the toy into one of his leather saddlebags. He made an ordeal of snapping it closed. "Johnnie has a pretty unique collection. Maybe you could buy one on the internet or something. They got damn near everything."

"No. Not toy," Kane said, struggling with his words.

I put a hand on the wooden handlebars of the bike and smiled. "We've been thinking about getting a fun car. Something to take to shows. Is there a life-sized version of that car, the Firebird, that might be for sale? Purple's his favorite color."

"It is?" Dock traced his eyes up to Kane. This took a moment. "Don't look like a fella who'd favor purple, to be honest."

I shrugged. "Big Prince fan."

Dock pulled off his straw hat, scratched his head, then put it back on. "That only makes it weirder, I reckon."

"Have you seen?" Kane said, his voice nearly a growl.

Once again, I leaned in. "Do you know anyone who might sell a real one of those? But in purple."

The old guy eyeballed the two of us for a moment then flipped a toggle on his bike and hit the starter. The motorcycle came alive once again with a throaty rumble. "I'm not sure what the two of you are playin' at, but I think we should head over to my trailer," he said, saddling up straight and toeing the kickstand.

"Is that a 'yes,' then?" I said, not yet letting go of the handlebars.

Dock looked down and turned them sharply, and my hand fell away.

"Follow me up the road here," he said, revving the engine a few times. The bike coughed out a plume of smoke. "I got a primo spot, and we can get this story straight."

"You *have* seen the purple car?" Kane said, agitated.

"Yes, I seen one. And the chaos that came with it," Dock said, slowly puttering away. He nodded forward. "Trailer."

Chapter Eleven

We walked behind the bike as Dock steered through the crowd. Normally, it would have been a thirty-second ride or a two-minute walk. However, the man on the unusual motorcycle had to stop every few feet to talk to friends and strangers alike.

Everyone wanted to revel in his creation.

I watched Dock smile and nod, telling his story as he went. The guy was a charmer and a bit of a showman. And, it seemed, was doing everything he could to make anyone interested feel special.

In turn, many would recount an old uncle or grandfather who'd made stuff with their hands years ago in the family garage, a cramped workshop, or a backyard strewn with rusting bits of this and that.

Dock's wooden bike gave people a chance to share a bit of themselves.

Trading stories might be the most ancient and pure form of barter humans ever came up with. If we'd only stuck to that, I think our species would have been better off.

When we finally got to the trailer, which was set up next to one of the covered paddocks, Dock parked the bike under the shade of a large red-and-white awning. He directed us toward a square picnic table stacked up with pamphlets and brochures. Many were still in boxes with their lids torn off.

"You two want anything to drink? I got domestic only. No imports, now."

Kane nodded. "Do you have fresh milk?"

"Uh, no," Dock said, halfway up into his trailer, which shined in the midday sun like a big, squat silver pill. It was made from brushed steel, with metal bands wrapping around its belly. Big enough for two people, but I didn't spot his frugal wife inside.

The old man began to say something else, thought better of it, and disappeared inside his home on wheels.

Sitting at the picnic table opposite Kane, I examined the boxes. "These are all for car shows." I slid another open box closer. "This one's for Milwaukee. That other one's for Winona, Minnesota." Leaning forward, I pointed to three other stacks between them. "Wausau. That's in Wisconsin. Duluth. Grand Forks."

The big man frowned and looked away. "Are you saying these things to make me feel stupid?"

"What? No. Why would—"

"I have trouble reading any of this," Kane said, sweeping his big hand over the glossy brochures. "You know I cannot. And yet you say this to make me feel stupid. Yes?"

"No." I reached out to grab his hand. "I'm just getting our bearings here, not trying to make fun of you."

"Then you do without trying."

A bark of laughter erupted from the trailer's open door. "Lovers' quarrel now?" Dock said, hitting the bottom stair outside his door, shifting the entire trailer on its axis.

When he sat down in the lawn chair next to the table, he put a brown bottle in front of both of us. "That there's Leinenkugel," he said, grinning. "Leinies is what you call 'em if you want to fit in with the locals. Best brew you'll find in four states."

"Thank you." I tipped the bottle toward my mouth but didn't take a sip. I'd learned long ago not to take drinks from people I didn't know.

Kane stared at the bubbles rising in the bottle. "What is this?"

"Beer, son." Laughing, Dock slapped him on the back and shook his hand gingerly afterward. Flexing his fingers, he said, "Put hair on your chest."

"I have much hair on my chest." Kane said, eyeballing the bottle. "Hair everywhere. Although not as much as when I am—"

"Wintering!" I interrupted. "Kane lets it all grow out in the winter."

Dock blinked and smiled. "You get any more hair, and you'll look like a Wookie."

Kane frowned and cut his eyes toward me, and I shook him off with a single nod. For a beast of a man, the dude was very sensitive about the mere hint of slight.

"So," I said before Kane got mad. "The purple car. Rather, a purple car. If you know—"

"We can drop some of the pretense, I reckon," Dock said, taking a swig. He burped and smiled to himself. "It is 'the' purple car. And before we talk about that, I wanna know your interest in it."

Kane leaned forward and opened his mouth. He slammed his lips closed then reached down to rub his shin where a boot had knocked him a moment earlier.

I told our host, "As I said, he wants what he wants. And he's got money, so..."

Dock took another sip, leaned back, and folded his chubby hands over his chubby belly. He looked between the two strangers in front of him for a moment.

"There is a circuit, you see," he said, nodding at the pamphlets on the table. "From May to September, or thereabouts, we got a car show every weekend. Many of the folks here join us for the entire season. Some just a few shows. Some just one."

I asked, "So you saw the purple car at one of those shows?"

The old man grabbed his bottle and began peeling the label. "Sometime last year, it all—" Dock stopped, shook his head, and continued. "A young man turns up at the Gisborne show, up near Lake Mille Lacs. About two hours' drive north of Minneapolis."

Kane brightened. "Mille Lacs. Thousand Lakes. I like this name."

"That's right. You're French, ain't ya?" Dock smiled at the big man.

"Wait, it means Lake Thousand Lakes?" I said, scrunching my nose up. "Horrible."

"Well, the Frenchies probably named it. Not known for their creativity," Dock said, chuckling. "No offense intended, my friend."

"I am French Canadian." Kane shrugged. "Is different."

"Uh-huh," Dock said. He nodded deeper into the bustling car show. "So, one of our regulars, he took his Purple People Pleaser all up and yonder through the Midwest. Had five cars all up, but the Purple People Pleaser was his pride and joy."

"Ugh, that name is gross," I said. "Just... dudes."

"What happened to this"—Kane inched closer to the old man—"Portal Penal Peeper?"

Dock frowned. *"Purple People Pleaser."*

Kane shook his head. "Papal Peter Peeker."

"No, no," Dock said, staring at the big man. "Just call it 3P so you don't bruise your brain, son."

I leaned over the table. "Fine. Okay. What happened to 3P?"

Dock sighed. "Up at the Gisborne show, everything was going fine and dandy. Had a local rockabilly band playing. Sun shone every day, not the crazy rain like we've been seeing—"

"Please get to the point." I plastered a smile on my face. "What happened?"

The old man scratched his gray-white goatee. "This young fella turns up. Strong kid, looked like he mighta been military. We get a lot of them at our shows."

He fell quiet for a moment, and I rolled my hand to get the story going again.

"But he don't seem right. Then again, we're used to odd folks. But then he *steals* the Purp—um—3P and takes right off," Dock said, his voice low. "No one's seen him since, and boy, they went a-lookin'. Because he didn't just take the car. I mean, the way the boy looked... crazed, I call it. Others said it was something else."

"Like what?" My voice was a whisper.

"Haunted, maybe? If he was military, you could understand that if he'd been stationed over in the sandbox or something." Dock fingered his straw hat aside and scratched his head. I wondered if the sun had already taken its toll. "But more than that. Deranged. Manic. Whatever he was, the boy wasn't right. Not at all. Crazy kid tried to steal the 3P, but as I said, Charlie loved that vehicle. Tried to stop him and got bit! That boy *bit* Charlie Boynton, for chrissakes!"

Kane put his hands on his knees and leapt up from the table, his head brushing the awning. "Where is the man with the purple car now? Where can I find him?" He leaned in, towering over Dock.

"Now, hold on—"

"No, enough stories," Kane said, his fingers flexing. "I must find the man in the Parkour Penis Peever!"

Dock slid his chair back, cutting two gouges in the dirt and sand. Jaw hanging down, he shot a look at me.

I held a hand out to my friend. "It's fine. It's fine." I spoke calmly, soothing him. "We're finding out. He's telling us. Sit down, Kane."

The large man breathed a few times until he finally blinked. Slowly, he returned to his seat.

I turned to Dock. "Maybe skip to the important part about now, yeah?"

Dock nodded. "Listen, that moment... it changed everything for our shows. People are scared. We still get a good crowd, but most of them, I reckon, haven't heard the stories yet. But attendance is way off." He looked at his bottle on the table, went to reach for it, then pulled his arm back. "And people. People have been hurt. Probably worse. I wish I'd never seen that car. Or that young man that day."

"Wait," I said and huffed. "Okay, maybe that was too much skipping. What the hell happened?"

Dock sighed, and his eyes turned glassy. "Charlie went to the Gisborne hospital, and they gave him a tetanus shot for the bite. Checked him for a few things but gave him a clean bill and sent him along."

The man turned quiet.

I spoke in the same calming voice I'd used on Kane. "So he was okay?"

"Don't know," Dock said, rubbing his thumb over his eyes and taking a quick sip of beer. Most of it dribbled down onto his shirt. "Next morning, people went up to his trailer to check on him. Only he wasn't there no more." He exhaled, and it came out shaky. "You see, they didn't even have to knock because... the door? Torn clean off. Inside was like a tornado had come through. Good folks around here, they loaded up Charlie's remaining four cars, and we took them to the next show in Duluth. Hoping he'd show up."

"And did he?"

Dock shook his head. "Not Charlie, but some folks claim they saw that military kid."

I asked, "They were sure?"

"Had a sleeve tat," Dock said, motioning to his own arm, which was pink and nearly hairless. "Bunch of stuff, but you could make out the snake that went from his wrist to past his elbow."

Kane didn't respond, but I could sense from the way he stiffened that he was working hard not to.

Dock continued. "People said they'd seen him at night. Running between booths. In and out of display tents. I thought it was just storytellin', you know? Someone trying to gin up a bit of excitement. Who knows? Might even sell more tickets or something."

We waited as the man took another swig of his beer and stared at the cheerful crowds weaving in and out of red-roped displays, enjoying the show.

"Our regulars are good people. Maybe some weren't so good some years ago, but old cars got a way of getting your head right a lot of times. You appreciate life. We got more than a hundred families that travel in this show, and really, it's one big family."

I nodded, smiling. "I can see that."

"So then, someone *else* goes missing at the Pine Valley show, out near Alexandria, Minnesota. Bridget Mills, Lorney's wife. She's just gone, and he's worried." Dock sighed. "Called the local sheriff, and they take a look around, but they didn't find anything. They promised to come back in the morning."

Dock took another sip of his beer.

"When they did," Dock said, his voice shaking again, "Lorney's trailer..." The man's eyes unfocused, and his voice faded to nothing.

"His trailer?" I asked.

Another sigh. "It was like a slaughterhouse, miss. Worse. Like nothing you can imagine. We knew it was Lorney, but they'd had to confirm that with dental records."

My throat tensed. "Do they know who did it?"

"Well... from what I've heard, ol' Lorney wasn't kind to his wife. People had been whispering about that for years. So, who knows, maybe Bridget had had enough of it." Dock frowned and drew the tip of his tongue across his lower lip. "But the way that man had been torn up? No way it could have been her."

"Jesus," I said.

That drew a sad smile from Dock. "You religious at all, Emelda?"

"Not so much. Years ago, maybe. Me and God, we had a falling out."

"Well, I reckon that's what might have happened here. Or something like it." Dock pulled at the label on his beer again. "God blinked. That's what my mother used to say when something real bad happened. God blinked. Took his eyes off ya for a just a moment. Musta been what happened to Lorney, because other than the splatter and smear on the walls? Just nothing."

I put a hand to my mouth. "What do you mean nothing?"

"Nothing left of ol' Lorn. Just bones. All the flesh had been torn from his body," Dock said. He grabbed his beer bottle by its neck and arced it through the air. It landed in a rusted barrel next to his trailer with a clang. "Eaten, Miss Emelda. The man was eaten."

Chapter Twelve

I watched for the next minute as Dock tried to continue his story. And yeah, this story needed continuing.

He'd started with a half-hearted laugh, but the words wouldn't come.

Then he took a deep breath as if he'd decided maybe he'd treat this like we were all sitting in the break room at work, avoiding the daily slog, and he was just telling us about some show he'd watched the night before. But after the shaky breath, he'd come up short.

When sadness pulled at his sagging face, I thought he might try again. Instead, he just looked at the two of us and gave us a weary, damp smile. He stood up and walked into his trailer.

Clearly, Dock was still struggling with whatever had happened. He hadn't yet worked everything out, or maybe any of it, to be able to finish his story.

Instead of facts, he had feelings. Emotions. That was how he'd known the story, I guessed.

For Dock, the details of what followed Lorney Mills being *eaten* were written in emotion. Feelings. None of them good. How did you tell a story when you didn't have words but instead sadness, regret, horror, and whatever else he'd suffered through?

We watched the small door slam as he slipped inside the metal trailer. Kane looked at me.

"Is this cliffhanger?"

"I think he's chucking some cold water on his face." I watched as the slats of the kitchen window wound closed. "Maybe taking a few shots. Or Xanax."

Kane nodded along, but I knew he only really understood half of what I was saying. I wondered if I purposely was saying shit in a way that he wouldn't get it. And since he was too proud to actually ask what I meant, he'd take my explanation as, well, an explanation.

Just one that he didn't understand.

I watched the pill-shaped home on wheels shift, dipping slightly, guessing Dock was using his toilet. When I heard him talking softly, I assumed he'd been chatting to his wife. But all the time we'd been out on his makeshift patio, I'd not heard anyone inside.

"Man, I dunno. This is a level of weirdness I just didn't sign up for."

My large friend looked at me. First, his face bore a wide expression that I was certain would turn to anger. But then his big eyebrows knit together.

"It sounds much too dangerous, yes. It may be best that Sad Girl doesn't follow."

"Dangerous, it—" I blinked. "Hold on. What do you mean follow?"

Kane nodded at the trailer. "Wherever this eating happened, there will be answers there."

"You can't know that."

I looked to the trailer, watching Dock as he louvered the blinds open once more.

"If that young military dude is eating people, man, he doesn't have answers," I said. "He's got a bottle of barbecue sauce and a blood-smeared bib, and he's looking for his next goddamn meal!"

Kane looked at me with sad eyes. "You think I do not know this? He attacked me as I stood to protect my pack. I know what kind of animal I face."

"Fine, fine," I said, throwing up my hands. "It's like you're back in the woods again, right? Animal versus animal. Fight to the death. Tooth and claw!"

Surprisingly, Kane smiled at this. "You are right. This is a world I know well. The wolf world."

"Well, you need *me* in the human world." I crossed my arms. "Do they drive in the *wolf world*? Because there ain't no way you're getting to wherever you think you're going. Not like you could get on a bus. With your reading level, you'd end up in Belize."

The large man frowned. "These attacks happen in Pine Valley. And near Lake Thousand Lakes."

"Dock said Gisborne."

He tilted his massive melon head. "Which is closer?"

I pulled my phone out, checked the map app, and gave him the answer.

Kane said, "Then Pine Valley is where I must go."

"Fine. I'll take you," I said, gritting my teeth. "But I want to get paid double."

"Double?"

"Hazard pay."

Kane shrugged. "Double is fair. I accept your new terms."

I tugged on my grandmother's locket, rolling it through my fingers. Jamming my thumbnail in to split it open, I was staring down at the tiny image when the door to the trailer creaked open. Dock descended, looking even older than he had when he'd gone in.

His face flushed and eyes red, he lowered himself into the chair again.

My big companion looked at me. Social graces weren't really the sort of arrows he had in his mental quiver. Hell, if the dude actually *had* a quiver, they'd all just be arrows. Gnarly things. Blood tipped. Spike tipped.

I shook him off, indicating for him to wait. If nothing else, Kane read body language better than anyone I'd ever met before. He folded his hands and waited for the other man.

When Dock lifted his head, his eyes landed on me. Then they slid to Kane.

"I feel kind of bad because," he said, nodding to the trailer, "I mean, the thing's made of metal, so it picks up sound like a drum. You can damn near hear a mouse fart out here from the inside."

I frowned. "What does that mean?"

"Well, first off, it means before you expect to get a good night's sleep, you gotta get rid of the mice," Dock said and smiled sadly. Ah, old-dude jokes. This was one he'd told a hundred times. However, not even he found it funny this time.

Kane picked up on the meaning before I did.

"We have no secrets," he said. "Make no apologies for overhearing. If we did not want you to know, we would have said nothing."

Me, I'm a bit slower sometimes. "Wait. What? You were listening?"

"Not actively," Dock said, lifting his hands in surrender. He looked at me with puffy eyes. "But it sounds like your big friend here is looking for the man who's been terrorizing people around these parts for the better part of a year."

"He's been seen again?"

"Not him so much." Dock swallowed and licked his lips. "But there have been stories of people going missing. Hard to say what it might have been because they just vanished. Maybe it's easy to blame the kid because, you know, he's the bogeyman right now to all these folks."

Kane leaned forward. "But not only missing people?"

Looking at me, Dock pointed a crooked finger at my friend. "He's smarter than he looks."

"Well, he'd have to be, right?" I said.

Dock nodded. "Farmers have reported livestock torn up. Animals, smaller ones, like dogs and cats. Some neighborhoods damn near cleared out. Vanished. Not too sad about the cats, truth be told. But some of the larger animals..." He drifted away for a moment then came back. "Ripped apart and, well, worse than that. In my professional life, the term I would have used is exsanguinated. A few drops, splatter here and there, but mostly, all the blood is gone."

I shuttered then chuckled. "So you got vampires too?"

"Please, we have lost good people." The old man frowned at me, and I felt a bit shitty. "Police have looked into it, and since the people who've gone missing just went missing... Well, people go missing all the time. Pick up and leave for a better life, maybe."

"It happens," I said, surprised how quickly those words fell out of my mouth.

"The mutilated animals," Dock said, letting out a long breath, "they're just blaming other animals."

"It is not," Kane said.

"No, it's that boy Cal, I reckon. Something sent him astray in the worst possible way," Dock said, sighing. He angled his eyes toward Kane. "You're going after him? Why?"

I spoke first. "Someone we know, we think, might have been attacked by the guy. You said his name is Cal?"

Dock looked between the two of us, and I could tell he wasn't wholly buying our story. He nodded toward where we'd first seen him on the wooden motorcycle.

"That crew with the buzz-cut guy, who parked a bike on your boy here," he said. "That wasn't the first time we've seen them. They've been asking about a guy named Cal Davis. It's not a big leap of logic to deduce that's the same young man who's caused all this trouble."

Kane shot me a look. We were getting somewhere!

I asked Dock, "What do you know about Cal Davis?"

"Probably *Calvin*, I suppose. Searched around on Google, nothing came of it. A few of our people here are law enforcement, but the name didn't set any alarm bells off, either."

"The name doesn't come up?"

"Oh, it comes up. Just common enough for a bunch of Cals out there, but nothing that would point to anyone who could do this." Dock shifted his weight slightly and hit us both with a hard stare. "That name mean anything to you guys?"

I shook my head.

Kane said nothing, which was standard Kane. Despite that, I knew he'd be jazzed, in his own way.

Finally, the Biting Man had a name.

Chapter Thirteen

It felt good to be back on the road.

Okay, that might have been an overstatement. At least, it felt good to be away from the tiny Wisconsin town and doing something. Heading somewhere.

There's something about movement that brings a calm in me. Like the advancement toward something, somewhere. Or just moving away from whatever trouble I was leaving behind.

We were heading toward the Lake Mille Lacs area, a town called Pine Valley, because, according to Dock, that was where the latest reports of animal attacks had come from. He'd been wary though, warning us that could all be just rumor, speculation, and possibly bullshit.

With a supposed monster on the loose, people could take advantage of that.

Most wouldn't. They'd lock their doors at night and check on the neighbors when they could. But some would see a phantom threat in the area as an opportunity.

Farmers with sick livestock could, in theory, destroy the animals themselves, maybe telling their insurance people some strange, ravenous animal hunting tore them up. *Haven't you heard the stories?*

Hell, the Cal Davis monster could be blamed for some missing granddad. The one who'd promised to pass down his home when he died and then selfishly kept living.

Sure, those were my dark thoughts, but I didn't have a whole hell of a lot of faith in humans. That thought made me smile. I looked over at the massive, snoozing dude in the passenger seat beside me.

Maybe that was why I was hanging with Kane.

* * *

It had taken most of the day and two stops at gas stations, which included threats to my boss that if he left the car for anything other than a pee break—no going inside and weirding out the locals—I'd put him in the trunk.

My ex had once told me Audi sedans had trunks the size of two average-sized people stacked on top of each other. I never asked him how he knew that but did file away that info in case it came up.

When we finally pulled into Pine Valley, Minnesota, the sun had run low on batteries, turning our world the color of two-day-old egg yolk.

Kane stared out the window. "This is a good place."

"How would you know?" All I saw was another rundown Minnesota town, and I'd seen plenty. "That some sort of wolf-sense you've got you hadn't told me about?"

He pointed out the window. "Trees. They have built this town but not cleared so much of the forest away."

I slowed at a stoplight, looked left and right, then made a turn. We'd need to find somewhere to stay for the night.

"Cutting down trees and clearing bushes ain't cheap."

The big man nodded to himself. "A town and forest more in harmony than most."

"Uh-huh."

"And they also have an Arby's," he said, pointing as we passed the familiar cowboy hat sign. "I do like the mocha shakes."

"Uh-huh."

It took me twenty minutes to find a place to stay because most were closed. Maybe it was the off-season.

Finally, I found a motel on the far edge of what appeared to be the main strip.

In the two weeks I'd known Kane, we'd spent every evening indoors. Not because of monsters because, hell, the way he told it, he *was* a monster. On the third night, he'd told me he had to avoid the moonlight.

Of course, that first morning, I'd seen the results of that change from dog to human. But even then, I'd had a hard time getting my head around that this was some new shiny truth in my bleak world.

Maybe, for me, Kane represented some hope that I'd gotten the world wrong. There was more to it. Mystery. It held more promise that I'd imagined. Or just more weirdness.

But when you're twenty-four and all you've ever known is assholes trying to take advantage of other assholes and jobs that only gave you enough dough to keep working for yet another week?

I'd embrace anything that suggested the world was otherwise.

It wasn't quite hope but something close to it. A hope suburb, I supposed. It would do for now.

Checking my phone, I flipped through the weather app, which told me the local sunset would be in about an hour. That should be enough time to ask around about the animal attacks.

That would give Kane somewhere to start come morning.

We pulled into the damp circular driveway, the neon orange reflection from the "vacancy" sign warbling in the puddles. Kane grabbed our bags from the trunk, and we walked toward the motel's entrance.

We triggered the motion detector, but the glass double doors just clanked and didn't part. Instead of walking into the lobby, I just watched my twin nearly bang into me.

I waited.

Peering through the fingerprint-bedazzled window, I saw a flicker of light just beyond the counter. Someone inside was watching television. Or playing with sparklers. Probably the TV thing, though.

A shadow passed over the office door, and a woman's head poked around the corner. When she saw me, she started forward. Then caught sight of my friend and hesitated.

Finally resolved that we weren't ax-wielding Minnesotans on holiday—if that's a thing—she crossed behind the counter and headed our way. She clutched a ring of keys, several of them poking between her thick fingers.

Resolutely, she plastered on a smile, eyeballed me for a quick moment, then pressed one key into the lock.

The door didn't move, so she waved me back, staring up at something above her head. She waved me forward, and they finally parted.

"Sorry for that," she said, sounding not particularly sorry. "Door sticks sometimes."

From the back trickled out the sounds of a television, turned up high enough where I could hear the occasional word. Music swells and arguing. The voice-over was louder, tinny and harsh.

She turned and quickly slid behind the counter. Her safe place, maybe. Or possibly she just wanted something solid between her and the people who'd just walked through the door.

"Sorry about the racket." The woman introduced herself as Olivia as she shuffled the mouse of her computer to wake it up. "Watching *Housewives*, and I don't want to miss anything good. Claws are about to come out." She popped her eyebrows at me. Then I watched those eyebrows nearly meet her hairline as she traced her vision up to the face of the man next to me. "You're a big fella, ain't ya?"

Before Kane could answer—because whatever he might say was not going to help—I put a hand on the counter, drawing her attention.

I said, "We just need a place—"

The television squawked behind her, and she flinched. I then realized that hadn't been the television. The program was at a lower volume than the voices I was hearing now. They were scratchy and flat, and I couldn't make out what they were saying.

When Olivia looked at my face, she offered an apologetic smile.

"Police scanner," she said and shrugged. "Everybody's got one of them now even though Barry up at the Cub Foods said nobody was supposed to have 'em. Illegal or something."

"It's illegal to have a police scanner, Olivia?"

"Dunno. Not that anyone pays attention to that. Not no more."

As she clicked away at her keyboard, I traced my eyes around the lobby.

Next to the office door, eight faux-wood plaques had been stacked one above the next. Each had a brass plate, and they got shinier the lower down the wall they went. The top one was missing, leaving behind a crisp, plaque-shaped patch of blue paint on the dull gray wall.

In a glass enclosed atrium to my left, a half-dozen square tables had been shoved together. Chairs pressed against the folds of big, heavy red-velvet curtains that had been drawn. On the far wall, longer tables held three of those silver serving stations. Their handles lifted, they lay open revealing rags, cleaning supplies, and a few clay pots with brittle brown twigs poking out of their dry-as-dust dirt.

No breakfast buffet, then.

Olivia asked me. "How many nights, hon?"

"Um, one? Maybe two. Do I have to say ahead of time?"

She shook her head, struggling to keep the sliver of a smile on her face. "No, that's all right. Just as long as you pay each day in advance, you can stay as long as you like," she said and waved at a wall of hooks behind her. They were all empty.

I frowned. "Do you have rooms available?"

When she noticed the look on my face, she blushed. "Oh, right. We don't use actual keys no more. And we're not really in season for, you know, tourists and the like. Plenty of room."

She pulled out a pen and small index card and pushed it toward me. Kane had become intensely interested in the procedure, looming over my shoulder like some cement gargoyle atop an old government building. I pulled the card toward me with a raised eyebrow and held out the pen to him. He frowned and stepped back.

I filled in my own name because I didn't know how guilty it would look to put in some sort of alias. That had always looked cool in the old movies, but writing a fake name somehow felt criminal.

Of course, in a town where people flaunted authority with their contraband police scanners, if I were a criminal, maybe I'd fit right in.

When I'd finished, Olivia spun the card around and smiled. "That's a pretty name, Emelda. Don't see ones like that anymore," she said, staring at it for a moment. Then she turned to her computer. "Lots of Emmas and Avas and Ariels these days. I blame Walt Disney."

Again, the police radio squelched behind her. A rat-a-tat missive of words spilled out of it over the *"You bitch!"* of the television.

Olivia reached into a small box, removed what looked like a blank credit card, slapped it into a black plastic holder, and pressed a rectangular red button. The light turned from red to green. She handed me the keycard.

"You okay with the one key, or do you need two?"

"One's fine. Anywhere close by you'd recommend for dinner? Steak place would be good."

She did a final few clicks of her mouse. "Eighty-five for the night."

I elbowed Kane, who had kept surprisingly quiet during our entire exchange. Maybe I was training him? Or maybe he was bored. Either way, I was thankful for the silence.

He pulled a couple of bills from his jeans, fumbling a bit slowly, so I grabbed them, snatched what I needed to pay the bill, and stuffed what remained into the pocket of my leather jacket.

This drew a tiny smile from Olivia.

I looked up to see Kane's reaction, but he was staring out the large bay windows.

The motel woman scooped the bills up, banged their crisp edges on the counter, and stuffed them into a cash drawer.

As she laid out the change, she said, "If you need to make any phone calls, you'll have to leave a credit card."

I held up my phone, and she smiled.

"Yeah, nobody uses the phone anymore. I'll be honest, I don't even know if the damn things work anymore."

I stuffed the change into my pocket, noting I'd made an extra thirty-five bucks just checking in.

Moments earlier, I'd been happy to have the blissful, nondramatic silence of the big man beside me. Now, his silence was beginning to rattle me. And that damn police scanner, with its squelching and squawking, was only fraying my already-rattled nerves.

Olivia smiled. "There's a laminated sheet in the room that's got numbers to get some food delivered, but—"

"We've been in a car all day," I said, sighing. "I'd like to stretch the legs a bit. Anyplace close?"

She nodded slowly and pointed toward the door, and I turned. But she'd said nothing. When I spun back, her eyes had glassed. Her mouth hung open with words that had gotten stuck somewhere in her teeth.

"You..." she started then tried again. "You'd best order in, hon. But to be honest, you might have to call around a bit. Not sure if many delivery drivers are going to be on the roads tonight."

I laughed. "Roll up the carpets a bit early around here, don't you?"

"You... you should know that tonight don't seem like a good night to be walking around." She nodded behind her. "You've got room eleven. Just around the corner, you'll find the ice maker and vending machines. It ain't fine cuisine or anything, but it's safer."

When I turned to look at Kane, he was focused intensely on the doors. I hated the feeling that I was somehow left out of some joke everyone else knew about.

"Safe?" I said, my frustration banging at the lid on my emotions. "I'm tired and hungry. I don't want to eat goddamn Funyuns for dinner."

Another squawk sounded on the radio behind her. This time she turned, cocking an ear. Had she heard a phrase or a word, some signal or code? Or was she just delaying telling me what I needed to know?

"I've lived in this town my entire life," she said, not looking at me. "More than—well, a long time. But this ain't the town I grew up in."

I clenched my fists, shifting from foot to foot. "What aren't you saying?"

She leaned forward, clasping her hands together. "What I'm saying, Emelda, is that there's someone out there. Some*thing* out there. It's been a good while now since there's been a problem, but the last few nights..." Her voice faded.

Kane took a step toward the door then stopped and looked at me like he'd only just remembered I'd been there.

He said, "I must go."

Chapter Fourteen

First driving into the town, I'd thought Pine Valley seemed sleepy. Quaint. Now, it seemed on edge.

The air felt heavy after the storm that had swept through before we'd arrived. Now, in the dimming light, the tiny town began to lose its color like an old photograph being drained of its vibrance. Its life. As if some entity were feeding on it, building up strength.

A few blocks down the damp, empty street, a flashing caught my eye. A bank's electronic sign was flipping between the current time and temperature like an old man repeatedly checking his watch.

"It's going to be dark soon," I said, following Kane as he took long strides toward the sidewalk. His eyes scanning left and right, up and down the road, he'd struggled over a row of bushes lining the motel's entryway. If he'd not been so serious, I might have laughed.

When he reached the path, the big man cocked his head.

I cut through a path in the hedge and bopped him in the arm.

Kane didn't respond.

"You know, I'm tired. And getting more tired of everyone being so jittery," I said, watching a lone car a few streets over cut a turn fast enough to make the tires squeal. Above, the traffic light flashed yellow.

"I can hear him," Kane said in a calm voice. "But there is too much noise here."

"What? It's a goddamn ghost town right now."

He looked at me, frowning. "Ghosts?"

"I just mean," I said, stepping into the street, waving my arms around, "no one's around. Place is deserted."

Kane shook his head slowly. "Loud but not here. There are voices, but..." The big man raised his hands, palms caressing the air. "Too much other noise. Dogs barking. Car engines. Machine sounds. A woman is yelling at some man to put his pants back on."

I chuckled and cupped my ears. Hell, I didn't even hear birds. Glancing back at the bank clock, I walked over and pulled on Kane's elbow.

"If you want to get indoors before it's dark, we should get to the room."

He turned his face upward then to the west. Standing there, washed in the burnt-orange light of the dying sun, he looked like he was posing for an album cover. Some eighties rocker who'd gone solo, hoping to squeeze a few more dollars out of a fading career.

Kane stepped out into the middle of the street, the exact spot I'd been moments earlier, and looked to the sky.

I said, "If you howl, I'm out of here."

Head titled back, he popped his eyes open, and for the first time since we'd stopped at the night's accommodations, he grinned at me. "You carefully choose the moments to do such things," he said. "Yes, this town is on edge. Worry. I can smell the fear."

I nodded to the dark building behind him. "That's probably the KFC."

He walked toward me and put his hands on my shoulders. It struck me how a man so large could be so gentle.

"Go back to the room," he said. "I do not think it is safe out here."

"I think I'm safe with *you*, Kane," I said, surprising even myself when I said it. "What's wrong?"

"I believe Cal Davis is here," he said. "And he is hunting."

* * *

We needed information, so I went hunting. Look at me. Solving problems.

Or, hell, just finding new ones.

"What are they saying on the scanner?" I asked, striding back into the motel lobby. Thankfully, Olivia hadn't yet secured the lock on the door.

The colors were now sharper in the back room, harshly lit and more pronounced. As I walked, my shadow stretched before me as if leading the way. It was oddly comforting.

Olivia peered out of the office, like she was ready to slam the door if things didn't look right. "Turned it off," she said, jamming a nail into her mouth.

"What?" I put both hands flat on the counter, letting the cool surface pull the heat from my sweating palms. "Why did you do that?"

"Heard enough. Sounds like it's starting up again." She shrugged. "Hard to tell."

I huffed and rounded the counter, past the tacit no-go zone for customers. It felt like a violation, but at that moment, I felt like a little violating.

Olivia pushed the door wider so I could come into the back room. Maybe she just wanted someone else nearby. Or another warm body between her and the entrance.

She muted the television but didn't turn it off. On the screen, some woman in what looked like a prom dress—despite being about thirty years from her latest prom—was brandishing a bread roll at another woman dressed even more garishly. Undoubtedly, the roll was about to be weaponized, but I didn't care about any of that.

Olivia reached for the police scanner, her hand hesitating for a moment, then she clicked it back on.

At first, it was silent.

We both waited. To fill the quiet, she started filling me in.

"We get reports most nights, but a lot of that is just panic," she said, her voice flat. "A sighting here. Missing animals or someone's boyfriend hasn't come home yet."

"Panic? The police are panicking?"

She shook her head vigorously, leaned forward in her chair, which squawked under her bulk, and fished a handheld radio out from a desk drawer. When she clicked it on, the red light came alive at the top. Olivia set the radio next to the police scanner.

"Half the town has a radio."

I stared at both transmitters. Neither made a sound. "You guys don't believe in cell phones?"

"Too slow." She shook her head, looking at me. "And the way things have been going, slow ain't gonna cut it. It's better for everything to get out as quick as possible. But, like I said, it can be a bit of a free-for-all."

"Panic."

She pointed at the handheld. "Mrs. Jenkins piped in last night. Got a little terrier with a horrible name like Princess or something, and she came on and was in a froth. 'I ain't see her. It's got her.' All that sort of thing."

Olivia let out a long breath. "Paul, he works for Barry at the Cub Foods, and he's known their family for years. Dated the Jenkins daughter at one point, but she didn't want to end up being married to the grocery store guy, so she—"

"The dog?" I said, trying to keep Olivia on track.

"Oh, right. Princess or Queenie or whatever had died a few *years* ago. Had nothing to do with what's going on now. Mrs. J just, you know, forgot. She's old."

I rubbed my temples. "So what is going on now? *Right* now?"

Olivia turned to the radios like she was explaining her high school science project.

"Each night, we listen in. All started maybe ten months back or so. There was this car show in town—"

I rolled my fingers to fast-forward the story. "We know about the car show. Some guy went haywire, stole a car, attacked the owner."

"*Bit* a man in Gisborne named Charlie Boynton! What kind of person bites people?" Another fingernail got sent to the toothy gallows. "We only found out about *that* after Lorney died the following weekend when the show rolled into town here. Now, Lorney was an asshole who treated his wife Bridget something awful, but nobody deserves to go like that."

For someone who loved a good gossip, it surprised me that Olivia hadn't gone into the gory detail of Lorney Mill's death. From how Dock had described it, the trailer had looked like a slaughter house. Maybe all that was a bit too real.

"The next day, Bridget, she's gone AWOL. Maybe she saw it as her chance to get out or..." Olivia turned and looked out the office door, as if the woman might be standing there at the entrance looking to come in.

"You okay, Olivia?" I asked and put a hand on her arm.

She nodded, gave me a wan smile, then started up again. "About a month later, pets started going missing, but no one paid much attention to that. Things got more real when the livestock were mutilated."

"Jesus," I said. "Mutilated?"

"Chewed on. Big chunks taken out," she said, her face growing paler. "Vet went out to take a look because, of course, everyone thought we just had some animals running low on food in the forest. Maybe bears or wolves. But we don't really get wolves in the city."

Well, I know of one, I thought to myself.

Olivia's voice dropped to a whisper. "Vet says teeth marks were *human.*" She swallowed and took a furtive glance at the front-door glass again. "I guess it's easy enough to tell, or maybe they train you for that sort of thing in veterinarian school. Does seem like an odd thing to teach animal doctors, now I think about it."

I nodded vigorously. *Jesus.* The woman spoke in frustrating tangents. Reality TV worming its way into her brain. Or maybe she was just nervous.

"No more missing pets, but there were more livestock attacks." She pointed at the radios. "Every other week, it seemed. And that, according to Barclay, he's Pine Valley's police chief, was a worry."

"Yeah, you've got some predator running around. At least people weren't losing animals they loved, I guess."

Olivia shook her head. "Barclay didn't see it that way. None of us do anymore."

"How do you see it?"

"This predator, as you say, had graduated from pets to larger animals. So what might be on the menu next?"

That thought sent a chill through my body.

"A few weeks back, the Wilkins girl went missing. She'd been coming home from a friend's house but..."

"Never got there."

A shake of the head. "Now, she'd always been a wild one. Some people thought she'd met some boy on the internet and headed out west or something. But Ruby, that's her mother, she didn't think so."

A voice split the silence. The police radio.

"Thirteen, base."

A pause then another voice: *"Go ahead, Barclay."*

"Got flagged down just outside the Clarrat farm on Bent River Road. Same as that night last week. Animals making a racket."

Another pause then: *"And? Anything?"*

Over the radio, the other voice, Barclay, grunted. Then came the sound of a car door slamming. *"Heading over."*

"Reports of an attack?"

"Too early to tell. But the neighbor thinks they may have heard gunshots. Wasn't sure but not so unusual out at Clarrats'."

"Keep us posted, Barclay. Be safe, and don't do anything dumb."

A laugh warbled over the line. *"I'll take that under advisement. Thirteen out."*

The radio turned to static, which grew in volume until everything went silent. I looked to Olivia.

"Gunshots?"

She nodded. "They're shooting at something. Or someone."

Chapter Fifteen

When I was a kid, we had a young woman in our part of town who had made a big splash, as it were, as an Olympic hopeful. One of those students who excelled at everything. Straight A's. Student newspaper. Yearbook. Healthy following on social media, where she earned endless praise for talking about mental health.

Turns out, God just likes some people more than others. Or at least, that's always been my take on it. I'd never been one of them.

But He did like Ruhi Mukherji. She of the four-point-oh grade average had also been blessed with a swimmer's body. Swimmer's lungs. Swimmer's muscles. And parents who could pay top dollar for the best swimmer's lessons.

Excited about the prospect of being the hometown of an Olympic hero, the school had fund-raised for a top-notch high dive to be put into our pool. The money had flowed in. The pool had to be deepened too. No expense too great for Ruhi Mukherji.

Some of the other families had complained, naturally. Not against the golden girl. But they'd tried for years to improve the facilities. The fields were a shambles. Lockers in the dressing rooms were rusted and busted.

As a compromise, if it was a compromise, the high dive would not be the domain of Ruhi alone. If a student went through the proper training and got the appropriate permissions—and their parents had signed the necessary liability waivers—they too could use the Olympic-style high dive.

Such permissions came with a red wristband. If you had a wristband, you were allowed to head up the ladder and, if you were brave enough, stand at the edge of the high-altitude concrete platform and leap off.

I'd never gone through the training. And I'd never been one to ask for permission.

Swiping a red wristband from the locker room when another girl had been in the showers, I'd strode over to the high dive and begun climbing the ladder. The lifeguard glanced over at me and saw the Red Strap of the Chosen and thought nothing of it.

The other kids knew better.

Knew I didn't belong up there.

Of course, none of them were going to say anything. Not out of respect or deference to me. They all sat back and watched. Maybe they might see someone die today. Phones had come out in that all-too-familiar stance. Tiny arms extended, bent at the elbow, camera faces pointed at The Event.

The twenty-first century's *shit's gonna get real* salute.

Climbing the cold metal ladder, I began to lose feeling in my fingers. My only goal, really, had been to steal the red wristband. Like it had been some treasure not afforded to people like me and I was setting the record straight.

Now, here I was climbing up with no plan.

No idea what I would do at the top.

Well, I knew *what* people did at the top, but I hadn't been a diver. I hadn't even considered what it would take to go through the motions to leap thirty feet into the air and land below.

However, I felt like I represented something. Maybe I'd been breaking barriers. See, even the poor kids can do this shit!

That had been the asshole side of my brain just rationalizing my actions.

In truth, I had all eyes on me now. And part of me, sure, was in screw-you mode. But most of me just didn't want to look like a coward.

At the top, I didn't even hesitate. Something in my mind had taken over. Like it had observed the white-knuckle fear within, thought it was quaint, and had rationalized this as merely a transactional moment.

The sum total of my world was just going from where I was on the ladder over the edge. That was it. Here to there. That was the only thought in my brain.

Here to there.

The moment my feet hit the concrete slab, I strode toward the edge. I knew if I had thought about it, I'd have been too busy shitting myself to actually jump.

Here to there.

Four strides from stepping off the ladder, I was airborne.

Two seconds later, I was in the water.

Two minutes after that, I was in the principal's office, still dripping wet, with two big red welts on the backs of my thighs and a grin from ear to ear.

That moment had changed me. I'd considered it a success because, chiefly, I hadn't died. It had also gotten me a reputation as someone not to mess with. Someone who knew no limits. Or at least, that was what other people thought.

But for ten years now, I'd been a person who, once I'd committed to something, never turned back. Ignored all those shrill voices in my head that said "this is a bad idea." However, sometimes, those voices had a point.

So here I was, in a strange town with a very strange guy and, well, a monster named Cal Davis on the loose. Of course, the only thing to do was go find the monster.

Shrill voices be damned.

Once Olivia had shown me on my phone where the farm was, I left the office and headed outside once again. The street was so quiet, it felt like the entire town had emptied out elsewhere. One part of my brain tried to rationalize it. Maybe there was a high school football game going on?

No.

As I stood on the cracked concrete sidewalk that ran parallel to the road, the only other figure near me was my shadow. It had grown taller in the minutes since I'd stood there last. The sun had begun its long kiss goodnight to the horizon.

"Kane?" I called out a bit too quietly but got no answer. I tried again, louder. Nothing.

I felt alone and stupid.

Swallowing my self-pity, the only thing in my stomach at that moment, I reset my head. He hadn't bolted because he was an asshole. Sure, he was a self-centered, arrogant... whatever he was. But I'd seen real concern in his eyes. He hadn't wanted me to get hurt.

And I knew where he'd gone. Despite his fear of the night, he'd headed out toward the voices he'd heard. He was hunting Cal Davis.

I began to turn back to my car but stopped when I heard the throaty rumble of a vehicle. Standing there like an idiot, I looked toward the sound as it grew louder and louder. The streetlights to my left flashed yellow with a mechanical thunk.

A moment later, a hulking black truck with wrap-around pipes burst from behind a gas station on the corner. The thing was jacked up so high from its wheels, it looked like the vehicle moved independently from its tires.

It hesitated at the intersection.

The truck did a staggered stop, and I squinted in the fading light, but the windows were dark. Not tinted, just shaded. I took a step toward it. Inside the cab, I saw movement. Someone in the passenger seat was waving their arms.

The black truck peeled into the intersection and turned, its taillights blazing and angry. But before it had turned, I'd caught a quick glimpse of the face of the man in the passenger seat.

"Gregor," I said aloud, my jaw aching as I uttered the word. The tech sergeant had found us.

As I watched the red taillights bend around the next intersection and disappear back in the direction they'd come, one street over, something about that didn't make any sense.

How the hell had the asshole and his sidekicks ended up in this town? Had he returned to the car show and asked where we'd gone?

That didn't seem likely. If they had, I didn't feel they'd get a warm reception.

My brain told me I'd been stupid. Missing something.

Sure, I hadn't been staring at my mirror the entire drive from Wisconsin, but no way would I have not seen that baby monster truck back there if they'd been trailing us. And had they been heading the same way, why wouldn't they have just overtaken us on the highway?

Or, worse, overrun us at a gas station. Kicked in the bathroom stall door.

There was only one answer. At least, I only had one answer.

My car was still in the half-moon driveway of the motel entryway. Walking around it, I searched for what I felt had to be there.

I checked the wheel wells, running my hand above each of the four tires. All I got from that effort was a dirty hand. Popping the trunk, I yanked out a pair of old work boots without laces, a few crushed cans, and some other trash that the previous owner hadn't cleared out. Then I lifted the false bottom to where the spare tire was held.

Note to self: I needed to get a spare tire.

All I'd found in the spare tire-shaped space was the dried-out carcass of a dead bird.

But no GPS tracking device. Not that I even knew what to look for. And yeah, I was under no illusions that all I needed to find was a black box with a blinking red light. If they'd put a tracker in my car, it would be hidden.

But a tracker would have been the only way they could have followed us. *If* they'd followed us.

My phone? Maybe. But that would mean, possibly, some government intervention. And while, sure, Kane had called him "tech sergeant," I got the distinct feeling this guy had been off book.

After I jammed all the stuff back inside and slammed the truck, I nearly jumped.

Olivia stood there, hands clasped in front of her. The expression on her face was dark. But I soon realized that hadn't been directed at me.

"My ex was a bastard. A cheater himself, so naturally, he thought I'd been fooling around," she said then stood back and eyeballed my car. "He put one of them boxes on my car to see where I was going. I only realized it when he showed up at my aunt's house one night."

"No, I just—"

Before I could finish, she waved my words away. "No judgments, hon. Whoever did whatever, that ain't on you."

Her eyes tweaked, and she pointed at the hood.

"You came from out of town, so maybe whoever put something on your car had meant it to send out a signal a long way. Battery packs are bulky and go dead over time." She walked over and stood at the front of my vehicle. "It might mean it's wired to your car battery somehow."

Saying nothing, I leaned into the driver's-side window and popped the hood.

Olivia was in full *oh-no-you-didn't Housewives* drama mode, wasting no time in lifting the hood and drawing up the metal bar to keep it elevated.

The bright lights of the motel overhang shined into my engine compartment. We both stared.

The Audi was a few years old and in pretty good shape. From what he'd told me, my old neighbor had originally bought it from a used-car lot and had always taken care of it. But like any relationship, that care had faded after time.

Under the hood, there were black plastic coverings hiding engine components below. I slotted a fingernail into one of the fat plastic screw heads that held down one of four clamshell housings. A minute later, I had the cover off. We both examined the battery.

I didn't really know what to look for. If there was a device leeching power, I didn't see any stray wires that revealed it.

"Huh." Olivia said, running her thick fingers over the poles and leaning down. Then she pointed up toward the windshield. "This got them connectors up by the wipers?"

I shrugged. "Not my car."

"What?"

"The big guy with me. Kane," I lied. "It's his."

She walked around the side of the car, chuckling. "Are you two, um, together or something?"

"Something," I said, watching her fingers pull at the lining under the windshield. When I saw her smile grow bigger, I amended my answer. "Not *that*. He's a friend."

"He's gorgeous."

I was eager to change the subject. "What are you looking for?"

Her answer came not in words but in the cracking sound of plastic and metal. Something had snapped.

"Oh, shit," she said, holding up a long black piece. "Sorry about that. I'm sure Valerie up the road can help you get that back on. Must have missed a screw or something."

Coming around beside her, I grabbed the covering, popped open the passenger door, and chucked it into the back. When I closed the door, Olivia was staring at me. Her eyes were big, her arm extended.

"I think this is what you're looking for, hon."

When I looked down, I saw what her chubby finger was resting on.

At the base of the window was a channel, and there were two metal poles surrounded by rubber. One red, one black. She'd peeled back the red one and indeed found a wire. It wasn't hard to find the device. It was sitting right next to the red pole, nestled snuggly in the gap.

A black, rectangular box that definitely looked aftermarket. When I tried to pull it out, I found that they had secured it with some epoxy or glue. It budged like a few hard yanks might free it. A thick black wire led to the red battery lead.

"It's probably grounded to the chassis," she said. Then she traced her finger to a smaller wire that led to the bottom of the windshield. "Dunno what this thin wire's for."

I guessed but felt I was right. And it answered a question I'd posed earlier in the day.

"The car antenna is in the windshield. Instead of pulling a signal into the radio, it's probably using it to send a signal out."

After complaining about the crappy choice of radio stations on the way *to* the car show that afternoon, I'd lamented how it had been impossible to get any station *after* we'd left. The antenna had been hijacked by this device.

Hijacked by Tech Sergeant Gregor.

I suspected that the asshole had gotten one of his goon-bros to install it while we'd been at the car show. The radio had worked just fine before that.

"I've got some tools in the office, so you can get that piece of shit out of there," she said and started to turn.

I put a hand on her arm. "Leave it for a moment." I stared at it, trying to stop my world from spinning. "If nothing else, they don't know I know it's there. Might come in handy."

That stopped Olivia, and she put a hand on my cheek. "*They?*" she said, and her eyes darkened. "Hon, what kind of trouble are you in?"

I couldn't help but laugh. "No more or less than I usually get into," I said, though even I didn't believe that. "I'm okay. Thanks for helping me find this."

She shrugged and smiled then looked around. "Where'd your big, beautiful friend go?"

I closed the hood of the car and moved toward the driver's-side door. "My best guess?" I said, hopping inside. "Nowhere good."

I fired up the car, but before I could leave, she pulled the handheld radio off her belt and gave it to me. I thanked her, threw a wave to my motel conspirator, and pulled out of the circular drive. Looking down at my phone, I headed toward the dot.

Kane would be heading that way.

Chapter Sixteen

Kane

Once again, I am the hunter.

Through my powerful muscles, I can feel the blood course. Fueling me and pushing me forward. As I pump my long legs, still a queer experience for me, I find I no longer struggle as much with balance in this form.

A lifetime on four legs, now two. It had been harder in the beginning.

But I adapt. Then I master. I have become a supreme being in this new form. I am—

"Ooof."

I had not seen the rock.

A boulder, for sure, for it would take something large to affect me in this farm's poorly plowed field. Standing once again, I brush off the dirt and bits of dead grass. A curious thing, that. I had never overly concerned myself with such things. Dirt, this never bothered me.

Not that it does now, for a hunter does not trouble himself with such things. However, I do prefer my jean pants to be tidy.

But not too tidy. The lady humans like men who are rugged but not wholly untidy. This is a confusing ritual. I have learned that my jean pants should be weathered but not dirty. Some holes are fine. In fact, this is preferred. However, too many holes, and I am asked to leave the cafes where the lady humans like to run in packs.

Not that I am seeking a lady human. I have a wolf wife and will forever be devoted to her, my alpha partner. But entrancing the lady humans with my wolf wiles can earn me favor in other matters. Offerings. Like pigs' feet.

Tonight, I welcome the dirt. Many times in the past, when my fur might get matted with mud and grass and debris, I had used this as cover. Camouflage, I have heard the humans call it. Except in cafes, as I have learned.

I must accept that I am one of them. For now. Only for now. One day, soon, that will be a memory.

Getting back up again, standing upon my rear paws—

Feet. They are feet!

—I must remember to cast an eye down to watch out for things I may stumble upon. So much more efficient to travel on four legs. However, in this form that does not bode well. It's cumbersome. And it upsets the humans.

I have that unnatural scent in my nostrils now, the one I seek. And so many others, too, but I must discern between them. There is something else now.

Sweat. The smell of oil. Excrement. And... meat? I am unsure.

A flicker of sound catches my ear. Beneath the sounds of tearing, there is blood in the air, flesh being stripped apart. I hear another. Teeth against—

"You there, mighty hunter!"

I turn and see a man dressed in colors I recognize as authority with humans. He is wearing a strange cap. And, more concerning, a gun strapped to his waist. I see his hand go to his belt, hovering there.

In his other, he is holding something. It looks strange. Smells like flesh. Has he made a fresh kill and is feeding upon his victory?

No.

That cannot be it. It smells cooked. This is how humans eat, destroying the flavor. Although I do smell something appealing within the odors wafting from the meat he is clutching in his paw.

Hand. It is a hand!

I stop running. Men with guns, I have learned, seek reasons to utilize them. I do not want to be the purpose he bends to this need.

My own instincts tell me I must appear as though I belong. This is my territory. I must convey this.

"What a fine evening," I say to the police man, my hands extended to show I am not similarly armed. "How are you, my friend?"

"I accept your dominance," he says. Not so much with his mouth but his face and eyes. "But I am wary of such a powerful creature as yourself. May I inquire as to the nature of your presence?"

I laugh to show I am unafraid. "This is my hour to engage in our ritual of recreational running. The air, it cools, as the sun travels to the dark side."

"My apologies for asking, since you are my better." The man's eyes shift from me to where I had come. "However, this is my duty to do so. In what manner do you claim passage upon this territory?"

I lift myself higher in stature, flexing my powerful arms and chest. Not to incite but maybe to intimidate. This comes naturally to me; it is the wolf way.

"This is my territory," I say to him. "And I have much work to do."

"I understand and, again, apologize for questioning you, since I have no right," he says with words and expression. He puts the strange meat to his mouth, removes a tiny piece, and chews nervously. "Be wary of others in such a place. Blood is in the air."

I nod, affording this low creature with his wide middle section and missing button my approval.

"Good travels, mighty hunter. And beware the teeth that flash and claws hidden by the night."

"Um," I say and chastise myself. Such utterances are more human than wolf. But I am human, so I allow it. "You too."

I begin my running again, slow at first. Then, when I feel the distance between me and the man with the meat stick is great enough, I run faster. Toward the sounds of screams. The sounds of gnashing and clawing.

It's only when I pass from the trees that I realize that it has begun. First in my lower extremities. Then my mind starts to swirl.

I have stepped into the moonlight.

Chapter Seventeen

"Turn left," my phone said just as I passed the lane, which I hadn't seen in the dark.

"Shit!" When I jammed on the brakes, the car slid sideways just a little. "Goddamn gravel roads."

As I reversed, I felt the car rise slightly then drop. Some pothole or a chunk of rock in the middle of the lane.

"Turn left."

Close enough now where I knew I just needed to go straight, I exited from the app's turn-by-turn directions. Out here, it didn't seem to do any good anyhow.

I hadn't been entirely sure if I was going the right way. Until I saw the cop, of course.

His patrol car had been parked at an angle, partially blocking the road. I'd had a thought about just flooring it and weaving around him, but I expected the local cops wouldn't take kindly to some stranger in an out-of-town Audi racing away from them.

I slowed, and he walked up to my window. When he leaned in, I could smell the beef jerky on his breath.

"You lost?"

"Is it that obvious?" I offered the guy a smile and dropped my shoulder. "Trying to get back to my uncle's farm, but all the roads start to look the same in the dark."

The cop tore off another strip of beef jerky and then stuffed the foil package into his upper pocket. A dull brass tag clinging to his shirt read *Barclay*.

"Who's your uncle?"

Thinking back to my conversation with Olivia, I threw out the first name that came to my mind.

"At the Clarrat farm," I said, looking through the windshield. "Should just be up this road."

The cop looked in the same direction as I had then nodded slowly.

"Yeah, trouble up there at the moment." He took a step back, thumbs dug into the tight gap between his belt and pants. I could see a bit of skin poking through his shirt where he was missing a button. "Might be best if you hang back with me here until things calm down."

"Trouble?"

He nodded up the road. "Ah, probably just some locals messing with the livestock." He flashed me a grin. There was beef jerky in his teeth. Gross. "Could be foxes. Might be timber wolves, but we don't see many of them in these parts."

I gripped the wheel. "Maybe I should go check on my uncle. I'm worried about him now."

The cop's hand moved just slightly on his belt, his fingers more tense than they'd been a moment before. "Wouldn't do that," he said. 'We've had some problems up this way the past year. Animals attacked. Not a pretty scene."

I chuckled. "I spent my summers on farms. I've seen a lot of less-than-pretty scenes."

The cop looked around, his eyes dancing. Looking for something. He said, "Had another guy through here a moment ago, weirdest thing."

Oh shit. "Really?"

"Didn't recognize him and had a funny accent, so I don't think he was from around here."

I shrugged. "Maybe a farmhand. I know Uncle gets some seasonal hires. They come from all over."

"Yeah, yeah," the cop said, pulling his cap down to scratch a spot on his scalp. "Big dude. I mean huge. Said he was out jogging. Can you believe that?"

"Nice night for a jog."

"Who jogs in blue jeans, though?" He stared just off behind him, his voice a whisper. "Never seen a guy that big move so fast."

"Oh, that's probably, um, François," I said and internally groaned. *Christ. François?* It made Kane sound like a Parisian pastry chef. "He's harmless. And, yeah, real fitness nut."

The cop shot a look at me. "That dude was probably many things, but 'harmless' ain't a word that comes to mind."

The cop's radio squawked, and he moved toward his car.

When he did, the trees shivered in the breeze, the branches playing with the light. Then I realized it.

Dropping the car into gear, I rolled around the squad. Behind me, I heard him call out, and I leaned into the accelerator.

The light I'd seen, of course, was moonlight. The night was about to get a whole hell of a lot more interesting for the locals.

Chapter Eighteen

I'd switched to high beams because out here in the sticks, it was real 1899. No streetlights. No road signs. The radio I'd gotten from Olivia squelched, and I heard a panicked man's voice.

"Four, maybe five!" the voice said.

There was a long pause, and I looked down to see if the device's battery had died. The red light bounced, and I looked up to see I'd almost driven off the road.

"Dammit, pay attention," I chastised myself.

The radio came to life again. "No, no! They're... I mean, they're all torn up. Worse than before. I think it's making a run down the raceway."

Another long silence told me I was only hearing half a conversation.

Up ahead to my left, I could see a burst of light, reflections against metal, and what might have been some water. It was hard to tell. Squinting as I drove, I tried to pull the images out of the blue-black darkness.

The radio squawked again. "...sheds! I threw the breakers open from here. But if you can get a clean shot, take it." Another long pause, then, "The goddamn milking sheds. It's heading that way!"

My car lurched to the left and spun, jamming the seat belt against my neck, and I nearly blacked out from the strain. The air filled with gravel, dust, and exhaust.

I coughed, my eyes watering as the haze played in the beams of the car's headlights.

Still dizzy, I clicked out of the seat belt and opened the door.

My left front tire had caught the edge of the ditch then slid and got caught in the muck of the road's drainage lines. Eyeballing it, I knew that if I tried to pull straight out, my tire would just spin and spin. Goddamn German car would have that limited-slip differential.

Jumping back into the driver's seat, I cranked the wheel hard to the left and dropped it into reverse. Instead of pulling straight back out, going down the groove I'd just cut into the muck, this would grip against the gravel road.

I leaned into the accelerator, not hard, just enough to get rolling. Once it cleared, I gave it a bit more gas.

A moment later, I was back on the road.

I'd considered turning the radio off, since that distraction had almost left me in the ditch and carless. But what I needed to know was if the "it" running down the raceway was Cal Davis or a big, lumbering French Canadian.

I looked up at the moonlight, worried at what I might find when I got up there.

The Clarrat farm was on my left, and undoubtedly, that was where the calls of panic had come from. I knew that if I'd heard them, it was likely the asshole tech sergeant had too.

He and his moron crew would be out here somewhere, likely monitoring radio chatter.

At a lonely streetlight, I hooked left toward the farm but met a gate within a few hundred feet. I got out to see if I could yank it open, but it had an electronic lock.

I pulled the car into a copse of trees, hidden from anyone passing by.

Jamming the keys into my pocket, I ran up the gravel road toward the reflecting light.

The smell hit me, rattling the dusty covers of my memories of my uncle's farm all those years ago. Shit, basically. You got used to the air smelling like excrement. For some reason, though, animal shit isn't as off-putting as the human variety.

Not because of the odor itself. Maybe it has something to do with its, um, manufacturer. When you smell human excrement, you get visions of how the person made their deposit. Squatting and grunting. Animals shit like they breathe. Just drop it where they stand.

On cue, I heard mooing to my left and turned.

There stood three cows pressed up against the fence. Their bulging eyes pleading with me. I'd been around cattle a lot in years past, and they'd all had the same expressions. Bored, passive, maybe a bit judgy.

I'd never seen cattle... scared?

Was I anthropomorphizing? Can cows be scared?

When I moved closer, they stirred even more. I reached out but then snapped my hand back when I felt the electric tingle at my fingertips.

The cows were pressing against an electrified fence. Those jolts had to be coursing through their bodies. Still, they didn't budge.

When I looked beyond them, deeper into the paddock, I could see where they'd decked it to the ground. That was what my uncle had called it when the cows would chew up all the grass, right down to the dirt.

But about fifty feet beyond that, I saw the clumps, big ones, where a few of the animals had been felled. I didn't think they'd be sleeping. Not if their girlfriends were smashed up against the electric fence.

I put a hand on one of the fenceposts and hopped over, landing on my knees.

"Gross," I said, hoping the dampness was night dew or something.

One cow pulled away from the fence and began to follow me. To be honest, I was happy for the company. It was creepy as hell, and I could smell something metallic mixed in with the rotting hay, mud, and shit odors.

As I grew closer, moonlight lit the way.

About fifteen feet away, I stopped.

In front of me, two of the cattle—maybe three; it was impossible to tell—had been gutted. Their flanks torn open, their necks shredded. One of the cows' heads had been shorn off entirely. I could see the body but not the rest.

I'd wondered if it had been taken or just flung away in the fight.

But there hadn't been a fight. Cows didn't fight back. This had just been carnage, a feast for Cal Davis. Was he not even human anymore? Part of me wanted to get back to the car and wait this out. But Kane would be chasing him.

And like that high dive all those years ago, I was now committed.

Here to there. Here to there.

With the moonlight blazing over the field, I had no idea if Kane had turned or what he might have turned into. If he was anything like I'd seen him two weeks earlier, a tiny dog with big bulbous eyes, he'd have no chance against whatever had slaughtered the cattle.

I turned to the cow, which was now standing next to me.

"A smart woman would get the hell out of here," I said to her.

She had no opinion either way because, you know, cow. As she gazed at me with those big bovine eyes, I guessed she thought the human before her was an idiot.

Maybe she was right.

I trotted through the paddock, leaving judgy Bessie behind me, until I got to the raceway. It was easy enough to find—a low gravel path that split the paddocks. I could see lumps of shit that hadn't been cleared when the cows had come down the raceway toward the milking sheds earlier in the day.

Could be the farmer had just been lazy about it.

Or they'd gotten distracted.

Up ahead, I heard *snarling*. I needed a weapon, something to defend myself.

Running up the raceway, I scanned constantly, so that whatever had attacked the cattle didn't see me as a midnight snack.

A green work tractor lay idle next to the effluent sump, which smelled like hell. The light from the milk sheds was brighter here, so I kept my head low.

Pulling the wire gate aside, I moved past the stone trap all the solids fall into. There, I found what I'd been looking for. At least, one of the dozens of things I'd been looking for. Sure, a machine gun would have been great. Or a flamethrower. I'd have taken that too.

Instead, I found what looked like a reinforced pitchfork.

I'd spent two summers cleaning out traps like this one, in the blazing Minnesota sun, ankle deep in cow shit. If that doesn't delete all interest in raising cattle for a living, nothing will.

It certainly did in me.

With the pitchfork in my hands, I moved up toward the brightly lit milking sheds. The snarling I'd heard earlier grew louder.

That was when I saw it.

It.

A tall, naked human was clawing and digging into the remains of a calf. Even after all the shit I'd seen on the farm, it still churned my stomach. Blood dripped from elbows, splattered across elongated, hairy thighs. I saw the person begin to lift their head, sniffing the air.

Shit.

But before they could turn toward me, a shotgun blast erupted from just opposite the sheds. I dropped to the ground, the pitchfork jamming into the dirt as I did.

Another snarl then a yell. A scream.

Cal Davis had run *toward* who'd ever fired the shot, racing down the hill, arms clawing the air. Down below sat another older shed, this one wooden.

I ran up to the farmer who'd fired the shot. Flat on his back, he looked dead.

When I came close, he lifted the barrel of the shotgun toward me, and I stopped, dropping the pitchfork.

"Holy shit, don't shoot, man!"

For a long, long moment, I stared at the holes in the shotgun barrel as it shook and bounced but never tracked away from me. Slowly, he lowered it and collapsed back to the ground. With his free hand, he reached over and grabbed his shoulder. Blood oozed through his fingers.

I leaned down, hovering over the weathered face of a lifelong farmer. Dirt muddied a full head of snow-white hair. "Are you okay, Mr. Clarrat?"

"Who the hell are you?" He stared at me as if he wasn't exactly sure I was real.

"Um, I'm with animal control," I said, flexing my bullshit muscle hard. "From out of town. We're... Are you okay?"

"Goddamn thing clawed at me as it went by," he said with a voice that sounded like he gargled with barbed wire. "I think I got a shot into its belly, but I can't tell."

I nodded into the dark. "What's down there?"

"Old milk shed. Don't use it no more," Clarrat said, leaning up on an elbow and craning his neck. "No animals in there, so don't know what it's after."

"Hiding, maybe," I guessed.

Pain deepened the wrinkles in the old guy's smile. "Don't seem like the hiding type."

I nodded, stood, and picked up the pitchfork. As I stepped forward, the old guy caught my foot with a hand, and I stopped, looking back.

"You going to poke it with that?" He motioned toward the farm implement in my hand then lifted the shotgun toward me. "Know how to use one of these?"

Right. I grabbed the stock of the weapon and hefted it against my shoulder. "Aim the pointy end and pull the trigger."

He chuckled. "If you're going, I won't talk you out of it. But if you can trap it in the old milk shed—"

I started running, not interested in hearing the old guy's plan. So far, his plan had nearly gotten him killed and had given him a helluva story for bathing-suit season. But he had a point.

Kane needed Cal Davis alive. He needed to find out who had done, well, what they'd done to Cal. If Kane knew how he'd been infected, there was a chance he could reverse it. Become wolf again.

Christ, was I really starting to believe that crazy story?

Shouldering the gun, I walked down the stony path that curved around the old milk shed. My fingers were slippery on the trigger, my heart thumping like some drum-and-bass track cranked up full volume.

I could taste blood in my mouth. I'd bitten the inside of my cheek.

"Heeey," I said, my voice unsteady. "Just want to talk, Cal. No need for any, um, eating me or anything."

From the dark, I heard a low, guttural growl.

Not directly in front of me but to my left. In the wooden stalls. I considered lowering the shotgun to show I didn't mean any harm. But the very idea of it made me feel exposed. Naked.

As my vision adjusted to the dark, I could make out a figure, hunched and heaving with breath. Naked in the dark, muscles wound tight like an animal ready to leap up at me.

"I just—"

It lurched, all bloodied teeth and flesh, amber eyes blazing, hitting me in a full sprint, knocking me onto my back as it leapt off my chest. The wind knocked out of me, I fought the black and sparkles at the edges of my vision. Above my head, I could hear thumping feet coming back around toward me. Clutching the shotgun under my arm, I rolled left down a slope, making the world spin and spin.

The creature had leapt at me and ended up tumbling end over end in the dirt.

I wouldn't be so lucky again.

When it turned back toward me, I saw its face—a horrifying mask of dirt, blood, and fury. It stared at me. Crazed. Human but no longer human. Then those eyes flared, and with limbs spraying gore, it was running toward me again, its long, powerful legs stretching awkwardly.

Up on one knee, I leveled the shotgun and fired off a blast, but still, it kept coming. I pulled the trigger again and only got a sharp click.

Two rounds in the shotgun.

The old guy had fired one, and I'd fired the other. I was out.

I flipped the shotgun around, hoping to use it as a club, but if the goddamn gun blast hadn't done anything, how would I—

The creature leaped into the air, arms wide and mouth open. When I noticed the fine details of dirt and blood in its teeth, a red-line split in its blackened gumline, I realized time had done that thing where it slowed the world around me.

Maybe it's due to adrenaline or panic or both. Maybe it's a god, disapproving of us, who slows down those last moments so you can really contemplate all the awful shit you've done wrong in your life.

Because that life?

It's about to end.

Hope you enjoyed the show.

Arching through the air, the hands came closer, reaching for my throat, the head tilted and jaw distended, ready to bite.

Then the creature shifted, bent, and fell to the side. It tumbled again and again with something fat and white clinging to its chest.

I jumped to my feet and saw what had knocked it out of the air. What had saved my life.

A pug. A goddamn pug dog.

"Kane!"

Chapter Nineteen

The two creatures rolled away in the dirt, tumbling down the short hill.

My brain felt like an icy hand had squeezed that gray mush into a tiny ball, leaving nothing but a flatline whine of fear ringing my ears. I watched as they bounced down the slope and got swallowed by the darkness of the milk shed.

Kane needed my help, but my legs had turned to cement. Frozen in fear.

Breathing deeply, I thought: *From here to there. From here to there.*

I heard the snarling of the little gray dog and the scream of the creature that had been inches away from tearing out my throat. Images formed in the darkness, and it was only then that I realized I was running toward that chaos.

The exterior walls of the old milk shed had been warped by decades of summer's punishing sun and spring's endless rain. As I sprinted under the massive awning, held aloft by a half dozen wooden poles, the smell of rot and mildew nearly threw me back.

At the rear, a dozen stalls once held cattle for milking, many years ago. Some of their individual doors were raised, some lowered, and many were chipped and rotting like an old woman's teeth.

Between me and those stalls, thrashing on a floor of dirt and decaying straw, the monster lay on its back as the tiny pug clawed and snapped at its chest.

Clutching the dog with both hands, it turned sideways and dug in its teeth.

Kane yelped, howling in pain.

He then twisted his thick pug body and bit into the neck of the other, clamping down hard. They tumbled once again, locked in a desperate, clawing battle, and rolled into one of the open sheds, their bodies smashing up against the far wall.

"Kane!" I shouted, searching for something other than an empty shotgun to use as a weapon. But the shed hadn't been used in years, abandoned after a newer, upgraded structure had appeared on the hill above. The only thing left behind were the tired, wooden bones of a now-forgotten friend—its job not finished, just taken up by another.

It offered nothing to fight off a monster.

Inside the stall, the dog rose to its feet, wobbly, and glanced toward me. In the dim light, the pug looked weary, glassy-eyed, and did the most curious thing. It shook its head.

Then the bloody creature was upon it again. I heard a yelp then another snap of teeth.

I burst toward them with the shotgun barrel in my hands and ran into the stall. Lifting the stock like a club, I bashed at the head of the frenzied, naked human. It collapsed, then quickly leaped on all fours, and looked up to me. The only parts of it not caked in mud were its crazed eyes.

Wide and full of bloodlust.

The pug reared up on its hind legs and went for its neck again, but the monster, so much stronger than the dog, so much stronger than any other human, just batted it away, raking its claws across dense fur. Kane flew five feet and smashed against the far side of the shed.

In the darkness, the creature lifted itself from the dirt and straw and stepped closer. Then it snapped its head to something behind me.

The gate to the stall slammed shut, and I heard the metallic slap of the locking mechanism. When I turned, I saw the face of Tech Sergeant Gregor. Grinning.

Then he was gone, slipping back into the thick envelope of night on the other side.

I heard the sound of smashing glass then a *whoosh!*

Enraged, the creature tore at the stall door's vertical metal bars, shaking them. It screamed, a voice half human, half animal.

The shotgun had flown from my hands when I'd struck the monster and was now lost beneath the clumps of straw of dirt at my feet. I searched for some kind of weapon, any kind of weapon, but before it could turn back on me, a new threat emerged.

Smoke. Suffocating heat. Licking flames.

Gregor had set the fucking milk shed on fire.

The creature slunk back to a corner, its naked frame nearly folding down to my height, eyes reflecting the angry flames. As the light from the fire grew, I finally got a look at its face. At its body.

This was not Cal Davis.

"Who?" I said, stammering. "W-Who are you?"

The feral woman, rotting straw clinging to her mud-caked body, looked through me at the growing flames. Her eyes were animal, lips pulled back in a snarl exposing flesh-flecked teeth. I glanced over at Kane. He wasn't moving.

She pointed at the pug dog.

"It... it is... is yours?"

I wondered if her distended jaw made it difficult to form words, or if she just hadn't used her voice for anything but full-throated screaming. The utterances came out guttural and staccato.

I nodded, my vision blurring. My heart ached for this woman, because I knew this blood-thirsty chaos had been thrust upon her. She hadn't chosen this. Her life had been ripped away and replaced with something unnatural. Her humanity corrupted, she was now a beast.

Like a mirror to Kane.

"Bridget?" I said, and she flinched, looking away. When I shifted my feet, she cocked her head at me, her teeth bared once again. "Bridget Mills?"

At the sound of her name, her twisted expression went slack, and I could see an echo of the woman who'd once been there. She blinked then pointed at the pug dog laying on its side and drawing in shallow, hitched breaths.

"It... it attacking. Me," she grunted. Her tongue then raked across her teeth as if scraping off the bitter taste of human words.

An explosion knocked us both sideways as angry flames reached and clawed for us through the bars. I could feel heat press upon my face as I lay there, trying to get my wits back. Coughing on smoke, my vision watery and dancing, I watched the woman claw her way up the side of the stall, skittering and shifting, and then try to squeeze through a space between the locked gate and the dark ceiling.

Something cracked. I couldn't tell if it had been wood or bone.

She wailed as she pressed her body through the gap then fell to the ground on the other side.

"Wait!" I shouted. But she didn't turn back. She was finally free and racing away from the flames.

The throaty exultation of an engine shook the night air. Blinking through the smoke, I saw the crimson headlights of a truck wheel up behind her. Chasing.

Hunting.

The tech sergeant and his crew were in pursuit, the vehicle's taillights bouncing like demon eyes across the uneven field. The red lights blazed brighter, and I heard the crack of a rifle.

The naked woman, just a silhouette in the moonlight, hitched awkwardly. Another shot rang out, and she dropped, disappearing into the shadows on the ground.

Something fluttered in the moonlight like a strange, impossibly large butterfly made from thick, spiderweb threads.

From their black truck, they'd launched a net, which twirled and spun until it landed upon the fallen woman. Through the crackle and heaving breath of the flames, I heard the snap of a winch as the netting was pulled taut.

The smoke stinging my vision snaked its way deep into my lungs. I coughed and rubbed my eyes, blinking away tears as I tried to watch the unreal scene play out on the other side of the locked gate. Two figures leaped from the truck. Then three. Hauling their prize toward the hulking, rumbling vehicle, they cinched the bloodied and bound woman within the net.

A mountain of a man threw her over his shoulder, her head lolling as he ran. She didn't move. The woman who'd once been Bridget Mills looked dead.

A moment later, the big man rounded the vehicle and chucked her through an open door in the back then slammed it. The men scuttled around like happy beetles, laughing and whooping, until they slipped back into the cab.

The engine whined, and they sped away, those devil eyes winking and dancing through the black void outside. The truck bounced down the field and out of my view.

The tech sergeant had tracked us all the way to Pine Valley but not because he'd had an interest in Kane himself. Gregor had known that Kane would pursue Cal Davis. He let us do the work, and he'd waited to collect the trophy.

Had they expected to find the woman instead?

No time for those questions.

The horror show outside my cage had all played out in less than thirty seconds. And in that time, the flames had begun licking the inside of the shed.

My hands stung, and I looked down to see the rusted bars between my fingers. I couldn't even remember gripping them. I spun around and ran toward the pug splayed out in the dirt and long-dead straw.

"Kane," I said, coughing. "Kane, we've got to get out of here."

He didn't move. His eyelids parted for just a moment. Then, once again, he was out.

I could feel the heat on my back. The fire had been robbed of the woman's flesh, and now it was coming for us.

Searching for a place to grab the pug dog, I tried to find some spot that wasn't already covered in blood or gashed by the feral woman's nails and teeth. There wasn't any.

My heart caught in my throat as I lifted Kane in this form. I couldn't tell if he was even breathing.

"Hold on," I whispered and hoisted his thick, limp body under my arm.

When I turned toward the stall's metal gate, I froze. It was locked from the outside. But I knew from my time on my uncle's farm that it wouldn't require a key.

These stalls had been designed to keep in animals, not people.

I just had to reach through the bars, find the mechanism, and lift it away.

But when I stepped forward, the scorching heat pushed me back like a demon giant's palm playing with its prize. I crouched low, hoping to get under the radiating energy. Scooting toward the gate, I tried to peer through the smoke and flames but only saw an angry, billowing haze.

Lifting Kane to my hip as if he was a toddler, I reached up toward the bars.

I yanked my fingers back, howling. "Fuck, that's hot!"

The iron slats had heated, far too hot to touch. The flames got bolder, inching forward, and the damp straw around us began to smolder. Once it got hot enough, that, too, would catch fire.

About a foot away from the door hung a large chunk of rusted iron at the end of some rope. Not rope. That would have burned away. It was hanging from a long strand of braided wire.

With the surrounding air swirling, a vortex of heat and smoke and dust, the metal bar swung slightly. It was cylindrical but tapered, about as long as my forearm. Like a rolling pin without the handles.

Something about the shape, the way it swung, tickled a faint memory, but when I tried to reach for it, panic and adrenaline batted it away.

I couldn't fathom its purpose. Probably some way to keep the cows in line? Or somewhere to hang a milk bucket? I had no idea. I reached for it, but after my painful encounter with the gate, I knew the metal would be far too hot.

Instead, I turned back to the gate and pressed my tennis shoe against a flat panel at the base. It moved just a little.

Maybe I could kick it away?

Hell, the locking mechanism might have even melted at these temperatures. One swift kick might do the trick!

Lowering Kane onto the damp straw once again, I lay on my back and lifted my knees to my chest. Then I lashed out with both feet. The gate rattled but didn't open. Instead, a chunk of burning wood from the top of the gate split and fell.

I had to roll out of the way as it landed, just inches above my head. Behind me, I could feel the thud of impact. Sparks belched out, and it felt like white-hot fleas biting at my back and neck. When I spun around to look, embers had begun steaming the damp straw below. Panicked, I searched for a bucket of water or feed that I could use to put out the nascent flames.

Nothing.

This was an old, forgotten milk shed. Anything of use or value had long ago been stripped out.

I jumped up and kicked at the tiny fires on the ground, but that only busted up the burning beam, spreading its embers farther. For now, the flames were just flickers. That wouldn't last.

"We gotta get out of here," I croaked to the pug dog, which lay on its side, unmoving. My breath caught in my throat as I stared. "Kane? Kane, are you...?"

He didn't move.

Angry tears mixed in with the ones squeezed out by the smoke. He looked dead.

Finally, I saw his eyes crack open just a little and noticed him staring up at my grandmother's locket hanging below my chin, reflecting the firelight. I stripped it off and wrapped it around his tiny neck, looping it a few times to secure it.

"For luck," I whispered.

Then I saw his tiny tummy rise and fall. Just a little. Kane was still alive. But for how long? The thick smoke felt like drawing in breaths of dirty water. I had to get him out of there.

Hell, I had to get *myself* out of there!

The locked gate was out of the question. It seemed like the only thing holding up the roof right now. If I bashed it again, the burning ceiling above us would come crashing down.

I looked to the stalls on both sides, but with the high walls—walls that were burning—I couldn't fathom a way into either.

Then I saw something.

In one of the neighboring stalls, some of the wood had been busted away at the back. It seemed thinner than the rest of the wall. Coughing and squinting, trying to push the smoke out of the way to get a better look, I realized that there'd been a rectangular shape against the back wall and part of that had come away.

Kicked by an animal or busted by some machinery?

Didn't care, didn't matter.

When I looked to the back of our stall, I saw a similar design. With a thin frame, it looked like, well, a doggie door. Or, rather, a cow door.

I glanced over at Kane. Still breathing.

I crossed the smoldering hay to the back wall, found the small panel, and gave it a push. Nope. Unlike doggie doors, apparently, cow doors slid up not out.

Tracing my fingers around its edges, I could feel the top of it, pressed the heels of my palms under its lip, and lifted.

It wouldn't budge.

"Goddammit!"

I heard Kane moan, but when I turned, he stirred for only a moment. Then he passed out once again.

Kicking at the door only shook the entire structure, which was disintegrating by the second. I stopped kicking and flopped onto my back. Using my heels under the lip, I could just lift it, but shit, it was heavy!

I crawled over, gripped the unconscious pug in my shaking fingers, and pulled him to the back wall.

On my back again, I tried to push the door up with my legs. If I could open it just a crack, I could at least slide Kane through. Then I'd have to find some way to follow.

I couldn't lift it high enough.

"Come on!" I shouted, willing the muscles in my legs to push harder. I was going to die if I didn't get out of there in the next half minute. Wasn't my rage supposed to give me super strength or something?

"Fuckin' Bruce Banner bullshit," I screamed as I pressed, but the gap opened only wide enough to tease out blissfully cool night air that caressed the backs of my thighs. Spent, I dropped the door, and it slid down the meager six inches I'd been able to lift it.

Above me, I heard a rattle. Something clanged and rang out.

I stood, hunched over, and finally noticed a series of eyelets, thick screws with circlets at the ends. A wire had been strung through them that bit into the cow door, which had been fitted into its wooden track.

I stepped over and pressed my head against the back wall to see better. The wire traced down the boards in a groove and attached to the top of the small door.

But what is it attached...?

The hanging metal bar.

Then I realized what it had reminded me of. Like those old grandfather clocks with something swinging at the bottom. It was a counterweight. A counterweight for the cow door.

I frog-crawled the three steps it took to get next to the hanging iron and went to grab it. Too hot. Jesus, it was roasting in there. We were literally cooking!

I just needed to—

On the far end of the cowshed, just a few stalls away, the ceiling collapsed, eaten away by the fire. When the flaming boards fell, they ignited the straw below. At another crash behind me, I spun around. That side, the roof, had caved in too. More flames feasted over there.

We had fire on all sides of us.

No time left.

Pulling off my leather jacket, I stripped out of my shirt, which was soaked in sweat and Kane's blood. I wrapped it around the counterweight and pulled down. It moved easily, and I nearly cried with joy when the door opened.

But the moment I let go, the door fell again.

Another crash. The roof above us buckled.

Putting the jacket back on, I was glad there weren't any mirrors. With a black jacket over a black bra, I would have looked like some wannabe punk rocker.

I scanned from corner to corner to corner of the tiny enclosure. There was nothing to weigh the metal bar down with but a bloody, half-dead pug dog. But that wasn't going to happen. Could I yank it and run through?

I tried that, but the moment I let go, the door fell back down like a wooden guillotine.

Looking around again, I saw nothing. There were no rocks, no bags of grain, no empty buckets left behind by happy milkmaids, *nothing*. All I had were my clothes, but that would never be enough.

I'd end up just burning to death naked.

Frustrated and terrified, I punched the fucking weight with my fist.

That had been a mistake. Christ, it hurt like a mother! But I didn't care. I had my way out right there in front of me, and all it had done was show me I could do nothing to escape. I kicked at the weight, and it flew toward the locked gate, banging against it, sending a shower of sparks toward me.

I yelped and fell back.

But when I did, I saw something strange.

The cow door had come open. Briefly. It had lifted up then snapped back down.

When I looked toward the gate, I saw the counterweight swinging toward me, passing a few feet above my head. When it swung back, it slipped through the bars, the braided wire bending as it hit the crossbar. There was a small thunk behind me.

Jumping up, I grabbed Kane under my arm, holding him to my bare skin beneath my jacket.

Another crash, and the stall next to us filled with flames and red-yellow embers. My body was drenched in sweat as I waited for the iron bar to swing back my way. When it reached the height of its arc on my side, I kicked again, as hard as I could.

It swung away faster, and I turned.

The door lifted halfway then fell again. I screamed and screamed.

Another crash, somewhere to my left, but this time, I ignored it. I was out of time.

Once again, I paused as the counterweight made its circuit, swinging back my way. This time, I roared at it, lifted my foot high in the air, and kicked it with everything I had. It flew away from me, but I didn't bother to watch it this time.

I turned and bolted. With two steps to go, I leaped just as the cow door was opening, but there was no stopping. Behind me, I heard the *whoosh-whoosh-whoosh clang* of wire on metal, and the door flew up just as we got to it.

We burst through the gap, and I went blind and deaf in a snap. But after the inferno, it felt joyous, like leaping off a high cliff into an icy mountainside lake.

Suspended in the air, I clutched the pug dog and pulled my knees up, waiting for the impact. When we landed, we rolled and rolled until we stopped in the deep trench that had been carved out by a tractor tire.

When I looked up, I saw stars.

I sucked in deep, beautifully pure breaths and screamed out, "Yeah, mother—"

My voice was drowned out by the final, explosive cry of the ancient milk shed as it collapsed in flames and spitting sparks. The fire seemed angry, furious, that I had denied it its meal.

Beyond it, I saw the flashing red and blue lights of two patrol cars. A large tanker was coming down the hill, filled, I assumed, with water. Hell, maybe it was milk.

Either way, the fire was their problem now.

With trembling arms, I raised Kane to eye level and gave him a little shake.

"You alive?"

Slowly, the pug's eyelids parted. Then he opened his mouth, and I swear, I thought the tiny thing laughed.

"You think that's funny?"

Instead of answering, Kane licked my face once then passed out again.

I blinked once, felt a wave of nausea and fatigue wash over me, and joined him in the black.

Chapter Twenty

Waking up has never been a pleasant experience for me.

Those first few seconds after cracking open, my eyes slowly fill with the disappointment that I've just been stolen away from somewhere safe. Well, maybe not safe. Just not here.

Dreams were the domain of the mind, and despite whatever detritus of the day had washed up on nightmare shores, I always knew in that synaptic landscape, I was queen.

I had been in control.

That thought made me laugh. Arguably, you're at your most vulnerable when sleeping. In the real world, immobile and unconscious, you couldn't be *more* vulnerable.

But in the dream world? I was powerful. I was the threat.

When I awoke, the lights forced me to squint, as if the rays emitted from the overhead fluorescents had come down in razor-sharp blades. I lifted my hand to cover my eyes and felt a pinch at my wrist then a tugging sensation.

A bolt of fear shot through me when I realized I was strapped down. Bound.

"You're all right, hon," a deep, soothing voice rolled from somewhere behind me. "That's just the IV."

Trying to see the person who'd spoken, I wrenched my shoulder, twisting my body. A hand shot out and steadied my arm.

"Don't fuss now," the man said, his touch strong but soft. "You'll just pull the darn thing out."

When he came around, blotting out some of the harsh light, I saw his face. A bit thin and haggard, but there was kindness in his eyes. A mustache on his upper lip bent upward. In my daze, it looked like eyebrows over his mouth.

Relief washed over me when I lifted my arms and saw that they moved freely.

"What am I doing here?" My words came out in a croak, stinging my throat, and I bent forward slightly, coughing. I felt the steady hand on my arm again, gentle but firm, making sure I didn't squirm too much.

"You were in a fire a few hours ago," he said as he placed a soothing hand at the back of my head, guiding me back down to the starchy pillow. "I'm Nurse Taylor. You're in the night clinic."

"Night clinic?"

He laughed then scrunched up his nose. "Saying the word 'hospital' always sounds so dramatic, especially when someone's just coming to. I prefer clinic."

At first, I thought this might be just a wing of the night clinic, since there were only four beds. But considering the size of Pine Valley, this might have been the entire facility. Aside from my bed, only one other was occupied, its threadbare curtain drawn around for what probably passed for privacy. Through the gap, I could see an older woman who might have been sleeping or, depending on the capabilities of the country clinic, dead.

The peeling walls had been repeatedly painted over, inadvertently creating a modern slap brush pattern. This may have made patients like my roomie more comfortable since the texture matched her wrinkled skin.

Lines crisscrossed the worn linoleum floor where the chairs stacked along the wall opposite me could be dragged bedside for visiting friends and family.

Still woozy from exhaustion, I realized Nurse Taylor had still been talking. I hadn't heard a word and asked him to rewind.

"Shorter version, then?" He grinned. "The fire crew found you just on the other side of a burnt-out milk shed on the Clarrat farm. Well, they found you after they'd put it out."

When I glanced down at his hand on my wrist, he pulled it away and lifted his palms to show he was no threat. That was when I noticed my sleeve wasn't my sleeve.

I wrinkled my nose at the blue speckled pattern of a hospital gown. Or maybe he preferred "clinic gown"?

"Where are my clothes?"

"Like I was saying, the fire team—they're volunteer, mostly, but dedicated—they'd put out the milk shed and then some. You would be the 'then some' of that statement. You got soaked." Nurse Taylor nodded over to a hanger. "I ran them through the wash for you, but the dryer ain't the best. They're still a little damp."

My mind began to clear like a morning haze burning off in the sun. Another bolt of panic cracked through me.

"Where's Kane?"

The nurse frowned and took a half step closer. He cocked his head.

"My *friend*," I said, my words coming fast. "He was next to me, and he didn't look so good. He's a big—"

"Oh!" Taylor chuckled and clapped his hands in front of his mouth. Then the smile fell away. "Right. He didn't fare as well as you, I'm afraid."

"What?" My eyes blazed. "Is he...?" I couldn't finish the sentence. Kane had looked pretty awful, but had his injuries been mortal wounds? Hell, I didn't even know what a mortal wound looked like.

"Ah, no, no, darlin'. Don't worry," he said, tugging at the thin blanket. "They took him over to Doc Blakelee's."

I sat up again, which drew an exasperated sigh from the nurse. That had given me a modicum of pleasure. My antiauthority streak, obviously, had not been injured.

"He's here? Kane's in the hospital?" I shook my head, trying to get all the words lined up. "In the, um, night clinic?"

Taylor laughed. "Here? No, that's—"

"Where is he?"

"I told you, he's at Doc Blakelee's," Taylor said and jammed his hands into his pink-and-gray smock. "He's got a clinic over on Baylor Road, a few blocks west. Doc's outta town until tomorrow, but they'll look after him."

I rolled my hands into fists. "Why is he there, and I'm here? Why did you separate us?"

Taylor blinked, grinning queerly. "Because people go to people hospitals and dogs go to doggie hospitals. They really don't like to mix the two."

Oh. Right.

A wave of dizziness hit me, the flash-flood of adrenaline draining from my brain, and I lay back onto the pillow. Baylor was just up the street just on the other side of the motel, so he'd be close. But I couldn't let him stay the night.

Come sunup, they'd walk in on a surprise I didn't think this town could handle. Hell, I could barely handle it. But a big, naked French Canadian man stuffed into some tiny cage would likely raise some eyebrows.

I scanned the room as the nurse fitted the sheet tighter at the bed's edges. It was unnecessary, but he was just being there for me. A kindness. I was disoriented, and he was hanging around to help me feel safe.

Thank God there are people in the world like that. That kind of empathy in people was so alien, in my experience. Like some beautiful birth defect, a gift to the world. I wondered, with all that love pouring out, how much people like Nurse Taylor had left for themselves.

For now, though, I was comforted by it. A little.

But I had to get the hell out of there.

Kane was in trouble.

Chapter Twenty-One

Kane

I am being held prisoner by the humans.

When the large man in plastic clothes had grabbed me back at the farm, I had bared my teeth to ward him off. The foul-smelling human, covered in the odor of many burnt things, only laughed.

I'd tried to establish my dominance, cry out to frighten him, but this only weakened me further. Yes, of course, he would have felt my strength. Feared me. Been at my every command.

However, sleep had taken me.

When I'd eventually awoken, I had not fully realized it because the dark, it continued.

I'd stood, lifting this tiny body from a very scratchy blanket. Not just scratchy. It smelled bad. Urine and spittle. Greasy meat. It reeked of dog.

Walking across the foul material, trying to clear my vision, I smack into cold steel bars.

But I cannot be held by steel!

I will bend it with...

Damn.

The steel is rather strong. In this tiny animal body with rat-like fur, I could be held by a paper bag!

But no.

I do have claws. Not very good ones, however. But they are a defense. They are an armament as well. I feel confident that if it comes to it, I will be able to escape a paper-bag confinement.

This is what Sad Girl has called "positive thinking." This is good, to learn the human things.

However, I am not enwrapped in shopping market material. I am in a small cage.

There is something tapping against my neck. When I lift a paw to touch it, I remember that Sad Girl had given me her necklace.

"For luck," she had said to me.

If I am alive, she must be as well. I do not understand this idea of luck, but I do know how much the necklace means to her. I will keep it safe until we are reunited.

A barking sound erupts from my left, and I brace for the attack. In the dim light, my vision adjusts, and I see the eyes of another. Some other creature's cage is next to mine. They got a larger one. What an insult!

Another gruff sound from elsewhere.

On the right of me, another cage and another creature. This one's eyes look dull and stupid.

"A cat," I mumble, and the foul beast, with its stupid fuzzy face, yawns at me. It would make a fine meal.

The first animal barks once again. I have deduced this is a dog.

Good.

Good.

I am working this out because I am crafty. Intelligent. Fierce.

I am learning about my surroundings. This is what the wolf does. Learns the territory and then uses it, bends it to his will. I walk to my left and once again feel the steel mesh bang against my tiny pink nose.

No, not tiny! It is also fierce and terrifying.

But it also now stings. However, only slightly. My dog eyes, they water.

Blinking the dampness away, I spot a dull light emitting from the far wall. Red and angular. I know this to be a clock. It is still night, and this is good. I have trouble with written human words and letters, but numbers are easier because there are fewer to remember.

The clock tells me it is not yet midnight.

However, midnight does not concern me. The dawn does.

A strange crackling sound perks my ears, confusing me further. For now, I ignore it because there are bigger concerns.

I cannot be in this tiny space when the sun once again rises and I return to the human form. Of course, I expect I could then bend the cage, for in that body, I am more powerful. But if I return to that form, the cage will cut and split my skin. Possibly break bones.

I must make my escape.

There is no fear in my heart. Despite my confinement, despite these other lower creatures fouling my air, I am the alpha wolf. In diminutive form, this is still true. I am the dominant creature in this strange metal forest.

Woof!

That sounds like a big one.

I cannot see this creature from my imprisonment, but I have deduced this is also a dog. Besides me, two dogs and one cat. Why have the humans imprisoned their animals?

What crimes have these creatures committed? I do not belong within their numbers. I am not criminal. I dislike to be in the presence of those who flout the way things should be. I must also allow that these creatures may be wrongly accused. Captive without crime.

The cat, yes, I can understand. They should all be imprisoned. Made slaves. However, they would be useless slaves, for they are lazy. And have tiny paws. Terrible creatures. God's error.

But tasty.

I chastise myself for such a thought. Mère and Père taught me of God and His ways. They would not like that I have thought myself worthy enough to pass judgment on His will. Still, the cat thing troubles me.

Woof!

Something has stirred the large creature, this unseen animal somewhere to my right. I hear thumping paws and scraping claws. The dog, a very big one, has also been imprisoned. I do not know his crime. However, I hope it is not that he likes to eat smaller dogs.

Woof!

What has troubled Large Dog?

The crackling I'd heard earlier, I now deduce, was the sound of car tires in an adjoining lot. For there is now something at the door. Only now do I see it because of the light that flicked on from above.

A jingling sound hits my ears, but it is not this that has my focus. The silhouette, so oddly formed. It looks like a human but with a ramrod-straight tail. Thick and menacing.

The strange tail moves, one side to another. Then I hear a key in a lock.

It is not a tail. This is a man. I can smell him. Sweat and dirt and, possibly, Axe body spray. But the tail is not a tail. He is holding something. Something large. A weapon.

And he is coming.

Chapter Twenty-Two

Nurse Taylor busied himself around my hospital room, refilling dispensers, wiping counters, jotting notes in a spiral notebook that hung from one cabinet. As best I could, I tried to look tired. Wasn't too hard; I was exhausted.

And, I had to remember, not one hundred percent. However, I couldn't remember when I'd last felt one hundred percent. But maybe that was just the whiny part of my brain. Self-pity was a comfort but never offered more than the false assurance that my troubles weren't my fault.

You can get drunk on that sort of denial. Or at least a little buzzed.

However, the hangover from that sort of self-delusion was always worse than the original low. The moment you realize, yes, this really is all you. That's the only conclusion you can come to when you're the only one left around.

But I wasn't the only one in my life, not at the moment.

I had a friend. Or employer. Whatever.

And whatever Kane was, I knew that he was in trouble. Out of either obligation or a mildly warming cockle of my heart, I knew I had to get him out of it.

Sure, he was a massive human. Despite, of course, not being human. Not fully. In that form, he was the largest man I'd ever met. But where fairy tales about the moon and those supernaturally affected by it had always promised gnashing teeth and claws, I'd only seen him transform twice.

Well, I'd seen the *results* of it twice, not actually ever witnessing that moment.

"I dunno if I want to see that," I mumbled to myself.

"What?"

The nurse spun toward me, a tiny smile bending his face. Taylor had a big heart, eager to please. Or help. It seemed he was waiting for any request from me or the sleeping lump in the other bed, ready to save the day.

I blinked slowly, hooding my eyes and forcing a smile of my own. "Oh, sorry," I said, rubbing my eyes. "Must have drifted off. I talk in my sleep sometimes."

Taylor took a step closer. "Giving away your secrets?"

"Don't really have any."

"We've all got secrets, hon."

I scrunched up my nose. "Yeah? What are yours?"

He laughed. "If I told you, they wouldn't be secrets." He capped a pen and slid it into his shirt pocket. "Although mine are boring. I work here, go home. Not much to do at night recently, but hopefully, that's about to change."

That piqued my interest. I raised my eyebrows, and he took this as some cue, sitting on the corner of my bed.

"What was that like?" His words were coming quickly now. "At the farm. Was it scary? Were you scared taking that thing on?"

Then I realized it.

Taylor hadn't been hanging around just out of kindness and the benevolent need to heal and comfort the sick. I didn't doubt that he had that trait; I'd seen it in his eyes.

But he'd busied himself in the room, close, looking for an opportunity to talk about the local monster. I hadn't really given him an opening, so he'd found one.

"Mostly, I remember the fire," I said, nodding to myself. "The smoke and just how fast it all began to burn around me."

Taylor laid a comforting hand on my blanket-covered shin. "I can't imagine. I think that's my greatest fear—burning to death. That and tiny dogs dressed in people clothes."

I chuckled.

He put an expression of mock seriousness on his face. "You don't dress little Kane up in doggie clothes, do you? Tell me you don't. I was hoping we might be friends."

I laughed harder at the thought and winced at the pain on my belly. My fingers went to where it hurt, and I felt two short, raised lines. I hadn't noticed those before.

"You had a couple of scratches there, which we stitched up," he said and held his fingers together. "Tiny stitches, so it shouldn't leave much of a scar. Do you know how you got those?"

I didn't. But he was watching me closely for the answer.

"I got thrown around a bit, knocked down. And then when I was fighting to get out of the burning barn—"

"Milk shed."

"Right. Either way, I was pretty frantic. I might have done it to myself." I thought for a moment. "Or rolling down the hill a bit when I got out. It's all a bit fuzzy."

Taylor nodded then looked casually at his hands. "That must have been scary as hell, coming face-to-face with that thing." He looked at me as if that had been a question, but when I didn't answer, he continued, "It's been a terror around here since last year. Although most people in town played it off as some starving bear or foxes."

"They come into town much?"

"Some, but the older folks said it wasn't like anything they'd seen," Taylor said, frowning. "Still, it was super grim. Chickens slaughtered in their coops with just feathers and blood and giblets left behind. That's why they thought it was foxes or dogs."

"But the whole town got spooked?"

"Bigger animals got attacked, which dogs and foxes don't really do," he said, staring off at the blank hospital wall. "Goats, even the ones with horns. Throats slashed. Sometimes that's all they found. Not much blood, though, so the rumors got, you know, otherworldly."

I shrugged. "People always search for the strangest of explanations. I think it helps us feel better about the weirdness in our own lives if we think there are unnatural forces out there toying with us."

That got a big smile out of him. "You didn't say you were a philosopher." He let out a long breath, and I could smell the faint tinge of cigarette smoke on it. "There was a call for a hunt to find the bear or wolf or whatever. They went out every night for a week until all the buzz sort of faded away. Time has a way of calming the jitters, I think."

"Calmer heads."

"Right, but that changed after Audrey Schmidt got into the middle of it," he said with a wan smile. "She's always been a busybody, making outlandish claims. Audrey has a couple acres across town, small farm.

Lifestyle block, she called it, but she's from out of town. Maybe out of country, the way she talks. Clipped accent, hard to place."

I waited patiently then bobbled my head. *Go on.*

He did.

"Audrey had been a teacher for years at the old high school but retired when the new high school up the road came in and they shut ours down. Bussed the kids out." He lifted his head, and I noticed the patient in the next bed stir. He stared for a moment, but when there was no more movement, he continued. "In her last year there, they'd had some gym equipment stolen. Coach Maylor put up some security cameras, and they caught the kids. I suppose that's where she'd gotten the idea."

I got it. "She put up cameras on her property."

"Just the one, because they're not cheap, and she was retired." He shrugged. "Audrey had tucked it up in the corner of her barn, where she'd had a bunch of chickens inside. It wasn't quite free range. They couldn't wander outside, but she hadn't had the heart to put them in cages."

"I get that."

"When there was a mini town meeting about 'the video,' Barclay, our police chief, said the placed had smelled like shit and death." Taylor laughed. "Audrey, no shame, said it always smelled like that."

As he dropped his head, I looked over at the time. Midnight. I had to get out of there and find Kane. But I needed to hear the rest of his story. If he'd just finish the damn thing.

"You mentioned a video?"

"Right, right," he said, raising his hands in mock surrender then dropping them back into his lap. "She put it up on the screens in the sports bar where we'd all met up. Everyone wanted to see the video, so that made sense."

I wrinkled my nose. "Must have been gross."

"Chief Barclay showed us all pictures of the aftermath, but the video was super spooky." Taylor paused for effect. He was enjoying telling the story. "Just a big barn of chickens wandering around, eating and shitting. We're all waiting to see a wolf or bear or dog or whatever, but the camera shifts violently and goes dark. That was it."

"That was it? That's what got everyone so spooked?"

Taylor's mood darkened. "Audrey rewound the video and stopped it in one frame. She knew the frame exactly. I could see she'd written the time code down on her arm. It was just before the camera tilted and went off. You could see a hand."

"A hand?"

"Blurred some, but right there—fingers splayed, reaching for the camera." He sighed. "A bunch of people threw their arms up at that. Blamed Audrey herself, saying she'd done that to get attention. But then, of course, were the pictures of the chicken massacre. Long way to go for someone looking for attention. And it wasn't like she could afford to lose all her chickens just to have a moment in the sun."

He quieted for a moment, staring at his fingers. When he didn't speak up, lost in thought, I prompted him. "What did you think?"

Taylor looked directly at me. "Girl, I've spent years looking after people in this town. I've seen parts of them they ain't even seen themselves. In fact, Audrey had busted her thumb a few years back when she'd tried to put up a gate, and I'd worked her through some physical therapy."

I picked up on his hint. "Not her hand on the video, then."

"It was blurry, but... no, I didn't think so," he said. "Fingers were too long and not, you know, kind of plump like Audrey's. Crazy, long nails like claws. Some didn't buy it, but many people did. She hadn't been the only one to see a 'someone' out slashing through the farm animals. That's when it comes out, right there in the bar."

"What comes out?"

"People said, 'I saw him running through the woods, naked, covered in blood.' Another says they'd seen him late at night at the side of the road. Just a glance and he'd skittered off."

That didn't sync with what I knew. "Him? I haven't seen a him. The person I saw was a woman."

Taylor almost leaped from the edge of my bed. "So you *did* see him—er, her!"

I nodded, but I didn't like being interrogated. I tried to take control of the conversation again. "Why did everyone think it was a him?"

"Cal Davis," he said as if it was obvious. "Everyone had heard the name by then. He'd attacked someone at the car show, naked from head to toe. Crazed. Then ran off. It was after that, just a few weeks, maybe, that all this craziness started up. At first, of course, everyone thought it was some animal."

"But then Audrey's video changed that," I said and got a nod. "Do you know who it was?"

A shrug. "Most thought it was still Cal. If it was a woman, though..."

"What?"

Another shrug. Dude was going to get powerful shoulders if he kept that up.

"Bunch of folks thought Cal had taken a local woman named Bridget Mills when the car show came to Pine Valley. Locked her in a dank cellar somewhere or worse. But maybe whatever had made Cal Davis crazy made Bridget crazy too?"

Keeping a stone face at the mention of Bridget's name, I asked, "Like a cult?"

That got a laugh, and it looked as if Taylor had needed it. "No, like some, I don't know... virus. Rabies, maybe, because that makes you crazy. Could explain all the dead animals everywhere. Doc says it can't be rabies because that'll kill you in weeks, and this has been going on for the better part of a year. But we're all virus experts now, right, after the pandemic and all that. We know that a virus can mutate and change. It could be a new strain of rabies. That seems to make the most sense."

"Sure."

Taylor dropped his voice to a whisper. "And could explain why Bridget's husband looked like he got dropped into a Ninja Blender the day after she disappeared." He leaned back and sighed. "The way he treated that poor woman... If she had gone psycho, the first person on her kill list would have been that poop-head Lorney."

I rubbed my face, feigning exhaustion, and caught another glimpse of the clock. Just past midnight. I was running out of time.

"I'm tired," I said, forcing a yawn. "I'm going to get some sleep."

That got me a smile. "Well, you've earned it. Heroes need their rest too."

"Hero?"

The nurse gave me a wry smile. "That's the word Stu Clarrat used, and I'm not one to argue with him. Especially the shape he'd been in."

It was my turn to shrug.

"They took him into the Cities in a helicopter for surgery," Taylor said. "Had three great slashes across his belly. Last thing he said was you went down there, charging in to take on the creature with one bullet!"

Yeah, I wish he'd told me it had just the one round, I thought.

"Sorry for prying." Taylor tucked the corners of my sheet in. "But are you part of some, I don't know, special SWAT team or, I dunno—ha!—a monster-hunting squad? Cops said when they headed down to the fire, they seen part of your group net the creature, chuck it in the back of their truck."

"Saw that too," I said.

"They got busy trying to contain the fire," Taylor continued. "But the truck had hauled ass outta there before they'd gotten down the hill. Those your people, then?"

Tech Sergeant Gregor and his crew were *not* my people. But I learned long ago that silence is often the best answer when you don't know the best way to respond. I said nothing.

Taylor checked my IV and changed out the bag as he spoke. "The chief's office has been asking about you, but I told them to come back in the morning. They'll be really interested in hearing your story. If you feel up for it now..."

I shook my head. "In the morning sounds good. That way, I can get some of it straight in my head too."

Nurse Taylor nodded once, and I noticed the tiny smile had returned. I thought he enjoyed being the only one in town who had another small piece of the puzzle. The man with no secrets, for a few hours, would finally have one of his own.

After a quick check of my vitals, we said our goodnights, and he snapped off the light, slowly closing the door.

The moment it clicked, I stripped off the IV and rummaged around for my clothes. I hadn't seen them nearby, but he had said they'd been hanging to dry. Making a circuit around the small room, quietly so I didn't wake the sleeping lump, I came up empty.

That was when I noticed two closets, one door smaller than the other.

The smaller one contained supplies. More hospital gowns, bedpans, all types of pads and bandages and tubes, but no clothes.

At the other—"Bingo!"

Then I frowned. I'd never said "bingo" in my entire life. Maybe I was still loopy.

Turns out I was a bit loopy, because when I put one leg into my pants and tried the other, I fell back and landed on my ass. On the floor, though, it was easier to put the pants on.

Fully dressed, I dug into my pockets. I panicked for a moment until I remembered that I'd stashed Kane's passport wallet in the Audi when I'd hidden it in the trees near the Clarrat farm. I could get that later. For now, I needed to find Kane.

Dawn was coming.

Slowly, I tiptoed to the door. When I reached for it, a voice split the quiet behind me.

"If you're trying to sneak out, you don't want to go that way," the voice said.

When I turned back, I saw a frail old woman leaning up on a bony arm.

"I get chucked in here every few weeks for whatever. They watch the doors. The back door's got an alarm and one of those internet cameras."

I whispered. "Where, then?"

She pointed at the windows on the far side of the room.

"They push open easy enough," she said, then lay back down. "I can't climb out of them, or I'll bust my bones, so I guess they don't worry about it."

I crept over, pulled the lever to the left, then turned and thanked her.

"Be careful, girl," she said to me, nodding. "This world is a lot stranger than they ever told us. I saw the video the nurse was talking about, too, and I don't know what to make of it. But I'd seen what that *whatever* did all over town. It's not natural. It's animal, maybe, but not natural."

"Got it," I said, hoping she'd shut up because all the talking could bring Taylor back. "Thanks."

She chuckled and leaned back onto her gray pillows, raising a thin arm over her head. "I used to be like you. Adventurous, daring." She rubbed two bony fingers up and down the side of her head, just beneath a gauze wrap. "Still am. A little."

Nodding, I pushed the window open. I had to get out of there.

"Bit of advice, darlin', from an old woman who's been there." She crossed her arms and closed her eyes. "Doesn't matter whether it's on two legs or four."

I got one foot outside, balanced on the ledge, then slung my other foot around. Dropping to the soft, wet grass, I still had my head inside the room. I lifted it and tried to think of a polite way to say goodbye.

She continued, "What I'm saying is, we are animals too. All of us. Sometimes, we just forget," she said. "But if that thing out there isn't locked up or dead, and you come up against it again, just remember—you're animal too."

That gave me pause. "I should feel sorry for it?"

"No, hell no," she said and leaned up again. "What I'm saying is you may not have much time to think. Trust your gut. Animal instincts. All you got sometimes."

"Thank you," I said, ducking my head under the window. "Um, get some sleep. And, you know, sweet dreams."

As I pulled by head away, she waved and said, "All I got left are dreams."

Nodding, because I didn't want the conversation to go further, I slowly closed the window and tramped toward the veterinary clinic.

Get Kane and get out.

This town was far too weird to hang around much longer.

Chapter Twenty-Three

Kane

The large dog in a cage resting on the dirty, tiled floor makes a chuffing protestation, which bangs off the clinic's walls. It is half warning, half worry, and half anger.

I think I need to talk with Sad Girl about math. It confuses me.

The smell of fear sullies the air, but I do not think it emanates from the man who has entered the room carrying his odd stick. My heart darkens further when he begins to whistle.

I do not trust whistlers.

A foul habit. Attention seeking. And you can never quite work out the melody. So maddening.

There is a skittering to my left. The smaller dog, smaller than I. Female, so I will have to keep vigilant, for I do not want her lustful attentions. I have a powerful musk, so this will be difficult.

The man dressed in stained coveralls stumbles and swears then coughs. Balancing on his weapon, he fumbles for the wall, and I brace, ready for his attack. For now, I am protected by the cage. However, I need no protection.

I am wolf.

In a pug dog body, yes. But I am fierce and powerful despite my many wounds. I feel them across my flank and neck. The pain is there, but I can handle pain. But the injuries drain me. I must fight that weakness.

The light clicks on, which fires broken diamonds of harsh light into my brain, but I do not flinch. The man closes the door with the heel of his dirty boot. That's when he spots me.

"What chu in for?" he says and laughs as if he's told a joke only he understands.

The weapon in his hand, that is the joke. A long wooden pole with, what? A mop of hair at the end of it. How stupid—

Ah, yes.

It is a mop.

Again, the large dog in the cage near the floor makes a throaty sound. Not aggressive; the tone is fearful. I walk to the edge of my cage and press my face against the wire mesh.

In the harsh light, I can now see that this is a big dog. A toddler human could ride it.

Why is this impressive animal afraid of the man with the mop?

My ears pick up the sound of shuffling, and when I look over, my face still pressed against the steel mesh, I brace.

The man is standing over my cage. His eyes are glassy, his protruding lips glistening. He laughs again, so close that I get a blast of his rank breath. He smells like pot pies and rotgut liquor. Unpleasant.

"They get you diggin' in the neighbor's garden?" he says, and his laugh comes in stomach-churning phlegmy waves. This is a man who does not take care of himself. "Looks like someone whooped you pretty good for it if'n ya did."

The smelly man pulls a flask from his coat, flicks the top of it, and tips liquid into his mouth. He swallows loudly and, in a practiced motion, thumbs the silvery top back into place.

His bloodshot eyes never leave me.

"Maybe you here so they can chop off those tiny balls of yours." His foul words knit together in a way that it's hard to tell when one ends and the other begins. The man tries to tuck the silver flask into his coat but misses his pocket, and it falls to the floor. Uttering a string of belching curses, he reaches down to pick it up.

This gives me a chance to plot. Make a plan.

I look to the dog to my left, the female. Its hair is packed in tight curls, cut in queer patterns. There is a pink bow atop its tiny head. Why has this shivering creature adorned itself in this way?

I motion toward the man, eyeing Pink Bow as I seek an advocate in the coming fight.

The dog trembles and urinates.

Frowning, I am unsure what she's trying to tell me. Strange way to communicate.

The man stands again, makes a show of opening his coat, sways slightly, and then replaces the flask. Another chuffing from the massive dog to my right.

This complaint angers the man, and he smacks the large cage, eliciting a sharp bark from the animal inside. He turns the mop around so that the wooden end is held out like a staff. Jamming it through the bars, he pokes the creature within.

More barking, then a growl.

The man's ruddy face darkens, his teeth bare, and he lifts himself and comes down again harder. This earns him a whimper.

I have respect for the large animal, caged so, yet still showing defiance.

The dirty man's violence does not illicit fear in me. I just have to be smarter than him. This does not seem like an exhaustive challenge. However, I am the caged one. He is not.

The sound of drizzling now, to my left.

I turn and see that the urine from the curly dog has exited the cage and is now streaming to the floor. The man has heard it as well.

"You little fucking—" he shouts and crosses past my cage. As he does, I reach with my paw, but I am too slow. I would love nothing more than to wring his neck, choke the life from him, and take his blood water.

However, this would be difficult in my current form. I have no thumbs.

Yes, I have done much in my years as a wolf without them, but since becoming human, I have grown to appreciate thumbs. They're so handy.

I laugh because I have made a joke. I need to remember to tell that one to Sad—

"The fuck are you huffing about?" the man says, now towering over my cage. I growl, staring up at him defiantly. He turns the mop around once again, and I stare at him with malice pouring from my tiny dog eyes. This only seems to enrage him more.

To my left, the sounds of another stream snap his attention away.

More urinating from Pink Bow, and this further angers him. I look to the animal and wonder if she'd done that on purpose to pull his attention away. If so, she is far braver than I gave her credit for.

The man raises his mop, bringing it down on the curly dog's cage. The metallic whack and ringing clatter sting my sensitive ears.

Pink Bow cowers deeper into the cage, but there is only so far she can go. Her fur is poking out the back in fuzzy bulbs. She has run out of room.

The man lifts the mop, a weapon once more, and bashes the wire again, bending it slightly.

This does not concern him. I can smell his rage and alcohol. I anger further, since it seems Pink Bow may have drawn the attention to protect me. However, I need no protection.

I growl at him, and it comes out more wolf than dog, which draws a curious expression from the man.

He takes a half step back. I expect I didn't emit an utterance congruent with my breed, but I am *not* a dog. The strangeness of it only angers the man further, and he now steps toward me. Instead of lifting it to strike my cage, he turns the mop around to use it as a wooden lance.

I hold my ground. That is, I hold my scratchy blanket.

I can withstand his wrath despite my many injuries. I am wolf. I am—

"Hey!"

The man turns, and his arms curl in sheepishly as the voice from behind, from the window, yells again.

"Hey, asshole!"

I step to the far side of the cage, only a step, but it's enough to see who is yelling. But I already know. I recognize the voice.

"Get away from him!" Sad Girl says, her eyes blazing with rage through the dirty window.

Chapter Twenty-Four

I stood at the vet clinic's window, shivering now that I wasn't running anymore.

My damp clothes had leeched heat away from my body. But none of that concerned me as I watched the asshole with the mop standing over Kane's cage.

Through the glass, I pointed at him then stepped back, looking for the door.

It was late, and I had to consider that I was about to step into a dark building with no one else around.

Strangely, the voice of the old woman in the hospital bed came to mind.

"Doesn't matter whether it's on two legs or four. Hell, even six or eight. It's all animals."

The man looked like some night cleaner. Stringy, matted hair. Bony arms. He didn't look terribly strong, but he was still, as she'd said, an animal. And he had been waving the mop around like a weapon. If I charged in there, I could get that right up the side of my head.

I wasn't armed.

But it was only a few hours until dawn. I had to get Kane out of there and back to the motel or, preferably, the hell out of town.

"It's all animals,"she'd said. "Just remember—you're animal too."

Screw this guy. I was going to show him some fucking animal!

I ran to the door, yanked on the handle, and threw the door open. Inside, I could see a poodle with a pink bow to the right, a massive Great Dane to the far left. A gray cat.

Then I saw the pug dog. Even though its body was bruised and bloodied, I could tell the expression on its face was recognition. But more than that.

I froze in that moment, staring at the pug dog's face. Kane had spoken to me, often, about how humans relied too much on words. How, as a race, we'd almost entirely lost the ability to read expression and gesture. And how these were a more pure and true way to communicate.

The look on his pug dog face. I felt I could read those thoughts, and they were words I never thought I'd ever hear him say. A flush of elation washed over me.

Three words.

Three perfect words written in furrow and frown.

Maybe I'd been imagining them, willed them to be there, because they're the three most important words in the world, at least to me. Ones I had always yearned to hear but never had. Those around me had always made me feel like such a burden. A drain on their lives. Yet here, now, I felt this tiny creature was emoting those three perfect words to me.

I need you.

The most amazing words in the human language. Hidden from me my entire life until now. Was I just imagining it? Hoping to see what I yearned to hear?

I need you.

"I'm here!" I shouted as angry yet joyful tears filled my eyes.

The man inside took a step back, throwing down his mop. "You can't be—"

I didn't hear the rest of what he said.

From behind, I felt hands grip my body tightly. Someone large lifted me off my feet, spinning my vision in a kaleidoscope of light, and carried me like a rag doll toward a truck. I knew whose truck that was.

Then I saw Tech Sergeant Gregor pass me, a wry smile on his smug face.

"Put her in the cab," he said then glanced toward the vet clinic's open door and shrugged.

I got shoved inside and moved to kick the massive guy who'd carried me.

"Ah, ah," a woman said. She was in the passenger's seat, pointing a pistol at me. "Quick chat. Best if you just chill."

Before I could answer, the big guy slid into the back seat next to me. Quickly, I fumbled my phone out of my pocket to call for help, but it fell from my shaking fingers and dropped to the floor. *Damn it!*

The cramped space was barely big enough for the giant human who'd snatched me, so when he got in and closed the door, he squished me against the cab's wall. He reached behind his head. I braced.

Then the gorilla-sized man pulled down a seat belt clasp and grinned at me. "Buckle up for safety."

Gregor climbed inside next to the massive dude, crunching my body further, and the truck sped off.

He leaned across the other man, a huge grin on his face. "We've got some questions," he said, his eyes dead. "You answer them right, and you'll see tomorrow. But I wouldn't get your hopes up."

Chapter Twenty-Five

Kane

I howl and howl but can only watch through tiny stupid pug eyes as Sad Girl is dragged away.

Gregor has taken her!

I must leave this place. Must find where he has taken her. And killing Gregor, too, this would be good. Despite Sad Girl saying killing is bad, sometimes it is good. It strikes me that this is a simple outlook. However, truth is always simple.

"This town is gettin' to where it ain't safe to walk around at night," Mop Man says as he watches the tech sergeant's truck speed away. Then he turns and casts his rheumy eyes over all of us.

He once again grabs his mop stick, and the large dog whimpers. Coward! The large ones *know* they can intimidate but are so easily cowed.

Once, I knew a bear like this in our part of the forest. Not a proper bear. A few growls, and he would turn and run. Not bear. Pussy. Pussy bear.

I step forward and bare my teeth. I am the alpha wolf!

"Ain't you full of piss and... Hell, now, that's a pretty thing." He is looking directly at me, and I sigh inwardly. Long ago, I accepted that females find me irresistible. There have been males, too, sure, but no brood can come from such a mating.

And, of course, I am betrothed. I have a wolf wife. Or had. I don't know if I will ever see my life mate again, and this saddens me so.

He steps closer. I do not care for his lustful attention, but this is my curse—wanted by so many—and one I have grown accustomed to. This smelly man also wants Kane, but he cannot have me.

I do have standards.

When Mop Man reaches for me with wanton hands, I bare my teeth. As his fingers get closer, I snap my puny jaws and growl.

"You little..." he says, his rancid breath nearly buckling my tiny dog knees.

When he pulls back, I think it's over and look over at the cat. It stares, licking its paw. Disdain in its eyes. I will eat those eyes. And the rest of it, once—

Whack.

Everything goes black for a moment, and I feel the scratchy blanket on the side of my face. I have fallen to the bottom of the cage. When I open my eyes, the world dances before me, unwilling to behave.

I see pink worms. Why do I see pink worms? Where did such terrifying worms come from, the way they bend and wiggle? Horrifying! The worms reach for me.

No. Worms do not reach.

"Got it," the man says and snaps the worms away. They were not worms. Fingers. However, they did smell like dirt and feces, so I allow the error.

I force myself to unsteady feet, ready to face the Mop Man again. If he tries to smack me with his stick, I will grab it, wrench it from his grasp!

However, he is not interested in me at the moment. Something dangles between his fingers.

No!

I try to look down at my neck, but my stupid little pug face will not bend in that direction. How horrible this body is! I lift a paw and feel below my chin. Sad Girl's necklace is gone. Mop Man has stolen it.

"This must be what your little friend came looking for," he says and stuffs it into his windbreaker jacket pocket, patting the spot with his worm fingers. "Mine now."

The large dog finds his spine once again and barks, which makes the man shudder. However, the dog is caged. Cannot get to Mop Man. This emboldens the human, and he reaches up, grabbing a hose hanging from the ceiling.

Spinning a red flower-circle above his head, he points the hose nozzle at the large dog and blasts the creature with the water. This elicits howling. Terror. The large dog's despair disturbs the curly dog to my left, who then begins to join in with her own call.

This also earns Pink Bow a torrent of water. She is flung rearward and smacks the back of her cage.

The man points the nozzle at me now as if daring me to make a noise. However, wolves make their own choices. Even when they are pugs. I give him nothing.

With a shrug, he fires a stream of water at the cat.

Fine. That has earned him a few points in my book. And good, because it is better that the cat is washed before I eat it.

He steps forward, raising the nozzle toward me, close. At this range, it will be powerful enough to knock me down. But I can brace. I can withstand.

Pink Bow howls then growls at the man. When I look, she is baring her teeth. Catching her pheromones, I realize... she is protecting me. I am smaller, and she is drawing his anger.

For this, she earns another blast from the rubber hose.

I feel the blood pump through my body, my breath quickening. My anger has risen, and I want to rip the man's head off. But Sad Girl has said, calm. She says anger leads to stupid.

Better to... What was it she said was better to do?

"Y'all stink like hell," the man says. He grabs his metal flask again, tilts his head back for another swallow, then replaces it. "Baths for everyone!" He turns the red circle above his head once again. "Let's go full volume to getcha real clean. Hell, we only turn 'er up this high when we're gettin' shit off the walls, so it'll do the job."

Through the red haze of anger, I hear Sad Girl's voice.

Anger only makes a bad situation worse. Talk. Use your words.

So I do.

I step forward and look up at the man. "Don't do that."

Chapter Twenty-Six

When we arrived at the closed bar, only a few blocks away, I was relieved to finally be out of the vehicle. Smashed up against the big dude in the back seat of the cab, I could barely take a breath.

The gorilla guy tried to pull me along, but I pushed him off.

"I can walk, asshole!"

I instinctively flinched when he raised his big meat sack of a hand, the back of it ready to take my head off. But Gregor stopped it with a few words. None of which I found encouraging.

"Plenty of time for that inside," he said, casually looking around the dark parking area at the back of the building.

The woman leaned forward and typed a few digits into the door's key-pad. A moment later, she shoved it open, and Gorilla pushed me forward. At some point, I was going to find a way to hurt that prick.

As I passed over the threshold, the florescent lights came alive. A kitchen prep area. I knew that world pretty well, worked in enough of them over the years, and I cast my eyes around. It didn't take long to find what I'd been looking for. There'd be dozens of them here.

Gregor noticed my gaze. "Don't even," he said and lazily lifted his pistol, waggling it in the air.

I let my stare fall from the long line of knives clinging to the white-tiled wall.

Another push from Gorilla, and we passed from the cold, sterile kitchen into the warmth of a country tavern closed for the night.

As the five of us piled in, our shuffling feet were silenced by low-pile red carpet of the dining area. I could make out a few blotchy stains on the floor where drinks had been spilled, which had probably elicited a round of applause at the time.

The bar area had been cleaned well enough to hold a sermon there; the wood countertop buffed to a shine reflected the shimmering glow of the hanging stemmed glasses that swayed in the silence.

The big gorilla pulled a chair off the closest table, dropped it to the floor, and pushed me into the seat. He sat at a chair to my left, and when he leaned forward, he took up half of the damn tabletop.

"You got bigger tits than I do," I said, frowning at him.

This got a smile out of him. "Thank you."

Obviously, Gorilla Tits was not the leader of the crew. But I knew that already. This was Gregor's show. He spoke with the woman as she pulled a barstool off a stack, stored for the night for the early-morning clean-up crew. Then she sat, back of her head leaning against the wall, listening to her boss as if she had better things to do.

"How long we got this place?" Gregor asked.

She shrugged. "It's totally fine. It's part of the Org."

Org? Whatever.

"Just gotta clear out before three," she added, shifting her head into a gap on a wall that was covered floor to ceiling with old license plates. Country bar décor.

Gregor shrugged and turned toward me. "We'll be long gone by that time. Doc Hammer's waiting for the Mills woman and wants her breathing when we deliver."

I ran my hands through my purple hair to stop them from shaking, hoping it would make me look casual. They were talking way too much for my comfort. Whatever they were into—orgs and docs and hammers, oh my—they didn't care that I heard any of that.

Could just be they were sloppy. Or that it wasn't a big deal.

But something told me it *was* a big deal. They didn't care what I heard because I'd never be able to repeat it to anyone if I was dead.

Sure, maybe that was an overreaction. Too many shitty movies and British cop shows.

One look in the tech sergeant's eyes, and I thought maybe it wasn't an overreaction at all. Which reminded me.

I asked, "You guys in the army or something?"

Gregor laughed, leaned over the bar with a grunt, and grabbed a bottle off the rail. He snatched a rocks glass from the runner, flipped it to himself, and caught it again. The tech sergeant sat in a chair across from me, blowing out a long breath.

"Hell of a day, huh?" he said then spun the cap on the bottle and tipped some of the clear liquid into the glass.

I frowned when I saw the label. "Anisette?" I said. "Who drinks liquid black licorice?"

He looked at me with eyes devoid of color; a black pupil in a pool of milk white. Gregor lifted the glass to his lips, sucked at the thick sluice, then smiled. "You're full of spirit, aren't you?" Arching an eyebrow, he lifted the bottle toward me.

"No." I crossed my arms. "I'm not twelve."

He laughed again, having the time of his life, and put another couple shots into his glass.

I was definitely going to die.

Chapter Twenty-Seven

Kane

The Mop Man has stopped screaming.

This is good. The Downgrade from wolf to human or dog has carried with it problems and issues, especially when it comes to evacuating—very troublesome in these varying forms—but it has not dulled my hearing.

Ma mère once told me a wolf can hear for up to two miles, although I believe it is much farther. Maybe just for me. I am an alpha wolf and better than most.

Alas, with such fine-tuned hearing, the childlike screams of the man make my head spin.

Now that he is on the floor, shaking, and having buried his face in the thick strands of his mop, I can no longer hear his wailing.

When I had first tried to calm him, so that I could reason with such an inferior creature, this only elicited more screaming. So I stopped.

I am wary to begin again, but Sad Girl is in trouble. I must go.

"Listen to me, urine-smelling man," I say, and he stiffens, his shoulders folding in as if to protect his head. Or cover his ears. "You are a foul creature. Lowly. And I find you offensive. And that is not just the smell. However, that is also very bad."

His hands fly to his ears, and his knees lift, pushing the dirty mop ropes into his face. I fear he may suffocate himself. That, of course, would be best for everyone. But not before he releases me.

Before I can speak again, I hear him muttering. Is he speaking to me? I listen closer and recognize the words.

I used to hear Mère say these words over me as I slept. A protection, she felt, I was sure of it. However, the lovely incantation means little coming from his foul man.

He is speaking what Mère called the Lord's Prayer.

He is fearful.

He is lost.

Good. I can use that shit against him.

"Listen unto me," I say and quietly offer a solemn apology to Mère, who I know is watching over me. She was devout and won't like this. "The Lord speaketh through me. For you are a weak man who has done... bad things."

He lifts his head.

I should have paid more attention to Mère when she would pray. I try again.

"You must redeem yourself for your life of foul deeds." There was much redemption talk in the services she had taken me to. Also another word bandied around. P-word. Meaning you have to make up for bad things you have done.

If only I had paid better—

"W-W-What? H-How?" he mutters, staring at me between twisted strands of mop fibers and what appears to be a discarded Cheeto. One of the bendy hot ones, if I am not mistaken.

What *was* that word? P...

"You will have to—" I squeeze my eyes together, trying to remember "—make... *pants* for what you have done. Do you understand?"

Mop Man lifts his head, his eyes dancing around the room. He does not want to look at the talking pug dog.

"N-No," he says, now gazing toward the ceiling. "What are you saying?"

"You have offended the Lord the way you have disgraced yourself," I say, stepping forward and throwing as much heft as I can into the voice of this puny body. "This thrashing of these creatures."

Near me, the big dog chuffs once more. When I look over, I can see it's pressing its big stupid head against the side of the cage. Confused?

It doesn't matter.

A well-timed utterance, that. The man thinks the big oaf dog has agreed with me.

"You have been judged and found unworthy." I had always liked that phrase. Although I think it was from a television show. No matter. Sounds religiousy.

His voice stammers, "I-I-I..."

"Yes," I proclaim. "It is always about you, you, you. Very selfish creature." I need to push the man lower so that he will do what I need without question. "The terrible food you put in this wretched body, a gift given unto you. The consumption of spirits that weaken an already soft mind." I roll the dice. "Using the Netflix passwords of others."

His face flashes up to me, mouth hanging open. "No! I... That... I wasn't... They changed the rules—"

"Enough!" I shout loud enough to rattle the cage. This hurts my wounds some. With less shouting, I continue. "You will have to make pants for what you have done."

He blinks at me. "Pants?"

"Yes. To do so, this will require—"

"Are you sayin'... penance?"

Damn. That is the word. Must cover. "I am French Canadian. It is how we say it where I am from."

"You're *what*?"

"I will ask the questions!" I shout. It hurts again, just a little. But worth it! I see a small puddle grow beneath the man's thighs. He is trembling again. "However, question time is over. You have displeased the Lord. Here's what... *Stop whimpering into the mop!*"

Trembling again, the man lifts his head toward me.

I fix him with a powerful stare. A wolf stare. His mind belongs to me. Not so much a treasure, sure. But he will do what I say now.

"You will release us." I take a step back and puff out my dog chest. "Now. Without another word."

The man jumps up, and the wafting smell of urine makes my eyes water. He goes to the cage on the floor first.

"Wait, my—" I begin to say, but when the door comes open, the large dog leaps at him, snapping at his face. The man struggles as he tries to hold the angry creature off.

"No!" I step up to the cage mesh. "Sit. Bad dog! Play dead!"

The stupid animal ignores me. Instead, it uses the man's chest to launch itself upward, scratching his chest. The man howls in pain. And then the big dumb dog runs through the open door, disappearing into the night.

I say, "Now, quickly—"

The man opens the door to the cat's cage. The cat looks at him with impassive eyes and licks a paw. Finally, Mop Man opens my cage, and I waste no time, leaping out and landing on the floor. I must get to Sad Girl.

As I reach the door's threshold, I hear whining behind me.

I turn and sigh, roll my eyes, and look at the man, who just stares at me. When he catches my gaze, he falls to his knees, head lowered, arms outstretched.

Pink Bow whimpers again.

"Fine, yes," I say, nodding. "Release the curly dog. Then I must go."

He reaches up and quickly unlatches the small door. The curly dog bursts out of the cage before it's fully open and follows the same path the large dog did. She is gone.

The cat just steps to the open door of its enclosure and watches us. I frown at it. It blinks.

No time to waste. I turn.

But before I can leave, once again, the man calls out. "What is my penance?" he says, his voice shaking. "What do I have to do to make things right? I don't want to... I want to make things right." His lips are trembling, and a line of spittle drips off.

"All good," I say and lift a single paw. "Fine. Just be better from now on."

"No!" the man wails and lifts two fists up to the sides of his head. "I need—I have to make it right." He crawls closer to me on his knees and palms. "What must I do? What is my penance?"

With no time, I come up with something simple.

However, the thought of it makes me smile.

Chapter Twenty-Eight

"You didn't answer my question," I said, squeezing my hands between my thighs. "Army? Air Force? Ska band?"

Gregor shook his head. "I don't think you're clear about this"—he waved his hand in a circle around the room—"scenario. *I'm* not here to answer *your* questions. You've got that part, right?"

I could feel my saliva get sticky. Just keep talking. If nothing else, it might stop my heart from fluttering my shirt.

"Just curious, Tech Sergeant," I said and tried to shrug casually. Instead, I expect I looked like I was having a spasm. "Checking your bona fides."

That got another laugh out of him, but the humor didn't make it to his eyes this time. I knew I was pushing him. And I wasn't sure if that was a good or bad thing. But anger—if I could anger him—makes people do stupid shit.

I told Kane that all the time. Not that he ever listened to me. Stupid wolf. Wolf man. Man wolf. Whatever.

"We are just ants, this little crew." Gregor lifted his hands and, so weird, began moving them like a conductor. "Ants rolling a grain of sand across the bottom of a boot at the back of a closet in a cruise ship..." He paused, hands still raised, and looked around the room. The woman leaning against the wall of license plates had closed her eyes, so he looked to Gorilla Tits.

"Rolling on the waves of a hurricane sea," the big man said, finishing the strange verse, his face stone. He wasn't having as much fun with it as his boss.

Gregor dropped his hands and looked at me, waiting for what, I didn't know. The room fell silent, and, eyes still closed, the woman finally spoke up. "Can we get on with it? I need some rack time, and we still got a drive ahead."

"Too true," Gregor said and again slugged the sickly-sweet liquid, smacking his lips. This guy was goddamn bananas. "Too true."

Outside, I heard the full-throated wail of what had to be the feral woman who'd been in the back of the truck. Bridget Mills wasn't dead, then. At least not yet.

"Oh, darn. The baby's awake," Gregor said and hopped up. He pointed at me. "Pardon me, would you?"

He took a few strides and disappeared into the kitchen. A moment later, I heard the bar's back door open.

I glanced to the woman, who was resting her head, and caught her looking at me. Her lids fell closed again, but I couldn't miss the tiny expression. Her lips turned down, tweaking slightly.

Not anger.

Not resentment.

I'd seen looks like that in the past. When I'd gone to the grocery store as a kid, years ago. And my mother, when she was having one of her "bad days," would go full noise right in the aisle. I'd have done something to anger her and probably had earned the tongue-lashing.

But the volume had shaken the entire store. Only as an adult, looking back, did I know that it was way, way too much. Back then, though, all I felt was shame.

And the looks from people around me? They almost never said a word, but all of them bore that same down-turned, tweaking expression I'd gotten from the woman at the wall.

Pity.

My mouth went dry.

Chapter Twenty-Nine

Kane

I am the night.

I am the creature that stalks and hunts.

I am far too tiny in this stupid pug body and its tiny pug legs.

I am winded.

Once again, I lift my face to the light breeze, and I pick up Sad Girl's scent. That is the greatest, if only, advantage this form has. My adoptive parents told me of this. One hundred thousand times more powerful than a human.

Running to find Sad Girl, I am also running away from Mop Man, from the rank of his urine and sweat and cheap alcohol that makes my eyes water. Out here somewhere now. I hope he's downwind of me.

When I glance around, taking a breath, I see two eyes in the night. I wince at the foul smell of the gray cat. Why is it following me? Stupid creature.

Only getting accustomed to pug life, I cannot yet tell how close Sad Girl is. However, her scent grows stronger as I run down the sidewalk. Either I am far more capable—and, yes, I am—or she is close. Very close.

There is light ahead.

A small tavern. Ma mère would always warn me of such places. Do not go, she would tell me, where people poison their bodies and minds. Where women, the guardians of this species, lose themselves. Although mon père did say taverns had the darts, which he would watch on the television.

However, I believe he would say this only to frustrate his kind wife.

I miss them.

Another scent on the air now. It is... more familiar.

As I cross in front of a tavern, I notice the warm glow of light inside. This is the only building nearby that has any illumination.

Leaping onto a rock and then a trash receptacle, my thick nails clicking as I try to balance, I can see inside.

Sad Girl is here! She is in a chair across from a very large man. Very large. That scent, that odor I cannot identify, has grown stronger. No time for that, however.

The large man strikes Sad Girl, and the anger roils through me.

On an opposite wall, a woman is watching. Concern on her face, in her expression, the way she holds her body. It is not clear if this is for her or for my friend.

Voices.

Around the side of the building.

I leap to the ground, bashing my chin on the peaty earth. It is very hard to get used to this pug body. And I constantly have the urge to lick my genitals. What foul creatures.

Once I am at the edge of the building, I push my snout past the wall and observe two men speaking. I can smell a strange chemical musk coming from nearby. Strange but familiar.

Gregor is berating a man in a ball cap.

"How much?" the tech sergeant says and approaches the truck, peering in the window. From the darkness inside, a palm strikes the glass then slides down, leaving a trail of dampness and blood.

"All we had of it," the skinny man with the ball cap says. "Goddamn tried to reach for the popper too! She woulda taken my hand off."

"You had two vials in the rifle," Gregor says, staring intently into the cab of the truck. "I thought you said that would keep her out until we got back to camp."

"I'm not a doctor, man. Or, in her case, a veterinarian."

"How much was left?"

"Not a full dose like the first one, but should keep her calm. Or just calmer," Ball Cap says. "Don't peek in the glass. That'll just rile her up."

Inside, I see sparks then hear a low moan that arcs into a growl. Then quiet.

Gregor steps toward the other. "The cage holding, then?"

A nod and a queer smile from Ball Cap.

"Well, if she tries to test it anymore, you won't need the knockout drugs," Gregor says. "The juice in the cage wire will fry her brain."

"It ain't the brain they're after. It's the blood."

The tech sergeant points at the cab as he walks away. "Keep her alive."

"How the hell am I supposed to do that? It's on her."

"She dies before we get back, then you die," Gregor says at the open door of the tavern. "We clear?"

"Crys-tal."

As the tech sergeant heads inside, Ball Cap takes a half step toward the back window of the truck. Then he turns away and enters the vehicle on the driver's-side door. I watch for a minute. Then two. Observe, evaluate, act.

This is the wolf way.

Slowly, I creep up to the back of the truck, my nails clicking as I do. I lift them so I am walking on the rough pads, but the clicking continues.

I spin around. I am being followed.

Standing at the corner of the building. The gray cat. It sits, staring, licking its paw. Stupid, vile creature. It is a spy, but for whom, I do not know. No matter. At least my next meal is close.

I return my attention to the rear of the running vehicle once more.

The dark line between the door and the truck bed tells me it is not fully secured. This is a moment of good fortune I need.

Stepping up, I put a paw upon the bumper and lift my snout to the door, pulling at it to make the black line larger. The door creaks slightly, and I freeze. I drop off the small step, where a license plate glows, then peek around the side of the truck.

Thankfully, the sounds of the engine have covered my noises.

Ball Cap is still there. With his head against the side of the vehicle, he appears to be sleeping. If not sleeping, he is close. His body is still.

I am running out of time!

Stepping back to the door, I take a quick glance at the cat. It's staring off into the night, away from me, as if I am of no consequence. Insulting creature.

The door is weighted and does not want to open entirely, so I push my nose between the door and its metal frame and slip inside.

Powerful, pungent odors here.

To my left, I see a small collection of weapons and thick, black clothing.

I have encountered these people several times but still do not know who they are. What their purpose is.

A duffel bag draws my attention, and when I sniff it, I am sure there is more weaponry inside. Next to this is a toolbox. There is also a short bank of blinking lights. Upon closer inspection, I can see these are walkie-talkie mounts. Three stations, and all but one are missing.

There is movement closer from the front of the cab, and I tense. But it is not Ball Cap. Still, his head lolls as he rests.

Inside a cage that takes up half of the rear enclosure is the beast woman. She appears to be sleeping, although her limbs twitch and slide. When I step closer, her eyes pop open, and her teeth bare. She slinks toward me, reaching, but is stopped by the cage.

Her eyes roll as she grips the wire, and when she pulls her hand away, arc light follows her fingers until she falls back.

"Quiet back there," Ball Cap shouts, his voice muffled. He elbows the rectangular window between the cab and the back of the truck. "Keep it down."

The woman lies on her side, her eyes glassy. She sniffs the air as she stares at me then frowns. In return, I also check for the scent. Something is familiar here. Her sweat. I smell something that is known to me.

Then I realize there is something within those notes that is my own. Not wolf. Something else.

No time for that.

I have to free Sad Girl, but there is little this pug body can do. That is why I am here.

This woman will do that for me.

Chapter Thirty

From the bar floor, I lifted my face toward Gorilla Tits. I tried to scowl at him, but the numbness in my cheek dragged the expression off kilter. I'd wanted to look threatening, but it probably looked more pitiful than pissed.

He'd moved so fast, I hadn't even seen his hand. Just the burst of light from inside my skull and the dull ringing it left behind. I'd flown from the chair, my head spinning.

Unimpressed by my less-than-mean face, the big man rounded the table, grabbed my hair, and yanked me from the floor.

It hurt like a mother, but I refused to call out or scream. I gritted my teeth. Everything in me wanted to growl at him, "Let me go." But I knew what came after I said those words.

They never let you go. Just more punches. More pain.

He dropped me back into the chair, and with my head wobbly on my body like a neck bolt had come loose, I began to slide out the other side. A meaty hand came out and pushed me back into place. When I lolled my head up and looked at him, the dude hadn't even glanced over.

As if this was a thing he did all the time. Bash, lift, drop, bop. Like it was routine.

Hell, it probably was.

Ten seconds or a minute or five minutes later, I couldn't tell, Gregor strolled back into the room. All the playfulness had gone out of him, and he slapped the wall hard with his hand. The woman, just inches away from that slap, didn't even flinch.

"You said that shit would put the woman out for hours, Mon!"

"That is not *exactly* a woman." She looked at him, bored. "If you can't tell."

Gregor took a step back, having found a modicum of his cool again. "Tits and ass for all the world to see. Looks like a woman to me."

"Shoot her with the stuff again." Mon yawned. "It'll give us enough time to get back," she said then leaned forward and spoke louder, "if we leave soon!"

"Did that, of course." Gregor threw a hand toward the wall, dismissing her.

When he turned, she glared at the back of his head then closed her eyes again.

"Where were we?" the tech sergeant said, spinning the chair around and gripping the back of it with curled fingers. Noticing the welt rising on my cheek, he smiled queerly then cast a glance at the big bastard to my left. Looking my way again, he said, "I'm impressed you got out of that barn. Well done."

"Milk shed," I said.

I turned toward the bar, catching my reflection in the mirror. My hair was going a million directions, like each strand was trying to escape, displaying more black than purple tint. A wash of red lifted off the side of my face where Gorilla Tits had hit me.

"Fine, fine. Whatever. Listen, I do need to speed this up, because I've got Beast Lady in the back of my truck, and the only reason she's being remotely quiet is because she's doped up to the gills and my sketchy friend Bobby is driving a rifle butt into her calf every time she makes a noise." He shook his head as if to say, "What a day, right?"

I gulped. Time to be quiet.

He rested his chin on folded hands. "I just wanted this little tête-à-tête, quick chat, and then you can go back to whatever people like you do."

It was my turn to laugh. I pointed to the back door. "Bobby." Then I raised my eyebrows.

Gregor shrugged. "Yeah."

I motioned around the room. "Mon, maybe Monica? And you're Gregor. This guy is Gorilla Tits."

That got a laugh out of Gregor, who shot his hand up to catch the fist flying my way. Shit, these guys were both fast. Maybe they teach them that ninja stuff in the Army. Or Air Force. Or whoever these guys were.

"Great, so we all know each other," Gregor said. "One big happy whatever."

I shook my head. "You're not letting me out of here. I know all your names, asshole."

That got a howl of laughter from Gregor. Even Gorilla Tits joined. The woman at the wall, Mon—maybe Monique?—she didn't find it funny. Stone-faced.

"Just so I'm clear," Gregor said, giggling and wiping away actual tears. "You got our names and that's, what? Prime intel? You gonna go to the cops and say, 'Bobby hurt the lady'?" He laughed harder, his voice rising higher and higher in pitch.

Dude was seriously creeping me the hell out.

"So you're not planning on killing me?" I said, trying to keep my voice steady.

"Oh no." Gregor shook his head then leaned forward and rested his chin on the back of the chair. "Yes, *definitely* killing. That's in the day planner. Night planner, whatever."

I crossed my arms, feeling the rabbiting *thump-thump-thump* of my heart against my wrists.

"So why would I answer any of your questions if you're going to—?"

"Kill you anyway?" Gregor said then folded his hands. "You can die good, or you can die bad, or you can die at the hands of... Gorilla Tits."

This time, the big guy smiled.

Gregor snapped his fingers to get my attention. He had it.

"Why is that big bastard, Kane, so interested in our business?" Gregor said, all the humor gone now. "He's not law enforcement. Not government."

"What do you mean?"

"I mean, Kane. Why is Kane showing up in the middle of all of this? Who is he working for?"

I couldn't help it. "Whom."

"What?"

"It's 'whom is he working for.' Object of the preposition."

For a long, long moment, the boss man just looked at me as if trying to read my face, but he didn't have wolf skills like *my* boss.

"This antiauthority streak of yours may have been big fun in the past," Gregor said. "In this room, it'll get you pain."

He reached into the pocket of his jacket and pulled out what at first looked like a battery pack that could jump-start a sixteen-wheeler. Thick and rubberized, there were grips for three fingers on one side and the thumb on the other. Initially what I'd thought was some hand strap in fact appeared to be a data cable that fed from the top, looping down and secured at the bottom.

"Petty theft, some breaking-and-entering. Two assault cases, but those charges against you were both dropped, Emelda Thorne," Gregor said, reading off his next-gen smartphone. He jutted his clefted chin toward me, staring down his nose. "How'd you manage that?"

He'd been trying to get a rise out of me by revealing he knew my name, but I didn't give it to him. So what? "I had a good lawyer."

He barked out another laugh and went back to fiddling with his phone. Probably a Candy Crush guy.

I could have told him that my boyfriend, ex-boyfriend, had been *connected*. That was the word Roy had always liked to use. After he'd gone to prison, I found out he'd been a low-level enforcer for a North Minneapolis criminal outfit. Nothing to really brag about but it had been that connection which encouraged the two guys I'd bashed with a tire iron to drop all charges.

Seemed only fair at the time, at least to me, because they'd been the ones to lock me in their trunk. The police had arrested me after they'd both ended up in hospital. My ex's boss had an arrangement with the bashed-up bozos' boss, his competition, and the charges disappeared.

I still owed on that debt. Another reason for me clearing out of the Twin Cities with Kane when I did.

Gregor's smile grew wider as he fingered the screen of his phone. Swiping left, swiping right. Swiping left, swiping right.

"For *whom*," Gregor said, swiping again, the grotesque pleasure on his face unsettling me, "is Kane working?"

"H-He..." My voice trembled, but I couldn't get it to behave. "Kane doesn't work for anyone."

The edge of his mouth twitched—swipe left, swipe right—and his eyes narrowed. He looked to me with an impish grin. With a slow tilt of his head, he spoke to the big bastard.

"This is what happens when a child grows up without a father in the home," he said then theatrically held a flat hand to the side of his mouth. "Daddy was army and got blowed up overseas." Gorilla Tits nodded thoughtfully, trying to hid his own smile. "Even so, weren't you taught *not* to lie?"

The tech sergeant draped one arm over the back of the chair and with his other held out his phone. My mouth went dry. The bones in my spine felt like they'd melted, oozing out between my muscles and organs, making it hard to sit straight.

I stared at the video feed of my mother, washed in green hues and unnaturally black shadow.

"Didn't mommy teach you that you should never lie?" he said, pressing the punishing image closer to my face. Diane Thorne lay in what I assumed was her San Bernardino living room. She'd fallen asleep on the couch. Light from an unseen television danced across her placid face. Between her fingers, a long-dead cigarette.

Disgust snaked through the sickening panic in my brain. My mother lay unaware, lost in that perfect and sacred bliss of just being at home. Being safe. Away from the harsh world, hidden from the eyes of strangers who felt they had every right to judge you. Without a second thought, and because he felt possessing some high-tech wizardry eclipsed her fundamental right to privacy *in her own home*, he'd violated her.

I hated him for it.

Seething with rage, I wanted to reach for the phone, but before I could will my body to move, Gregor snatched it back.

Swipe.

Resting his chin on the back of the chair, he hooked his arm around the side, and my mind screamed at these new images, *Jesus, no!*

"Didn't your dear granny tell you not to lie?"

The person I loved more than anyone else lay sleeping in her bed, drenched in that same sickening greenish tint. Some sort of night vision software within whatever hidden camera had been pointed at her.

The two-pane window above the bed was now dark, but I remembered how she'd smile and wave from that very spot as she watched me in the sunny backyard. Where I used to play, after dad died, and my mother would slip from under our home's oily, suffocating blanket of grief and be gone for days on end.

In the grainy image, Grandma's cane leaned up against the dresser. At the top of those drawers, angled toward the bed, lay a picture frame. Her "favorite face in the world."

It crushed my heart to think that, hundreds of miles away, she had me watching over her as she slept. And now, "her favorite face" had put her in danger.

Gregor leaned back, scanning my eyes. Without looking down, he opened his jacket with one hand; with the other, he dropped the phone back into his pocket and tapped the fabric twice.

"Soooooo," he said, singsonging the word. "Who is Kane working for?"

"No one!" I shouted, fighting back tears. Whatever he'd hoped for, I'd never give him that.

Despite his stone-faced expression, the blood rose up in the tech sergeant's cheeks. Mechanically, he leaned forward and gripped both sides of the chair. I jumped as it snapped and cracked between his strong hands as he pressed them together.

He held the wooden pieces above his head for a moment, like some prey animal he'd pulled from the safety of its hole, then threw them to the floor. They banged and clattered across the dirty carpet.

Putting two fingers to his hairline, he flamboyantly flicked away faux sweat.

Without the chairback between us, I felt exposed. Like he could reach over and tear my throat out.

"But, ha... he just *knows* where to look?" Gregor lifted his hands up, blood trickling from splinters that had torn the pads of several fingers. "Someone's got to be feeding him intel. Who?"

I shook my head. "He's good with people. Asks the right questions."

"*Why is he even asking questions*?!" Gregor boomed, and the sheer volume of it seemed to lift him off his chair. "Why? Why? Why? Why-why-why-why?"

I turned away and caught the look on the woman's face, her eyes pleading with me. I didn't think she was on my side. Maybe she'd just seen too many people like this, sitting in front of her boss, and what happened when he got nuts.

What was I supposed to say?

Kane? Oh, he's just searching for the guy, Cal Davis, who bit him and turned him from wolf into man, because he thinks that guy will know how he can get back. Be a wolf again. See?

If I even tried to sell him on that truth, Mon at the wall would see another violent death.

When they'd grabbed me in front of the vet clinic, Gregor had barely taken a second glance at the animals inside. That meant he didn't know about Kane's *uniqueness*.

That felt like an advantage.

I wracked my brain for who the hell would be looking into shit like this. A reporter wouldn't work—this guy, he wouldn't remotely like the idea of any press being involved. I needed someone who'd be interested but harmless. A curious person with no clout. No threat.

"He's... He's writing a book."

Gregor opened his mouth then closed it again. He sat back down, stared at the ruin of the chair, which looked like a bottom mandible of broken teeth, then rolled his hand for more.

"Kane is an author. Well, wanna-be author, and, you know, there's all this talk of two scary monsters running around. He's... He's researching."

Gregor wrinkled his nose. "For a book."

"Right. But it'll never get published. He's got nothing but rumor and—"

"What kind of rumor?"

Shit!

"Nothing. I don't know. He hasn't shown me anything. I'm just his driver."

That got a laugh out of Gregor, but it sounded hollow. He was rolling the story over in his mind. "Driver? He's got money, then? Resources? Backers?"

Shit, shit! I needed to stop making it worse.

"No, he just can't drive, you know, here in the U.S. He's French Canadian."

That got an odd look from Gregor, who made an "oooh" face and looked over at Gorilla Tits, who just shook his head, whatever that meant.

"That explains a lot," Gregor said. "But not enough."

"Why not?"

He shrugged. "Because I don't *believe* you."

Chapter Thirty-One

Kane

Inside the truck's cargo bay, the woman stares at me intensely. She crawls toward the cage wall, eying it. When I lean in, I can smell oxidation from the wires.

Znnt!

I leaned in too close.

Stars flash in my eyes, and there is blood in my mouth. I may have bitten my tongue. The cage is electrified. However, this may have been a hasty addition. I can see a pair of leads snaking from its side, where fat welds keep them in place.

Tracing the cables, I can see they are attached to a large, square battery bolted to the floor. A car battery.

On her side now, the woman watches me, but her eyes roll back occasionally. This must be from drugs they have administered. She is fighting them but not always winning.

If I want to use this woman to help Sad Girl, I must disable the battery.

However, I do not know how I can do that. The only thing I know about batteries is from mon père's teachings. His warnings about...

Wire.

Is there a wire?

If I could find a wire, how would I even grab it? No thumbs. Very troubling. I have gotten used to thumbs. I approve muchly of thumbs.

Teeth, these I could use. But the thought of clamping my mouth down on an electrified wire puts pressure on my bladder. Odd dog sensation.

I hear a smashing from within the tavern. Wood clattering as it hits the floor. Then Gregor yelling in anger. I must hurry.

Scanning the small truck cargo area, my eyes land on the red toolbox. I lift the lid with my nose, but it exposes no wire. Just tools. I suppose I should have deduced this from the container's name.

The clanking of the box lid has stirred the ball cap man. Again, he raps on the glass with his elbow.

"Keep 'er down in there," he says without lifting his head. "Go to sleep. Night-night time, yeah?" He laughs to himself. Horrible human.

If I could lift the toolbox shelf out, there may be wire underneath. With this, I could connect the poles and short the battery. This is more of mon père's teachings.

However, disturbing the tools, this, too, will make noise. Before me is a series of tiny circles. Sockets, my father told me. Those will do nothing.

But the handle, the long handle where the circles go, this I grab.

It takes me a moment to free it. The handle tastes like grease and fast food. Disgusting. Finally, I nuzzle it free and clamp the metal rod between my teeth. Behind the electrified cage, the woman lies on the floor, watching me, her eyes fluttering. Again, her odor wafts toward me. Sweat, anger, fear, and something else underneath it all.

So familiar.

I walk back over to the battery with the metal bar, hovering over it. When mon père showed me how a car battery works, much of it did not make sense. There is water and metal inside. Acid, he warned me. Much of this was confusing.

However, it was his warning I remember.

Connecting the two metal spikes, the poles he called them, is bad. Never do.

But this is what I will do.

Drawing in a deep breath, bracing myself, I get ready to drop and run away quickly. I lower the metal bar close so that when it quietly lands, it will connect the two poles.

Drop!

It did not connect the two poles. I now see a plastic cover, a red cap, covering one side.

More commotion inside the tavern.

How can I connect the two? The metal is very close but not touching. I could get the tiny circles and drop those in, but that will take time and the red rubber guard is blocking. No wire. Nothing else.

Water!

Père told me that water is also a wire. Although he did not say it in such a way. I scan around the truck cabin but do not see any water. No cups or bottles. Only tools and weapons.

Of course, I have water.

I fear this is going to sting in a place I do not want stinging.

But Sad Girl needs me!

Resolved, I turn and align next to the battery. I cast a quick glance at the woman, whose eyes are once again closed. I lift my leg and produce a stream of water. I am surprised by how much I have, this tiny—

Zzzzzztntt!

I howl in pain, and this draws the head of Ball Cap up. He spins and looks to the cage but does not see me. I am stealth pug, hiding in the darkness. I am stealth pug, and it feels like I have melted my tiny pink crayon! So hot.

The man up front is agitated, searching for the noise. The woman's eyes open again, watching me, but she does not move.

Ball Cap *is* moving, so I must move faster.

I approach the cage and, gingerly, I press my nose against it. It still sparkles and hurts! I have failed Sad Girl.

A crackling sound behind me then smoke. The smell of putrid acid and vapor rises.

I race to the door of the truck and feel the concussive blast as the battery explodes. Tumbling to the ground outside, I go end over end until all I can see is gravel. There is grit in my mouth.

Getting back up to my wobbly feet, slowly, I turn and see the ball cap man throwing the door open to the back of the truck.

"What the fu—?"

She leaps on top of him, arms outstretched and fingers splayed. The feral woman grabs the back of the man's head, taking two clumps of hair tightly. Then, as if she were biting into an overripe plum, she clamps down and takes a chunk out of his neck.

The man's wails are weak and feeble as he collapses. His hands fling out as if spring-loaded, but he makes no attempt to break his fall. The sounds of chewing and slurping nauseate me. So much blood, and she takes it in like a person dying of thirst who's found a desert oasis.

A need.

A hunger.

I feel a rush flow through me as this same need compels me now, the thirst for blood, but I cannot. I have fought these urges before, and they are strong. But I am strong. I am wolf.

Voices grow louder inside the tavern, but Bridget Mills pays them no attention. She is feeding.

Sad Girl is inside, and I need this woman to help free her. When the men come out with their rifles, my chance will be lost.

Growling, I approach the woman, and she lifts her head, bits of torn flesh still in her teeth. Blood paints her face, neck, and hands. Her eyes are wild as she stares at me. I pivot toward the tavern door because I know it will open soon.

I *need* her to pursue me into the building. This is how I will save Sad Girl.

I hope.

The feral woman lifts her head and smells the air. She blinks then growls and goes back to feeding.

There is something in me that she can sense. I am not prey. I am like her. I can smell that familiarity too. My heart turns black. She will not pursue me.

Noises clang in the tavern room on the opposite side of the wall. Angry voices, the sounds of metal pots crashing to stone floors.

She takes a quick glance at the sound but then continues to feed.

When Gregor and his crew emerge, they will see her and put a bullet in her skull. My chance to save Sad Girl will explode like the battery.

How can I tempt her from the meal before her?

There is a bang at the door. They are coming. More arguing.

I scan the lot to find something, anything, I may wield. Nothing.

I bark to draw her attention, and it earns me only a withering look. She returns to her feast. Frustrated, I spin around, shouting in anger.

That's when I see the judgy cat staring at me from its rock perch at the corner of the building. Shoving its tiny pink tongue between its fingernails as if it were laughing at my failure!

Oh. Oh, yes.

I have an idea.

Chapter Thirty-Two

The hollow boom from outside shook the room, belching dust from the ceiling. I held my breath for a moment, not wanting to breathe any of that shit in. My three captors snapped their heads and stared at a wall of old sports photos swaying from the tremor. The small picture frames scraped left to right, right to left, sounding like a dozen lazy cats pawing at the door to go outside.

Glassware that had been hanging above the bar swung and clinked until a large snifter shattered, sprinkling shards down onto the laminated wood below.

This snapped the three black-clad assholes out of their stupor. Gregor turned to the woman, nodding toward the door. "Go see what the hell that was."

She smirked. "Probably Bobby shooting the woman. Dude's not right in the head."

"That wasn't from a rifle," her boss said. "Mon, go check!"

Lifting off the wall, she threw a look my way. Casual at first then darker. She moved toward the kitchen.

"Don't let these guys kill me, Mon," I pled.

Glancing over her shoulder, she laughed. "Like I can tell these meat sacks what to do?"

But her expression didn't match the look on her face. A flash of something else. As she walked past Gregor, she grabbed his sleeve, pulling him along. He went with her.

Maybe those two were more than just boss and lackey. Or maybe they were clearing the room so the big man could get started. He'd watched them go, and I took my shot, grabbing the highball glass Gregor had been drinking from and smashing it against the big man's head.

Shards exploded and sparkled in the light like angry, dancing fireflies.

Gorilla Tits didn't even flinch.

A trickle of blood traced down the side of his face, dripping onto his collar. The big bastard only wiped away a few specks of glass. When his fingers caught on a piece, he pulled it from his face, held it between his finger and thumb, and flicked it at me.

"After I kill you," he said, pushing the chair back, "I'll go through your pockets and look for some spare change. Pay for the glass you broke." He laughed, a big belly laugh, as if he was the funniest guy in the world.

We both turned when the voices rose in the kitchen. The woman was making my case, but from the tone of the voices—I couldn't actually hear the words—I knew Gregor had already made his mind up. He roared at her, and pots and pans clattered.

With Gorilla Tits leaning over to see his friends argue, I burst out of my seat and ran toward the front of the tavern, into that darkness, knocking down chairs and barstools. I couldn't see jack and ran full steam into a low table.

"Shit!" I shouted and faceplanted onto the dank carpet.

Behind me, I could hear laughter from the big man. When I turned, I saw his silhouette against the light. Not moving fast. Just walking toward me.

The big ape was loving this. Loving my fear.

I scrambled on hands and feet toward the front door. When I got to the host station, I grabbed the ostentatiously large reservation book and hurled it at him. He lifted an arm to block it, and it ricocheted off, flapping to the floor like a wounded bird. The only thing in the shadow I could see was the gleaming of his teeth.

And the baton.

Not a gun or knife. A small, thick bat.

Sure, a knife would have been more terrifying. A gun would have meant a quick death, but hell, a quick death is still dying.

Still, something about the idea of this man swinging his club, in rapturous joy with every strike, beating me to death? That was the most horrifying thing I could imagine.

He stalked forward, stepping into a column of light cast from a streetlamp outside through a gap in the curtains.

I turned to the front door and fumbled at the lock. But there was no mechanism on this side. You needed a key even from the inside! The big man kept coming, and I spun, defiant.

The windows were closed and barred. No going that way. And with the tables and chairs stacked so tightly in the front of the restaurant, I'd never get around the big prick.

Still, he kept coming. Slowly. Enjoying the moment.

Gorilla Tits didn't even turn when some clattering rose from the kitchen. I tried to peer around him, and he only laughed.

"No one's coming for you," he said, his voice hitching, excited. He was relishing this, feeding off my fear. "Just me and you, girl."

Still a few yards away from me, he palmed the baton and spun it in his hand. I took a big step forward to the host station and grabbed the only thing available. I held up the cheap brass pen like a knife. This only made the big man laugh harder.

He gripped the baton, and I looked around him, searching for a place to run, even just to hide. Time slowed for just a moment, a reflection, and the queerest feeling came over me.

I realized I didn't want to die.

For all the dark thoughts I'd had over the past year—and the things I'd almost done—it was only now, with my death imminent, that I came to the realization.

I didn't *want* to die.

My brain had picked a messed-up time to work that out.

Bursting forward, I tried to go under the asshole's outstretched arm, but he only clamped down and held me, squeezing so hard I felt like I might burst like a zit.

When I opened my eyes, my head was spinning. He gripped harder, sending sparks into the edges of my vision.

I couldn't even draw a breath.

He wasn't going to beat me to death. He was going to suffocate me. My lungs burned, and my eyes fluttered as I struggled.

My mind began playing tricks on me.

Only way to explain it.

I was hallucinating.

Because if I wasn't hallucinating, it meant that a tiny dog was actually running through the restaurant, right at me, a wild woman behind him, with arms raised above her head like talons, covered in blood.

I squeaked out, "Kane?"

The big man turned, and I dropped painfully to the floor. When I looked up, the pug dog leaped over me. That was when I noticed he had something in his mouth. Large and fuzzy.

I heard the cat hiss and moan, its claws swiping at my head as Kane passed above me.

The beast woman screamed as she found a new target. Bridget Mills locked her arms onto the big man, trying to get her teeth into the flesh of his throat. He shouted back then roared at her, but she was so strong!

How could she even hold on to the big bastard?

A muffled voice beside me said, "Must go, Sad Girl!"

When I turned to look at Kane, his little doggie face was wild-eyed, his gaze fixed on me. He was panting, making the fur in his mouth billow out in tiny, undulating waves.

"Where?" I whispered to him. The cat in his mouth growled low, not enjoying the experience. Not a bit.

Kane nodded toward the back of the room, and I leaped up, my vision momentarily strobing between light and darkness. I reached out and steadied myself on the host station. In front of me, the two monsters battled, and I could see where she'd raked her claws down his arm, splitting his pale skin in three long, leaky slits.

The metallic smell of blood tainted the air.

I ran to the side wall, around the tables, as a chair exploded to my right. The combatants had fallen, arms wrapped around each other, and turned the wood into splinters.

I wove between tables and around more chairs until we were back in the kitchen, the harsh fluorescents making my eyes instantly water.

Scanning for Mon and Gregor, I saw no signs of them. When I spotted the tall walk-in cooler, I realized they'd hidden inside when the woman had burst into the restaurant, chasing Kane.

And the cat in his mouth.

"Hold on," I said.

His muffled voice came out in ragged breaths: "Must go!"

I went to the long metal strip with the series of knives, each successively larger than the last. I grabbed a long, thin one then hurried up to the walk-in cooler, jamming the white plastic butt of the knife between the handle and the door.

It wouldn't hold long, but it should slow them down.

Turning to the rear door again, it was so bizarre, I almost laughed. The sounds of the bloody battle taking place one room over—the smashing and growling and screaming. Standing in front of me was a fat little pug with a pissed-off cat in its mouth.

"Okay," I said and rounded the corner past them and out the back door.

The cool air slapped my sweaty skin, sending my frayed nerves into overdrive.

The truck was still humming in the parking lot. I couldn't see the driver anymore. Then, with a look to my left, I did, and wished I hadn't.

The guy with the ball cap, who Gregor had called Bobby, lay sprawled out on the ground, his arms and legs in awkward positions. Bent at impossible angles. His chest and neck had been torn open and splayed, like he'd grown a series of small, toothless mouths on his body. His eyes, still open, stared up at the night sky, a question in them that would never be answered.

I slapped the quarter panel of the truck and shouted, "Get in!"

Running around the hood, I yanked opened the door and hopped inside. Then I remembered.

"Shit."

I hopped back out and came around the hood again to open the door for Kane. His tiny doggie hands—er, paws—wouldn't be able to work the handle. When I looked at him, he was coughing.

"Are you okay?"

"Yes, fine," he said, clearing his throat.

I looked around the lot. "Where's the cat?"

He lifted his tiny dog shoulders. "Ran away." He then spat out a tiny clump of something gray.

Scowling, I pulled the door open. He hopped inside, and I closed it behind him.

Back in the driver's seat, I saw only a battered old fence and Dumpsters in front of me, so I dropped the truck into reverse and punched the gas.

When I felt the damp *tha-da-dump* under the tires, I whispered, "Sorry, Bobby."

I cranked the wheel and pointed the nose of the truck toward the exit and smashed the accelerator again, but I had to jam the brakes a second later.

"What the hell?"

The guy I'd seen from the vet clinic, the asshole who'd been hovering over Kane and the other animals, was now running down the street, stripping off his clothes. He was muttering something. I rolled down the window to listen.

"I am a bad dog. I am a bad dog," he repeated over and over, peeling off his jacket and kicking off his shoes as he ran.

"This is the weirdest city I've ever—"

"His coat," Kane said, lying on the passenger seat, wheezing. His wounds were weeping. His skin was mottled with welts and long red marks—the infancy of what would be angry bruises. "Your necklace is in his coat."

I hadn't even realized that Kane was no longer wearing it. I jumped out, took a quick look back, and saw no one had exited the bar. Not yet, at least. The half-naked guy was halfway down the street, so I snatched the jacket up, dug into the pocket, and grabbed my locket.

Shots rang out from within the tavern, and I saw muzzle flashes flare behind the windows. I ran back to the truck and jumped inside. I shifted into drive and, once again, floored the accelerator.

Chapter Thirty-Three

I had to drive the tech sergeant's truck with the windows down because of the acrid fumes wafting into the cab from the back. Halfway to the Clarrat farm to retrieve the Audi, I'd stopped and dug around in the back of the cab to find the blankets I'd seen earlier.

Crawling over the seat, I stuffed the covers into a hole in the cab's window. It had been partially blown out, and bits of glass sparkled in the fabric below. Plugging it helped some, but the eye-watering smell still hung in the air.

When I'd looked into the back of the truck, I'd seen a mess. Items were strewn across the floor, and the bent door of a cage hung open at an awkward angle. Black scoring traced out from an area off to the side.

"Looks like a bomb went off back there," I said, scrambling back behind the wheel. I got us moving again.

"Not bomb," Kane said, wheezing as he spoke. "Battery."

His little doggie eyes closed, and he told me how that had happened. I couldn't help but smile. Part of me wished I'd seen it. Except for the part where the driver had gotten mauled. I'd seen the results of that and had no interest in the visual image of his final moments.

Once I got back to the road leading to the farm, I searched for the copse of trees where I'd hidden the car. Kane had either passed out or fallen asleep next to me. I let him rest as I searched. But I knew time was ticking down on us—undoubtedly, there'd be some sort of tracker on the truck.

Instinctively, I knew that would be true, but I wasn't sure why. But I thought it was something that Gregor had said back in the tavern.

The bit about being an ant on the bottom of a boot on a ship in the ocean or whatever.

That implied their merry band of murderers was some small cog in some vast… I didn't know. Organization? One of them had said the word "org."

But if he were to be believed—that they were the little guys in a big machine—they would be beholden to a whole line of bosses and middlemen.

Whether that was a military or corporate outfit, I didn't know. Those two organizational structures had grown more and more similar over the years, one much better armed than the other. But the military had good weapons too.

However, if they were pawns, then the king—or queen—would very likely monitor their every move. Hell, even UPS drivers got tracked by their bosses.

I had to ditch the truck fast.

Of course, I had to get rid of the tracker on my vehicle as well. I wasn't sure if that would be enough, but hopefully, it would buy us the time to find a safe place for Kane to recover.

When I finally found the old Audi, I saw the first blood of daylight seep across the eastern horizon. As I quickly parked, I looked over at Kane in his pug dog form. He had gashes across his body and wounds on his head and paws.

I left him to rest. He'd earned it.

Digging around the back of the truck, I searched for anything useful. Of course, I did not *know* what would be useful to us in the coming days and weeks. The fumes still strong, my eyes watered as I popped open the cabinets lining the ceiling.

I found a couple of sleeping bags, a lantern, and a few propane tanks like they use for camping stoves. A field laptop I'd considered taking, but it was dead, and I couldn't see a way to charge it.

The last cabinet held what I needed: a first aid kit.

Not your everyday setup you might find in the office canteen. This one had gauze pads, antibacterial gel, and even a field kit to stitch up open wounds. I'd done a little sewing over the years—the benefits of being endlessly flat broke—but had never put needle to skin.

At least, not to sew it.

I hoped it wouldn't come to that, but I had no idea how Kane's injuries might manifest when he became human again. If he became human again. I had no clue how any of that worked.

Was he too injured to change?

Or was I just assuming that when the sun came up, he would *naturally* return to the brooding, hulking man I'd spent the last few weeks with?

"Naturally," I muttered to myself and laughed. "There's nothing natural about that."

I heard a rustling in the truck's cab—maybe Kane reacting to the sound of my voice.

It was time to go. I wasn't sure how safe we'd be in the Audi, but, for now, that felt like the only option.

When I got back to the truck, sure enough, there was all six foot seven of Kane, lying across the seat. His massive arm, as big as my leg, hung down into the footwell of the front seat.

"Hey, big fella," I said, opening the door. The moon might have gone away in the sky, but right there in front of me was a new one. Big and hairy. I leaned the seat down to grab the blankets I'd stuffed into the window. "How are you feeling?"

"I am good," he said, his face jammed against the door.

He wasn't good. He was bruised, busted up, and bloody.

I shook the blankets free of a few pebbles of glass then chucked them over the top of his naked body.

"You need me to help you out?"

"No." He lifted himself, his arms trembling a little. "I will manage."

I turned away. Not so much to give him privacy—Kane didn't care a whip about nakedness. It meant nothing to him because *I am wolf* and all that. But the welts all up and down his back and legs made my heart hurt.

Across the back of his right thigh was a gash that, yep, I'd likely have to sew up.

When he'd first stepped out of the truck, he was wobbly, so I offered a shoulder. Surprisingly, he didn't fight me about it. However, I wasn't sure how much help I was giving him. In his human form, Kane was a giant man, easily two hundred fifty pounds.

I didn't even weight half that, and I could feel his bulk compacting my spine as we hobbled toward the car. I'd left the rear door open because I didn't feel he could sit upright in the front.

Once inside, he collapsed onto the vinyl fabric. Then, he was out like a light. I had to fight to get his big Fred Flintstone feet into the car just to get the door closed. He hadn't helped at all. Fast asleep, he was actually snoring.

Kane secured, I hopped into the car, dug the keys out from under the seat, slammed them into the ignition, and fired up the car.

Pulling out, I stopped and realized, once again, I had no idea where to go.

I stared over the hood at the orange-red sun setting the horizon on fire. Should we just drive out of town? No. There was that tracker I'd seen earlier in the day. Rather, the day before.

Christ, I was so tired.

I'd been up a day and a half, and except for maybe an hour at the hospital, I had had no sleep.

First things first. I popped the hood, dug around for the tracker, and went to yank it out. It didn't budge.

As the sun grew warmer, I could feel my heart speed up. I didn't have time to screw around. Running around to the trunk, I dug around for something I could use to dislodge the tracker. In the spare tire well, I was down one spare tire. But the jack was there, and so was the long, metal bar used to expand it upward.

The end of it tapered into a flat edge, like the tip of a massive flathead screwdriver.

Back under the hood, I wedged the bar between the device and the body of the Audi and put my weight into it. After some splintering plastic, it came free.

I yanked it clear of the wires and chucked it into the bushes.

Back in the driver's seat, I was faced with the same dilemma I'd had moments earlier.

"Where to?"

If Gregor was looking for us, he'd first check the motel. Would he stake it out and wait until we showed up?

After turning ball-capped Bobby into a blood Slurpee, the beast woman had likely killed Gorilla Tits as well. Hell, by now, she might have even torn into the walk-in cooler.

But there had been shots inside the bar. In the end, who had been left standing?

If any of the tech sergeant's assholes were left, they would be searching for the truck. *Maybe* thinking we'd know it would be far too stupid to return to the motel.

I said, "Okay, then—let's get stupid."

Chapter Thirty-Four

I raced down the pock-marked road listening to the rhythmic bumping of Kane's head against the Audi's backseat door. At this time of morning, just after dawn, I hadn't expected too many people on the streets.

But if anyone did see us whipping through town, we'd get looks. The blankets swaddling Kane had fallen to the floorboards. From the outside, he'd look naked.

I'd seen the slices across his body—injuries from feral Bridget Mills gnashing him with teeth and nails during our milk-shed adventure. The cuts and bruises had elongated when he'd materialized back into his human form.

Jeez, that phrase sounded batshit. "Human form." But that was my life now.

Leaning around the headrest, I draped the blankets over his body again. Then I ran my finger over his skin, which felt cold to the touch.

"Does it hurt?"

I snatched my hand away when he lifted himself and sat up in the back seat, his broad shoulders slumped. "Wolves do not feel pain."

"Yes, they do."

Kane cracked his eyes open and looked at me, a grin bending his bearded face. "Yes. You are right. They do. It hurts, but not so bad. I will be fine."

He didn't look like he was going to be fine. He looked like he'd fallen down the side of a mountain and hit every rock on the way down. Maybe a few pissed-off billy goats had even given him a whack as he tumbled by.

Looking at Kane in the rearview mirror, I said, "I thought, you know, werewolves were supposed to be immune to injury or whatever. Bullets bounce off you unless they're silver or something."

"I am not werewolf." Kane chuckled. "I know of some of these legends. But they are just that. Legends."

"I don't know any weredog legends. Seems like the worst superpower ever."

"Is no superpower."

"No shit," I said. "So you can get hurt?"

He swiveled his head and parted the blanket slightly, showing me his stomach and chest. It looked like an old woman's cutting board. At least the wounds weren't weeping anymore.

Back in town, I took the first turn at the yellow-flashing lights. This would take us back to the motel, but even with the tracker yanked out, I wouldn't feel safe there. We'd have to get our stuff and go fast.

And, yeah, find another car.

"Have you ever been shot?"

Kane shrugged and didn't answer. He closed his eyes again.

"Okay, what's with the moon thing, then?" I pressed. "Somehow, that part is kinda true. I mean, you don't turn into a snarling hell-beast or anything. I've only seen you as a tiny dog and a less tiny dog. Do you only turn into dogs, then?"

Another shrug.

"Well, so if all the other stuff is bullshit, why would the moon thing be true?"

I made the turn into the motel lot, banged up the low-rise curb, and heard the sound of a skull thunking on the ceiling.

"Sorry," I said.

"It is fine. As for moon, I do not know," he said as I pulled up in front of our room. "But I would say all legends have some element of truth. This is how they become legends. Then humans muddy them with all their fantasy and folklore."

I dropped the car into park. "Um, *you* are human right now, Kane. Welcome to the species."

He glared at me, but it didn't have any heat behind it. "I am wolf."

Chapter Thirty-Five

As dawn fried off the early-morning mist, I hurried out of the car and ran up to the door to our room. I jammed my hands into my pockets.

"Damn."

Kane held onto the door and roof of the Audi, trying to not look like he was steadying himself. With the death grip he'd used to stay upright, the big man looked like he could pull the top of the car off.

"You have lost the key," he said, breathing out a shaky breath. The blankets tumbled down, and he stood there buck naked again.

"No!" I said. "It was in my phone case."

He wobbled his big watermelon head toward me and cocked an eyebrow. "Which you have lost."

"I didn't lose it, it..." For a moment, I tried to remember what the hell had happened to my phone. Then I remembered being shoved into the back of the truck and trying to reach for it, only to have it slip from my grip. "It fell out."

"Good," he said, grabbing the blankets in a ball under his arm and pushing the car door closed. "At least you did not lose it."

"Sarcasm? See, you're learning to be more human every day."

I looked up and down the row of rooms along the long wall. Each door had been painted a different color, recessed in the white-painted concrete that had been dulled by years of harsh sun.

There were no other cars in the lot, but that didn't mean no one else lay sleeping in their beds. Waking up and getting an eye full of a six-foot-seven beast of a man's bare ass might not be the first thing they wanted to see.

Although, I had to say, my boss was in shape. It wouldn't be the last thing, either.

"Wait here," I said, trotting toward the front office. Then, I spun around and called back. "And wrap yourself up, will you? Humans have a bit of modesty."

I ran faster because we were already pressing our luck. The tavern was only a few blocks over. If the tech sergeant's crew decided to see if we were here, it would take them less than five minutes to cross that distance.

When I rounded the corner, I nearly fell over.

"It's okay!" Olivia said, her palms raised toward me. "Only me. I saw you guys pull in—"

"I need a key," I said, my breath a bit ragged. I forced a smile. "I lost mine. Must have..."

The look on Olivia's face stole my words away. She'd lifted her outstretched hand to her mouth, slowly shaking her head. Her eyes instantly began to water.

"Oh, dear girl," she said, her voice hitching. "Are you okay?"

I realized she'd been looking at the welts on my face and arms, already beginning to rise into greenish bruises.

"I'm fine. We got into a wreck—"

"No, you didn't," she said, taking a step closer to me.

At first, I flinched, but her eyes were kind.

"I heard it on my back-up scanner last night, but only bits and pieces. Officer Barclay called to the police station that some young girl had gone to the farm. That was you."

It wasn't a question. I nodded, unsure of what to say.

"I called Stu Clarrat, and he told me what you did," she said, tracing her fingers across my cuts. "Girl, what were you thinking?"

I didn't know how to respond to that because I didn't know what exactly "what you did" had implied. Did she mean fight it out with a she-beast? Nearly die in a fire? Break out of a hospital? Get taken hostage by jacked-up lunatics?

Then I recalled Clarrat had owned the farm. He'd been the one who'd handed me the shotgun with one shell. I asked, "Is he all right?"

Olivia put a hand to her throat, smiling. "He'll be fine, and he'll have some nasty scars to brag about for years."

It had been a long night, and if I had any hope of a tomorrow, we had to get the hell out of Dodge. Or Pine Valley, Minnesota, as it were.

"I need another room key," I said, pointing to the desk through the glass behind her. "Mine got lost in the... It got lost."

Olivia snapped her head to the road, looking up and down the street. When she turned back to me, her eyes had gone from kind to something else. Frightened.

"A man and a woman came by, looking for you, about a half hour ago," she said, her words coming quickly. "Didn't like the look of them, all keyed up and strange, and since your car wasn't here, I told them you'd cleared out of town."

"They bought that?"

She shrugged. "I don't know, but they bugged out of here pretty quick. But I didn't trust them."

"What makes you say that?"

"Because they were driving one of Ben's tavern supply vans, and they certainly didn't look like help, neither of them," she said, wiping her damp hands on her skirt. "I called the police because I think they stole it."

"Shit, okay," I said. "Can we get into the room and grab our stuff?"

Instead of spinning around into the building, she burst past me, calling for me to follow. When we rounded the corner, she stopped, and I banged into her.

"Oh my lord," she said.

I peered around her shoulder. Then I frowned. "Kane, will you please drape those blankets around you?"

Olivia tiptoed forward. "Don't bother on my account," she said, her voice taking on a playful tone. "Whatever makes you feel comfortable. We had a whole nudist convention here a few weeks before all the trouble." The motel manager stopped at our door then looked over at Kane, who was sitting on the hood of the car, smashing its chassis into the curb. "None of them were"—she waved a red key card in the air toward my friend—"um, as in shape as you are, though. Do you work out?"

"Olivia?" I pointed at the door. "Open."

Inside, I dumped all my stuff into my backpack then did a quick check around the room for my phone, just in case I had dropped it and, in the panic of being kidnapped and all, I'd just gotten my brain wires crossed.

Not there.

When I went back outside, I saw Kane lying across the hood of our car. He looked like he was sleeping. Gashes across his torso and legs, his face banged up. What I didn't understand was why he was naked again.

Olivia turned toward me, her face reddening. She had the blankets balled up in her arms.

"Ah, I told your friend that I'd wash these," she said, her eyes drifting back to Kane. "They're covered in dog hair and..." Her voice trailed off for a moment. "Is he, um, dead?"

I shouted, "Kane!"

He flinched, sat up, and rolled off the car and landed on the pavement.

"Nope," I said to her. "Not dead."

Hefting the bag over my shoulder, I ran around the naked guy to drop it into the trunk.

Olivia put a hand on the lid.

"You can't take this car, can you?" she said, her voice low. "Those people.... They're a danger to you, yes?"

Having no idea of what to say, I just nodded.

"They'll be looking for this Audi," she said, fishing in her pocket. She pulled out a key chain with a pink rabbit's foot and two keys on it. She nodded to an F-150 parked by the entrance of the motel. "Those are to my truck."

"You can't give me your truck, Olivia."

"Heavens, no," she said and grabbed my bag. "Help your friend up. I'll meet you over there."

When I rounded the car, Kane was wobbling to his feet, dressed in only bruises, cuts, and scrapes. Well, that and some gravel and dirt now that he'd dropped his ass onto the parking lot.

"I fell down."

"Yes, I saw that," I said then draped one of his arms over my shoulders. When he leaned on me, I nearly fell to the ground myself. "Hey, big fella, you're going to have to help me out."

"I am helping."

Moving us forward, I grunted, "More helping, please."

When we got to the truck, it was already running. My backpack was in the open tailgate behind it, and both doors were wide open.

I smiled as I dragged Kane forward. "All I gotta do is hit the accelerator, girl. You've done everything else."

"This ain't my first get-the-hell-out rodeo," she said. "I may be the town's cat lady, but I wasn't always the town's cat lady." She laughed at her own joke.

Standing at the passenger-side door, I paused. "Olivia, I really don't want to take your ride."

"Why not? I cleaned it up real good just yesterday," she said as she helped me get Kane into the passenger seat. She spent far, far too much time getting his seat belt on and making sure it was snug.

"I think he's good," I said. "But I don't think—"

"You're not *taking* my truck," she said. "Good friend of mine, Miss Florida, has a property just outside of town, and she's had an old Jeep sitting in her barn for the last five years. Her older son went over to Europe between high school and college and just stayed."

"A Jeep."

Olivia nodded. "You'll have to charge up the battery and might have to drain the gas after all this time, but I think that Audi of yours is burnt."

"Burnt?" I said, smiling. "You watch a lot of cop dramas, don't you?"

"I watch a lot of TV, but that's one of the perks of the job," she said, gently closing the door. When Kane's head lolled out and thunked against the frame, she simply reached up and slowly pushed it back to the headrest and shut the door again. "For the past few years, I've been a registered Nielsen family."

I felt embarrassed. "Oh, I didn't even ask you. You and your husband have kids?"

"No, it's really just me at home," she said, waving me toward the driver's side. "But you get paid more if you've got a spouse and rug rats. I've got Fred, Fred junior, Daphne, and our youngest, Velma, who is six so that she qualifies for the five-plus ratings."

Wrinkling my nose, I said, "You gave your fake family the names of the Scooby Doo gang?"

"Family of five," she said, gently pushing me inside the cab. "I get paid extra. And, coincidentally, they're all big fans of all the shows I love. So maybe they won't cancel them."

Once I stepped up into the driver's seat, she slammed my door for me then leaned into the open window. For the next minute, she pointed as she spoke, giving me directions to Miss Florida's house.

"It's a farm on the outskirts of town," she'd clarified.

It was a twenty-minute drive. I hoped that would be far enough away, but I had no business complaining. This near-complete stranger had loaned me a vehicle and found a place for us to stay. Minnesota nice is underrated.

Olivia asked me if she should write down the directions.

"It's three right turns?" I said and got a pleased, rapid nod. "I've got it."

Dropping the truck into gear, I pulled out of the space quicker than I meant to. The truck had some balls to it. Kane made a *glluhhh* sound when the seat belt snapped tight and caught his neck.

Olivia hurried around the passenger side of the truck. "Oh, dear, that's not sitting very well on him, let me just adjust—"

"Olivia!" I said, putting a smile in my voice so I didn't sound annoyed. "He'll be fine."

Disappointed, she stopped. Standing at his door, she took a quick peek, blushed, then came back around my side.

"Thank you," I said and extended a hand to her. Olivia moved toward my hand then leaned in for a hug. My heart tweaked a bit until I realized she was probably getting one last look at naked Kane behind me.

However, when she broke away, her eyes were just coming open. I smiled.

"I'll have a wrecker tow your car to a yard on the other side of town," she said and took a step back. "If you can't get the Jeep started, then maybe give it a few days. Till the heat dies down. We can have the shop boys sweep it for bugs if need be."

Heat? Sweep for bugs? I chuckled.

"Okay," I said. Then a realization flooded over me. "Wait, so this Miss Florida person knows we're coming, right?"

Olivia shook her head. "She'll be fine with it. Miss Florida is good people, always willing to help. Once you bug outta here, I'll give her a call and let her know."

"How... I mean, what if she isn't interested in two strangers showing up at her place?"

That got a big, warm smile out of Olivia. "You're not strangers in this town. Not no more."

"What does that mean?"

Up the street, a car came to a skidding halt at a red light, and we both tensed. Inside the vehicle, I saw a couple of teenagers, one of them punching his laughing friend. The puncher had pink milkshake all down his shirt.

"You gotta go," Olivia said. "I'll call ahead. And thank you! Thank you both!"

I called out, "You're wel—" then I stopped. I was supposed to be thanking *her*.

Why was she thanking *us*?

Chapter Thirty-Six

Olivia's directions had been easy to follow, although it felt like I'd earlier taken some pill that induced panic on a time-release, and a crippling bolt of terror wiped my mind blank. As if I'd had the three turns up on some whiteboard in front of me, and when my adrenaline drained, it had dragged a dirty rag all down the cool surface.

Kane lay passed out in the seat next to me, and I slowed for a few minutes, trying to get the directions back into my head.

It hadn't been a wholly alien experience.

When I'd been just a kid, I'd had far too much time on my hands after school. After dad died, my mother found ways to not be at home. I only realized later this was because everything within those walls reminded her of him. The couch they'd both hauled back from the thrift store. The cat tower she'd bought and he'd spent a weekend, cursing and hollering, putting together.

One night, late, I'd woken up to the sounds of wailing and found her leaning against their closet wall. Daddy's shirts, all hanging askew, were draped across her trembling body.

During the day, she worked. Often weekends too. Her daddy, my grandfather, encouraged this and put pressure on me to do the same as he sat around and sipped his warm beer all hours.

It hadn't helped bringing up that *he* never worked. Not that he could by that time. Gnarled hands, bad heart, worse breath. I guess he felt he'd put his time in, and all that was left was to tell the younger generations in our home they weren't working hard enough.

Whatever.

After school, knowing he was the only one at home, I usually kept busy away from the house. And it often meant getting into trouble. That had never been the plan, but if you're wandering the neighborhood for hours on end, trouble has a way of finding you.

I don't recall how many times I'd done something stupid—or one of my friends had—and found myself tearing through bushes and backyards, trying to get away from the resulting chaos.

Panic would shake my mind like a snow globe. Scattered flakes of thought swirling around in my head. Then they would eventually fall, leaving nothing behind.

That same feeling, the blank slate, hit me as I sat in the truck.

Slowing my breathing, concentrating on nothing at all, I slowly lifted the memories back, like fingerprint ridges rising on cooling glass.

As I dropped our speed down to forty then thirty—I felt stopping might wake the big man next to me—I breathed in the country air.

Eventually, the road names came back to me. There were just the two left, so not a lot of data to retrieve.

What had also helped was the rail-thin woman in the flowery dress and sun hat standing at the end of her gravel drive with a big wave and even bigger smile. Her skin was a few shades darker than mine, but it radiated light far beyond just the sun reflecting off her face.

"Just pull our girl's truck down there by the barn," Miss Florida said with a big, gap-toothed smile. "I can get Denny to take it over to her place later tonight."

"Denny?" I said, mainly because I did not know what else to say. I was just following my nose at that point.

Miss Florida put her hands on her hips and sighed, the smile never far from her face.

"That is my younger son, but you won't likely see much of him," she said and waved me forward. Olivia had said the older boy had gone overseas. She hadn't mentioned any Denny. "He's still got dreams of joining a band and being some famous guitar player. Fat chance of that, though."

I wrinkled my nose. "He's that bad?"

"No, he don't know how to play guitar."

She'd peeked inside and seen Kane lying there, sleeping. The cuts, bruises, and gashes on him dimmed her smile by a few watts. Without another word, Miss Florida pointed down the gravel road and walked behind me. I felt the truck dip slightly.

She'd hopped onto the bumper and sat, her arm wrapped around the inside of the truck's tailgate.

I liked this woman.

Rolling down the gravel driveway, I stopped when the stones turned to shortcut grass. Stepping out of the truck, farmhouse images from my uncle's property that had rooted in my brain were replaced by the glorious bounty before me.

The wooden structure, though several decades old, had been lovingly maintained over the years. Its white exterior was now tinged with a slight yellow patina, giving it a warm and inviting feel.

The wraparound porch offered a place where one could spend endless afternoons lounging in the sun. The wooden planks creaked underfoot as I wandered toward the front door, a welcoming sound that whispered secrets about the house's long history.

In the distance, I could see unused farm equipment scattered about the fields, now lying dormant. The once-cultivated crops had now given way to grasslands, their vibrant green hues waving in the gentle breeze.

The door was open, and as I stepped inside the two-story home, I was struck by the sense of coziness that enveloped me. The rooms were filled with natural light; the floor sighed softly beneath my feet.

It was clear that this was a home filled with love and warmth, a place where memories had been made and new ones were waiting to be created.

Back outside, it had taken a few minutes to get Kane moving toward the house. I'd draped the blankets around him like some Roman toga, but bits and pieces of him still kept poking out. Thankfully, our host didn't make a fuss about it.

She'd called for her son to come down and help but got no answer from him.

Denny did eventually show up, just as we laid Kane down onto the mattress in one of the first-floor bedrooms. Dressed in a hoodie that looked like he lived in it, he balanced a large mixing bowl on the top of a paunch of a belly, jamming spoonfuls of something orange and crunchy into his dark bearded face.

"Who are these people?"

Miss Florida was pulling the covers over Kane's prone body. I stood in the far corner, peeking out the window.

"Perfect timing, as usual," she said, thumbing a strand of dark hair away from her damp face. "Where you been?"

He shrugged. "Breakfast."

When he said the word, I realized I was starving.

"I'm Emelda Thorne. That sleeping lump there is Kane." I smiled at him as kindly as I could. "What ya eatin'?"

Another shrug. "Mac and cheese."

"What's the crunchy bit?" I said, looking at him. "You got croutons in there or something?"

"Just mac and cheese."

I winced. "Maybe you didn't cook it long enough."

"Couldn't find matches for the stove," he said as if that was all the explanation necessary, which I supposed it was. When I said nothing more, he rolled his shoulder off the door and padded down the hall.

Miss Florida tucked the bed covers in, fussing over Kane in a sweet way. "Your man is dead to the world, ain't he?"

I laughed. "He's not my man." When that got me a look, I clarified, "He's my employer. I drive for him."

"Right, that makes a bit of sense, I suppose. How you guys operate is no business of mine, as long as it works." She hit me with a big smile again then told me to follow her into the kitchen and let Kane sleep.

I did.

As we walked, I replayed the last part of the conversation in my mind, but, so tired, I couldn't work out what the hell she was saying.

How we *operate*?

Chapter Thirty-Seven

"Is there something I should call you other than Miss Florida?" I asked, sitting at the kitchen table and watching her dig through the cupboards.

"You can call me Florida if you'd like," she said, dipping her tiny fingers into a green ceramic jar marked "Flour" and pulling out a box of matches. She shook them and smiled at me. "Some folks do. Sounds less formal, maybe."

"What do you prefer?"

Snapping a match across the box, she turned one of the gas knobs and lit the chipped, ceramic stove. She blew the match out and dropped the smoldering stick into a slot at the top of a tiny clay rooster resting on the counter. "Either one. But I *earned* the title, so I wouldn't be too sad if you kept with the 'Miss' part."

"Earned?" I said, my eyes still locked on the window, scanning for movement. "What does that mean?"

As she dug in the fridge, she cleared her throat dramatically to get my attention then threw a nod to the far side of the kitchen.

Nearly floor to ceiling, photographs of a young woman filled the wall. Smaller ones at the edges of the collage filled in the gaps left by the larger ones. In the middle was a poster-sized image of the woman making me breakfast. Draped over that was a banner—a sash, really—that read "Miss Florida."

"You were *actually* Miss Florida?"

A pan slid over the blue-white flame, and I watched a lump of butter get dropped into its center. Miss Florida—like an actual Miss Florida—laughed.

"Many years ago," she said then sighed. "Many, many years ago now."

I looked back to the largest photograph. She'd put on the years but not the pounds that usually come with that. She was in very good shape for someone who had to be—what? Sixties? Maybe a hard fifties.

I knew better than to inquire about *that*.

Instead, I said, "Can I ask what your real name is?"

She gazed at the poster, a faraway look in her eyes. Blinking the years away and returning to the present, she smiled and looked at me.

"Florida," she said, cracking a few eggs into the pan. "Florida Newman, but the only folks who call me Miss Newman are those asking for money." She laughed at her own joke.

I smiled. "Florida becomes Miss Florida. That's serendipitous." I leaned back in the chair and let out a long breath. "Is there a story behind that?"

Miss Florida shrugged. "There's a story behind all life's big moments, but never quite as good as you expect."

"You're probably right."

She pointed a spatula at the back bedroom. "Which brings me to your friend."

"Kane."

"How'd you get hooked up with that fine man? You say you're his driver?"

For the briefest of moments, I actually considered telling her the truth. Well, what I understood of it. Instead, I lied. "That story may not be as good as you'd expect."

Miss Florida tapped the cooking utensil to her head once, pointed it at me, and smiled.

I sat quietly for a few minutes as she finished up, tossing in cheese, some diced tomatoes, and peppers. Me, I'm not a big fan of peppers, but as hungry as I was, I would have eaten a plate of jalapeños at that moment.

As we ate, she told me about their town. Or more specifically, the past year. Since I'd met her, this was the first time that her smile vanished entirely.

"When it first started up, there was the usual bluster that comes with these sorts of things. Older folks in town, older than me, had seen stuff like that before. Dogs and cats went missing. Some chickens as well. Bunch of yahoo farmers went out with rifles and shotguns every night for a week, but they never did find anything."

"Were people scared?" I shoveled in a big helping of scrambled eggs as I listened.

Miss Florida just picked at her plate. I guessed that she'd already had breakfast that morning but had made herself up a serving just so I didn't feel self-conscious about eating in front of her. I liked her even more for that.

"Scared? Not at first, no. I mean, not really. But when people started locking up the dogs and cats—the ones that were left—and securing chicken coops—" Her eyes darkened. "A bunch of us went up to the Richter place to see the mess after one of their Herefords, beef cattle, had gotten killed."

She stood and grabbed our empty plates, taking them to the sink. "You need any more, hon?"

I shook my head. "What happened to the cow?"

Sitting back down, her shoulders rolled forward, making her look small. Older.

"People thought it was a bear or a wolf, maybe," she said and let out a sad chuckle. "Or at least, that's what they told themselves and each other. But a cow's probably too big for animals like that. We all knew it, even if no one was brave enough to say." Her face darkened.

I just listened.

"The hunting groups went out and were full of bravado, but what it had done to the cow?" Miss Florida shook her head, closing her eyes. Her voice fell to a whisper. "There were chunks of it missing. Throat slashed."

"It... it had eaten a whole cow right in the field?"

She shook her head again, eyes opening slowly. "That was the most unsettling part, I think. They found the chunks here and there around. Some of it gnawed on, maybe eaten, who knows. But, Emelda, the cow had been drained."

"Drained?"

"No blood left. Or at least nothing to speak of," she said and rubbed one of her eyebrows a bit too hard. "Whatever it had been, it had taken the blood."

"Jesus." I felt the buzz of adrenaline weakly drizzling through my body. I was tapped out by this time, running on reserves.

"Johnny Feltmann, far as I know, he was the first to see it," she said, staring out the window again. "Or at least he claimed to be the first. They'd been out hitting the trees, searching."

"Hitting the trees?"

"The sound will spook some animals. You get a bunch of folks on one side banging the trees with sticks and pipes, and the animal will run out the other." She laughed darkly. "Good plan, right? According to Johnny, this thing, huge, comes out. Pitch black but he says he saw long muscular limbs and blood and teeth. He's bricking it, so he never fires off a shot. Thing just ran past and deeper into the woods."

I jumped at the sound of a single knock on the door. My head whipped toward it, and I pushed my chair back, standing, ready to run. Where I would run, I had no idea.

When I looked back at my host, she smiled weakly and lifted a hand.

"It's fine. Don't worry about that." Miss Florida motioned for me to sit again. I did. "Now, Johnny wouldn't have ever admitted nearly soiling his pants. Instead, he said he had good reason not to shoot."

"Which was?" I said, breathing out the words, my eyes still cutting toward the door.

She reached forward and put a hand to the side of my head, tilting my eyes toward her.

"He said, even in the dark, the shape of it looked human. But not, you know, *human* human. Bigger, stronger, and, of course, covered in blood, which, if true, would have scared the hell out of anyone. But to hear him tell it, the creature was taller than him by a head. And, he thought, maybe naked, but with all the blood and it running away, he wasn't sure."

When I'd seen her, she had been naked. And, yeah, big. I didn't know if I should tell her Johnny's story had been true. At this point, I wasn't sure it mattered.

I asked her, "Were there more attacks, then?"

"Some, but I think at that point, people stopped talking about it," Miss Florida said. "I was never sure if that had been some, you know, arrangement. Maybe the mayor had said something on the down-low or something."

"Why?"

"Because people started leaving." She smiled, and her eyes dampened. "Tourists got warned off. Then some new families who'd just moved in, they sold their lots and moved. Probably for a loss, too, because who was going to buy in a town that had a monster?"

"Can't really blame them, can you?"

Before she could answer, there was another knock at the door, this one a bit louder and sharper. I looked to her, and she gave me a warm smile.

My nerves were fried. "What *is* that?"

"Give it a minute, and I'll take care of it," she said, which did nothing to calm me. Instead, she continued her story. "Damn near killed the town. Nobody left to work, all but one grocery store closed up. Some say temporary, but I seen them selling their stock to the Cub Foods, since it was still open."

My eyes went to the door again, and I could feel my palms sweat. Something was going on.

She saw my expression, pushed away from the table, and walked toward the entrance. Passing the window, she stopped, took a quick peek outside, then looked at me strangely.

Not menacing—I wasn't sure she could make a face like that—but strange with the hint of that smile. I wanted that smile back in full.

"Olivia's really got the only accommodation left in town, but it's her family's business. Her mom and dad ran it for years. It's all they got." When she reached the door, she put her hand on the knob then turned toward me.

She gave me a big grin. "But I think that's all about to change."

Miss Florida pulled the door open, and I braced. Would something leap through the crack? Why was she so calm?

She put her hands to her mouth and chuckled then threw the door open wider.

Stepping aside, she leaned up against the side of the door frame. "I think maybe this town has a chance of coming back," she said, smiling, with tears now falling from her eyes. "People coming back."

I stood on shaky legs and walked closer to see what was at the door. Two strange shapes, both covered with cloth. Like... like an offering? What the hell was this town into?

Miss Florida bent down and lifted one of the rounded, rectangular shapes and sniffed it.

When she pulled aside the thin towel, it revealed a white casserole dish filled with red liquid with some translucent green things the size of a kid's fist.

"I bet that's from Norma Lancaster," she said and smelled it again with a big smile.

Speechless, I stood there as she handed it to me. I winced. The bowl was very warm, which gave me chills. When I spun around to put it on the table and turned back, she handed me the other. Tears were on her cheeks now, the smile even wider.

"Right. Good man made that one," she said and clutched her hands to her chest.

I opened my mouth to ask her a question, but then she jumped and quickly closed the door. She put a finger to her lips and moved away from the window.

"Another one's coming," she whispered and hiked her shoulders.

I looked to her, then to the door, then back to the table where the casserole dishes sat. I nearly leaped out of my skin when I heard the knock. Just the one.

"What—?" I started, then she put a finger to her lips. I waited.

After a minute, she finally nodded and got up to look out the window again.

"What the hell is going on, Miss Florida?" I said, pointing at the table. "What's in those dishes?"

Casting a glance at me, she grinned wickedly. She opened the door slowly at first, then all the way. Another clothed offering lay on her stoop. Everything in me told me to get the hell out of there. But with Kane laid up, dead to the world, what could I do?

The old woman bent down and picked up the next item, this one covered in clear plastic wrap. It was chunky and brown and white and—had bits of what looked like flesh? Jesus Christ, was that flesh?

"I hope you like mushrooms," Miss Florida said.

I stopped. Looked back to the table and pointed, but no words came out. My host walked over to the table, put the new plate down, and went to the first, pulling back the damp dish towel.

"Cabbage rolls," she said and sniffed it again. "Norma's for sure. She makes the best cabbage rolls in town. Everybody says so."

I repeated the words. "Cabbage rolls."

She pointed to the second that had arrived. "That will be Aaron Planks's lasagna," she said and fanned her face. "It's more like pasta soup, sure, but the man tries. His wife died some years ago, and cooking's never been his strong suit. But he tries."

Leaning down to the third one, she pulled back the plastic, and a small puff of steam rose out. She laughed out loud, big and full-throated.

"That could only be Irma. She's British. Or Australian, I can never tell," she said then pointed down at the dish and dropped into her chair. Unsure what to do, I did the same. "Sheppard's pie, they call it. Sounds awful, but it tastes wonderful. Potatoes and hamburger, mushrooms and sauce. Cheese on top. It's good, but you'll have one plate of it and not have to eat for a week."

My head spun as the panic seeped from my body, taking what little energy I had left with it. I stared at the three dishes on the table.

"Why are they bringing you food?" I said then swung my face toward her. "Are you sick?"

Miss Florida looked at me with a quirky expression. "What?" She spread her arms over the table. "No, dear. These are for you, of course! Well, you and your big friend. We should go check—"

"In a minute," I said, slamming my palm on the table. "What do you mean, those are for me? Why are they sneaking up to the door?"

She lifted out of her chair and came around to where I was sitting, getting down on one knee. Cradling my face in her hands, she searched my eyes for something as she spoke.

"We're just country folks out here, love," she said softly. "Many are shy around strangers, and we haven't had many of those in the past year. That's why they're knocking and going like that."

I put my hands on her wrists, too tired to pull them away. "How do they even know we're here? We might... There may be people after us, Florida."

"You're safe here."

"How do you know that?"

She stood and went to the window, pulling back the curtain. "On top of that ridge is an old fire watch. Benjamin MacMillan is up there with a rifle and a radio, watching the road you came down." She slid to the other side of the window. "Esther Lloyd is in a deer stand on the property across from my drive. She's watching the other access road, and I don't want to know what she's packing. Bit of a gun nut."

"You know about the guys after us?"

She nodded then sat in the chair next to me. "Olivia isn't the best at keeping secrets, truth be told. Within five minutes of you leaving the motel, she told us to keep an eye out for the big black truck and the horrible people after you."

"She did?"

Miss Florida nodded. "But more importantly, she told us what you did last night. On the farm. Stu Clarrat and his wife had already gotten the whisper train rolling. They said when he went down, you ran right into the thick of it, chasing after the creature. When the fire started, they thought..." Her eyes misted, and she cleared her throat. "They thought the worst. Then Elma, she's in the hospital again, she told Francine that she'd seen *you* there and that you'd gone and snuck out the window!"

I recalled the old woman, the one-time young troublemaker, and nodded. Elma.

"Olivia filled in the rest and asked me if I still had that old Jeep, which I do." She nodded out the window toward a weather-beaten barn. "It'll need a bit of lovin' to get back into shape, but it'll run just fine. It's yours if you want it."

"Why?" I shook my head, missing something. "Why are people bringing us food? Why are you letting us stay? Why are people protecting us in... in deer blinds?"

"For saving this town, Emelda," she said and put her hand on mine. "For killing our monster."

Chapter Thirty-Eight

When I woke up hours later, my back and neck were screaming. I'd fallen asleep in the chair next to Kane's bed and took a few moments to reset my head.

The quiet unsettled me.

I'd been living in that basement apartment in North Minneapolis for about half a year and had gotten used to the city soundtrack—the rumble of predatory menace skittering off the top of my skull from the street-level windows above me.

That said, my subterranean cave felt safe. Or had given me that impression. Cinder-block walls and several tons of dirt cocooning me in a false sense of security.

On Miss Florida's farm, wide open fields surrounded us. I stared out the bedroom window and had dark thoughts of a sniper lining up on me, a mile away, and taking the shot. Hell, he could have fired a few seconds ago, watching for the result through one of those mono-lenses like in the Bourne films.

The first few days in my old apartment had been depressing. Passing cars or those parked at the curb, waiting for one of the drug dealers on the floors above to stumble down the stairs with their delivery, had belched toxic fumes into my home.

After a while, I just got used to it. And, as these things go, began to feel like I had somehow become some part of all that rot.

But the farm smelled like life. Damp grass, the sweet scent of flowers. Dirt, sure, but not like the toxic shit that used to splatter my old windows. The odor here was more earthen. Some promise that if you dropped a seed into it, after a little while, something would poke out of the dirt and reach for the sun.

And the only soundtrack out here was the song from the light breeze playing through the cattails and the chattering insects looking for love.

That thought made me smile. Insect love, baby!

Kane grunted, shifting a little under the light covers. Good. At least he was still breathing. He hadn't moved since I'd awoken.

And he did look better. Much better than he should have after the beating he'd received the night before. The cuts he'd had on his face, arms, torso, everywhere, had stopped shining angry red. Already, scabs had formed.

His bruises had turned from green and yellow and were whipping through their angry purple stage. I remembered one on his flank that looked like the state of Texas. Now it looked more like Missouri or Louisiana. Maybe Idaho? I'd never been great with state shapes.

"Where is this place?" he said, his voice gravelly.

I slid out of the chair, sat on the edge of the bed, and put my hand on his forehead. He seemed hot, but I had no idea if a wolf-turned-man ran naturally hot.

"We're safe."

He blinked and frowned at me. "We are not safe. Not from Gregor."

"Well, Miss Florida—an actual Miss Florida at one point—this is her house, and we've got Ben with a rifle covering one part of the road and Esther watching the other. I wandered over there to check a few hours ago, and I think she may have a machine gun."

"W-What? We have to leave, Sad Girl."

I shook my head. "Not until Denny finishes up with the Jeep. Just needs a few belts and plugs, he says, and those have been ordered. But they won't be in until tomorrow at the earliest. Most likely the day after."

"Who is Denny?"

"Miss Florida's son." I dropped back into my chair and drew in a deep, clean breath of farm air. "And we've got about a dozen casseroles out there. Well, one of them, I'm told, is more of a pasta soup. Plenty of food to get your strength back."

Kane shuffled slowly and lifted himself up, leaning against the headboard. His face twisted a little, and he lifted his covers, looking down.

"Oh, I found you some pajama bottoms," I said, not able to keep the grin off my face. "They don't go all the way down to your feet, but they fit you otherwise. Got them from Denny, so sorry about the—"

"Why do I have a sponge person on my pants?"

I shook my head. "They're not pants, they're PJs. And how do you not know SpongeBob? He's world famous."

"Who is this SpongeBob? Why is he honored with his likeness on pants?"

Laughing, I said, "He's a brave little sponge that lives on the bottom of the sea with his best friend, Patrick."

Kane frowned. "I know those words were supposed to explain the pants, but they do not."

"It doesn't matter."

The big man nodded slowly then cut his eyes toward me. "Why are these people helping us?"

I leaned forward and went down on one knee, facing him. "They think we killed the monster."

"We did not. Bridget Mills almost killed us."

I put a finger to my lips and pointed to the closed door. "We played our part. We, you know, distracted her. Then Gregor's assholes nabbed her. They couldn't have done that without us."

Kane considered my rationalization, and I thought it offended his wolf morality. Or something. "This feels like a deception to get a Jeep and pasta soup."

"Not wholly," I said, shrugging. "We helped. In our own way."

Kane started to get up. "We should go back to the tavern. Find out what has happened—"

I gently put a hand on his chest and eased him back.

"They've bugged out. According to the bar owner—that's the dude out there with the rifle—they'd trashed up the place, but when he got there with the cops, they'd cleared out."

"Where have they gone?"

"Dunno. This ain't a big CCTV town, so once they'd left the parking lot, they pretty much vanished. That still doesn't explain what they're up to."

"What do you mean?"

I sat back in the chair, thinking, thumbing the locket at my neck. "Why did they cage that woman?" I said. "And why was Gregor asking about you?"

That got a sideways glance from Kane. "What did he say?"

"They just wanted to know where you were. What you were up to. Why?"

"They know I am searching for Cal Davis. I believe they think I may know where he is."

"Okay," I said, growling in frustration. Sometimes, conversations with him were like questioning a coffee tin of old lard. "Fine. So *why* are *they* searching for Cal Davis?"

Kane smiled at me weakly. "Because he has been terrorizing the towns around here."

I shook my head. "The monster on the Clarrat farm wasn't Cal, and you know it. It was Bridget." I watched him as I spoke. "Miss Florida showed me a newspaper article about her when she went missing. The speculation was she'd been taken by someone."

"I remember the man with the wooden motorcycle telling us about this thing."

"Right, Dock had brought her up. This town's monster was definitely Bridget Mills. More muscles, a foot or two taller, and had traded long black hair for stubble. But the same person."

Kane looked out the window at the squat hills beyond the glass. He blinked slowly. "Then she was perhaps bitten by Cal Davis."

I'd had the same thought. "Like you." Movement outside startled me, but then saw Denny carrying handfuls of trash to a large metal drum. "Does Gregor know that? About you?"

"No, because I am not... as she was," he said, shaking his head. "I think whatever did this to me also changed Bridget Mills. Into something different."

I told Kane about what had happened in the tavern. The way Gregor's crew seemed on edge. And how they'd rolled into town with military gear, an electrified cage, and drugs to take down a rhino. Or monster.

"They'd planned on not killing some monster but taking it captive. They may have been as surprised as anyone that the creature wasn't Cal but Bridget instead." I closed my eyes and rubbed my temples. "But why do you think they want Cal Davis? And the woman?"

He shrugged. "Maybe *they* are the true monster hunters who deserve the pasta soup."

That didn't sound right to me. "Is that why they're after you?"

"I do not understand. Have you just called me a monster?"

"Ha, no. A wolf-who-turned-into-a-man-who-turns-into-tiny dogs is not a monster."

Kane shrugged.

"But they *were* looking for you, Kane."

"Maybe to find Cal Davis before I do."

It still didn't make sense to me. How had they connected Kane to Cal in the first place? Of course, the big guy had shown up all over, asking about him.

"We better find him first," I said. "You find out what you need to know, and then we hand him over."

Kane hit me with a look that told me he wasn't into giving *anything* to Gregor.

"If they don't know about"—I said and pointed at him—"your particular biological quirk, then the only way this is over is if they've got Cal."

"It will not be over until I have returned to my pack."

I threw my hands up. "Really? You think they're waiting for you?"

"They will wait. My wolf wife, she will wait."

"How do you know that? Plenty of other, you know, wolves in the forest. Or whatever."

He looked out the window again, his eyes falling closed.

"Wolf is not like human. My wife, she awaits me. I must return to her."

Kane's head lolled to the side, and he once again closed his eyes. For as horrifying as the past twenty-four hours had been, he seemed so at ease with all of it. Like it was business as usual.

I asked him, "What was your life like back then? You know, before."

"When I was wolf."

"Yeah, when you had, you know, a family. A pack."

He shifted his weight, turning toward me. As he stared toward the floor, a small smile crept across his ashen face.

"Hard to mesh those memories with my human ones. But I remember... seeking shelter from storms. Hunger, always hunger. The danger of night and being exposed to enemies by day."

I shuddered. "And you miss that?"

"Also, as you say, family. My wolf wife and three others. We hunted as a pack and traded warmth in the night. Always one of us keeping an eye out for danger. Threats."

"The five of you, then. Were they your, um, kids?"

He shook his head. "No, but... relations. Bloodlines, yes?"

"I understand, sure."

"The three were progeny of the former alpha male," he said, his words slurring slightly from exhaustion. "I was... bloodline... but not a child of alpha."

Nodding, I tried to understand. "I thought you were the alpha. No?"

"Six of us before. Then battle changes this." Kane lowered his head, eyes closed, and grimaced. "Hard to make memories work."

"It's okay," I said, because I could see the recollections upset him. "You don't have to—"

"Fighting in the forest one time, and alpha commands we... take cover in the forest nearby."

"To fight alone?"

Kane thought for a moment then gave me a half nod. "To protect us. From the threat. This was unusual, but the alpha was larger than I and powerful. Strong. So strong."

I keep quiet. It was clear what happened next. Part of me wanted to tell him to stop and not finish the story. He seemed upset by it. But I said nothing.

"Afterward, we find his body. Broken. Dead. We honor him by consuming what we can. I am second best, so I am alpha now," he told me. "But... always, I know, I will always be the lesser alpha."

"I doubt that." I smiled, trying to be light. He was in no mood for it, though. Still, I tried to lift his mood. "I bet you were a badass alpha."

Once again, he closed his eyes. "Sometime later, we had made a fresh kill. Deer. My wolf wife and I had feasted first, for this is our way. Before the others could feed, Cal Davis attacked my pack." Kane got a faraway look in his eyes. "He must have smelled the blood from our kill. Or seen it from the road in his purple car."

"The blood?"

Kane ignored my question and continued his story. "Like old alpha had done, I tell the others to find safety. I... I am not sure why. We are stronger as a pack, yes. But this was the better alpha's way, and I try to do the same."

I knew the story from there. Cal, wild with fever, sickness, or whatever had been coursing through him, nearly killed Kane. I still didn't understand how a man could not only conceive of taking on a wolf but then overcome it.

"I would have died and should have. Only the warning shot from mon père—this I understand later from his telling of it—that is why I do not die. After, I am in the barn of the old couple who will become my human parents."

When I tried to speak again, I found my own emotion gumming up the words. Drawing the back of my hand across my eyes, I cleared my throat.

"We'll get you back to them, Kane," I told him, and I meant it. "Cal will have your answers. He'll know what needs to be done. Then you can return to your pack again. They need their badass alpha back, right?"

Kane's eyes fell closed. "Second best, still," he said. Then his head lolled to the pillow, and he fell asleep.

Chapter Thirty-Nine

Over the next few days, I helped Denny to get the Jeep back in shape while Kane slowly recovered from his injuries.

Each night, Miss Florida prepared dinner—a simple task given the number of casserole gifts that filled her fridge. Still, I assisted her in the kitchen not because she needed it, but because I found being around the woman a delight.

She always found joy in the simplest tasks, and it was hard not to get wonderfully infected by her enthusiasm.

We dined at the kitchen table. Her son would swoop in, grab his supper, and head upstairs to eat and play video games with overseas friends he'd never met and never would. When he'd come in, that had given me a chance to take a plate to Kane, who rarely left the dark bedroom.

He hadn't been a fan of the heavy dishes, but I felt asking for slabs of raw steak might get me raised eyebrows and questions I didn't want to answer. In the end, Kane had favored Aaron Plank's watery lasagna.

He'd eaten that, and only that, three nights running.

* * *

After we'd pulled the Jeep out to get it running again, the barn was left in disarray. In the years since Miss Florida's older son had left, the old vehicle ended up storing items disused but too loved to be discarded. Removing the vehicle had left behind what Denny had jokingly referred to as a "redneck yard sale."

I'd spent the fourth day tidying up their barn, which, as things always go, ended up being a far bigger task than it seemed when I'd first embarked upon it.

Once finished, I went to the back bedroom and fell onto the cot Miss Florida had told Denny to set up next to the bed days earlier.

Despite the bright afternoon sun outside, I was out in minutes.

When I finally woke up, the sky had turned dark. I pulled the curtains to block the stars and moonlight and let Kane sleep.

Catching a whiff of myself, I winced.

What I needed was a lot of water and a change of clothes. I'd been wearing the same ones for days now. Nasty.

I grabbed my bag and went to hunt down the shower and a towel. Or just a shower. I could drip dry for all I cared. I just needed to defunk a bit.

When I entered the kitchen, I saw Denny eating from one of the casserole dishes with a wooden spoon. There was red sauce all over his face, an image that made me shiver at first. When he looked up at me, though, his mouth hung open in surprise, ringed by crimson goo, and I couldn't help but laugh.

"Nice," I said. "I'd take a picture if I could and hang it on your mom's wall."

"Don't do that," he said, little sprinkles of cheese and sauce falling back into the dish.

I made a mental note to cross that item off my dinner list.

"Don't worry, I lost my phone. No pictures."

He nodded, scooped up another big serving of red glop, and shoveled it in. I looked in the refrigerator and saw it still half filled with stacks of casserole dishes. The thought made me smile. I had never felt that appreciated for anything in my entire life.

I liked it. I *really* liked it.

Even if, in a small way, we hadn't been wholly responsible for ridding the town of its evil monster menace. But, like I'd said to Kane, we'd played a part. We'd definitely played a part. I wasn't sure if it was a fifteen-casserole-worth part, but who was I to argue?

Dinner after a long shower.

Between slurping gulps, Denny told me if I were going to shower, I had to be quiet. Apparently, Miss Florida had gone to bed early. He said something about "beauty sleep" and laughed to himself.

When I turned to go, Denny called after me.

"So, where'd you lose your phone?"

* * *

"I'm sure the battery is dead by now," I said, looking around Denny's room for the first time. Rock posters on his walls. Guitar magazines on every flat surface. At least the laptop seemed kind of nice.

"Doesn't matter," he said, licking his fingers. "It probably sent up a signal flare."

I sighed. "Just pretend, you know, I asked you what that was."

"The phone knows when it's dying, so just before it does, it'll tell its network, 'here I am.' Or 'was,' I suppose."

I'd told Denny that I hadn't remembered where I'd dropped the phone because I didn't want to get into it. Last time I saw it, I'd been smashed like a bug in the back of Gregor's truck days earlier.

It might have fallen to the floor or outside in the lot. If it had been in the lot, it probably would have gotten smashed by a tire or the she-beast.

But Denny was now in that "dude tech" mode that just thrilled some guys. I'd seen it in my old boyfriend Roy so many times. They had all the old electronic gear they'd hoarded for years—the guy-standard box of tangled cables, dongles, adapters, and wires—and now, dammit, this guy had a chance to use it!

Why take away that joy?

At his insistence, I logged into the Google account connected to my phone, and it spent a minute searching. Nothing.

"Ah, well," I said, looking toward the hallway. There, a shower beckoned my stinky body. "Worth a shot."

"Hold up. We can see where that last signal was if nothing else." A few more keystrokes, one-handed, mind you. I made a mental note to not sit anywhere in Denny's room.

A red pin appeared on the screen with a timestamp indicating the last signal flare had been three days earlier.

"Great," I said then tried to locate the cross streets. But I couldn't see any on the map. "I don't know where that is. Is that the tavern?"

Denny shook his head and refreshed the screen. The map disappeared for a moment.

"Why did you do that? What the fu—"

"Just doing another search for it," he said, holding red-stained fingers up at me. "The data's there. It ain't going anywhere. It just..."

Panicking, I watched the screen while it recycled. As before, he went to the archival signals, and the fat red pin returned.

"Phew, great. Don't do that again," I said, searching for streets. Shitty map didn't have any. "Where is that?"

Denny chewed on the pad of his thumb, staring at the screen. "It's up in the hills. There's a lake there, good for fishing. Me and my buddies go down there in the spring most years. Not this year because all the rain washed the roads out."

"Are you saying my phone got washed down there?" I looked at him, frowning.

"No. Um, maybe," he said. Then he leaned into the map. "I don't know how it got there, but that's not the weird part."

I raised my eyebrows and rolled my hand to get him to finish.

"The weird part is, like I said, me and my buds have gone down there for years," he said, smacking his lips. "Even if you don't catch any fish, it's a good place to hide away from everyone. Because it dips down a bit, and there's not a cell tower for miles and miles."

"Okay." I shrugged. "That matters why?"

Denny clicked through the archival data, tracing his finger down the screen. "Four. I count four times your phone pinged out there." He wiped a thin line of casserole sauce off the screen and leaned back. "But that's just not possible because it's a dead zone. There's no way for your phone to have done that."

Again, I shrugged. "But it did. So what does that mean?"

"Well, it could mean that the family that owns the land around that area finally caved to the telecoms and let them put up a tower, but there's zero chance of that. Their grandpa—"

"Denny!" I said, putting a hand up. "Do I look like I'm whittling? I don't want to hear any back country stories right now. Did someone put a cell tower up, or not?"

"No chance," he said, shaking his head. "Only one way a signal got out."

"Which is?"

"Somebody set up a temporary tower," he said and whistled. "Have no idea why. The fishing ain't that good. But I can tell you tech like that ain't exactly cheap."

Somebody.

I could guess who that somebody was. Kane was still out for the count and would be until the next morning, maybe longer. But I had no idea how long that *somebody* might stick around.

Obviously, I didn't give a damn about my phone.

Because of me, my family was now in danger. Gregor had made that crystal clear, brandishing his fancy smartphone like a weapon. The sickly green images of my mother in California and my grandmother in Minneapolis.

How connected was the guy to not only dig into my past but to get hidden cameras into the homes of my family? And he'd done it so quickly!

But what could I do?

Denny looked up at me, waiting. At first, I didn't know what the hell that was about; I didn't have any answers. Then, I realized, he was waiting to hear the plan from their new monster hunter in residence.

Me.

As if I were some kind of expert in... all of this.

No one had ever looked to me as an expert in anything. But this town saw me as a *fifteen*-casserole-level monster hunting pro.

Emboldened by his faith in me that I didn't have myself, I dipped my finger into Denny's bowl, took a glop, and licked my finger.

With the images of my mother and grandmother still in my mind, I said: "That Jeep ready to roll, Denny?"

Chapter Forty

"I don't think Mom will be happy about me driving around here at night," he said, hunched over his wheel and scanning the woods from side to side. "In fact, I ain't been out in town at night for the better part of a year."

"Don't worry," I said. "We've secured the threat, Denny."

Secured the threat!

I felt very professional.

The Jeep, in fact, had not been ready to roll. It still needed gas transfusion and new tires.

Instead, we took his car, which smelled like a fast-food dumpster.

Denny had suckered his phone to the dash somehow. I hadn't seen him chuck it up there, but it didn't look like anything he might have nabbed off Amazon during some late-night, drunken, retail doomscrolling. A bit of black tubing snaked into the air vent, and strapped to that was some bit of thin, flat metal with a series of holes.

From there, I had no idea what was securing it in place. But it was apparent he'd fashioned the holder himself.

He'd also come up with another holder exactly the size of a hip flask. I knew that because there lay a glass bottle within its grasp. Denny saw me looking at it and got a very self-satisfied look on his face.

"You want a belt?"

The words sent a chill rippling through me—I'd heard variations of that challenge all through my childhood—until I realized he was talking about the rotgut. I declined.

On "the job" and all that.

"You're not worried you'll get busted for drinking and driving?" I said, wishing I was behind the wheel. "Cop comes up to the window and spots the—"

Denny pulled a black plastic lever I hadn't seen, and the bottle and its mesh holder dropped a few inches. When he yanked the handle farther down, the arm of it looped down and disappeared under the dash.

"Neat, huh?"

I grimaced. "You get to the point where you're MacGyvering parts of your car to hide your hooch, maybe you should seek some help."

"Didn't need no help." He lifted the lever, and the bottle popped back up again, not a drop spilled. "Did it all by myself."

Uh-huh.

Despite the headlights valiantly cutting through the night, it was hard to see anything but the gravel road ahead of us. Had it not been for the fat, lopsided moon in the sky, it would have been as dark as a dead man's dreams.

Almost as if he could read my mind, Denny clicked his lights off.

"What the hell, man?" I said, grabbing the handle above the window. "Turn those on!"

He did and shrugged. "I've lived in this shithole my entire life. I can get there blindfolded."

"Can you get there with two black fucking eyes?" I said, leaning toward him and baring my teeth. "Would that be a challenge?"

Denny flinched away from me but, impressively, he hadn't swerved. He mumbled an apology and went quiet for the next ten minutes.

About an inch away from the red dot, the spot that had sent up the "signal flare" from my phone, he slowed. I was about to ask why he was easing off the speed when I saw the road ahead. Or what was left of it.

"Shit," I muttered.

"Told you. Got washed out in all the flooding we've had recently. There's no..."

I turned to him to see what had happened to the rest of his words. He stared at the mess of dirt, silt, bramble, rock, and branches.

Jabbing a finger into his shoulder, I asked him, "What?"

"Ow," he said softly, rubbing the spot. He reached out, grabbed his flask, and took a drink. He wiped his mouth with the back of his hand then pointed the bottle ahead. "Someone's gone around that."

"Great. Let's do that."

A low, throaty sound rumbled out of him, and I realized he was laughing.

"Those tire tracks are fat, and they go down deep. Whatever they were driving, it was made for bad terrain. This shitbox ain't."

I reached for the door handle. "I'll walk the rest of the way."

"Hold on, now! There's a monster out—" Denny started to say then stopped. He laughed to himself. "Well, I guess there ain't a monster anymore. You guys took care of that."

One foot out the door, I paused to get my bearings. I glanced back at the map with the tiny dot. Just up this road and...

Right. And? Then what?

Denny's voice split the silence. "Why do you guys, you know, do what you do?"

"What?"

"This monster-hunter business," he said and smiled again. "If it's a *business*, I don't know. Seems like the scariest damn thing in the world. People around here, they didn't even leave their houses most days. Well, the ones who hadn't left their houses altogether."

That strange alien feeling came over me again, but I pushed it aside and instead pointed toward the washed-out road in the headlights. "How far up is it?"

He ignored the question. "Well, whatever reason you're doing it," he said and swallowed hard, "thank you. I can finally get back to the city. Got some things lined up."

"Uh-huh," I said and laughed. "Guitar player, right?"

He shook his head. "Naw, but I know the business pretty good. I manage two bands in the Twin Cities. Lining up a third."

That surprised me. This guy didn't look like he could manage getting dressed in the morning without a YouTube instructional video.

"Now," he continued, "I can get back to it. Only came up here to look after my mom when, you know, all the trouble started."

I turned toward him, the lights of the dash illuminating his face. I could see him blinking away dampness.

"You came back to watch over your mom?"

He shrugged. "She's not one to ask for help, but she's all alone in that big house after my brother left. I wasn't sure what I could do, but sometimes, just being there is enough, you know." When I didn't say anything, he added, "I ain't no monster hunter like you, but I had to be there for my mom. World's crazy-ass shit is sometimes only tolerable when you got someone in the shit with you." He laughed and wiped his nose then did a quick brush of his eyes.

I put a hand on his arm softly, so he didn't think I was going to jab him with a finger again.

"You're a good son, then."

Denny cleared his throat. "And a helluva fisherman. There's a turnoff back there, just dirt, but it'll get us around some of this. Won't take you all the way down to the lake, but it'll give you a bird's-eye view."

* * *

When we'd come to the crest of the hill, I'd told Denny to click the lights off and got a frown.

"Now you want the lights off? This ain't a road up here."

Eventually, he complied, and about ten yards from the top, we stopped. I hopped out and walked up the rest of the way. Denny waited in the car.

On his phone's map, the area was just a wishbone lake, designated by a blue upside-down U-shape with pale green surrounding it. On the east side of that was my red pin.

As I stood at the top of the hill, below me was a void.

I crouched, waiting for my eyes to adjust. That took a few minutes, and when the moon peeked out from behind a cloud, I could see right down into the lake valley. The light glimmered off the water, mimicking the shape I'd seen on the map.

Around the lake, I could see dim sparkling. If it had been brighter, it would have almost looked like a halo around the water.

On the west side, I noticed glinting at the shoreline, but something else too. Large and angular.

"That's our pontoon boat."

"Jesus," I hissed then turned to Denny. How did a guy like that sneak up on me?

"Sorry."

Tracing my eyes toward where the red pin had been on the map, I saw only darkness. Nothing was there.

I sighed and waved a hand toward the lake. "It's pretty. And sparkly."

"That's the rock beach around the edges." He'd brought his flask with him and took another belt.

I looked back at the car and seriously considered walking home.

"Big boulders all slick with moss and stuff. Others the size of stoves or microwave ovens. Some about as big as a toaster."

Looking at him with hooded eyes, I asked, "Are all your units of measurement devices that cook food?"

Even in the dim light, I could see he'd blushed. Maybe it was time to not be such an asshole to the guy? Yeah, probably.

"There's nothing here," I said, nodding back down to the lake. "The spot where my phone supposedly pinged is empty."

Denny rubbed his lips. "Could be just the towers around here picked up some ghost signal and dropped a pin," he said. Then he took a step forward. "Weird that it woulda done it three or four times in the same spot."

"Technology, right? Who knows—"

"But that down there, it's all black," he said, pointing with his bottle.

"Yeah, got that."

He looked at me and shook his head. "No, what I mean is... I been out here plenty at night. A lot of fellas do, you know, because of the pretty lake and sparkle. We'd take, um, girls up here. And stuff."

"And stuff?"

Denny raised an eyebrow. "Personal stuff."

"Right, Romeo," I said and stepped toward the car. I didn't feel like walking and planned to hop into the driver's seat before he did. "I don't want to hear about your conquests. I don't think the pasta soup is settling too well."

"That's not what I'm talking about," he said, and I turned around. "See, it's a, you know, romantic spot because of the ring."

"Ring?"

"The shale beach that surrounds the lake. In the moonlight, it glistens like it's magic. Pretty, really."

I stepped back and looked to where he was pointing now.

"But that chunk over there? It ain't sparkling." Denny lifted the bottle to his lips but then lowered it again without taking a sip. "It should be. Always has before."

Sometimes, I'm slow, but I get there in the end. Finally, I understood what he was saying.

"Something's there."

Chapter Forty-One

It had taken me much longer to climb down the hill then I'd hoped. Aside from those summers on my uncle's farm, I'm a city girl through and through. So when I get into the big, wide-open spaces, I've got no bearings to judge distances. In the urban sprawl of my mind, everything is a block or two up. You see something in the distance, and it's a ten-minute walk.

Beyond that, in a city, you can't really see anything.

From the top of the hill, the blackout area down on the beach looked like it would be one of those ten-minute walks. It had taken me at least twenty. Maybe longer. I wasn't any good at judging time, either.

I'd only fallen twice, which was three less than Denny had estimated, so I put that down as a win. Walking down the hill, even with its bumps and ridges, hadn't been too difficult.

But once I'd hit the rock beach, a bit cooler down here than above, it was a different story entirely. And he'd been right: some of the boulders in their various food-making-device sizes were slippery as shit, at least the ones closer to the lake.

When the smaller pebbles began crunching under my feet, I felt suddenly exposed. Thankfully, the night sounds of cicadas masked my steps. I felt a nauseating tingle on the back of my tongue and swallowed, hoping those emotions got squeezed down into my gut and consumed by the churning acid.

To my left was the flat, steel surface of the small wishbone lake.

I hadn't seen a river or stream on the map feeding the water but hadn't really looked that closely. I'd wondered if this had been a quarry at some time, abandoned when some optimism about the housing market got eviscerated by the cold, hard reality of human wants and wills and a consumer-based economy.

Yeah, I was stalling.

Not thinking about what I needed to do. What I needed to do was get closer to whatever structure or structures lay about fifty yards up the stony beach.

That was when another thought—another distraction, maybe—hit me.

Why did I need to get there?

If I really wanted to protect my family, I could likely call them up and tell them to get out of their homes. Go somewhere safe. Or just somewhere else for a while.

Only ten days earlier, I'd been living a normal life. Boring and depressing but normal. Then I met Kane, and everything went topsy-turvy. Like I'd gotten tagged in some wrestling match I hadn't even known I'd been a part of: you go in.

So what the hell was I doing?

This was Kane's thing. Searching for Cal Davis, running from people with guns and cages and from blood-sucking monsters. Exposed as I was, maybe this wasn't the best place for an existential crisis.

The rational part of my brain screamed at me to run back up the hill and forget all of this. But my legs had other ideas.

If I was going to move forward, I had to do it quickly.

But I still had to work out why the hell I was doing this!

Then it occurred to me.

That look.

The look on Denny's face when he talked about the "work" Kane and I were doing. How his voice hung in the air like a cool mist and rained down upon me.

The knocks at Miss Florida's door.

Just one at a time. The door opening to reveal an offering of appreciation for something we'd kind of done. No, we'd done it. Had it not been for our involvement, that beast woman would surely still have been running around out here, terrorizing the locals.

People still afraid to leave their homes. Go to the store. Go to bars. Have dinner with friends in a restaurant. Now, maybe normal life would return. Slowly, but now it had a chance of coming back.

And Denny, Miss Florida, Olivia, Stu Clarrat, and dozens of others with various levels of baking skills—and maybe hundreds more—now looked to me and Kane as *heroes*.

No, I didn't have any deep need to be a hero. Never had.

But for the first time in my memory, people hadn't looked in my direction and just stared right through, looking for something better. People hadn't quietly scowled, disappointed. Hadn't ignored me entirely.

I'd been appreciated. Valued.

I had *value*.

And I wanted to feel more of that.

I needed to.

I needed it more than food, more than water, more than air to breathe. In the past few hours, it had been like a reawakening. Or being reanimated. I had a purpose, and people were looking to *me* as someone who wasn't a total loser.

I felt that elusive drug coursing through my veins. One I'd been starved of my entire life. I was needed. People *needed* me.

Enough navel-gazing.

Time for overanalyzing my inner workings could come later. Hopefully, it would come later. If the Black-Clad Mafia were about, these were the assholes who, no question, had been ready to kill me the day before. And here I was, sneaking up on them.

The moon shone like a penitentiary spotlight, so I moved farther up the beach toward the rise in the hill again. Once there, I traced that bottom ridge, moving closer to the encampment.

That was what it was.

My eyes adjusted, and I could see three black tents, the farthest of which was more of a covering, a dark tarp spread out over six black poles. Beneath that was the truck I'd been thrown into when Tech Sergeant Gregor and his crew had nabbed me outside the vet clinic. Next to that looked like a converted mail van, also jet black. Of course.

I could hear my heartbeat just beneath a dull ringing in my ears. My blood pressure was up, and my hands were sweating. Indecision gripped me. Well, that and sheer terror. I wasn't any sort of adrenaline junkie and had run away from danger.

Creeping forward, I slipped behind some dead brush and crouched.

In front of the makeshift carport, I saw two large tents, both made from the same black material hiding the truck. From this vantage point, I spotted dim red lights with hoods above them. That was why we couldn't see them from above. Any and all light was being reflected downward.

It was odd that that same light didn't reflect off the sparkly beach. The moonlight had. Then I noticed black mats circling the tents, thick rubber things covered in coarse fibers like wool, leading down one side all the way to the truck.

They were absorbing the faint light from above.

Sure, they didn't want to be spotted, but who the hell would see them in the middle of nowhere, deep in some lake valley? I looked up and only saw the lopsided moon and a clear night sky. I couldn't imagine there'd be any air traffic out this way.

I flinched when I heard the bark of a laugh in the far tent, followed by another voice shushing the first. I'd recognized Laughing Boy's voice: Gorilla Tits.

How the hell had he survived that battle with the beast woman?

Didn't matter.

I sat and listened. How many people were in there? Was it just the three or—?

My answer came the moment I posed the question. Two people, one tall and one short, walked out of the far tent, heading toward the truck. Dressed head to toe in black, they kept to the mats, so I couldn't hear their footfalls.

Under the carport, the light caught a face I recognized.

"Gregor," I whispered to myself.

He and the other person walked past the boxy black van and disappeared around the side. The van dipped, and I heard the quiet click of a door. They'd gone inside.

I guessed—and I could only guess—that it was some sort of camper, even though it didn't really look like one from here. Hell, maybe it was some radio room like in the movies? A dim red light clicked on inside, but its illumination was quickly swallowed by the sea of darkness around the camp.

Another minute later, and a beast of a human came out of the far tent, same as the others had, and loped toward the van.

Gorilla Tits was calling it a night? Or going for supper. That thought made me smile slightly. I bet no one had left them two weeks' worth of dinners at their doorstep.

Time to move. The longer I stayed out there, the bigger the chance I'd get seen. The bushes didn't hide me well, and if anyone looked over here, they'd pick me out soon enough.

Slowly, I crept across the rocky beach, making as little sound as possible. Each gritty crunch made my heart bang against my ribs. When I finally got to the mat, I calmed. Only slightly.

Tent One was right next to me, but the voices had come from Tent Two. I crept over and listened as I walked. Through a gap in the window flap, I could hear two voices. I got bits and pieces of their conversation.

"... doesn't help now. She's gone, so we need..."

"I know what we need."

"Then what? We wait?"

A woman sounded close. The other was flat and strange. I realized the second voice was coming from a speaker. A radio? Why would she radio her crew if they were just in the van nearby?

"Just stick it out. Especially now, for god's sake," a man's voice over the radio said.

The woman laughed quietly. "Easy for you to say."

"Fine." The man's voice crackled. "I'll call it if you can't hack it."

"And then?"

"I don't know," the man on the radio said. "But I don't think they'll be happy with you. Way above my pay grade."

The woman in the tent sighed. "We are just a speck of sand, being rolled around by an ant..."

"Sounds like you're buying into their bullshit already, Mon."

He'd said "Mon." The woman I'd seen in the bar.

I wiped my hands down my jeans and slowly crept away from the temporary structure. I heard footfalls closer to the flap and skittered back, slipping between the two tents. A moment later, I heard the flap open.

I held my breath.

The sounds of the feet stopped. Quiet.

Had she heard me?

All it would take would be for Mon to walk two steps to her right, and if she looked between the tents, I'd be done.

Thankfully, I heard footsteps again, trailing away—I assumed—toward the carport. If she was joining the other two, that should give me at least a few minutes.

I desperately wanted to get a peek into Tent Two, but I wasn't entirely sure she'd cleared out. And I was already rolling the dice just by being there.

Creeping as slowly as I could, I stepped back onto the mat and found the entrance for Tent One. I had no illusions that I'd be safe there. I had to get in and out fast. Hopefully, I'd find something out about this crew in that time.

If I didn't? Screw it. I'd pressed my luck enough already.

At the entrance, I could see it was secured with a simple hook-and-eye set up. All it took was to lift the corner away, and the tent lay open to me. I went inside and replaced the flap.

A long wire snaked around one of the thin black poles that curved to keep the tent upright. At the terminus of that wire, at the top, was a single bulb, hanging down like a blood-red teardrop and casting a hazy light.

I could see two long tables and what looked like some sort of bureau on the far wall. My hammering pulse was making my head spin. I felt the sharp edges of those snow globe flecks in my brain begin to stir and breathed slowly to calm myself.

In and out. In and out.

Across the first table were radios, nylon straps, and a small arsenal. Two automatic rifles lay side by side with magazines stacked next to them. A wooden box held fist-sized devices I'd only seen on television. Grenades. Actual grenades.

Who are these people?

Without thinking, I grabbed one and slipped it into my pocket. Did they have serial numbers that could be traced? Who knew? I'd ask Kane about it when I got back. I took a step and felt the grenade bang against my thigh, and my stomach lurched.

Yeah, so, I had an explosive bumping against my body. I was all about new experiences, but I would have been happy to leave that one alone.

Farther down the bang-bang-boom table were small tools that I didn't recognize. One had a bit of a hook at the end, another a long brush scored with black material. Next to that sat a small bottle with a long nipple at the top. Looked like oil.

I guessed, and I could only guess, this was stuff to clean their weapons. As they waited for their next move, they were making sure all their gear was ready to go.

A black steel box sat on the corner of the table, but when I tried to open it, no surprise, I found that it was locked. I considered picking it up and shaking it, but that would have made noise. Either a rattling sound, which I couldn't risk, or—if there were explosives inside—a boom sound that would likely take my hands with it.

I left the box alone.

The next table over offered up a large map of the area, with grease pencil markings I couldn't understand. For the high-tech commando squad, the physical map seemed incongruous. But if they'd put a high value on secrecy—by using black tents and hooded lights in the well of a lake—maybe this was a way of keeping their movements offline.

That would imply they weren't just trying to keep out of sight of any locals who might stumble upon their encampment.

Someone else, then?

I thought about how, from above, we couldn't even see the encampment.

Maybe they hadn't just been avoiding curious eyeballs but also anything that might pass above. Planes? Satellites?

I had no idea. No use speculating.

A field laptop sat up on its metal case, also black, so on-brand. I checked the flap at the door, swallowing hard. Couldn't see anything. And couldn't hear anything.

The latter made me nervous but also curious. I could no longer hear the chattering of insects outside. They hadn't gone quiet—something about the tent's fabric dampened the sound. I realized the only way I'd heard the woman speaking on the radio was because the window flap had shifted slightly.

With a trembling finger, I swiped across the laptop's touchpad. The screen lit up, and I gasped.

Fuck!

I'd felt like I'd shouted, "Hey, I'm just in here going through your shit!"

Had I been loud, or was it just because my utterance had been in my own head and seemed loud to me? Screw it. I'd pressed my luck enough. Time to get the fu—

A face on the laptop screen stopped me.

A young-looking man in a military outfit, maybe Army? His picture took up the upper quarter of the screen. Next to his face, a name: Cal Davis.

I looked toward the door again, sure I'd heard something. I was jittery as hell, and I wished I'd had my phone so I could just take a picture and run. But the damn thing was likely jammed under the seat of the truck fifty feet from me.

Sure, I could go get it.

I decided, *Ah, no. Not doing that.*

As quickly as I could, I scanned what was some kind of dossier.

Cal Davis had served in the Army and had reenlisted for a second term. An athlete, he'd excelled in a variety of sports, including basketball and football. His academic scores were all high, too, but not some genius level. A personality assessment labeled the man as brave to the point of fearless. There was a hyperlink next to this with a (1) above it.

Taking a chance, I clicked on it, and a window popped up. It didn't populate with text right away. The wheel spun for a moment, and I worried it was logging in somewhere. A moment later, the words *Decryption Complete* appeared.

At the top of the pop-out box was a warning about the sensitive material, secrets, blah blah. In the upper corner was the number thirty.

I scanned past the boilerplate shit and found a passage that appeared to have been copied from some personnel notes. In italics, it read:

Pvt Davis shows an incredible aptitude for quickly assessing changing circumstances and taking action. We've run him through the Breighton-Mansoul tests and not seen better results in any other candidate.

When stressed, Davis shows total calm and clear thought.

Decisive and fearless (2).

Some hesitation in the morality measurements for this candidate, as—

The borders of the screen flashed. Once. Twice. That was when I noticed the "thirty" up in the corner had been a timer. Three seconds left.

I read quickly, and my panicked brain only picked up a few scraps of information before, three flashes later, the decrypted text box disappeared.

My finger hovered over the (1) again, but I hesitated. Would opening it a second time set off some alarm? Why had there even been a countdown?

That was when I noticed Cal Davis's bio information on the primary screen's dossier.

Born in Barlow Creek, British Columbia. His home address was listed as Terrace, BC.

His mother: Linda Davis, deceased.

His father: John Davis, deceased.

Both deaths had been on the same date. A car crash? There was also a hyperlink next to that date, but I hesitated, worried about making the software ping off any alarms and, in truth, what did I care about the guy's dead parents?

I heard a noise outside. Maybe.

My nerves were fried. Could have been my imagination.

As I turned to leave, something on the screen caught my eye. I had to blink a few times to be clear about what I was looking at. Beneath the notation about his parents was another line of text.

Siblings: Brother, Kane Davis, deceased.

What the hell?

Could that be my Kane? It couldn't. For one, he wasn't deceased. But how many Kanes were there out there?

I took a step back, shaking my head. What the hell had I gotten into?

Something pressed against the middle of my back, and I realized that I'd stumbled against a bureau along the far wall. When I turned, I saw it wasn't a piece of furniture. A long black cloth covered a rounded base.

I shot another look at the door, the flap hanging open. Hadn't I closed it?

Didn't matter. I had to get the hell out, but curiosity got the best of me. I lifted the heavy cloth and found glass underneath. Rounded, dark inside.

The red light was too dim at the far side of the tent, so I stepped over to the gear table and found a penlight, went back to the long glass cabinet, lifted the cloth again, and clicked it on.

I covered my mouth so I didn't cry out.

Pine Valley's monster lay beneath the glass, undeniably dead. The body of Bridget Mills was long and muscular, but the limbs were distended and strange. The skin looked rippled and stretched, as if she'd had a growth spurt in her thirties.

Her body was beaten, bruised, and smashed. I had to stifle a crackle of acid from my stomach that was desperately trying to rise up into my throat as my eyes passed over her.

Skin flayed. Bones split.

Someone had carefully sliced through her legs, splaying out muscle fibers, tendons, and snaking blood vessels. The skin had been grotesquely flayed opened and pinned into what appeared to be a thick bed of black wax. What had been her right foot was now only a bloody pulp, and I fought the urge to gag.

This had all taken time.

I shined the penlight's beam up to her face. High cheekbones, large protruding forehead. Her lips parted into a gruesome scowl revealing oversized teeth flecked with black.

The amber eyes that had been so fierce were now glassy and dull.

Her last moment of defiance had been captured in death like a photograph she now wore on her face.

But this monster had once been just a woman in town doing her best to get by, day after day. Went to work. Maybe cheered the local boys at Friday night Pine Valley football games. Gossiped with friends in the cereal aisle of Cub Foods.

Then after a chance run-in with a crazed, infected man at a car show, that life ended. The one solace may have been that she'd likely also ended the life of her wife-beating husband.

But she's never asked for this. She'd never *wanted* this. And now, she lay dead and broken and pinned up like a goddamn high school science experiment, stripped of everything that had once made her human.

My lip trembled as I tenderly reached toward the glass. I whispered, "I'm sorry for what happened to you."

A voice rose behind me. "What the hell are you doing here?"

Chapter Forty-Two

The voice shot an electric punch up my body, nearly taking my head off when it reached the top. I spun around and saw the woman called Mon standing at the tent flap, her rifle swung off her back and pointed at me.

When she snapped on a light just beneath the muzzle of the barrel, my entire world turned white. I held up a trembling hand to shield my eyes from the glare.

"Jesus. You?" she whispered. "What in the hell are you doing?"

I stepped forward, and the light bobbed higher. She'd pointed the rifle at my head.

But she hadn't called out to her comrades. Not yet. As my mind wove through panic that turned my stomach sour and my mouth dry, that puzzled me.

She hadn't shot me on the spot.

She hadn't called in her boss, Gregor.

Why not?

The beam of light dropped to the stony ground, reflecting tiny stars up her body and across the tent walls. Bathed in dull white sparkles, Mon looked to her right, and I braced for her to finally call out, bringing in Gorilla Tits, the tech sergeant, and whoever else was over there.

She didn't.

Mon took a step forward, and the starfield vanished. She'd raised her weapon, but this time, she hadn't pointed it right at me.

I tried to say something. Anything. Why had she hesitated?

"I just..." I started but lost my words.

She growled at me. "Are they checking up on me?"

I shook my head. I had no idea what else to do.

"Are *you* checking up on me?" She said in an angry whisper. When I didn't respond, she took a step closer, and my vision washed with white once again. "Wait. Show me your eyes."

Show her my eyes?

She was pointing the flashlight right in my face, so how the hell was I supposed to do that?

Mon stepped closer, the light knifing deeper into my brain. But in the darkness, the glare reflecting off my face had to be blinding her too. I took a chance.

Reaching into my pocket, I pulled out the grenade and chucked it at her feet. She pointed the beam down, saw the explosive, bent at the knees, and backflipped out of the tent.

What the hell?

She'd realize in seconds that I hadn't pulled the pin. I used those seconds to drop to my feet, find the bottom of the tent wall at my back, lift it, and roll outside.

Before me was the big glass lake and its glittering halo of stones. Sure, I could jump into the water, but that would make me an easy target. I started to run toward the hill but only got three steps before a rifle butt smacked me in the forehead, knocking me to the hard, cold stone below.

Mon stood over me, a wild look in her eyes.

"You've got five seconds," she said, her voice low but rippling with rage. "Who sent you?"

My mind was a jumble, not just from the bash to the head but because fear was ping-ponging thoughts around my brain, none of them cooperating. I was going to die on that stone beach as the cicadas chirped all around us, happy and indifferent to the petty concerns of humans.

She leaned forward and pressed the barrel to my tender forehead. "Did they send you?"

I had always prided myself on being a first-rate bullshit artist, but in that moment of terror, my art failed me. An image flashed in my mind, that of Bridget Mills lying on the table just a few feet from me on the other side of the tent.

Crazed eyes. Mouth forever frozen in an open-mouthed scream.

Would someone find me wearing a similar death mask days or weeks from now?

The world went black for a moment, and I realized that I'd closed my eyes.

No. No, stay in the game!

I had to fight. Somehow, I had to fight.

When I felt the rifle barrel lift from my head, I opened my eyes and saw Mon turning away from me. Something had caught her attention, and I just knew Gregor or his big gorilla henchman would roll up next to her with a big, shit-eating grin on his face.

That was when I heard the rumble.

No, not a rumble. A growl.

The commando woman took one step away from me, swinging her rifle around into the darkness. Her head darted left to right like a predatory bird's then back over her shoulder. She'd heard it, too, but couldn't work out where the sound had come from.

She spun back to me, baring her teeth. "Who else is out—?"

The shimmer of oily black skin flashed out of the darkness. Something, some *creature* had burst from the other side of the tent, its feet never touching the stones below.

Mon was on the ground, struggling to lift her rifle. Long rows of teeth clamped down on her forearm. She dropped the gun. Her free hand came up to clobber the creature with a fist, but it was too fast. Unnaturally fast.

Its muzzle released her right arm and, a fraction of a second later, clamped onto her throat. A burst of blood sprayed across Mon's face. Her expression contorted as some tumbler in her brain fell and her rage clicked over to fear.

She drew in a damp, ragged breath to scream.

Standing on her chest, its mouth bubbling red with her blood, a rottweiler twisted its massive head slightly, and I heard the crack of bone. The unborn scream died in her throat as she sucked in another damp breath. The pain had to be mind-bending.

Her next inhalation would be the last she'd ever take. The massive dog, easily as heavy as she was, dropped its hind end and launched at her open mouth, digging and gnawing. A pale hand came up in a weak, flailing attempt to push the animal off.

As I lay there, watching, horrified, the motion was so slight and languid, it almost looked as if she were stroking the beast amid some macabre, passionate kiss. She tensed, fingers curled as she drew her fingernails down its flank.

Another twist from the rottweiler's head, its powerful jaw now clamped in the hollow between her chin and neck, and blood sprayed.

She was dead.

My voice trembled as I spoke. "Kane?"

Aside from the initial low growl, the muscular dog hadn't made a single sound. Not a bark or guttural utterance at any point during the fierce attack. The only noise had been the two of them landing on top of the pebbled beach, barely audible over the insects merrily chattering all around us.

"Kane?" My mind slowly floated down to me, slipping itself back into my skull. Scraping my elbows against the stone, I backed away from the creature digging into her ruined throat.

No, not digging. It was... suckling?

Horrified, I muttered, "Jesus Chr—"

The dog snapped its head toward me, and my eyes stung as some warm dampness sprayed my face.

"You must be quiet," it said in a low, strange voice. Strange, yes, but it was Kane. Not that I was familiar with *speaking dogs*, for fuck's sake, but this one had a French-Canadian accent.

I stumbled to my feet, my head spinning. Putting my hand up to my face, I felt for the lump where Mon had smashed me with the rifle. When I pulled it away, I saw blood. That scared the shit out of me until I realized it wasn't mine.

Mon's blood.

The same life-giving liquid that my friend appeared to be drinking out of her now-dead body.

As I shook my head, my voice came out in a husky whisper. "What the fu...?"

Kane's head snapped up, chunks of pink flesh tumbling from his mouth. Yellow streaks of what may have been fat or viscera fell back onto the dead woman's face. The dog's ears perked, twisting in the night air like tiny electronic dishes looking for a radio signal.

He hopped off the woman, his weight so massive that her entire body appeared to shrug as if to say, "Well, I'm glad that's over!"

Shit, I'm losing it.

Staring at her, I hadn't noticed Kane come up next to me. He repeated a question, his ragged breath hot against my hip.

"Are you all right, Sad Girl?"

My eyes fell closed, and I fought tears. Nodding, I told him I was.

"Then we must go," he said, his head flicking toward the truck on the other side of the encampment. "Quickly and quietly."

I followed the massive black dog as it stalked through the darkness. He could move much quicker but kept his speed at one I could maintain. For most of the journey upward, I was only following the reflection of the moonlight off his sleek, black body.

Ten minutes later, we were back to the top of the hill, and we both turned and looked down.

I stared at the structure below. Earlier, it had looked like just a blank space by the lakeside. Now that I knew the layout, I could just make out the edges of the tents. The long dark tarp at the far side, I now knew, hid two vehicles. Inside the van were Gregor, Gorilla Tits, and at least one other.

Back in the tavern, Gregor had referred to a person I'd not seen yet: *"Doc Hammer's waiting for the Mills woman and wants her alive."*

That must have been the third person in the van. Doc Hammer had likely been the one who'd dissected the body of Bridget Mills.

From what I'd seen in the bar, despite the doctor's orders, the only way Gregor & Co. had survived the she-beast was by killing her. Had that screwed up their plans? Why would it matter if she were alive or dead?

My mind back in the present, I wondered how long it would be before they came looking for their missing comrade, Mon.

From here, I couldn't see her body. But it was there. I knew it was there.

"Jesus," I said, going down on one knee. "You killed her."

Kane nodded his massive black-brown head. "She would have killed you."

"Yes, but..."

"We must go."

"You—" I struggled to find the words. "I mean, the *blood*. Why?"

"Later. Not safe here."

He turned, and I thumped my head with the heel of my palm, trying to reset my brain. She *would* have definitely killed me. No question. For now, I had to put the thoughts of the dead woman out of my mind.

"At least this time, you didn't turn into a Labradoodle or something," I said, watching the huge animal's muscles ripple beneath its skin.

Not looking at me, he asked, "What is Labradoodle?"

"Doesn't matter," I said. "You've got some explaining to do, little doggie."

Kane turned to me, and I involuntarily took a half step back. The dark face was stained red with blood. His eyes searched mine, and something told me not to recoil. He was looking at me so oddly. I couldn't quite read it.

Then my thoughts went back to the woman who lay dead, alone, on the stony beach below.

"Did you have to... chew on her like that?" I shivered. "Shit, that was awful."

The dog chuffed. "Must sever the artery to the brain."

"She was obviously going to die without that, Kane."

"Maybe," he said. "Also, I needed her blood. Not having, this makes me weak."

I had so many questions, but right now wasn't the time. "Thank you, by the way," I said. "How did you even know I was here?"

The big head swung back toward the car, where the light from a phone lit Denny's face. "I followed."

"Followed? You followed a moving car?"

"It was not moving very fast," he said. He walked ahead of me, putting distance between us and the lake below. "It is a shitty car."

Chapter Forty-Three

Denny nearly jumped out of his seat when I walked up.

"Oh, thank God, I nearly came..." His voice trailed off as he stepped out of the vehicle. "What the hell happened to you?"

I laughed. I must have been a helluva sight coming out of the darkness, bruised and bashed. And despite my attempts to wipe Mon's blood off my mouth, I knew I hadn't gotten all of it.

"Ran into some old friends," I said with a wry smile.

Yes, yes. Okay.

I'd come up with that line on the two-minute trek from the hilltop back to the car. I knew I'd look like something out of a war movie when the guy saw me. And I wanted something badass to say, because I realized that was how Denny saw me.

That was how Miss Florida had.

How dozens of people with their casserole offerings had.

Me.

Emelda Thorne, badass.

I'd never, not ever in my entire life, been seen as a badass, and now I had a whole goddamn town who thought that. Despite the danger, the near-death experience—several of them, actually—I was a bit drunk on that feeling.

I had never felt powerful.

Or maybe it was just not feeling so weak. Sure, Kane played his part, but I had stood my ground with Mon. I'd been the one to sneak down into a camp filled with gun-toting... what? Beast fighters and back-flippers?

And I had lived.

Okay, in the end, I *had* lived because of Kane.

But everything up to that point, before the second time I'd almost died, yes, that had all been me.

The expression I'd seen on Denny's face earlier had been something like awe or admiration. Of me. This was all new territory.

Not a boastful, bragging, "look at me" thing.

It was just a good feeling, being valued, and I never wanted it to end. But I needed to be more careful. Had Kane not shown up, would I have made it back up here alive?

I pushed that thought aside and told Denny we had to leave. He rounded the car and yanked the driver's-side door open. When he turned to me, he was smiling.

That smile turned to horror a second time. "What the hell is that?"

Oh. Right.

I'd asked Kane to hang back a few paces despite his insistence that we had to clear out. I had planned on warning Denny about the appearance of a big, terrifying dog. Slipped my mind.

"It's okay," I said. "He's with me."

Booyah! I hadn't even planned on saying that one, it just came to me. I liked this badass shit.

Kane padded up to my side and chuffed. Our driver's eyes never left us as he slipped inside the car.

Standing at the open passenger door, I reached down and patted Kane on the head.

He sidestepped me and whispered. "Do not pet my head. I am not a dog."

"Um, you are," I whispered back.

"I am wolf."

I laughed. "Yeah, not so much."

* * *

As we drove, Denny's questions were endless. Mostly, I listened and watched Kane in the visor's mirror. I caught my driver stealing glances back too.

I told Denny as little as I could about what had happened below. Thankfully, he accepted most of my "I can't talk about that" answers. Of course. This guy saw me as some monster hunter. Did he think I was part of some government team? Freelance?

It didn't matter.

The implication, if nothing else, allowed me to brush off most of his questions.

"Where did *he* come from?" Denny asked, looking at the rearview mirror.

I shrugged and leaned my head against the window. The cool glass felt amazing against my skin. I smiled.

"Oh, I've got a special whistle," I said, trying to hide my smile. "He comes when I call him."

"Right," Denny said, as if this made total sense. "I'd heard stories that there was a dog at the farm the other night. You know, when you took down the creature."

That caught my attention. I looked over.

"No one knew much," he stammered. "Just rumors. But the guy who owns the place said he'd seen a dog. Not big like this one. Kinda small and fat."

Kane let out a low growl.

I shot a glance at him. *Don't do that.*

Denny didn't seem to notice. "Why didn't your boss go with you tonight if you knew there might be trouble?"

My boss? Oh, right. I had said that I was Kane's driver.

"Well, you know, bosses. You do all the hard work while they lie around all day."

"I heard *that*!" Denny said, laughing.

When I looked up into the visor's mirror, I nearly giggled at the face on the little doggie back there, his lip curling up in a snarl.

"Yeah," I said, laying my head back on the window again. "He'd get nothing done without me."

Chapter Forty-Four

By the time we got back to the farmhouse, clouds had started to move in. The gravel crunching under the tires sounded too loud as we slowly rolled up the driveway. I was still on edge. Glancing back at rottweiler Kane, I saw him scanning the darkness on the other side of the car's windows.

That didn't calm my sparking nerves. Not a bit.

"Oh, I wonder what that is," Denny said as he clicked off the ignition. I snapped my head in the direction he was looking.

"What?"

He eased out of the car, and I clicked out of my seat belt and opened the door. I got jostled as Kane bounded out, knocking my seat forward. Grunting more out of frustration than effort, I climbed out.

Denny was loping toward the farmhouse door. Above the stoop, a single light bulb was locked in battle with a thick swarm of flying insects. So far, it was winning.

"I'm hoping it's pie. I could use pie," he said, bending down and lifting yet another dish from the threshold. "Oh, not pie." He turned to me with a big smile.

I shrugged, wondering where Kane had run off to.

"What is it, then?"

"Smells sweet. Like apple crumble or something," he said and took a big, exaggerated sniff. "There is a god."

Once we got inside, Denny plopped the dish on the table and spun to the drawers. He pulled out a fork but then caught me walking in, blanched, and grabbed two plates. He smiled at me sheepishly.

"You want?"

I shook my head.

Then he looked behind me at the open door. "Where'd the big, scary dog go?"

"He's, um, scouting."

The monster hunter had spoken about her charge, and he'd taken that pitiful reasoning at face value. Maybe he was just deferring to my faux expertise. Or just really focused on the apple crumble.

I told him goodnight and quietly padded down the dark hallway toward our room. Halfway there, a door opened, and I flinched. Standing there was Miss Florida.

"This ain't a hotel, you know," she said, not unpleasantly. "You're as bad as my kid. Going out at all hours of the night."

Leaning back on the wall, I frowned. "Sorry about the noise."

"Not worried about the noise. Truth be told, it kind of brings the house alive." Miss Florida smiled widely. Then it lost a few watts, and she nodded toward the room I'd been heading toward. "Your big friend burst out of here right as you guys left. I peeked out the window after him, none of my business, but he must have been moving fast. I couldn't see him."

I almost asked whether she'd seen a black-and-tan dog out in the moonlight, but I just wanted to get to the room. I didn't have any answers, only more questions. Nothing I could say to her would be of any comfort.

"Oh, he's a fitness nut. Probably just out for a night jog."

She looked at me, her frown lines deepening as she examined my face. "Looks like it was a rough night. Figured it might be, so I put out some extra towels in the bathroom."

I thanked her.

She wished me goodnight and went back into her room.

Realizing she didn't want my "rough night" all over her linens, I trotted upstairs and took a two-minute shower. Then spent twice as long getting all the dirt, sand, and blood to go down the drain.

Back downstairs, I closed the door before I clicked on the light. Kane was sitting on the bed. I closed the window and drew the curtains.

"Where'd you go?" I whispered.

He shrugged, which is a strange mannerism to see in a dog, actually.

"Checked to see if we were being followed," he said, avoiding my eyes. "Quick check. Also, the boy was looking at me in a strange way. I felt it would be better if I was not there anymore."

Exhausted, I plopped down on the bed.

Kane looked toward the window, taking a half step toward it. "I should maybe do another quick—"

"Uh-uh, doggie dearest," I said, keeping my voice low. "I have so many questions."

He'd known this was coming. Kane turned back toward me like a child caught with cookie crumbs down his shirt.

"I do not have many answers. This is why I have been searching."

For the next few minutes, I told him about sneaking down to the encampment. About seeing Gregor, the big guy, Mon, and the other faceless lacky. I told him about finding Bridget Mills. The entire time, he just listened, expressionless.

I assumed he was expressionless. I'm no good at reading dog expressions.

When I stopped to organize what I was going to say next, he said, "You did very well. I stayed out of sight and only stepped in when I felt I must."

"What?" I felt my anger rise up but kept my voice low. "She had a rifle pointed at me in the tent, Kane!"

"You handled it. Nice trick with the tiny bomb."

Tiny bomb? Right.

"I got lucky with the grenade. I don't know jack about those things, so I had no idea if chucking it down might, I don't know, loosen something and set it off."

"You did fine."

"Thanks for the vote of confidence," I said. "You were hurt, I thought. Why did you risk following me?"

"We are a pack of two. It is my job to be sure you are okay."

That hit me like a gut punch. Not a bad one, mind you. I can tell the difference; I'd had plenty of the bad ones. Had he just called me family?

I shelved that thought. My questions needed answers.

"I saw some stuff about Cal Davis. A dossier," I said, then held up a single finger. "First time I've ever used that word in an unironic manner, by the way. This is my world, now."

This piqued his interest, and he moved a paw toward me. "Did it say where he is?"

Frowning, I shushed him, telling him to keep his voice down.

"No, Kane. There wasn't much," I said then glared at him. "But it said his brother is Kane Davis. *Kane.* Not a common name, is it?"

He pulled the paw back and looked down. That was all I needed to know something was up.

"What aren't you telling me?"

I waited.

After a moment, he shrugged again and said, "Not so much to tell."

"Fine, tell me what you do know. You kept that from me, so you owe me."

He nodded. "Cal Davis was the child of Mère and Père."

"Your parents."

"Human parents, yes."

It made sense and did explain something I'd wondered about.

"That's why he'd been way up in British Columbia, in the middle of nowhere. He'd been going to see his parents?"

Kane nodded. "I believe he was on the run. So felt his only refuge was his ancestral home." The big dog shifted its weight and turned his head away as he spoke. "From what I understand, from what Père told me, Cal Davis was close to the property when he spotted me with my pack after we'd made a fresh kill. I had gotten mine so had allowed the others to eat."

The thought of it sickened me slightly. "You were still a wolf, then?"

He nodded again. "But I think... the sight of the blood," he said, then clarified, "on me. Cal had been driving the stolen purple car, saw the blood, and was compelled by it. He came after me."

That got a dark chuckle out of me. "Some man taking on five hungry wolves? Jesus, he must have been batshit crazy."

"Part of it, yes. But he was not like other humans," Kane said, struggling with his words. "The memories are confusing—from my wolf body to this one—but Cal Davis was larger. Stronger. Stranger than other people me and my pack had encountered."

That tickled something in my brain. "Like Bridget Mills."

"Similar, yes. However Cal Davis changed me, it is clear he also changed them. Although differently because—"

"*You* are wolf, right." I nodded. "They became like him, some superhuman beast monster. Why did he attack you in the first place?"

"I stood my ground to protect my pack, thinking he would yield," he said. "He did not. I indicated to my family they should retreat to the woods. When I turned back, he leapt upon me. He moved impossibly fast."

"Jesus."

"Cal Davis broke both of my front... legs," Kane said, closing his eyes. "So fast. The entire time, he was salivating and licking the blood from my face."

"Oh my god."

"He had bared his teeth to take my neck, and I fought him. But I was only delaying. There would be no way to stop such a man. Not a man like that."

"How did you—?"

"Père fired a shot," he said. "I do not know if he knew his son Cal Davis had been coming. Maybe so. I think either Père or Mère had said that later, but back then, I did not understand your language."

"So your human dad had been out there to meet Cal, saw him attack you, and shot him?"

Kane shook his massive head. "Not shooting Cal Davis. A warning, maybe. I do not know. My attacker released me, ran to his purple vehicle, and sped off."

"But you were injured."

Another nod. "I passed out, as you say. When I awoke, it was because of shaking. I realized I was inside a vehicle."

Now I got it.

"Cal's dad picked you up. Put you in the car," I said and got a nod in return. "Why would he do that?"

"As I say, my memories are jumbled. But I do believe I had seen the old man before. We had never given him trouble, so..."

I waved him off. "It doesn't matter now. So he took you to his home."

"Yes. I had a place with blankets, in what I know now as a barn," he said, and a sad smile crossed his dog face. Weird. "Mère had come out and bound my forelegs with sticks and rope. She tended to my wounds. They were kind to me."

"Wait, you didn't, you know, attack them. You were a wolf, right?"

"I am still wolf," he said then looked down at himself. "Still wolf. But my brain was changing. Confused. Any thoughts of attacking or all of that... I could barely hold a thought. After Mère tended to me, I fell asleep in the barn." He hit me with a strange look. "The next morning when I awoke, my arms were screaming in pain."

"They were broken, Kane. I know how bad that—"

He shook his head. "No. I *had* arms. Not the legs of a wolf. Human arms. I was wailing, with strange sounds coming from me."

He told me that when the couple came out, they'd taken up a few minutes with frantic whispers, but he'd been wailing in pain and clawing—with human fingers—at his bindings. Eventually, they loosened them.

"But still broken arms," he said then chuckled. "And now I was human, it maybe seemed improper for me to be in barn. They took me inside. Allowed me to heal. Spoke to me, which was terrifying, but they were patient."

"How long did it take you to learn, you know, our language?"

"Yours? English?"

I nodded.

"Not English first. Père was French, and he spoke to me at first. I think he worried about Mère being left with me. French first, then English. I find English very much more confusing."

"Me too. But you eventually got it."

Kane lay down on the blankets, blinking slowly. "After a few days, I understood him in French."

"A few *days*?"

"Yes." Kane's eyes fell closed. "It had taken me some time."

"That's not a lot of time, Kane."

"By the next week, English, because Mère was English. She was nice. From Winnipeg. She knew French but preferred her native language."

"You learned French and English in a week?" I stared at him. "Damn, that makes me feel dumb."

"After that, they knew as a young man, if I was to remain in this form, that I needed... um... paperwork. Identification. Their younger son had died as a child. Kane. I became Kane."

Something about the story confused me.

"Wait, hold on," I said, still keeping my voice low. "You skipped over the part where two old Canadians in the hinterlands saw a wolf turn into a dude and they went, 'Yeah, makes total sense.'"

Kane opened one eye and chuckled. "The way humans look at their old as if they are somehow stupid. As if years and life make one dumb. Of course, it is obviously the opposite of this."

"Right," I said. My eyes were getting heavy, so I grabbed a pillow, propped it behind my head, and leaned back. "So in all that wizened experience, life, they totally bought that animals turn into people."

"I do not know," he said then looked toward the curtained window. "But there was a time, early, when I believe I saw Cal Davis outside the barn. Maybe not see. Hear. Voices. At that time, I did not know words, so I don't know what they spoke of."

I pointed at him. "You think Cal told them something. About you?"

"Maybe. Or maybe what had happened to him," he said, now opening both eyes, "which explained why the wolf became a man."

And that, really, explained Kane in a nutshell. He was just someone trying to find a way back to his old life. Me, I was the opposite—looking for a way out of the life I'd been living. Sometimes, that desire had taken me to embarrassing extremes.

Burying that thought, I put a hand out to his hand. Well, paw.

"Do you think your family misses you?" It was a stupid question, but I was trying to see the world through his eyes.

He thought about that for a moment. "With wolf, these are complicated emotions. Hard to translate into human ideas. There is a longing for the familiar because that is safe. Protected." Kane struggled to find the right words then sighed. "Yes, I believe they do miss me."

"Do you have, you know, wolf babies?" I couldn't help but laugh. "This is one of the most bizarre conversations I've ever had, by the way."

"Me too. But no, I do not have children. I hope to in the spring, but first I must return to my wolf wife."

I had a million other questions, but he and I were both tired.

And asking questions about his past seemed to only sadden my friend. He'd been through enough for the night.

"Get some rest," I said. I got up and clicked off the light. "In a few days, you should be healthy enough in your big human body to get on the road."

In the dark, I saw the two marbles of his eyes staring at me, light reflecting in tiny crescent arcs.

"Where? Where would we go?"

"Well, the monster hunters have done their work in this here town," I said, briefly affecting an old-timey cowboy voice. "If Cal had been heading back to your parents' house last year, maybe it wasn't just about seeing

Mom and Dad. Maybe there's someone else up there. An old friend. Or some hideaway of his. Worth a look, yeah?"

When he didn't answer, I noticed the two tiny reflected lights had gone dark.

Kane had fallen asleep.

Chapter Forty-Five

Despite crashing late, I was up before dawn. When I'd dragged the sheet up over Kane's body, his big doggie legs were twitching. I smiled. Was he chasing rabbits? Or were they wolf dreams? Chasing his wolf wife?

I clicked the door closed and padded quietly into the kitchen.

Miss Florida was already up. I'd heard her shuffling minutes earlier, and before I said a word, she reached into the cupboard to grab me a mug, silently promising the ambrosia of caffeine and warmth on a chilly morning.

For now, we were just two people watching the world get its shit together to begin its day. We took our coffee out on the wraparound porch as sunlight began to drizzle through the trees and hills around us.

"I spent a bunch of summers as a kid on a farm like this," I said, sipping my coffee. "Well, not like this. That place was probably three times the size. The land itself went for miles and miles."

"Good memories?"

I shrugged. "A few. Once I got past the smell, always took a day or two, I liked the animals. My aunt and uncle never stopped working until well past dark. Seems like a hard life."

"A hard life is doing a job you don't enjoy. If it's in ya, you love it even when it is hard. Maybe more then."

I cocked an eyebrow at her. "You a part-time philosopher?"

"Comes with being old, my dear. But sure, when I look back to the times I remember most in my life, it's never the easy-breezy times. It's like they don't have substance I can hold onto. Mostly, I recall the hard stuff, and how I got through it."

Looking down at the dark swirling liquid in my cup, I said. "Some of that, I'd rather forget."

"Ah, try to hold onto the part where you got out of it. The victory at the end. Or if not victory, just the fact you survived it."

"I get that."

"There had to be happy times on that farm, right? Maybe you've got a bit of farmer in you?"

"Ha, no," I said. "Most of my time, I spent running from two older cousins. Two and three years older. We played hunting games."

"Well, that sounds fun." Miss Florida screwed up her face. "Sorta."

"Not when you're the one being hunted."

She put a hand to her throat. "Oh, wow. That sounds kind of dangerous."

I shrugged. "Thankfully, they didn't use real guns. Paintball, but they had some pretty wicked setups. I tell you what, you get one of those in the back—or a dozen—and you feel it for a few days. Hurts like a mother—um, hurts like a mother."

Miss Florida laughed. "I ain't a prude, now. I can take some light cursing," she said. "You ever tell your aunt and uncle about it?"

Shaking my head, I said, "I was too stubborn. Or proud. Or worried my cousins would only beat the shit out of me if I did." I laughed to let her know it was okay if she did. She didn't but smiled.

"Doesn't seem very nice."

"Oh, after I paraded around in a bathing suit, covered in welts, the cousins finally evened the playing field. A little."

"You got your own paintball gun."

"No, those weren't cheap, and I don't think they liked even odds." I chuckled. "I could finally shoot the little paint pellets at them, but old-school style. They'd given me one of their old wrist rockets."

"A *what* now?"

I held one arm out straight, my other fist beside my chin. "Slingshot. Half the time, those little paintballs just mashed in my hand, so I had a rainbow of colors all down my wrist and arm. By the end of the day, I looked like I'd gotten into a fistfight with Bob Ross."

She covered her smile with a hand.

I told her, "But by that third summer, I got pretty damn good with the slingshot and had a whisper of a chance."

She was at a loss for words then but managed. "Did... did that make it any, you know, better?"

"Not really. I got a few good shots in, but the slingshot was terrible. Only way I could ever hit either of them was to get up close. At that range, I probably would have done more damage if I'd thrown the damn thing at their heads." I shrugged. "Which I did do on one glorious occasion, sure."

That brought her another laugh, and we fell into silence again, enjoying the new day.

For the next ten hours, I helped Denny with the final repairs on the Jeep. He had to make two trips into town. One was for the muffler, which had rusted through because this was Minnesota and mufflers were the state's archenemy. That and the undercarriages of cars. The second time was for a new set of tires, since the ones on the Jeep had been sliced after sitting on their rims for a few years.

I'd offered to pay—or, rather, let Kane pay—but Miss Florida wouldn't hear of it.

Later that afternoon, we were back on the porch once again. Kane hadn't once come out of the room, and I just let him sleep. In truth, it was nice to be with some normal folks for a while.

Sipping some iced tea, my host put her own glass down and leaned forward to get up. "We got a lotta casserole dishes to get through. I'll fire up the stove and—"

The sound of the phone ringing cut her off, and she looked toward the dimming sun. "Who the heck is calling at this hour?"

As she walked past me, I said, "Ha, did you just look at the sun to tell the time?"

She put a hand on my shoulder. "We only get a limited supply of nice moments, day in and day out. When you get a chance to look at something beautiful" —she motioned to the sun setting the treetops ablaze, its beams cutting ribbons through the late afternoon mist—"you take it."

"I'll do that," I said and squeezed her hand.

Once she'd left, I stared out at the quiet of the forest. Listening to the birds making last-minute plans for the day. The soft braying of a cow, just the one, tumbled through the grass. Maybe I could get used to living in the country.

The quiet.

The serenity.

When the screen door banged open, I felt the old woman's hand on my shoulder again. I looked up.

"There's been another attack."

Chapter Forty-Six

My heart was racing. Had Bridget Mills escaped? She'd been sliced and diced and split open! Jesus, could these monsters come back to life?

I couldn't handle that.

Sure, I hung around a massive human who moonlighted as a dog, but that had pushed me to my weirdness limit.

Despite the shitstorm I knew was coming, as Miss Florida's eyes grew wider, as she pressed her ear harder against the receiver, I smiled to myself.

Moonlights as a dog. That's a good one.

The entire time she listened, the old woman watched me. I don't think she blinked once. Her hand had gone to her mouth a few times.

"What?" I whispered and got a shake of the head in return. I understood the message: *Wait.*

I needed to wake Kane, so I headed down the hallway. He would still be beat to hell, but if Bridget had somehow gotten free, we weren't done. I wasn't sure if the farm would be the safest place. I needed to think.

"Yes, yes." Miss Florida nodded. "I got just the people."

I blinked and looked back. "What?"

Ignoring me, she spoke quickly into the phone. "Right. Yes, yes. I'll send them." She paused and then rolled her eyes. "Of course they will, Roger. This is what they do!"

Uh-oh.

She hung up the phone and spun toward me with her back against the wall. After taking a moment to compose her thoughts, she finally told me what was going on.

The attack had come just before dawn, when we'd been enjoying that first coffee and each other's company.

Like Pine Valley, the neighboring town of Gisborne had been under siege for the better part of a year. At least that's how the locals saw it, but same as here, no humans had been attacked so state authorities didn't get involved.

The same pattern of attacks. At first the creature had devoured pets, then, more recently, farm animals. This had to be the second monster Kane had mentioned: the original owner of the purple car. According to what our wooden-motorcycle-riding friend Dock had said, this was Charlie Boynton. Or whatever Charlie had become.

Miss Florida said the overnight encounter had, so far, just one casualty: a goat in a mall.

"In a mall?"

"Yes," she said. "It seems the folks down that way heard about our success—your success—here. You inspired them. Emboldened them. So they've got a mall that got shut down a while back because of all the flooding we've been getting."

"How did the goat—"

"I'm getting to that." She held up a hand. "The call came first from a man over there who raises hogs. Yesterday, he'd lost two, and they're big suckers, bigger than most people. This time, I guess, the fine people of Gisborne decided to do something about it."

I shook my head. "With a goat?"

"Right," she said. "You and your big friend proved these monsters could be stopped, so some of the people in the town put a goat in the mall over there. Chained up all the exits but one. Threw those doors open. They did it quietly because, of course, the corporation that owns that big complex would have never allowed it."

"How do you quietly bait a monster to come to a mall?"

"Small-town ingenuity involving buckets of offal," she said and shrugged. "Well, they got it. They never even saw the creature go inside, but they heard the goat screaming bloody murder."

"They've trapped it?"

She nodded, but then the lines in her face deepened. "But it didn't all go as planned."

"Of course."

Miss Florida sighed. “The creature, it’s been in there since early this morning. Tearing around. They’d waited for it to bust out and had people with rifles prepared to take it down.”

“It’s not a dumb animal,” I said. “It’ll work it out.”

Slowly she shook her head. “It’s not *coming* out. It’s still hunting.”

“More goats?”

Another shake of the head, then she looked out to the fading sun. This time, I didn’t think that beautiful image gave her any comfort.

“With all the flooding, the mall needs work to get back up and running again. Dozens of shops, jobs, people’s livelihoods are on hold until then. A lot of cleaning up—”

“Wait! What are you saying, Florida?”

She closed her eyes. “The clean-up crew,” she said, opening them slowly. “There are people in that mall.”

Chapter Forty-Seven

"What?"

She took a half step toward me. "They're not sure how many. Maybe a half dozen of them. The townsfolk think that crew heard the creature and locked themselves away somewhere. Hoped, maybe."

"And now it's hunting them." I cursed under my breath. "That's why it hasn't come out."

She nodded.

I spun away, striding down the hall toward our room. Busted-up Kane or not, we weren't done.

When I threw the door open, I yelped.

"Dammit, Kane," I said, covering my eyes to block out the naked human lying on the bed. I slipped in and closed the door. "Will you just... get into clothes already?"

"They are cumbersome," he said, reaching over for some sweatpants I'd left on the dresser.

"So are you, but I don't complain."

"You do complain," he said, sitting on the bed and slipping on the gray pants. "All the time."

I started to tell him about the new attack but then noticed something. I pointed at his skin. The sweats hadn't covered much of it.

"Your cuts and scrapes," I said and knelt on the bed. Pushing his head to the side, I saw that his massive back was pristine. "You're all better. In one day?"

He nodded and looked over my shoulder at me.

I lowered my voice. "Is that because you changed? Does that, you know, reset everything? Make you better?" It hadn't last time.

"No. I am better because of the blood."

I blinked and recalled the previous night, when he'd been suckling the life out of Mon's body. Of course, she would have died anyhow. But that didn't make thinking about those images less sickening.

"Why blood?"

He shook his head. "I only know that it is a hunger for it. Consuming gives strength."

"Which is why Cal hopped out of the car when he saw all that blood from your fresh kill," I said, hoping to not dredge up the sadness about his missing pack. "You're drawn to it?"

Another shake of the head. "There is much I do not understand."

"Like how you turn from this big-ass human into a lapdog?"

"There is that as well."

"At least when you went on paw patrol last night, you'd turned into a powerful killer canine," I said, smiling, trying to lighten his mood. "Any way you can bring *that* one out more often?"

"I have no control. Whatever happens happens."

Trying to read his face and work out what was going on in that big head of his, I noticed something else strange. I put my thumb on his chin.

"Wait, your skin is smoother, and you had crow's feet—" I said, and he raised an eyebrow. "Wrinkles around the eyes. But they're... they're gone."

"I slept well."

Thumbing his chin left, then right, I shook my head. "Are you *younger*?"

Before he could answer, a knock at the door made me jump. I told Miss Florida to come in.

"Denny has gassed up the Jeep for you guys," she said. She handed me a piece of lined paper with some written directions. "Here's how you get there. I've drawn a—"

"No, Ma." Denny came in around her and handed me a battered black device. "Here's one of my spare phones. It's prepaid, so don't use it so much for calling. But it's got mapping software. I've already plugged in where you need to go."

"We are going?" Kane said, looking at me.

"You've got another job," Miss Florida said with a ripple of excitement in her voice. "People need your help."

"Job?" Kane said, the word hanging in the air. Kane frowned at me but said nothing more. I didn't think he was afraid to go up against one of the creatures. It just hadn't been in our plans.

Now it was.

Chapter Forty-Eight

The mall was about forty-five minutes away, according to the digital map on the phone Denny had given me. Kane was digging through the duffle bag Miss Florida had handed us as we'd left.

I looked over, keeping one eye on the road. "Did she pack us a lunch?"

"Several lunches," he said, rummaging. "I do not see the pasta soup. We should go back."

"What?" I spun the wheel at the next turn. "There are people trapped in that mall, Kane. With one of those things in there."

He sighed. "So stupid. Why would they try to cage it so?"

"Because it's been terrorizing their town," I said and chewed on a fingernail. "Listen, you know who that is, right?"

Kane stared deep into the duffle, brooding. "The man who owned the purple car."

"Right, Charlie Boynton." Something occurred to me. "He used to live near Gisborne. I wonder why they stay local? Maybe it's some territorial thing."

My friend shrugged, still digging in the bag. I considered the timeline.

"So last year Cal Davis goes to the car show, attacks the owner of the purple Trans Am, and steals it."

Kane sighed and threw the bag into the back seat. "Charlie Boynton is now monster."

"Right. Cal's got his car now but then shows up at the Pine Valley showgrounds," I said, watching the dotted lines in the road disappear beneath the Jeep. "Bridget Mills gets attacked there."

"She becomes monster," Kane said, staring out his window at the fields racing past. "Later, ends up at Gregor's camp, dead and cut up like Christmas ham."

I grimaced at the coldness of it but pressed on. "After infecting Charlie and Bridget, Cal Davis heads north. Then he attacks you and your new adventure on two legs begins," I said. "Why do you think he ran home to Canada?"

"Why else?" Kane shrugged. "Gregor was hunting him."

That made sense. "Which explains our run-in with the tech sergeant a few days ago. The new season of car shows began, and he'd hoped Cal might turn up again. You ran into him in Minneapolis."

"I had been asking questions about purple car, yes. Tech sergeant confronted me, but I ran."

My jaw dropped. "You ran? How very un-wolf of you."

"Not running from Gregor," Kane said, then pointed to the ceiling of the Jeep. "Moon was coming out. But I did not run fast enough. In alley, I change into tiny dog. Humiliating."

I nodded. "And ended up under the boots of some asshole kids, right. That's when I found you. That's when I *saved* you."

He shrugged and muttered, "Yes."

My big friend rolled down the window. Leaning his head out for a moment, he let the wind tousle his thick mane of hair.

"There's a piece missing here," I said, tapping him on his big shoulder. He looked at me, hair dancing in the breeze. "If Cal Davis just needed a car, which is possible, why did he turn up at the car show in *another* town after he had one?"

Kane pulled his head in, looked at his hands, then to me.

"Right, of course," he said, nodding slowly. "He realized he does not like purple."

"What? No!" I looked over at him to see if he'd been joking, but with that stone face, I couldn't tell. "He went back because was searching for something at the car show and hadn't found it yet."

"Or someone."

* * *

When I pulled the Jeep up to the mall, we saw five pickups in the lot, all parked in a circle facing each other.

Beyond them, the darkened shopping complex lay like a giant that had been slain long ago. Its body left to rot. The rain had taken its toll on the building, leaving water stains on the walls and pooling on the floors inside.

At least a dozen people were out front, each with a rifle or shotgun. Not that these had helped them so far.

A man in a mud-stained cowboy hat called us over. We'd been expected.

I threw him a wave, and he turned to talk with his group. When I parked, I put a hand out over Kane's as he reached for the seat belt.

"Wait, before I forget. Last night, Mon said something I can't stop thinking about."

"Okay."

"She asked me something so strange," I said, trying to recall the exact wording. "Something like, 'Are they watching me? Are you with them?' It was along those lines."

"Okay."

"I think she thought I was part of some group and that's the only reason she didn't kill me right there and then. I don't know… like maybe we might be on the same side?"

"Okay."

"Stop saying 'okay,' okay?" I clicked out of my seat belt. "Who is the 'they'? What does any of that mean?"

Kane looked at me. "I understand none of this conversation."

Growling, I hopped out of the car and saw his big head lift past the passenger-side door. Then I watched the eyes of a dozen locals follow Kane as he stood. Their chattering had all fallen silent. If I was being honest, that warmed something deep inside me.

The man in the cowboy hat stepped up as we approached and introduced himself as Roger Peel. He'd been the one who'd called Miss Florida.

"You guys the monster hunters?"

"Yes," I said.

"No," Kane said.

Over the next few minutes, Roger filled us in on what was happening—or what they thought was happening—in the massive, dark mall in front of us.

As Miss Florida had explained, they'd chained all the doors and posted people at the exits. Farmers, shopkeepers, just everyday folks who wanted their nightmare to end like it had for Pine Valley.

"Our people are in pairs," Roger said. "Safer that way."

Kane frowned. "Or just doubles body count."

I elbowed him and prompted Roger to finish, twisting my grandmother's necklace between my fingers to calm my nerves. The more he spoke, the more it became clear that the thing they feared most—the thing an *entire town* feared—was what I was putting my hand up to go in and take on.

"We think," a woman who looked like the town's librarian said, laying a glossy mall map over the hood of one of the pickups, "that it's most likely the crew in there holed up in one of the maintenance tunnels. They run all through the back of the shops."

I'd worked in a mall years ago and knew all about those. "Don't those lead to a loading dock or an area where they can get out?"

Librarian Lady shook her head. "All that flooding weakened some of the structure. They had to fortify parts of it with big steel poles and such. Any exit out that way is blocked. Even if you could get around that way, if you moved a pole, it could bring the roof down on top of you."

"Damn," I said.

She turned and pointed at the building. "And that's three stories high. One floor goes out, and the other two could pancake down as well. The loading dock is not an option."

"Only way in is that door there," Roger said, nodding with his hat. "We can unlock it, but we won't leave it like that."

I laughed. "You want to lock us in?"

"Not just you," a balding, heavy-set man in overalls chimed in, pointing at a short woman with a ponytail pulled through her ball cap. "Janice is our police chief. Just before Roger suggested we ring you up, she called this in, so they're sending some team here. SWAT, I bet. You'll have, you know, backup."

Kane pushed through the group. "Only more people in danger," he said. "Unlock the door."

Roger called out, "Hold on, now. Don't you have gear or something?" He eyeballed Kane's sweatpants and the T-shirt Denny had loaned him, which stretched taut over his bulging chest. Across it were the words "Iron Maiden" atop a zombie-like creature holding a bloodied ax.

"No," Kane said over his shoulder as he walked away.

"Don't you got a big-ass rifle or anything?" Roger shouted to him.

I patted the man in the cowboy hat on his shoulder. "He's not a fan."

They all looked to me, and I swallowed then felt something in my brain move my legs and push me toward the door. What the hell was I doing?

Kane had the same thought.

When I came up next to him, he said, "Sad Girl should stay with the Fargo people."

"Fargo people?"

He nodded at the group. "Mère used to watch show. *Fargo*. They had same word sounds."

"Accents," I said. "And that's not actually—"

"No, you should stay."

I stopped as he continued to walk toward the mall's entrance. When I turned and saw the group, all eyes were on me. I ran up beside Kane again, matching his stride.

"Don't forget, I was the one who got you out of the burning milk shed, right?" I put a finger in his face. "Bridget Mills would have eaten your pug-dog body as an appetizer had it not been for me."

He didn't slow, but I did see a hint of indecision pass across his face.

"I won't put myself in danger, Kane."

His laugh sounded more like a bark. "Being *inside* is danger."

"So I'll just, you know, be behind you. You're big enough to block out the sun," I said and moved into his faint shadow to prove my point.

"No. Sad Girl must stay safe."

I skittered around him, blocking his path, and put out my arm to stop him.

"I am safest with you, Kane," I said, fighting the emotion bubbling into my voice. "If that thing gets out, I've only got the posse here to protect me. That doesn't fill me with confidence."

He shook his head but said nothing.

I moved closer, stood up on my toes, and put a hand on the side of his face to make him look at me.

"You and me are doing this," I said. "You have lost your pack for now. I get that. But I'm the one helping you get back to them. So for now, we are a pack."

Under his thick brow, Kane's eyes widened.

"We are a pack, you and me," I said. "We do this together."

"A pack of two?" he said with a half smile.

I sighed. "As big as you are, brother, more like two-point-five."

Chapter Forty-Nine

Janice the cop, not in uniform, by the way, jingled the keys on a massive metal loop, searching for the right one. After she found it, Janice took a long look inside, pulled a strap away from the top of the gun on her hip, and looked again.

"You sure you don't want to take a shotgun or something, darlin'?"

I frowned. "My name is Emelda. And no, I don't think it'll do much. I'll just end up shooting my foot."

"Or me," Kane said, his eyes scanning the darkness on the other side of the thick glass.

I could see another question was forming on her lips, but instead, she just nodded, unlocked the door, and looked at us. "Ready?"

We both nodded. A bit over dramatically, she counted down from three and pulled it open. Once we slipped inside, she slammed the door and reengaged the lock. Through the door's window, she gave us a wave, concern furrowing her brow.

"I kinda wish she wouldn't have slammed it," I said, my heart pounding so hard that my voice bubble-popped like a series of hiccups. "Won't that only draw Charlie Boynton closer to us?"

"This is what you want, is it not?"

"Is it?" Of course it was. We were going toward the thing everyone wanted to run away from. If it came toward us, even better.

Wait. *Was* that better?

What was I doing?

I was staying right behind the six-foot-seven French Canadian, that was what I was doing!

As we walked deeper inside, the sound of dripping water echoed throughout the empty space, a constant reminder of the flooding that had closed the mall. The darkness made it difficult to navigate, and I stumbled over debris scattered across the black tiled floor.

The stores that lined the hallways were dark, but I could see their merchandise still inside, secured by rollaway gates across their entrances.

On edge, I could feel my heart beat in my neck.

As I crossed from shadow to light and shadow again, I couldn't shake the feeling that we were being watched. The stillness of the air was suffocating and tasted like rot. Other than the constant drip of water, I could only hear our feet slapping the damp floors.

The sole light in the cavernous space was coming from the late-afternoon sun peeking through skylights above. Thankfully, those long windows ran the length of the ceiling. However, since they were three stories up, by the time the light got this far down, it was feeble and thin.

And, if I was being honest, spooky as shit.

"Oh, wow," I muttered, only realizing I'd said it out loud when Kane tensed, fell into a fighting stance, and scanned left and right.

I walked up to one darkened storefront and stared inside, pressing my nose to the glass. It had been years since I'd been in high school, but I recalled the thrill that had swirled all around me during prom season. A fever pitch of excitement that our home could never afford.

Before me, frilly outfits hung on display in bright colors, each promising a night to remember. In the center, a yellow dress, its bodice adorned with intricate beading and sequins that shimmered even in the dim light of the mall.

Spaghetti straps draped over the padded hanger like epaulets, waiting for a young woman to thread her arms through and be magically transformed into a vision that would either win hearts or break them.

Maybe both.

Kane leaned over my shoulder. "There is no time for window shopping."

"Just looking," I said and shrugged.

Walking farther into the shopping center, I spotted escalators that had once carried shoppers up and down the floors and which now stood still, covered in a layer of grime.

When I saw Kane's head twitching left and right again, I stopped walking. So did he.

"What is it?"

He tensed. "I can smell sweat. Cigarette. Axe body spray."

"Body spray?" I said. "I don't smell anything."

"I don't think that is the smell of Charlie Boynton."

"I dunno," I said, just talking to calm my nerves. "Maybe he came here to get ready for a date."

Kane frowned at me. "I think it must be the people who are trapped."

That squeezed whatever playfulness I'd been trying to fake right out of me. "You can smell them?"

"Yes."

"That's good, then. We know where to find them."

"No. If I can smell them, I believe Charlie Boynton can too." He started forward again.

We spoke in whispers as we walked.

Our plan, if it was a plan, was for Kane to get ahold of Charlie. How he was going to do that, I wasn't sure. And I had no idea how strong Charlie might be compared to my big friend. If they both had the same whatever coursing through their veins, maybe it would be an even fight.

Or would Kane have an advantage as a natural-born predator?

I didn't think about that. My job would be to get the trapped crew to the front of the store as quickly as possible and then out of the building.

"And not die," Kane said flatly. "That would be best as well."

"Good to know you care, Kane."

"Well, I cannot drive."

I looked at him and saw the grin on his face. Dude made a joke! I felt as if I was helping him grow into a real boy. Or something.

We rounded a corner, and an odd sound stopped us both. Distant pounding rang off the stone floors. Fists on a wall or door. Snarling, snuffling. In the darkness, we saw nothing ahead of us, but up ahead, somewhere in the twisty labyrinth of the mall, Charlie was there.

And by the sounds of it—and the look on Kane's face—the monster had found his prey.

"I hope they're barricaded in somewhere safe."

Kane frowned, his eyes darting to all the dark corners around us. "It won't matter. Charlie Boynton is smart, not a dumb animal. Still human. Mostly."

That had struck a chord in my brain. "He never went after people before. Neither had Bridget." I pulled Kane's chin to get him to look at me. "Why is he going after other humans now?"

"Hunger, maybe." My friend's eyes narrowed. "But there can be other reasons."

"Like?"

He opened his mouth to answer but stopped. Kane sniffed the air then growled and shook his head from side to side.

"Stupid human nose."

Creeping forward, we passed dark halls on our left and right that led to bathrooms and storage space. The snarling was getting louder. I could just hear it over the hammering of my heart.

We stopped at one juncture, and Kane looked around. When he pulled back, he looked at me and lowered his head. I leaned forward and saw the next short hallway was empty. Up about fifty feet, it bent to the left, another hall.

That was when I saw the dim shadow up ahead, dancing along the wall.

The monster was somewhere in the next hallway. We went through our plan again. Kane would first run in to pin Charlie down. I would hang back, and he'd call out when it was safe.

"Safe?" I whispered, smiling.

He clarified, "Safer." Kane stared at me.

I waited for him to say something then shrugged. "What?"

"Are you not supposed to count backward from three?"

I frowned. "Would that help?"

He shrugged. I shrugged back and put a finger to my lips.

Then I pumped my arm and held out three fingers.

Another pump: two fingers.

When I drew my arm back the final time, it felt as if my body had been dropped into a bathtub with a toaster shooting sparks on the bottom. My muscles tensed, freezing me in place. Beside me, I could hear the short, fast breaths of Kane.

We both fell back away from the hall, frozen, and staring up at the ceiling.

The electric current stopped, but my muscles had been overstimulated. I couldn't move. Then, in the darkness, a face came into view.

"Mall security." Gregor smiled as he looked down again. He nodded to someone else nearby, and the current fired up again.

My head exploded in a burst of light.

Then darkness took me.

Chapter Fifty

The slap to my face brought me back to consciousness, and I blinked away the crust of dried tears. I hadn't remembered crying.

My neck was aching, and all the other muscles in my body were screaming. I felt two hands on my shoulders holding me against a hard-backed chair. When I looked down, I saw Gregor's smug face, grinning as if it were all one big game.

"Ow, that hurts," I said, flinching away from his grasp. He had a two-tone snake of rope hooked in the crook of his arm and was wrapping one end of it around my outstretched hands.

He said in that singsong voice, "It'll all be over soon enough." Gregor came around and kneeled in front of me, hoping to savor whatever panicked look might be there. I scowled.

The tech sergeant yanked harder on my wrists as he bound them tight. I felt another set of hands on my shoulders squeeze me hard enough to break skin. I remembered those hands.

"Just hold still, little girl," Gorilla Tits said.

All those summers on the farm came back to me in a rush. With my older cousins treating me like I was part of some real-life mafia video game, I'd been tied up more times than I could count. I'd eventually learned it was best to comply but to do it on my terms.

I balled my hands into fists and watched as Gregor wrapped the rope around them. I think a part of him was disappointed I'd stopped struggling.

The big bastard behind me let go of my shoulders and fed another loop of rope around my chest. I began crying softly, taking deep breaths.

"You are hurting her," a deep voice rumbled from behind Gregor. "For every hurt you give to her, I will deliver that unto you tenfold."

This only made the tech sergeant laugh.

I cried harder and earned a frown from the guy.

"Enough with that," he said. "You're giving me a migraine with all that whining."

I stifled the sobs, intermittently holding my breath in big lungfuls. After a minute, the two of them were done. When they stepped away, I saw Kane across from me.

In any other scenario, I would have laughed. It looked comical.

Kane had been bound across his ankles, knees, thighs, and chest. Ropes had been snaked around his chair across his elbows, pinning them back. He had additional bonds across his forearms and his wrists.

"You think you got enough rope on him?" I asked, and Gregor looked at me curiously. I guessed he was surprised my tone had shifted so quickly from weeping girl to smart-mouthed woman.

Gorilla Tits stepped between us, holding a rifle. He whispered something in Gregor's ear and got a single nod in return. The big man walked behind me toward the door of what I now could see was some chain restaurant within the mall.

Christ, was I going to die in an Applebee's?

Gregor grabbed a chair and sat at an angle so he could see both of his captives.

I looked at Kane and saw him staring at me. He then flicked his gaze up behind me, toward the big bastard peering out the door into the dark mall.

"Emelda, so good to see you again," Gregor said, enjoying himself far too much. He nodded at Kane. "Aside from the occasional death threats, your friend is a quiet one," he said, but it had no playfulness to it. "FYI, that's not a healthy attitude to take."

How was Gregor even here? Had news of the monster come across some scanner? Or worse. Had Denny or Miss Florida told him.

No. No way.

I growled at the tech sergeant. "How did you find us?"

"*Find* you?" he said and laughed. "You found us. You do show up exactly where we want to be. That's curious to me."

"Bullshit. You put a tracker in my neck or something? How did you know to come here?"

"We got invited," he said, arms wide, leaning back onto two legs of the chair. "The terrified Gisborne townies had trapped a monster and, it being too much for them to handle, made a call. We just intercepted that call." He looked up to the gunman at the door. "Hell, these local hicks think we're the Feds or something. The cop asked for a badge, but I showed her an M4 and, well, they were happy for us to take care of their little creature problem."

"You're not here to help anyone," I spat. "You're not trying to save those people."

"I don't care two shits about those people, no," he said and nodded to Gorilla Tits—his part in some unspoken exchange with the guy behind me. I got a rifle barrel to the skull, which sent stars into my brain. I hadn't even heard the asshole come near. "And you're not the one who gets to ask questions. First time being tied up?"

I frowned at him. "Hardly."

"If you strike her again, I will rip your head off, Gregor," Kane said, his voice even, but the timbre of it sent a ripple of fear through even me.

The tech sergeant stared at me as he spoke with my friend. "You're strong, Kane. But not enough to get out of those ropes—they're of our own design. The other side has their nerds, we've got ours. Ours came up with those restraints for situations like this."

"Like this?" I asked.

"I don't know, some sort of enhanced fibers or whatever. I don't really care." Gregor's head lifted at the sound of a growl echoing through the cavernous mall. To his man, he said, "Go check that out."

"Go where?" Gorilla Tits said.

Gregor sighed. "Look out the window and see if it's coming this way. That would certainly speed this along."

The big guy huffed, and I heard his footballs moving away from me.

Gregor slapped both hands on his thighs and raised his eyebrows, looking at Kane then me. I supposed he thought I might be easier to talk to. Kane looked ready to kill him.

"Apologies to you both, but we've got a monster to catch, so I've got to make this quick," he said, taking a big breath and letting it out with a smile. "Whose blood was on the woman you killed last night?"

That wasn't remotely the question I'd expected.

Not that I knew what the hell the guy was on about, but his query was not even in the same universe as what I thought it would be. He pointed at me, waiting for an answer.

I shook my head. "What are you talking about?"

"Listen, I don't have time for this." Gregor grabbed a metal pole off a nearby table. As long as a mop handle, it had a ring of fat silver cylinders on one end near the loop of a rubber handle. Twin spikes jetted from the other end like fangs. "My comrade was busted all to hell—"

"You mean Mon?"

That stopped him for a moment. He eyeballed me then shrugged it off. "Yes, Monique. Are you the one she scratched?"

I recalled the woman raking her nails down Kane's side but clamped my lips shut.

"I'll ask again, and if I don't get an answer, I'll cut off a finger," he said then chuckled, waving the metal pole slowly between us like a metronome. "Then a hand, then, well, you know. It gets much worse from there."

Kane rattled against his bonds. "If you touch—"

Without even looking in my friend's direction, Gregor jammed the pole's fangs into Kane's neck, and it erupted with a rat-tat-tat and sizzling sound. Arc light streamed across my friend's clenched teeth.

I heard a breath escape from Kane then silence. His head lolled forward. He was out.

"Kane?" I called over. "Kane? Are you all right?"

Gregor looked down at his weapon. "Hard to tell the settings on this. New tech. Still working out the bugs."

"Did you kill my friend?"

The tech sergeant slithered to a knee in front of Kane. He sighed. "Well, he's breathing," he said and looked back over his shoulder. "For now. But I don't know how many shots like that he might be able to take. We could try a few more—"

"Just leave him alone!"

A low chuckle bubbled from the man when he turned away, his right shoulder tweaking and twitching as if trying to shoo away a bug. I tried to envision the look on the creep's face, then chased the unsettling image from my mind. His laughter rose in pitch just as his hand came up; the spiked metal pole swaying like a conductor's baton in front of my friend's placid face. Gregor's elbow lifted, and he jammed the spikes into Kane's throat.

Sparks bit into flesh, like a tiny, angry star trying to bore its way into his body. Still unconscious, Kane shook and writhed and jerked against the ropes. After several seconds, the smell of charred meat filled the air, and my eyes watered. I watched the skin beneath his chin blacken. Nothing I could say would stop the horrific abuse, so I bit my lip and quietly sniffed back a sob.

Then it stopped. Smoke from Kane's burnt throat drew wispy curtains across his face. A low wheezing sound dribbled from his lips.

Gregor went back to his chair, plopped down, and crossed his legs at the ankles, angling toward me. He kept his lightning rod trained on Kane.

"Who did Mon scratch?"

"She bashed me in the goddamn head," I said, gritting my teeth. "That's what I remember."

This prompted him to pull his legs back. He leaned closer to me.

"Did. She. Scratch. You?" He smiled wider with each word. "Was that your blood under her fingernails?"

I shrugged. "I don't remember."

He flicked his head toward my unconscious friend. "Or was it him? Was the big guy there?"

"No, the big guy wasn't there," I said, and he could see I was telling the truth. The big *guy* hadn't been there. Just a big dog.

"Then who?" Gregor roared at me, lifting out of his chair. I flinched. It was the first time I'd ever really seen him lose his shit. His eyes were wild, the cords in his neck straining, his face red.

Holy hell, this guy is unhinged.

"I-I don't really know," I said, feigning tears again. That came easily to me. "This animal came out of the dark and attacked. Knocked her down and it... fed on her."

"Animal?"

"Creature," I said, employing the same word he'd used earlier. Technically, it was true, although I didn't care about telling the truth. Truth has a different sound from a lie. Even a half-truth.

Gregor considered this, seemingly having an argument in his own mind. He looked up to the front of the restaurant, where his man was watching the door. Eyes still focused on the dark mall, he asked me, "Do you think it was that thing in there?"

"I don't know," I said. "Maybe."

He nodded and sighed. "That would explain..." His voice trailed off. Then he shook his head. "But the timing isn't right. From there to here? Possibly."

As he waded through murky indecision, I chanced a question. "Why are you asking about the blood?"

The man at the door made a tick-ticking sound with his lips, catching his attention.

Gregor snapped his head up, raising his eyebrows. When I craned my neck back, I saw his man shake his head sharply, raising his weapon. I tried to see what he was looking at, but my view was blocked by a thick wooden pole that ran from floor to ceiling.

But whatever he'd seen had him worried.

Without another word, Gregor got up, strapped his lighting rod onto his back, and grabbed a rifle off the nearby table. He stepped toward the door.

Now that they were out of earshot, I whispered, trying to get my friend's attention.

"Kane?" I said then louder. "Kane? Are you all right?"

"Be quiet over there!" The hoarse whisper had come from the big guy at the door.

I looked back to Kane. The shock had really knocked him out.

Behind me, I heard metal grinding against metal. When I turned, I saw Gregor and his gorilla buddy standing at the door to the restaurant. They'd disengaged the locks. The tech sergeant cast a quick glance at me then back out into the mall.

The two of them slowly crept out the door. It closed behind them.

I watched as they walked, arm's length apart, deeper into the mall's food court.

Out of the corner of my eye, I saw a massive shadow darken the windows on the far side of the restaurant. When I turned to get a better look, whatever it was had passed behind the thick wooden support beam.

Gregor and the other man moved forward, perpendicular to where the other had crossed. With them distracted, I looked back toward Kane then down at my hands.

When I was being tied up, I'd rotated my hands inward so my knuckles were pressed against each other. Now, I needed to twist them apart. This I'd worked out during my older cousins' Summers of Fun.

I'd learned that if I pressed my knuckles to each other as I was being bound, it would leave a space between my wrists. Afterward, I could relax my hands, and the gap would often be enough that I could wriggle free.

It didn't always work, but over the years, I'd gotten good at it. Not the kind of thing you want to be good at, but it might pay off now.

Shifting my hands back and forth, I found I had room. It hurt like hell, but I was slowly able to pull one hand out of the ropes, scraping the skin as I went.

There!

I had a hand out.

When I dropped my other arm toward the ground, the bonds fell to the floor, still in a tight coil. Now for the ropes around my chest. While feigning tears, I'd held my breath as those ropes had been tightened, expanding my chest so that when I exhaled, they'd loosen.

But it wasn't enough. Still, I had my hands free and—

Behind me, a roar split the air, rattling the glassware and the interior windows separating the restaurant from the bar. I saw the lightning rod shoot sparks, and the big shadow flew back the way it had come, massive arms flailing as it fell.

Gregor and his man stepped forward, eyes cast down. They were exchanging quick words, commands. I couldn't hear. A moment later, they passed behind the wooden pole. Once again, the lightning burst out, this time toward the ground.

I heard a howl of some creature in pain. I could just see one of their rifle tips poke around the other side of the pole. Their voices got louder.

"Again," I heard Gorilla Tits shout. "Hit it again. Then we can get Doc Hammer to bring the box."

Gregor's voice came up, but I couldn't make it out.

The other man said, more loudly, "Shit, look at its eyes."

They had the creature on the ground, but it wasn't going down easy. I looked down at the ropes around my chest. If they had it under control, they would be back here any second. I scanned the restaurant to see if they'd left a weapon behind.

Of course they hadn't.

I looked out the exterior windows, across the parking lot, to the circle of trucks. Those people had shotguns coming out of their ears. I just needed to untie Kane and get out the door. If I could convince—

Another roar, this one louder and throatier, erupted behind me. I spun back toward the windows in time to see a huge man—creature—pass by the stenciled glass. But the howling hadn't come from the direction Gregor and Gorilla Tits had been facing.

It had come from behind them.

How had the monster gotten around them? They had been stalking toward it. And it had been on the ground!

With most of my view blocked by the wooden pole, I heard one of the men's screams as the creature swiped through the air with its powerful limbs. Shouting and then more shouting. The yelling then turned to screams as I saw Gregor's body flung across my line of sight, arching upward and out of view.

I heard him smash into something down the hall.

How had it gotten behind them? How fast could this thing move?

And where was Gregor's lackey? He'd gone silent.

A shadow rose from the floor, slowly at first then to its full height.

But that was on the far side of the window, where the two men had attacked it. It didn't make sense. Could this thing dematerialize and pop in and out? Crazy thought, but I was getting a bit used to crazy.

The shadowed creature stood, shook for a moment, then passed behind the wooden pole, heading in the opposite direction. Heading back toward where the crew had likely holed up.

When it reappeared on the other side of the pole, everything finally made sense.

Because it hadn't come into view alone.

There were two of them.

We'd finally found Cal Davis.

Chapter Fifty-One

The two creatures—*monsters*, I had to remind myself—uttered such strange, damp, and throaty noises. Desperate and insistent, Charlie and Cal sounded as if they were squabbling. They silenced, bent down out of view, and then there were new sounds.

They began feeding on the man on the ground.

Gregor had been chucked aside like a dirtied rag, landing somewhere down the hall. But the big gorilla of a man who'd stalked me back at the tavern, the one who'd planned on beating me to death with his club—they were eating him.

No. Not eating. They were taking his blood. I knew that much now.

I glanced over at Kane, who looked dead. Alone in this bizarre, nightmare-carnival hell, I wanted to jump up, bang on the exterior glass and call out to all those people with their rifles and shotguns. With my hands free now, I could do that. But that would draw the attention of monsters.

For now, both Kane and I were hidden by the thick pole.

I was frozen. Terrified. I held my breath, bracing for the sound of plate glass breaking behind me that I was sure would come.

After the longest minute of my life, I heard them moving again, long nails clicking across the floor. Feet shuffling. I didn't dare turn to look, worried that the shine from my wide, horrified eyes might draw them over. Their next feed.

Reflected in the mirror behind the restaurant's bar, warped, watery images of the two giant creatures lurched by. For an instant, I thought one set of amber-colored eyes had met mine.

Then they were gone.

And I knew where they were going. There was more feeding to be done.

Quietly, I stretched my legs and rocked up onto my feet, carrying the chair with me. I sat down next to Kane and whispered in his ear.

"Kane! Kane, wake up, man!"

He didn't move.

The door that Charlie—or possibly Cal—had been banging on was down a series of turns. A short, causal stroll for two long-limbed monsters. How long would it take two of them to get through the door? And why had there only been one pounding on the door earlier?

Like Kane had said, these creatures were human smart. One had hidden in the shadows because they knew someone might be coming.

I needed Kane back on his feet.

But no matter how much I pushed and shoved him, he wouldn't awaken from the taser-induced unconsciousness. I tried to step around him, but I was still tied to the chair.

Trying to not make any noise, I sat back down and wriggled back and forth, clawing at the bonds to loosen them. It had only taken a few seconds to free myself, but in those precious seconds, deep inside the mall, I could hear the pounding and smashing once again. Two sets of fists now, banging out like the heart attack rhythm of a dying man.

I reached for the ropes wrapped around Kane. I grappled with the knots, but my fingers wouldn't be enough. Far too tight.

The bar. There would be a knife or fork or whatever, something, behind the bar. I could use that to slice the ropes. *Enhanced* ropes, Gregor had said.

How long would it take to cut them? Minutes? I didn't think the trapped crew had minutes now that both monsters were tearing at their door.

Again, I scanned the restaurant, looking for anything that I could use to free Kane, but could barely see around us. In the dead mall, the only light coming in was from the moon.

Moonlight.

Of course. If I could pull Kane into the moonlight, he'd change. Whatever variation of dog he might turn into, it would be smaller than the massive human slumped unconscious in the chair. When the ropes around him loosened, I could pull him free.

He'd no longer be the giant, powerful human. If he turned into some lapdog or a pug again, those people would die. The bull-like rottweiler *might* have a chance. It would be a gamble, a spin at the Devil's roulette table, but I had no other option.

Glancing over at the moonlight coming through the mall restaurant's windows, I picked a spot, grabbed Kane's chair, and pulled.

No damn way.

I couldn't move him. The guy had to weigh two hundred fifty pounds! I tried again from the other side. Trembling with the effort, I gritted my teeth until my jaw ached and pushed and pushed and only got a chair squeak in return.

It was useless.

I ran to the windows. The townspeople. I needed their help, so I raised my fist to pound on the glass. Would the sound bring the creatures back? Would I only endanger a dozen more innocents outside?

I stood there, frozen with my clutched hand in the air, then looked up to the moon, the big round brilliant orb in the sky. Somehow, that light changed Kane. He just needed the light.

Leaping away from the windows toward the bar, I found some cutlery in the drying rack next to a small sink and ran back.

Could I reflect the light toward him?

I chucked away the fork, which would be useless. The spoon only dispersed the light to nothing. The steak knife seemed promising, but its brushed metal yielded no reflection. I looked up, frustration spinning my mind off its axis, and saw my own ghostly reflection in the glass behind the bar.

Mirror.

I could break the bar mirror, sure. Again, that sound could bring the creatures back, but staring back at myself, I realized I had something better.

Reaching beneath my shirt, I pulled out my grandmother's locket.

I flipped the clasp and looked at what my grandmother had called her most "favorite face in the world."

My eyes filled with tears as I stared at my own reflection in the tiny mirror, only the size of my thumbnail. I nodded to the terrified woman I saw there, assuring her all would be okay.

It had to work.

Lifting the locket's mirror toward the window, I caught the moonlight and directed the tiny beam toward Kane. It landed on his shoulder, and I hoped.

Nothing.

Then I moved it down toward his leg. Still nothing.

But those areas were covered in clothes. If it was going to work, I needed skin. After all the times I'd scolded him for walking around naked, now, I wished he were. Where the rock music T-shirt and sweats didn't cover, his comically numerous bindings did.

I ran over to him and lifted his head, angling his face toward the outside. Back at the window, I tried again. When I looked up, I saw a dark haze creeping closer to the moon, a big massive black storm hunting its prey. But I was quicker.

The small, shimmering beam moved up his body, past his clothed leg and shoulder, then to his face.

When it struck skin, Kane's eyes shot open.

His pupils shrank to pinpricks against yellow, and his face turned into a silent scream. His body began to tremble and shake as his bones slid and buckled beneath undulating skin.

The mote of light cast by the mirror winked out. The cloud had swallowed the full moon whole. Then a thought struck me.

Weeks ago, he'd been just a tiny thing. One of those little purse dogs.

Three days earlier—four or two? I didn't recall—Kane had transformed into a pug. We'd barely made it out alive.

The night before, he'd been much stronger. Much fiercer. The rottweiler.

Our answer had always been there, hanging in the sky above us. Kane's transformations were dependent upon the phase of the moon. It made sense. How had he not worked that out?

Of course, after seeing how the moon had affected Kane, his parents had instructed him to avoid it. He'd tried to honor that as best he could, so he wouldn't have known.

As the light of the moon changed him now, I was transfixed.

What would the full moon do to him?

Chapter Fifty-Two

I had never witnessed Kane transform.

Not when he'd become a yippy lapdog. Not when he'd changed into the far more powerful rottweiler.

So I had no idea if what I was witnessing now was normal. Not that any of this was normal.

His transformation looked agonizing. A soul-crushing level of pain.

The flesh on Kane's body surged in ropey waves that twisted and rippled as the muscles expanded. Bulbous purple knots grew, receded, then swelled again as if ready to burst.

As his hands bloated, three times the size they'd been as a man, the bonds across his wrists cinched tighter, levering his crooked fingers upward. He clawed at the air as if fighting off some invisible attacker.

The cold surface of the restaurant's window pressed against my shoulders, and I realized I'd backed away until I could go no farther.

The ropes that hadn't even budged under my fingertips split as his body ballooned. The bonds around his chest and feet burst in succession, from chest to ankle, their enhanced fibers splaying like dry straw then snapping with a rising *pang-pang-pang* as if someone were tuning a demon's guitar.

Now freed, Kane grew larger, arching his back and drawing huge lungfuls of air that expanded his chest and tore the rock T-shirt to ribbons, exposing purple-dark, sinewy flesh and coarse black hair. His head lolled at a horrifying angle, his neck bending and twisting.

A moment later, his silent scream was over.

My head swam, and I sucked in air through my teeth. I'd been holding my breath.

Slowly, Kane lifted from the chair, ribbons of torn cloth and shredded rope tumbling to the floor like water flowing off his thick hide.

His massive head turned and, in the dim light of the restaurant, his fierce yellow eyes found me.

Staring up, I whispered, pressing myself harder against the glass, "Jesus Christ."

The monster stared. No, not monster. Not creature. This was still Kane. At least, I hoped it was still Kane.

For the first time, I saw the wolf within the man.

His dark, protruding canine snout hung open, exposing rows of thick, sharp teeth. Kane's brow had receded, smoothing behind those piercing eyes. Ears set back on a head of black, coarse hair.

He'd been large before, intimidating, in his human form.

Now, standing more than eight feet in height, towering above me, he was something out of Stephen King's nightmares.

Below the massive wolf-like head, black, fibrous hair curved along the oil-dark flesh of his body that made him look more ape than human. Thick, ropey muscles wound down his shoulders like twisting undersea cables, terminating in massive hands, capped by hooked claws.

I watched him scan his surroundings as if looking at the world with new eyes. Hell, they *were* new eyes, twice the size they'd been before! I wondered how much of the man I knew was left in him.

"Kane?" I said, my voice shaking.

He turned and looked at me, slowly stalking forward. His eyes never wavered as he bared his teeth, rows upon rows of jagged things, twice as many as a human might have.

"Kane? Are you—"

He kept coming, and I braced. Jesus, what had I done?

His massive arm reached for me, and I flinched away from it. His expression changed, and he slowly pulled it back.

"Are you okay, Sad Girl?"

I let out a bark of a laugh, expelling terror from my lungs. It had been half joy and half relief. I had no idea what the big hairy thing might have for a brain. But he still sounded like Kane. A bit rougher and more animal, but Kane none the less.

I nodded and touched his head, which looked like a combination of the powerful dog I'd seen the night before and, well, a wolf. I traced my fingers down his neck, shifting the thick hair as I did.

All the while, as I explored his new form with my fingertips, Kane didn't shrink from my caress. Didn't shy away. Instinctively, he knew I needed to reassure myself that yes, this was the man I knew.

Then, as if time had restarted again, the world around us came rushing back. I heard the banging echo down the hall and the terrified screams of the people trapped as two monsters tried to smash the barriers protecting them.

Kane had heard it to. He turned and took a half step back, raising his arms as if he were about to swing, then staggered. He asked me, "Who attacked us?"

"Gregor and the big guy," I said, worried that he'd somehow forgotten that. "Gorilla Tits is on the floor out there. Gregor got flung down the hall, but I can't imagine he survived that."

"What of the creature?"

"Not one," I said and pointed to the interior of the mall. "There are two of them now."

"Two?" he said, flashing his muzzle toward me.

Again, I nodded. "Charlie and—"

"Cal Davis."

"Yes."

He nodded. "Then I must go find him. You stay here."

"We need to help those people!"

Kane moved forward, banging his shoulders on the restaurant lamps; they swayed in his wake.

"I will if I can," he said, taking long strides toward the door, but his gait hitched, and he reached out to steady himself. I ran up and put a hand on his giant arm.

He looked down at me.

I said, "Pack of two, remember? I know you have to find Cal, but it's important to me that those people are okay."

Eyes a bit out of focus, Kane let out a long breath. "I will try."

"And I'll help," I said and reached for the door's handle, but he put out an arm to block me, shaking his head.

"Kane, I think you're still out of it because of those electric shocks," I said, but he wouldn't move his arm away. "Listen, I know you won't let anything happen to me. And those two are working together. I think they tricked Gregor and the other guy. That's how they killed them. Cal had been hiding in the shadows and came from up behind after they got distracted."

Kane frowned at me.

"I'll be *behind* you, watching back there to make sure one of them doesn't sneak up. Just a lookout."

Frowning, he nodded slowly. "Just a lookout."

Once outside the restaurant, we crept deeper into the mall, and I cast a quick glance back to where I'd seen Gregor's man attacked. I wished I hadn't. The big gorilla man was in pieces, few of which I could identify.

As we skulked down the winding hallway, the pounding on the door grew louder. Once at the final turn, we stopped. Using only hand gestures, I told my friend to wait while I peered around the corner. There stood two giant naked men with bizarrely elongated limbs bashing the door.

They'd gotten a corner of it free and were yanking at the split metal. I could hear the terrified screams of the people inside.

I slipped back around the corner and told Kane what I saw. He put a hand out, gently pushing me back.

"Go now," he said quietly. "It is not safe."

"You can't take on two!"

He shrugged and half nodded. "I will try."

When he started to step forward, I clutched a handful of his back hair and stopped him. If he were to step out there, eight feet of muscle, claws, and teeth, they would both come at him at full force.

I said, "I have a better idea."

Chapter Fifty-Three

Taking a deep, shaky breath, I cast a quick glance behind me. Thirty feet away, Kane stood watching from the bend in the hallway. I frowned and pointed my finger, jamming it a few times in the air.

He moved back to take cover around the corner. Still, I could see one of his yellow eyes watching me. That would have to do.

Turning back and looking at the wall's edge, knowing what lay beyond it, I tried to control my breathing.

Here to there.

I stepped into the next hallway.

The breath caught in my throat when I saw the two monsters tearing at the flayed edge of the door, which had bent and twisted like tinfoil. It wouldn't last much longer.

From within, I saw the crimson glow of emergency lights illuminating the black work shoes of several people, shuffling and twisting, trying to move away from the danger just a few feet away.

"Leave them alone!" I shouted.

The two attackers turned to me, startled, unsure of what they were looking at.

They were both massive men. Not men. Creatures. *Monsters.* Like Bridget Mills, their hair looked shorn, almost like it had been all ripped out at the roots and then grown back into a thin woolen cap.

Their naked bodies were mottled with dirt, blood, and dark patches of discoloration. Might be bruises or some effect of their transformation— a corruption of not just the mind but the body.

The one with darker skin had the muscular build of a football lineman and the height of a basketball star forward. His head looked mishappen, swollen, as if he'd jammed his face inside a wasps' nest and chewed at what he'd found there.

Charlie Boynton.

The lighter skinned man could have almost passed for human despite his inhuman size, a head taller than the other. When he shifted his stance to look at me, I saw the long snake tattoo. Its tail curved around a bulging bicep, winding down the forearm. When this one lifted his hand in my direction, the ink-snake's fangs seemed to rise up from the heel of his palm.

Cal Davis.

They exchanged quick glances, and maybe a word passed between them. I couldn't tell. Then Charlie came at me. Fast.

I ran.

His bare feet slapped the damp tile floor behind me as I pushed my own muscles to move faster and faster. Fear gripped my imagination. I could feel its breath on my neck, the fingers swiping through the air behind me. The short hallway didn't look so short anymore.

I heard the creature growl, snapping its teeth.

My head yanked back. It had gripped my hair and was pulling me toward the floor. My skull bounced off the hard tile, and lights exploded in my vision. When it cleared a second later, I saw a mouth coming down on me.

I screamed.

My arms were being crushed by its powerful hands, but then I was being lifted off the ground. It was pulling me up to its gnashing teeth!

I realized we were both being lifted.

Just beyond the creature's head, I saw Kane's face, his new wolfen one, lips drawn back in a snarl, teeth glistening in the dim light. He bent down to tear at the monster's neck, and I fell to the floor again. Charlie had lifted a fist and punched Kane, letting me go in the process.

The two of them tumbled into the next hallway, and I ran around them as they clawed and tore into one another on the wet tile floor.

Kane wrapped his muscular arms and legs around the creature, grunting and snarling, but trembled as he tried to hold on. I realized he'd been more weakened by the taser blast, *two* of them, than he'd let on. Gregor had hit Charlie with his lightning wand, too, but he seemed unaffected.

The monster fought against his attacker, clawing at his flank, unleashing a gush that sprayed the floor red.

Kane growled at me, "Go."

The creature hissed and bashed an elbow to his head, knocking him aside. Both flipped off their backs and onto all fours, lightning quick. The strange motion looked both animal and insectile.

As they faced off, Kane turned to me. "Go!"

Even if I'd wanted to stay—and I didn't—I was only distracting him. I raced down the hall so fast, the sweat on my face cooled like I'd been plunged into ice water.

At the next corner, I turned back to look.

Their two bodies entwined, rolling and flexing, both landing punches, but Kane seemed to be stronger. However, if the other at the door were to come, if Cal Davis heard the struggling, I didn't think Kane could take on both. I leapt back around the corner before he saw me again.

There was nothing I could do against superhumans. Hell, I'd been out of my depth the first moment I met Kane! I had done my part.

All at once, the fear I'd been ignoring hit me, washing over me like a cold mountain river. What the hell was I still doing in the mall?

Danger.

And I'd learned a long time ago, if I were to survive that, I had to run.

So I did.

Chapter Fifty-Four

Kane

I have fought powerful creatures before, but this one is different. Stronger, faster, and does not tire.

A fine warrior, but so am I.

The beast-man is cunning. As he launches toward me, teeth parted and wanting, I raise an arm to deflect, only to discover another strike in motion—his claws pierce my side as if he anticipated the move.

The elongated nails dig in, and I fight the urge to howl.

Such utterance would alert Cal Davis, and then I would be battling two of them.

Turning the pain into power, I smash my arm across the beast-man's head, hoping to dizzy him.

It works!

The creature releases my side, the retracted claws making a sickly sucking sound as they exit my flesh, and he tumbles to the floor. I leap up, splaying my legs to immobilize its arms, but as I land upon him, I only catch one. He moves so fast!

But I can be faster. I must be faster.

It is my turn to pierce flesh, and I rake my own claws across his chest and am rewarded by four red rivers splitting the skin. Before he can cry out, I drop to a knee and drive my elbow into his opening mouth.

A bad choice, I realize too late.

The beast-man clamps his jaw around my arm, and his teeth drill into my flesh. The wounds bleed but are not deep, but that limb has now been immobilized.

Stupid! Stupid move!

I must be better. And I am better—stronger and larger.

However, when I look to the red rivers of his chest, they are no longer flowing. I watch in horror as the flesh there begins to knit itself closed! It has begun repairing just seconds after I landed what should have been a fatal blow.

It is because he has taken some of my blood. Like me, this can heal him.

The wolf in me knows I should have gone for the throat. Always the throat. I will pay for such a mistake.

Wrenching my arm from its bloodied teeth, I feel my flesh tear away within the mouth of the... monster? Are they monsters?

Does such a designation give them undue power over me?

The creature reaches up with his free hand and clutches the hair on the back of my head, wrenching my neck—*so strong!*—and I am flung from his body. For a bizarre moment, I am floating in the air until the impact of the wall shoots lightening into my brain.

Everything turns dark, but I must move!

Back up on my hands and feet, wolflike once again, I can see him jumping toward me, and I make a leap of my own. The beast-man crashes into the stone wall and slides to the floor.

This is my chance, and I pounce atop him. The creature is a fine warrior and strong. I can be stronger.

For every move I make, he counters. He is not animal and not human. A deadly combination of both.

My limbs do not obey as they should, the nerves and muscles within still frayed by Gregor's electric weapon. However, I can hold the creature... until I cannot.

I slash at his neck, where he is vulnerable, but only leave a superficial wound. His eyes bore into me, and I catch the glimmer of a smile. As he does, once again, the slash beneath that grin begins to fix itself.

Staring, transfixed by the skin turning from ruined to repaired, I have lost focus. The man-beast takes advantage of this and flexes his legs, spinning us both in the air, until our positions reverse.

The impact steals my breath and waters my eyes.

On top now, the creature has me pinned.

I cannot lift my trembling arms to free myself. I raise my legs and dig my hind claws into him. He grunts but does not break. I tear at his skin, my nails scraping against the bone beneath the flesh. Still, he does not release me. The monster bares his teeth, plunging them into my shoulder.

But I do not heal like he does, and the blood pours quickly. No, not pouring. He is suckling, drawing in my blood, drinking my life away from me. It feels as if my mind drains with it.

However, a thought remains.

I am second best. Always, I will be second best.

And I know what second best must do.

Chapter Fifty-Five

I ran down hallways that seemed so much longer than before. Every time I got to one junction, the slapping of my boots ringing off the marble walls, I rounded the corner, only to find yet another stretch. It felt endless.

Finally, I saw the restaurant where Kane and I had been held, a dark, crumpled mass near its door that used to be a gorilla of a man. Racing past, I lost my footing and tumbled to the floor, bashing my forearm as I landed.

I'd slipped on something slick and viscous.

The smell rose and infected my nostrils, metallic and organic at the same time. Scrambling back to my feet again, I could see red stains down my pant legs.

"Goddamn it," I whispered, as if afraid saying the words too loud might wake the dead man.

Back on my feet, I scrambled to the mall's exit, where we'd come in earlier. Before I could even reach the door, Janice the cop was there, keys fluttering and sparkling in the moonlight.

As her trembling hands worked the lock, I slapped my palm on the glass.

"Come on!" I shouted.

Then it was open. She held it ajar, just a crack, trying to look past me. The woman hadn't said a word, but I knew she was looking to see if monsters might be close behind. Would she have slammed the door again, locked me back inside, if she'd seen one?

Finally, she threw it open and stood back.

"Let's go," Janice said, her voice a husky whisper.

Behind me, I could hear the raging battle echoing off the floors and walls. The gut-wrenching sounds of it snaked through those long hallways as if they'd chased me in a panic to get away, hoping to flee the chaos as I had.

The growling and snarling, the slap of skin against floor.

A howl of pain.

The cop shook the door, her eyes boring into me. She didn't speak another word, likely afraid that any utterance would draw the monsters within.

Why wasn't I moving?

From where I stood, I could see the circle of trucks, their lights on now. The townspeople had gathered in that pool of cool, illuminated safety. Their faces had turned my way, all silently waiting for me to join them.

Or worried one of the creatures would burst past me and attack.

"Come out, now," Janice said. "I gotta lock the door, ma'am."

The tone of her words was one I knew. Detached and floating above myself, I recognized the "cop voice." The one they use to get you to do what they want you to. Sure, that's usually what you should be doing. For your own safety.

But not always.

This time, though, of course, it would be. Outside would be safe. Steel and reinforced glass and chain locks between me and the threat from the darkness within.

However, I'd heard something else.

A voice.

At first, I couldn't make out the words. Or maybe I had and couldn't believe what my brain had heard. I froze, waiting.

Janice rattled the door again, imploring me to join them, the chains banging against the glass.

Then, I heard the voice again, desperate and plaintive, rolling across the floor and up my body.

"Emelda," the distant voice said. Then again, "Emelda."

Had that been why I'd stopped?

The cop bored her eyes into mine and said something about if I didn't come out, she was going to lock me back in again. But I barely heard her.

"Emelda," Kane called out, distant and echoing around me. "I need you."

Chapter Fifty-Six

Kane

The creature lifts an arm and leans into his blow, but I shift, and he smashes his fist into the floor below me. I hear the marble crack under the force of it.

I can smell his sweat and rage and my own blood. And that chemical scent once again. So strange. Emanating from his pores.

Then another scent, distant and faint.

Despite my call to her, a desperation, I must defeat the monster to keep her safe. Keeping her safe is how we came to be our pack of two.

That terrible night when I got caught in the moonlight, all those weeks ago. Stupid, so stupid! My parents warned me to keep from its gaze. My mistake had been once again trying to drive the human vehicles. They do not make sense to me; too many motions to just move forward.

But my questions about Cal Davis at the Minneapolis car show had drawn the attention of Gregor and his crew. Instinct had kicked in, and I knew I had to flee.

Still, the crash into fencing had surprised me. The blankets I had used to cover the vehicle's windows, to keep the moon's gaze off my human skin, had also blocked my view of obstacles in the street.

My brain jumbled from the impact, I had stepped out of the car and into the night. Into the moonlight. That queer, dizzying feeling overcame me. I had changed. My face was just inches from the ground.

The crash had earned me unwanted attention. I had become so tiny, chased by cruel boys with sticks. In my human form, I could have thrown each of them over the ruined fence!

But, alas, I was so small.

And, maybe, foolish. I had found a place to hide in an alley. With a chance glance through a basement window, I saw her for the first time. She sat alone in the dark apartment, and even through the tiniest crack in the glass, I could smell her sorrow.

Then I spotted the bottle. Broken and jagged. Held above her arm as if to strike herself.

After being pursued by the tech sergeant and his people, then the boys and their pain sticks, I had finally been safe. But seeing this sad person in trouble, if only by her own hand, I had been compelled. I tried to call out, however in that tiny, feeble body, my words tripped and stumbled over themselves.

Despite my failings, through the dirty glass of the window, I could see it had worked. The bottle lowered. Before she could turn, the boys had found me, and the beating began once more.

Already weakened, their blows dimmed my lights, and I fell into black.

The next day, I awoke, in human form again, to see the girl. My Sad Girl. We had both made it through the night.

This was the first day of our pack of two.

Pain rips my mind back to the present, carrying the echoes of that sorrow with it, as the beast-man smashes my wounded shoulder. I am dazed. Exhausted. Above me, the dim light dances across bloodied teeth.

The creature is going for my neck.

Yes, the throat.

Always the best choice.

Chapter Fifty-Seven

Behind me, I heard the door slam and the clanging of the thick chain against it. The cop didn't seem so worried about making noise now the lock was back in place.

Kane needed my help.

Me.

I'd been right about the taser blasts. That had to be it. He'd been weakened, unsteady, and that had given Charlie the monster an edge over a much stronger Kane.

As I pumped my fists, running back into the fight, I skidded to a stop. What the hell was I going to do? I needed a weapon.

Of course!

The lightning rod that Gregor and that big bastard had used. I raced back to the mound of flesh just outside the restaurant, fighting the urge to puke. The stench of cooling blood made my eyes water. But all I could see was lumps of shredded flesh and torn clothing.

Scowling, I had to dig through the lumps of gore. I didn't find the metal pole, but I found something even better.

Struggling with the strap of the automatic rifle, I dislodged bits and pieces of Gorilla Tits's body to lift it out.

"M4," I said, remembering what Gregor had called it. I didn't know jack shit about rifles but had seen enough action movies to know the pointy end spat out bullets. I lifted it to my shoulder, ignoring the smear of blood soaking into my clothes. Pointing it down the hall, I stared down the sights.

I didn't need to aim it well, just aim it at the monster!

And, of course, not hit Kane.

I lined up on a display for cellular service. An inflatable mobile phone, as tall as I was. Over the past few weeks, with the mall closed, it had lost some of its air and slumped sadly against the counter. I would end its misery.

I pulled the trigger... Nothing.

"Shit!"

I lifted the M4 closer to my face to find the safety. Off. Of course it would be; they'd been stepping into a monster fight. So why would it...

Holding the gun closer to my face, I could see a silvery metal pad on the front of the trigger. Did that need to be engaged or moved or...?

Once again, I hefted the rifle and tried to fire.

Nothing.

Would the weapons of Gregor's crew be somehow coded to their members? Did guns check for fingerprints before letting you use them like my old cell phone did?

Either way, the rifle was useless to me.

A howl of pain bounced off the walls around me. I recognized Kane's voice. It sounded weak. Desperate. He sounded like he was dying.

But I needed a weapon!

Where the hell was I going to find a weapon?

Of course. This was a goddamn mall. A mall in the United States. There would be some weapon, something, in one of these stores.

Tossing the rifle—it landed with a damp thump in the heap next to me—I ran down the first hall and the next.

In one store, I spotted a mannequin dressed like a pink skier geared up for a pricey Aspen holiday. Sporting goods? Peering in the window, I saw a display of camo jackets inside.

That seemed promising.

The door was locked and covered by a roll-down cage, so I pulled a nearby trash can from its holder, lifted it to my hip, and smashed the big display window. My arms got sliced by some of the falling glass before I could jump away. I'd have to tend to those cuts later.

Once inside, I scanned for anything I could use. But it was darker in the store than the mall outside. If I went too far in, I wouldn't be able to see a damn thing.

I picked up a ski, which I could maybe use as a bat? No. I tossed it aside.

Looking at the far wall, those summers on my uncle's farm flood back to me. A squared-off section held paintball guns. I'd never had one myself, but I damn sure knew how they worked!

I ran to the display, searching for the largest one.

"Jee-*sus*," I whispered, grabbing one of the air rifles that looked like a replica of Gorilla Tits's M4. But when I went to pull it way, it only came a few inches then clanked to a stop. A short wire encased in plastic held it in place. Theft deterrent.

At first, I thought to find something to cut it away. Then I'd have to find CO2 cartridges and paint balls and... Would a paintball gun really work against a monster?

Frustrated, I hung my head. Desperate. Angry.

Below, in the detritus of half-open boxes, packing material, and hangers, I saw something even more familiar to me. I reached down and grabbed the slingshot, its long rubber tube catching on a hook. I freed the tube and gripped the weapon, placing the curved cup of its wire brace atop my forearm.

The one I'd used against my cousins had been of a similar design. They'd called it a wrist rocket. Stupid name.

Holding the handle with its wishbone uprights, I grabbed the rubber tube. Where it came to a loop, there was a small metal cup in the shape of a road cone. I held this odd cap between my thumb and forefinger and pulled the rubber cord back. That was when I noticed another difference from my old, secondhand one.

Between those wishbone uprights was a piece of metal, cut at the top. Not a cut. It was a notch.

"What the...?"

When I looked at the box I'd pulled the weird slingshot from, I saw what the notch was for.

I smiled. "That'll work."

Chapter Fifty-Eight

Kane

I am fighting not only the beast man but the darkness in my head and eyes, which is trying to take me. My own mind has become an enemy.

However, my muscles do not obey as I will them to. From exhaustion of battle, they are weary.

Charlie Boynton, the man who became a monster, has me pinned against the stone floor, spittle dripping from his gaping mouth. He salivates, anticipating the taste of my blood once again. His eyes grow larger, fiercer, as hunger fuels his fury.

When he leans toward me once again, I raise a knee into his stomach, but he only grunts and endures my blow. Again, I strike him, and he lifts his hand, releasing me briefly, before smashing an elbow to my face.

Stars erupt in my brain, and my vision flips and blurs. I taste the bitterness of sweat, feel grit grind between my teeth.

I lift my free arm to block him, to push him away, but it is easily batted aside. With his forearm crushing my wrist, the beast-man clamps a powerful hand to the side of my face and presses down, exposing my neck. He leans forward, mouth open and teeth flashing.

No strength left in me, I can only await—

"Hey, Chuck!" a strange voice calls out.

The creature lifts his head from me.

Then his thoughts change.

His thoughts change so much, one of them pokes... out?

I am not sure how you think to make something poke out. What is this strange thing he can do?

What purpose would that serve?

The creature shudders and reaches up for the spike—no, not a spike. It is an arrow.

The arrow is sticking out of the side of his neck. Blood erupts from his lips, and his eyes glass over as he struggles to breathe. The man's body shudders and quakes.

When he gropes for the spike, he frees one of my arms. I do not hesitate, and with all my remaining strength, I reach up and grab the thought arrow and twist it hard, splitting his neck, nearly severing the man's head.

Blood gushes from his gaping wound, and I consume what is given to me, taking the life in with large, greedy swallows. I can feel strength once again return and course through my body. My wounds sting and bite as I heal.

I spin the arrow further, and his body shakes.

Energized, I wrap my legs around his torso and lift my claws to his neck, twisting and twisting and twisting! I hear a wet snap and toss his head to the side.

I turn and see Emelda as she steps into the moonlight slipping through the windows above. She is holding something strange, a rubber loop swaying from her fingertips.

And she is smiling.

Chapter Fifty-Nine

I ran over and knelt down by Kane and flinched when I saw his shredded shoulder. Strangely, in the time it takes me to strip my leather jacket off, which I'd planned to wrap around the wound, it stops bleeding. Did he run *out* of blood?

Putting the jacket back on, I asked him, "Are you okay?"

He flashed a weary look at me. "Yes, of course. I have defeated this creature."

"You?" I said and held up the weapon I'd commandeered from the store. "I'm the one who shot him. Not exactly where I meant to. I'd gone for the head, but close enough."

"Is..." Kane squinted at the device in my hand. "Is that where the thought spike came from?"

"The thought spike? It's a slingshot arrow... thingy," I said. "What the hell are you talking about?"

Before he could answer, we both heard the screams and looked to the adjoining hall.

Kane leaped to his feet, towering over me. "The people..."

"Yes, the people, Kane!" I shouted, running down the hall with the slingshot under my arm. I had a few more arrows tucked into the back of my jeans. "Come on!"

We ran around the corner to see the remaining creature on its knees and tearing at the door, a leg of one of the men inside caught in its grasp. I shouted at it.

"Stop!"

It turned toward us, and its animal panting slowed, a queer expression passing over its face. He blinked, looked down at the screaming man, then back to us.

Kane took a step forward. "Cal Davis."

Cal, naked and covered in blood and dirt, let go of the man. He stood and, as he stared at us, I moved behind Kane, preparing for the creature's attack. As I stared at my friend, his fury seemed to melt into confusion.

Then he ran.

Kane chased after him, and I charged at the busted door. The man who had nearly been yanked out was gushing blood from a long gash on his leg. I yanked hard, trying to open the door, but twisted on its jamb, it wouldn't budge.

Cal Davis had wrenched away just the edge, like lifting the corner on a tinfoil dinner hot out of the oven. That had created a gap only large enough to reach inside. Now freed of the monster's grasp, the injured man was bleeding out.

I screamed, "Kane! Kane, help me here!"

Cal had run up the mall steps, taking three at a time, heading for the upper floors. In pursuit and midway up, Kane gripped the rail and turned to me.

"I must go, Emelda!"

"No!" I shouted. "He'll die if we don't get him out of there. I can't open the door."

"But—!"

"Kane, please!" I pleaded. "Pack of two, remember? I need you."

He cast one last glance above then threw his head back and howled so loud my hands flew to my ears. A three-story tall window behind him actually cracked and spiderwebbed. The men behind the door screamed louder, terrified.

Hell, the sound of it had frightened me!

Kane's eyes met mine, glaring. Then they softened, and he jumped off the staircase, landing fifteen feet below and shaking the floor around us.

I asked, "Can you pull it open?"

He grasped the door, bracing his feet in a wide stance. When the crew inside saw sharp claws gripping the metal, they shuffled farther back, screaming once more. Kane twisted and pulled, howling as he did, but it finally broke free, and he flung the reinforced door down the hallway. It bounced and clattered and disappeared in the darkness.

The bleeding man looked up, saw the massive silhouette above him, and scuttled toward the others, leaving a smear of red on the floor.

"Thank you," I said to Kane. Then I nodded. "Go!"

He ran after the answers he'd sought for more than a year.

Chapter Sixty

There had been five people barricaded in the storage room—three men and two women. The guy who had gotten hurt and had been seconds away from becoming a blood Slurpee had been in pretty bad shape. Thankfully, one of the women on their crew was former military. She'd had some basic field-medicine training that had saved the guy's life.

Well, that and a wolf-turned-man, an eight-foot-tall... werewolf?

No, that wasn't right.

Werewolves were people who turned into wolf monsters. What did you call a wolf that turned into a human that turns into a wolf monster?

No, he wasn't a monster. In truth, I had no idea what he was.

But not a monster.

I felt a little guilty about all the glad-handing and hugs I'd gotten outside the store. Once we'd set up the bleeding guy in the awaiting ambulance, all eyes turned back to me.

There were tears and even laughter. It felt like the entire town had exhaled a breath it had been holding for a year.

My thoughts darkened when I saw a body being rolled out on a stretcher. It had been zipped up into a long, semireflective bag. An awful thought came to mind that it looked a little like a trash bag that one might drag out to the curb on any given Tuesday morning.

There was a person inside. Well, what was left of a person.

Of course, that person had been one of the crew who'd wanted to kill me. Given the size of the lump inside, I knew who it was: the asshole formerly known as Gorilla Tits.

As I watched the body roll by, I recalled their strange questions in the mall restaurant. Gregor had been very interested in some blood they'd found under their comrade's fingernails. I tried to think back and remember if Mon had scratched me. I'd had a few cuts and bruises but nothing that looked like nail marks.

Had to be Kane.

Were they just pissed about her death? Looking for revenge, and whoever's blood had been there, that would be the focus of that rage?

No use speculating. I didn't have any answers.

"Thank you," Janice said, extending a hand to me. She had a warm smile on her face, but her eyes searched *my* face for something. I'd had dozens of those eyes, cop eyes, stare me down over the years.

Nothing new.

"Where's your big friend? Didn't see him come out. Is he all right?"

I nodded a few times more than I needed to just to get the story lined up in my head.

Their monster was dead, laid out on the mall floor. What good would it do to say Kane had chased after another?

Did they deserve to know? Probably. But I didn't feel I owed these people that. Any conversation about Cal Davis would inevitably lead to questions about Kane I couldn't answer.

Hell, I had questions about Kane I couldn't answer.

Watching the door, bracing myself for the other body, I told the cop Kane was doing his due diligence—I'd read that phrase in a book once—and following the tracks back to where the monster had come from. That seemed to satisfy her. At least in part.

"Can you describe the man for me? The attacker?" She had a notebook out and was scribbling.

"You haven't seen the body yet?"

"No, actually," the cop said and sighed with the hint of a smile. "I used to work in the Twin Cities and Chicago before that. I've seen a few bodies in my time. Came out to these parts so I didn't have to anymore."

"How's that working out for you?" I said and gave her a weak grin.

"Not so good." She shrugged, and her smile collapsed. "Can you describe the attacker for me?"

"Listen, I'm beat." I pointed over to the coroner's van and saw the body of Gregor's dead buddy being loaded inside. "But you'll get a chance to examine it once they've hauled it out, right?"

The cop looked at me strangely. "No, the others have already taken it," she said, chewing her words a little. "You didn't know that? I thought those guys were with you."

The others?

"It was just me and Kane," I said. "Who are you talking about?"

She looked to the dark mall then back at me.

"Those two from some federal authority. Homeland Security was our best guess, but with our people trapped inside, no one was asking for badges." She nodded toward the coroner. "One of them didn't make it, of course. But the other came out just as this black van came up. Less than a minute later, he and some woman loaded up that thing and took it away. Good riddance, really."

"Wait. The other one got chucked down the hall," I said, remembering how Gregor had flown the length of the mall. "I heard the smash. You may want to check the info booth. Probably in a cubbyhole next to some glossy brochures."

It was a bit of dark humor, and I felt embarrassed for it. Now really wasn't the time.

The cop shook her head. "No, our people pulled out just the one. Well, what was left of him."

"What?"

"The other guy came out when you and the crew were working to make sure Richard didn't bleed out." She stepped closer and put a hand on my arm. "Again, thank you for that."

I shook my head. "He's alive?"

"Yes, thanks to you and your big friend. And Jessie, who had some train—"

"No, no. Not, um, Richard. The other guy, the one you called a fed, Gregor. I can't imagine he survived that."

The cop frowned at me. "When he came out, Roger went to talk with him and got stonewalled. That guy—Gregor, you said?—dude's an ass-hole."

"You don't know the half of it."

"He'd been jabbering on his radio as the van pulled up. The woman who'd hopped out told us all to keep back, and the words 'infection' and 'contagion' were bandied about. We didn't argue. They raced in, bagged up the body, and shot out of here with it before you and the maintenance crew came out."

"You guys just let them do that?"

"Miles and miles above my pay grade." Janice waved her hands around. "This entire town has been in a virtual lockdown for almost a year because of that thing. Or whatever he was. I think everyone was happy to see it gone. In truth, I was too. Now I can go back to checking fishing licenses. Chicken-eating psycho dudes, I can do without."

A few more of the locals had come up to shake my hand, and I tried to be gracious. I needed to get out of there and find Kane. Also, I wasn't up for any more questions about my friend, "the big guy," that I couldn't answer.

When I got back to the Jeep, I nearly jumped at the sight of a woman there waiting for me. I hadn't seen her earlier as part of the monster posse. She looked like she'd slept in her clothes, and her frizz of black hair was slightly matted on one side. Red-rimmed eyes told me she'd been crying. And not just today.

She extended a hand, and I shook it then reached for the car door. She watched me as I climbed inside. The woman came around and motioned for me to roll down the window. I did.

"Thank you for saving our town," she said, pulling a sweater closer across her shoulders. "Did you see him? It was Charlie, wasn't it?"

Not knowing what to say, I just nodded.

The woman winced. "Do *they* know that for certain? I mean, did you tell them it was—"

"No, I didn't get into it."

She let out a long breath and looked back to the mall. "I don't know what happened to Charlie, but the past year has been... It's been a horror."

"You knew him?"

She smiled weakly. "Charlie was my brother. He's been missing, but he used to do that as a kid. When he was gone and all this started happening, I was just happy he wasn't here for it. But one of the cleanup crew that those things tried to..." She inhaled and let out a shaky breath. "Well, we've been dating on and off, and he called me. Said he thought one of them looked like my brother." She turned away, squeezing herself. "Wasn't sure because he was... different. Or deformed in some way. I don't know what to make of any of this."

She'd come to me, looking for answers.

"I'm so sorry. I wish I could tell you more, but I really don't know anything."

For a moment, she thought about that then seemed to accept it. "It's been so bad, they called in a monster hunter, I suppose. But he wasn't a monster, okay? I think he just sort of lost himself."

Having no idea what to say, I just nodded.

She put a hand on my shoulder. "Thank you for, you know, ending this."

"It's... what we do," I said, and a strange feeling rippled through me. Not bad. It felt good, actually. Not something I was used to.

Pulling away, I watched her get smaller and smaller in my rearview mirror.

Chapter Sixty-One

For the rest of the night, I drove up and down the streets surrounding the mall looking for Kane but saw no sign of him.

Without any other place to go for now, I fueled up and got on the road back to Miss Florida's farmhouse. If nothing else, I could pick up what little stuff I had and...

Then what?

I felt alone.

Kane was now chasing Cal Davis. Hell, he could be two states away by now. I had no idea.

Halfway to my destination, the sun began to peek up over the horizon, and I couldn't help but smile. I wondered what state Kane might be in at that moment.

The big, hairy version of him had split not only his bonds but all of his clothes right off his body. A real Hulk moment. So my guess was he was out running around, naked head to toe. That would make him happy.

And that thought made me happy. A little.

Back at the farmhouse, I was met with a big breakfast and bigger hugs from my host. Over eggs, bacon, hash browns, and fried tomatoes, she caught me up on the buzz around town. Word had gotten out.

There had been two monsters—one in Pine Valley and another in Gisborne—and now both were gone because of a young woman and a very big French-Canadian man.

That both thrilled and worried me. I didn't like my name out there, even if it was attached to something as cool as "monster hunter."

There were people I really wanted to forget about me.

"Oh, no," Miss Florida said, chewing on her toast. "No names, now. Only me and Olivia know your true identities." She laughed at that.

"Ah-hem," Denny said, strolling into the room. Given the spread on the table, I was surprised it had taken him that long to get into the kitchen. "I know your names."

"I gotta worry about that?" I asked him.

"Nah, not at all."

Miss Florida pointed at the food. "Took you long enough. I would have thought you'd have smelled this a half hour ago."

"I did," Denny said and looked at me. "I was just, you know, setting up your website." He waited for an answer.

I looked at his mother, who only shrugged.

"You know," Denny added, "in case people need to contact you. If there's more trouble. Had we known about you two, hell, we could have ended this months ago."

"You set up a website?" I said, my eyes darting between the two of them.

Denny shook his head. "Just one of those free ones. WordPress thing. It's got a blind-box contact address."

"Jesus, now every crazy—"

"No, no." He raised his hands. "Don't worry. I'll go through them, and if there's something worth a call back, I'll let you know. I'll vet them."

That didn't sit well with me. "I don't know."

He shrugged. "Well, you guys got both of them, so it's over."

Of course, I said nothing about Cal Davis.

Miss Florida had insisted she tend to the cuts from when I'd broken into the mall's sporting goods store. I'd put that off until after breakfast, and once we'd finished, she pulled out a small box with hand-painted flowers. Inside were iodine and bandages.

Two hours later, I was loading our stuff into my new Jeep. Denny said they had paperwork for it tucked in some old boxes, and once he found it, he'd take care of transferring ownership officially. That reminded me of a bit of personal shame I had to do right by.

"Where's our old Audi?"

Denny rubbed a spot on the Jeep with his sleeve. "Up at the garage in one of the bays, so it's hidden. The Jeep is, you know, good and all. If you don't want—"

"No, the Jeep is great," I said, closing the door. From the driver's seat, I took a long look at Miss Florida's farm. It would be good to replace my old farm memories with new ones from my short time here. "I'd actually borrowed the Audi from a neighbor."

"Borrowed?" He gave me a half smile. Dude already knew me.

"Close enough. Is there a way I could get it towed back to the Cities?"

Denny shrugged, jamming his hands into his gray sweatpants. "You know, I could drive it back for you."

"I couldn't ask—"

"Not a problem, Em. Actually, now that this has all died down..." His voice fell silent as he stared off in the same direction I was. Imprinting his own fond memories, maybe. "There's some friends I can crash with in St. Paul. And if I want to start working with those bands, now's as good a time as any."

I turned to him, smiled, and texted my old neighbor's address to his phone. For a long moment, we just listened to the crickets and cicadas who had no interest in the world of humans. Or monsters.

Finally, Denny asked, "Where are you going?"

"Sorry," I said. "I can't really say."

He tapped his brow. "Gotcha."

I really didn't know where I was going. Kane had split, but I still had his bank card. That kind of money? I could live off it for years. That should have been a comforting thought. It wasn't.

For now, I would just drive. Maybe head to California?

I waved my goodbyes and rolled down the road, leaving the solace of the farm behind me. When I got to the end of the gravel driveway, I looked right and left. Which way?

I sat for a minute. Then another. I had a car, a full tank of gas, and tons of cash. But I had no idea where—

Ahead of me, I saw movement in the trees.

I looked to the back seat, where I'd stashed the slingshot-arrow contraption I'd nabbed from the mall. Something about having it felt like a "screw you" to all that shit in my past. But I couldn't keep calling it my "slingshot-arrow contraption." Needed a cool name.

When I looked up, I saw a huge man emerge from the forest and walk toward me. Biggest guy I'd ever seen. And despite the previous night's battle, there wasn't a scratch on him. I could tell because, except for a strap over his shoulder, he was all skin and hair from head to toe.

Human skin and hair, this time.

Kane reached over and opened the passenger-side door. When he got in, the suspension groaned. He threw a small backpack to the floor boards and, for a moment, just sat staring out into the forest.

Unable to fully suppress my smile, I rolled my grandmother's necklace between my fingers. Then I pointed to the back seat and, as casually as I could, said, "I got some clothes back there from Denny. Just in case you showed."

He grunted and put on his seat belt, naked as the day he was born.

Well, born the *second* time.

I asked, "You didn't find Cal?"

Kane shook his head. "Followed for a while. I could track his scent for some time, but then I could not. I searched but did not find."

"It's okay."

He wobbled his massive head toward me and scratched his beard. "Not okay."

I put a hand on his shoulder. "We'll find him."

He waved to the windshield, motioning to the world around us. "Where?"

"I think our earlier plan is the best idea," I said and turned down the road that would eventually take us north. "When you first encountered Cal, he'd been heading to his parents'. Or at least back to his hometown."

He shrugged, tired. We both were after being up since the day before.

"I'm thinking there's a reason for it," I said. "Maybe he was just looking for a place to lie low, or maybe he was searching for something."

"Like what?"

"Dunno, but there's only one way to find out."

Reaching into the back seat, he grabbed a hockey jersey that Denny had given us because he thought it might fit Kane better. And more gray sweats. Miss Florida's son had a lot of gray sweats.

"What is this?" he asked, his hairy butt pointing at our windshield. When he sat back down, the Jeep shifted, and I nearly steered off the road. He held out the device I'd picked up from the mall.

"I've decided to call it my slingdart," I said, smiling. "It needs a cool name."

"It is very puny."

I laughed. "Put an arrow through that beast dude, right?"

"Thank you for that." Kane sighed. "He would have bested me; I must accept this. I am only alive now because of you, Emelda."

Open-mouthed, I spun my head to him. "You just called me Emelda. No more Sad Girl?"

That lightened his mood, and he chuckled. "You prefer—?"

"No, I like the way you say my name." I looked back to the road. "Say it again."

"Emelda," he said, drawing my name out with a grin, "I could not have survived without your intervention. I need your help because I will always be second best."

"Listen, Kane," I said and leaned over and put a hand on his bare shoulder. "There's nothing wrong with needing someone else. Trusting another will lift you up when you stumble is brave. It makes you stronger, not weaker."

He stared off into the thicket of trees ahead of us, lost in thought. Then he turned to me.

"We are pack of two, yes?"

My vision blurred, and I tried to speak but didn't trust my own voice. I knit my fingers between his, my hand so laughably small compared to my big friend's. I squeezed once and then grabbed the wheel again.

For a few minutes, we drove, not saying a word. Kane broke the silence. "Canada, yes?"

"Sure," I said and leaned into the accelerator a little. "Good of a start as any."

"So you have not been to Canada before?"

I shook my head. "No. Nice?"

"Yes, very nice, although can be cold," he said then looked at me with a twinkle in his eye. "I think you are not wearing enough clothes."

I turned to him, theatrically looking his body up and down. The only thing he was wearing was a seat belt.

"Jokes?" I said, laughing. "You got jokes now? You're sitting there butt-ass naked, man."

He shrugged, leaned his head back, and closed his eyes.

"I am wolf."

At a juncture, I turned and noticed something at his feet. I pointed. "What's in the backpack? You didn't take Charlie's head or anything did you? I don't wanna be driving around with a head."

Kane reached down, grabbed the bag, and handed it to me. When I unzipped it and looked inside, I saw yellow, flowing material.

And sequins.

"I saw you look at it in the mall store," he said, not looking at me.

I grinned at him. "You stole it?"

"Borrow," he said and closed his eyes again as we rolled north, looking for answers. "Like you did with the Audi?"

###

Acknowledgments

This book would not have been possible without my incredible beta readers. They've got to slog through early edits and point out all the shit I screwed up. Each one of you makes this book better, and I thank you. Peggy Hackett, Grace Lehmann, Ron Daniel, Myrtle the Hag, Joe McCormick, Michael Pelto, Bill Thompson, Steve Lewis, and Nathan Folse.

I also wanted to express my heartfelt gratitude to NetGalley's Mark O'Brien. You were so gracious in guiding me through the process, despite my endless and inane questions.

As always, to my wife Tiffany. Thank you for letting me squirrel away for hours in our garage so I can play with my imaginary friends.

And, finally, to you the Reader. I hoped you enjoyed Kane and will join me on the adventures to come.

It's going to be fun.

Afterword

Basically, the idea for this book came from an old journalism adage: Dog bites man is *not* news. Man bites dog *is* news.

While researching *Live Shot*, I heard this mantra from news producers and reporters repeatedly. Enough times that it got stuck in my brain and, eventually, Kane popped out. I hope you enjoyed reading the book as much as I did writing it.

I do feel I should say something about cats.

They're great and furry and wonderful. We've got three of them at home—Millie, Gracie, and Jackson—and they are a big part of our family, and I love them dearly. Kane, of course, is not a fan of kitties But, who knows? We may bring him around.

If you've enjoyed Kane, please leave a review on Amazon. That helps other readers find the book, and convinces Amazon to keep showing it to potential readers. Every review is a big help.

Thank you for reading!

—Dick Wybrow, August 2023

Also By Dick Wybrow

THE HELL INC SERIES

Hell inc

Hell to Pay

Hell Raisers

The InBetween

The Night Vanishing

Past Life

Ride the Light

The Hangman

MELODY SUNDAY SERIES

Live Shot

Printed in Great Britain
by Amazon